Interstellar Epiphany

The Shoplifter

Clandestine Gospel

For more information, please visit: https://www.salgodoij.com

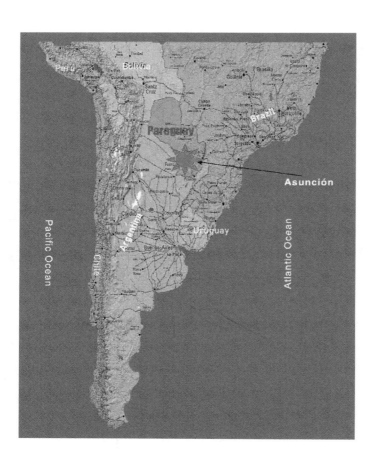

To Hannah
She who takes care of the writer

Part One

CAPRICIOUS RIVER

Asunción, June 1983

THE IMPOSSIBLE is but an obstacle we must overcome if we want to access greatness, is one of Werner's favourite maxims. Werner Mann, aged sixty-one, a German expatriate and ex-Nazi party member, was on his quest to find a diamonds field that a Native legend placed alongside the banks of an elusive river somewhere in the Amazon rainforest.

Forty years ago, the Nazi German government had gotten information on the diamonds field and, seeking unorthodox means to continue financing the war, had sent one secretive expedition, yet they had come back empty-handed. Their findings had indicated that it was all but a myth, based on an obscure Guaraní legend. Henceforth, the Nazis had disregarded further investigation. From his lower position within the ranks in his assigned workplace, Werner Mann had discreetly followed the development of this venture. Then, mulling upon the Nazi's failure, he had concluded that the diamond field was real. His conclusion had been: the German expedition had failed to find it because they couldn't interpret the legend correctly—the Indigenous worldview had concealed the river's actual location.

By the end of World War II, Werner had managed to steal the records on the venture from his *kameraden,* achieving it amidst the chaos of defeat. And then, he had planned to travel to South America to find such a place. Yet, it had taken him nearly forty years to act upon the fulfillment of his lifetime dream. And now, he was ready. He was in Asunción, the capital of the Republic of Paraguay. Asunción, a peaceful city with the Paraguay River languorously flowing at its feet.

In Asunción, Werner had found a partner whom he confessed some, if not all, of his dreams. Werner's partner was María Rosa Martinez, an attractive brunette in her late thirties. A divorcée with no children, María Rosa held a low-ranked clerical position in the right-wing governing political party's headquarters. Yet, unbeknownst to Werner—and government officers—María Rosa was a member of the clandestine Communist Party, promoting an uprising against Alfredo Stroessner, Paraguay's *de facto* president, notorious for his ruthless regime.

Thus, to María Rosa, Werner's success in finding the diamonds—although far-fetched in her view—was a chance she could not dismiss. If the Nazis wanted to fund their war program with the Paraguayan diamonds, why couldn't the Communists finance their revolutions? After all, *pecunia non olet—money does not stink.* Furthermore, if the diamonds were there as Werner sustained, there would be enough money to fund not only one but two or three revolutions, María Rosa thought, as it was Che Guevara's dream to create several Vietnams meaning guerrilla warfare of attrition against the American forces.

"Every poor in the world must become a Communist!" María Rosa's precept paraphrased Karl Marx's famous axiom: "Workers of the World, Unite!"

Her role model was Tamara Bunke, best known as Tania the Guerrilla, a German-Argentinian revolutionary. Tania died in an ambush set by the Bolivian army on August 31, 1967. While masking as a socialite in large cities, Tania's espionage activity had supported Che Guevara's guerrilla in the Bolivian jungle.

But María Rosa was not—and would not become—such a sophisticated spy. However, from her perspective, what she did was enough to keep her comrades aware, ahead of time, of course, about the government's reaction to the guerrilla's action. And so, María Rosa held casual acquaintances with some bureaucrats, overheard relevant information, and learned about the movement of troops in some critical regions of the country. Then, she passed this information through to different individuals—the grapevine system of the insurrectionary pyramid.

And although subsidizing a revolution with diamonds may sound paradoxical—but then, it was María Rosa's idealistic thought. She had a feeling for her older mate, too, for aside from her political principles, she was a romantic woman as she wanted Werner to fulfill his dream. Still, she was practical. She had perceived that Werner's age, health, and inexperience in the rainforest would stop him from reaching his goal, so she had involved young Ariel Gimmel in the adventure. But, at twenty, Ariel's aims were neither political nor financial, but to live in peace with his God—he was a Jew—his neighbours, and nature. Ariel, whom María Rosa knew well, worked as a mechanic apprentice in the car dealership where María Rosa serviced her car—as most government officers do.

Once upon a time, María Rosa Martinez attempted to enroll young Ariel in some of her group's covert activities. She had at first thought Ariel could be a courier, but he had shunned her lectures. Since the beginning of María Rosa's first attempts to enroll him, Ariel had not been interested in becoming a politician. *She may go on and practice her Jehovah's Witnesses kind of proselytism with someone else, somewhere else.* Ariel thought that all the sacrifices idealists were willing to make for the love of their cause were feats of pure romanticism.

"Like that woman, Tania," he said. *Like Che and others. Romantic heroes. There is a kind of longing in it,* he thought. *To die for a cause. A type of passion.* "My cause is nature," he said, but he would not die for it. "Nature brings life," he said—indeed, nature keeps life alive. Ariel loved wild landscapes. He wanted to become a hermit one day.

Nevertheless, Ariel accepted the role María Rosa imposed upon him to become Werner's guardian angel. But, on the other hand, Werner resisted the idea of sharing the diamonds with a Jew—once a Nazi, always a Nazi—and he pondered on the surprises which life persisted in startling him with, being such a Nazi loyalist as he had been, and a neo-fascist as he was. Thus, the idea that one day he, Werner, would be working together on a project with a Jew had never crossed his mind. And yet, being also an obstinate anti-Communist, he had not known nor suspected about María Rosa's leftist activities either. Still, regarding Ariel, María Rosa's advocacy had won over Werner's resistance, and finally, Werner had approved of María Rosa's choice of a companion, and he had agreed to meet Ariel.

And so, in three previous meetings, Werner had achieved to earn Ariel's attention, if not yet his friendship.

"Eventually, the friendship will come," María Rosa had said. "Be patient, Werner. Ariel is a great young man."

Werner's plan, although not yet fully disclosed, intrigued Ariel. In the three previous meetings, Werner had casually introduced the subject. And it seemed that he was, step by step, probing Ariel's discretion and ability to keep a secret. Because of his Nazi past, Werner had grown paranoid, which is, by the way, a highly valued condition in any country under a dictatorship—like Paraguay under Alfredo Stroessner—where the government's omniscient power is everywhere. But Ariel knew how to keep a secret. María Rosa's political trend, for example. Ariel knew most of it and kept it to himself.

Yet, Ariel wondered if María Rosa had already confessed to Werner, a declared anti-Communist, her ties with Communist radicals. Although Ariel considered, María Rosa might have indeed admitted to Werner her involvement in political activities. Indeed, she may have done so, but she had not told anybody about Werner's diamond quest. Certainly, María Rosa knew how to keep a secret, too, for she had made Werner's secret her own. And she would not share it with any member of her underground movement. With nobody. Well, not yet, because she was skeptical too unless she had the diamonds in her hands. "To see is to believe" could be another of her mottos.

Today's meeting was in *Yasy Retá*, the Hotel Guaraní's alfresco restaurant, across from Plaza de Los Héroes in downtown Asunción.

Like Big Brother from Orwell's *1984*, Alfredo Stroessner ogled at them from a giant poster set on one of the nearby buildings. *Peace, Work, and Social Welfare* claimed the caption below the photograph.

Farther below, behind the poster, beyond that building, the sun began its descending march, and the Paraguay River burst into fire. The first shadows brought a choir of croaking frogs, and the mosquitos started their annoying buzzing dance. And toward the east, high above the treetops, a white round moon waited her turn to admire itself on the river's water. And the cicadas started their singing. And it was hot and humid as it always was.

Werner treated Ariel to a pint of beer. Ariel courteously refused the drink, yet Werner insisted, and thus a waitress set two glasses of the coldest, foamy, delicious draft beer on their table. Broken conversations from the other tables covered their awkward silence like unrelenting rain. Werner sipped his beer. Instead, Ariel covered his glass as if he was warming his hands with it. And the clock ticked—

Werner gulped the rest of his beer down and relaxed in his chair. "For many years," he said, "I have been coming to this country, and I'm always surprised by the calmness of these people; there are all kinds of rumours about terrorism, military uprising, guerrilla, drug dealers, smuggling, and all of these seem to affect no one. Here, nobody ever dies of a heart attack."

"It's because of the weather," Ariel casually said.

"I beg your pardon?" Werner said, and straightened in his chair and got closer to Ariel, paying full attention to every word. He didn't want to miss a syllable from his young interlocutor's speech, as he was not yet fully acquainted with Ariel's accent.

And the same happened to Ariel, for Werner's Spanish hit his ears in guttural waves, sometimes leading to embarrassing misunderstandings.

"This heat is too much," Ariel said. "It takes from you whatever you have left to do anything."

Werner smiled. *The winter in Germany takes everything from you too,* he thought, *but you still have to work and do things. So weather should not be an excuse.*

"And also," Ariel said as if he had read Werner's thoughts, "That's the thing about fear, you know?"

"Indeed," Werner said, "The weather and fear. How interesting."

"It's true, Werner," Ariel said. "Here, nobody wants to be involved in anything, least of all in politics, you know? It's the law of the *ñembotagüy,* the best recipe to live a longer life."

Werner remained silent. He knew Ariel had spoken about a Guaraní version of the old proverb represented by the three wise monkeys—sees no evil, speaks no evil, and hears no evil. Of witnessing nothing—playing the fool rather than being involved in any business with the police. In a country governed by an absolutist regime, it was risky for a citizen to assume even slightly doubting the system's correctness. The mention of something contrary to the government may turn everybody hysterical—the perfect Orwellian society in which Werner's and Ariel's days went by.

"Sorry, what did you say?" Ariel said as he heard Werner mumbling about something not yet clear to him.

"Politicians," Werner said. He was speaking in whispers as if he were afraid of being caught talking about a taboo subject.

"What about them?"

"I said, it's the politicians' fault." He sipped his beer while his eyes smiled, waiting for Ariel's answer.

"Politicians should have the vocation of a teacher, Werner, with low pay, hard work, and the satisfaction and responsibility of forming the future of the country."

"Fair enough," Werner said and smiled.

There was a long awkward silence.

"And what about you?" Werner suddenly said as if he remembered something.

"About myself?" Ariel said as if Werner had asked, 'tell me about yourself' as in a job interview.

"Well, yes, Ariel. I mean, about your vocation. María Rosa told me that once upon a time, you wanted to become a teacher."

"A rural teacher—"

Again, Werner straightened in his chair and leaned over, and Ariel relaxed with his eyes closed as if recalling memories.

"It will be better," Ariel said after a while as if dismissing the previous subject and changing his mind upon reflecting on a divine commandment, "If instead, I talk to you about my father."

Werner noticed the glass in Ariel's hands and interrupted Ariel.

"Your beer must be already warm, my friend," Werner said as if Ariel's story couldn't continue without another pint of the coldest, foamy, delicious draft beer.

He turned about to call for the waitress' attention. Ariel extended his hand to stop Werner's action, but it was too late now. The waitress, a smiling, sensual young woman with long, braided, black hair, poured two pints of beer from the draft dispenser into two clean glasses and brought them on a tray. She leaned, placed the glasses on the table, and her breasts seemed to burst out of the thin fabric of her colourful *ao-po'i* blouse. Ariel blushed and looked away. The waitress stood there, playing with the tray in her hands.

"*¿Algo más desea, el señor?*" she said coquettishly, grinning at Werner.

"*No, no, gracias, señorita,*" was Werner's courteous but stiff answer. He got his wallet, paid for the beers, and added a tip.

The waitress smiled, took the money, collected the dirty glasses, and sashayed her way behind the counter.

Ariel's eyes followed her with the candid look of a child that followed the fluttering of a butterfly. And his mind drifted into reveries. He dreamed of becoming a hermit, living away in the countryside surrounded by plants and animals, away from civilization. And although his withdrawn personality attracted many young women, he had made no commitments.

Werner looked at his young acquaintance and smiled sympathetically—Ariel's boyish innocent look was an open book to him. Then, Werner turned his sight toward the Plaza de Los Héroes and again relaxed in his chair. People anxious to return home after a working day crowded Calle Oliva below. Beyond the Plaza de Los Héroes, the Paraguay River languorously flowed. Lovers contemplated the glittering, orange stream under the setting sun and made promises. Above, in the blue sky, the white, round moon became more and more noticeable. A warm feeling surrounded both men.

"My father . . ." Ariel said and then paused.

Again, Werner leaned over, this time even closer.

"My father's name was Seth," Ariel said in a burst of words as if he had suddenly remembered his duty as he urged himself to speak about his father. "Like Seth from the Torah in Genesis, the third child of Adam and Eve. My father was fifty years old when I was born. He had a strong voice, a stentorian voice. In the family, they used to say that my father was born with that quality. He would have been an extraordinary opera singer."

Werner actively listened.

"Because of a misunderstanding," Ariel continued his remembrance, "my father earned the name Aniceto, which was the Spanish name he carried the rest of his life. He took that name once he arrived in this country. He came in a group from Buenos Aires, Argentina, to their destination, Asunción del Paraguay. In those days, Asunción was little more than a village. Look at what it is now."

Werner raised his head and looked around as if he recognized the place for the first time. He didn't have to do that. He knew Asunción well. From the border of the Paraguay River, and every street, every building, its people, its foundations—

"They were a group of about ten families from Europe. All Jewish immigrants. Refugees from wars, racism, hunger, pogroms, religion, poverty, prejudices, politics, revolutions, all of the above evils the human race creates to disintegrate itself. Anyway, that day, the newcomers gathered around the immigration officer as if this civil servant were a prophet ready to announce the coming of the Messiah. My father was just a boy. He was travelling in the care of family friends. His parents could not make the trip, so they entrusted the child to their friends, who brought him to Buenos Aires and then to Asunción. They were all tired of their journey, the heat, the humidity, and the mosquitoes.

"Finally, the adults gathered in that crowded office in Asunción. And amidst the urgency to obtain the papers to stay in the country, they overlooked the boy, sitting alone with his sad eyes, his belly empty, and his arms around his meager belongings. However, from the height of his desk, the civil servant noticed the little boy, and I'm sure that the immigration officer felt sorry for the little one because he stood up from his chair behind his desk and said, '¡Eh tú, mita-í! ¿Cómo te llamás, che'raa?' The man was speaking *Jopará*, the way you already know the folks here talk, which is a mixture of Spanish and Guaraní.

"But, of course, my father didn't understand what the man was asking him. A neighbour translated the question into Yiddish, '*Vos iz deyn nomen, fraynd?*' And my father, upset because of the long journey, and perhaps hungry and thirsty, answered with that loud voice of his, but he did so in Hebrew, '*Ani Seth!*' Which means, 'I'm Seth.' Maybe my father's voice raised an echo in the immigration officer's memory because he left his desk at my father's answer, went to my father's side, and in an amicable tone, he said, '*Aniceto! ¿mba'éichapa che ra'a? ¡Vení aquí, ch'amigo!*' Which meant, 'Aniceto, how are you? Come over here, my friend!' And, as it turned out, the name of the immigration officer was Aniceto as well, so from then on, everybody called my father, Aniceto. Aniceto Gimmel. My father always laughed at the way that he got his Spanish name."

Werner chuckled.

Three boys came.

"¿*Lustrada, karaí?*" One of the boys said, showing the adults his shoeshine box.

The sweet voice of the boy addressing him so respectfully did not move Werner. The boys then ignored Werner and spoke to Ariel, this time in a choir.

"¿*Lustrada, karaí?*"

Ariel took some coins from his pocket.

"*No, lo mita-i,*" Ariel said and dropped the coins in one of the boys' hands.

The boy closed his hand and ran to a corner of the room to count the coins. His friends followed him.

Across the terrace, the Plaza de Los Héroes bustled with activity. Some festival was going on. Werner stretched in his chair and closed his eyes. The peace of the moment overwhelmed him.

"Well," Ariel said, "I was his only son. But, unfortunately, he passed away when I was a ten-year-old boy."

"I'm sorry to hear that," Werner said politely.

"Baruch Hashem," Ariel said, and he proceeded with the narrative as if he had found the thread of his life from his roots on. "My widowed mother accepted the help of her brothers, my uncles, who are residents in Chile. She sold the house we had here in Asunción, and with this and other savings, mom and I travelled through the wild greenery of the Chaco, crossed the Andes, and settled in Valparaiso, Chile. I was accepted in the Universidad de Valparaiso, but I had a change of mind, wanted to return to Asunción, spoke to my mother about it, and she agreed, spoke to my uncles about it, and they disagreed, but it's my life, so here I am."

"Why Asunción, Ariel?"

Ariel smiled and did not answer, at least not immediately. Werner nodded again understandingly, although he could have asked the question to himself as well. *Why did you choose Asunción, Werner? Well, because here is the base for my venture on my quest in search of the diamonds field about which the Guaraní legend gives such explicit clues,* he would answer. And that would be all of Werner's attachment to Asunción. But in Ariel's case, he could expand indefinitely about his preferred city—*Asunción is the city of my infancy,* he would say. And he could go on and on, explaining his motives to live in Asunción.

Indeed, Asunción agreed more with Ariel's melancholic character than Valparaiso, the vibrant Chilean city port. Still, Valparaiso had profoundly influenced his character. The cosmopolitan splendor of downtown had contrasted with the distressing inequity suffered by people surviving harshly in Valparaiso's hills and ravines. The disturbing scenery had turned Ariel into a skeptic regarding human social justice. Yet, he hadn't participated in the social-political maelstrom that took over Valparaiso—and the whole country. Instead, Ariel's rebellion had turned toward mystical channels that had taken him away from any social unrest.

Ariel had traveled to Santiago to help his uncle, Levi, in his store during the summers. Levi was a merchant of fabrics and textiles. The store faced Calle Puente, an animated artery in the Chilean capital. Ariel had witnessed the daily clashes between diverse political factions from his place behind the counter, the masses of protesters who, like an avalanche, used to gather downtown at the hour of the protests. And so, Ariel had observed the marching groups of the discontented, those neglected by the politicians, abandoned by society, homeless, families leaving in *campamentos* in deplorable conditions, men and women, children and elders, all of them marching, all of them demanding respect and a solution to their problems. Levi feared these people, so he ordered Ariel to lower the steel curtains that protected the display windows each time the picketers gathered in the neigbourhood.

And so, Ariel, too, had grown afraid of the masses. His constant search for self-satisfaction did not include cities. Above all, big cities scared him, threatened him. He could not understand how such a great city could abandon its citizens, a well-planned place in the affluent boroughs and forgotten in the poor neighbourhoods. And so many automobiles, pollution, smog, noise, and crime mixed with opportunities, shows, political scandals, and the anonymous life of the ordinary citizen.

Still, Ariel's employment as a mechanic apprentice in a car dealership in Asunción didn't fit into his scheme of life at all. He hoped that the job would not become a permanent occupation. Therefore, Werner's offer and the possibility of coming into the possession of capital enticed him. He would buy the land of his dreams if he successfully sold his share of the diamonds. After being disappointed in people early on in his life, Ariel dreamed of having enough money to buy an orchard far away from any city and to live the life of a hermit, growing his food. And he was in this mindset when Werner startled him by asking him why he had chosen to live in Asunción.

"Asunción has all that I need," Ariel finally said as if it had taken him a great effort to answer that question.

Werner nodded and smiled without digging further into Ariel's choice of a city. Life in *Yasy Retá* continued as it always did, with the murmur of conversations, an occasional laugh, and the waitresses constantly busy with their chores—and it was hot and humid as it always was.

"You know, Ariel?" Werner said as if an idea had just come to him. "Latin Americans subsist between political instability and striking natural sceneries."

"Striking natural sceneries that are rapidly vanishing, Werner."

"Because of political instability, Ariel. There is an underground fire burning."

Is it a rightist fire or a leftist one? Ariel did not respond as he seemed concerned about his own internal fire.

Werner shrugged at Ariel's disinterest as if he was the only one in the world who cared for the fate of the Latin American people. He brought the glass to his lips, and the explosion caught him while the beer still travelled down his throat. The glass shattered, and the clinking lost in the screams. Soldiers swiftly cordoned the area.

"No one goes out! No one comes in! Remain where you are! No sudden movements!" It was what they all heard through megaphones.

An army officer with dead eyes gave orders. "Men and women over fourteen years old must show a piece of identification!"

Werner ignored the order issued by the officer and went toward the exit door. Ariel followed him. They walked toward the gallery that connected the exterior with the hotel lobby. Two young soldiers stopped them there. One of them was almost a boy.

"What can a boy like this one do against a terrorist?" Werner whispered to Ariel and decidedly stepped forwards toward the soldiers, his passport high in his hand.

Ariel remained behind, intuiting what was going to happen. Werner's demeanor impressed the young soldiers, and so they militarily saluted as if Werner were an army general in civil clothes. Werner was about to exit when another army officer stopped him.

"Negative, *señor*!" the officer commanded. "Return to the hotel lobby!"

Werner stopped, came to attention, fixed his gaze in the officer's eyes, briskly raised his right hand to his temple, clicked his heels, turned around, and walked with martial steps back to the lobby. Ariel was there waiting for him with a smirk on his face.

In the hotel lobby, they sat on a sofa and waited. In there, everyone gave his or her version of the attack, the confusion grew.

Outside, there was a choir of emergency bells, and inside, the whispering of different mouths and various accents, languages, and dialects reached them: Guaraní, Spanish, Portuguese, English, and German, and even Korean, proof of the large immigrant population. And the Natives whispered in their peculiar parlance, which they call Jopará, a mix of Guaraní and Spanish, and in another, which they call *Portuñol*, a combination of Portuguese and Spanish.

"It was in the corner of the hotel!"

"No, it was a package left in a garbage can at the Ministry of Public Works' doors!"

"There are two dead! Two bystanders, innocent civilians!"

"No, there are more than five! I saw the bodies bleeding on the sidewalk!"

"No, there is no one hurt!"

Dozens of voices continued whispering contradictory information after the tragedy. Slowly, the gossiping ended, and it was all calm. Then, finally, the soldiers allowed people to leave.

"Let's go," Werner said.

They went out to the street and walked among the crowd. Everybody was in a hurry to leave the place. Behind them were the lights of the emergency vehicles. The police had set barriers in every street leading to and from Plaza de Los Héroes. Werner and Ariel showed their identification card at every halt.

"This arrangement is silly," Werner mumbled.

"What?" a distracted Ariel said.

"No matter what the police do, Ariel, there is always room for a break-in."

"What do you mean?"

"All of this security," Werner stopped and turned around, "is useless. The tighter it is, the more room for terrorists to break in. It might even be possible that those who did this are members of the same repressive arm of the government."

"What?"

"Indeed. This kind of repressive government always uses this tactic to justify repression."

"You are crazy, Werner! Why are they going to kill their own people?"

"They are creating martyrs, Ariel. Innocent victims are the best advertising, you know."

"No, I don't know, Werner, and I cannot believe it!"

"Anyhow, this will go for a long time. We know about it already. I told you that a subterranean war is going on."

A subterranean war. Ariel thought about María Rosa's possible involvement in this incident, scratched his head, but said nothing. Yet, Ariel knew that her underground work was dangerous. A small mistake might take her to the police headquarters where she would—yes, she would—reveal all that María Rosa knew, and probably most of what she did not know.

They approached a group of young men.

"*Aichelláranga lo perro, ch'amigo.*" The words gently dragged, pronounced in the soft Native accent, reaching Werner's ears as vibrant as another explosion. "*Lo pyragüé lo van a denunciar antes de que cante el gallo.*"

Werner looked at Ariel with a question in his eyes, and Ariel translated, answering the mute request of his friend, "I'm sorry for those guys, my friend. But, for sure, the *pyragüé* will turn them in before the rooster sings."

Ariel was talking about the government spies inserted into all areas of society. The *pyragüé,* people willing to denounce anybody in exchange for favours from the government.

That is it, Werner told himself. *The spies will denounce the suspicious ones to the police. And the police will torture those poor guys, so they will say what the law wants to hear. And under torture, many more, some innocents, will pay the price.*

—There are political systems in the world where a prisoner will swear that he or she is a thief, an adulterer, a common criminal, a bank robber, anything rather than recognizing his or her political affiliation and covert work. Indeed, in most dictatorial systems, common criminals, even assassins, have more chances to go free than a political prisoner ever does—

Ariel walked fast as if he wanted to escape from there, to disappear from the horror. As if the internal rebelliousness nestled in his heart had managed to come outside to cause that chaos. Werner followed him, also absorbed in his thoughts. Ariel's words had opened a path to his past, and so, in Werner's mind, these words turned into a whirlpool of memories. *Pyragüé.* Spies. *Das Spitlzen.* Repression. Torture. He knew these words well. He had seen all of this before in Germany, his old country, at other times. He had not only heard these words; he had felt them. Experiences that were already far in his past, although still alive in his mind—

"What a mess, Ariel."

"It's human nature, Werner."

"Human nature is to survive, Ariel, not to kill each other."

Ariel remained silent. That was not his subject. Political issues meant little to him, although he prayed to God regularly to illuminate those in political positions and never to forget the forsaken, the abandoned, those who suffer for one cause or another, the poor, the aging, and the sick people. *Baruch Attah Adonai Eloheynu Melech Ha-Olam.* And he concluded his prayers the way his father taught him when he was a little boy. *And I ask for me, and all of those in need of Your love and mercy.*

Pyragüé all over, Werner thought. He struggled with the meaning of this Guaraní word. He preferred to express his feeling about the same word in his Native German, *spitzel.*

"*Spitzel,*" Werner said aloud, and the word fell from his mouth like a rotten tooth. He realized what he had said and collected himself. He put his hand on his mouth.

"What?" Ariel said, caught by surprise with Werner's behaviour and because of the foreign word.

"Nothing. Nothing, Ariel," Werner said, dismissing his own words with a gesture of his hand.

They came into a German restaurant on Calle Palma, whereby then, Werner had become a regular. An old blonde waiter cheered Werner and directed him to a table. Ariel followed behind.

"Thank you, Dariusz," Werner said. "Two cold drafts, please."

"Today, the *schnitzel* is excellent, sir," the waiter said.

"Not for me now, and you, Ariel?"

"You know I don't enjoy pork, Werner."

"It actually is beef *schnitzel*, sir, and fresh *spargel*," the waiter said.

"That sounds well, Dariusz. Please bring one plate for my young friend here."

Dariusz nodded and left.

"I'm not used to people deciding for me, Werner."

"I'm so sorry there is no *kosher* food here, my friend."

"It is okay, Werner. It's not your fault." Ariel was naïve enough not to notice that Werner was cynical.

"Should we focus on our business then?"

"The hidden treasure?"

Werner noticed that Dariusz was coming back. The waiter brought one plate and one small bread basket in one hand and two beer jars in the other. Werner put an index finger on his lips. Dariusz placed his load on the table, Werner nodded approvingly, smiled, and Dariusz moved away.

Werner's eyes went to the waiter's back and then followed a couple who had just entered the restaurant. Dariusz went on to take care of them.

"Americans," Werner whispered, and then he focused on the still life watercolours on the wall.

Ariel followed Werner's edginess. He knew how uncomfortable Werner felt when there were people around him.

"No one is following us, Werner," Ariel whispered.

"You never know, Ariel," Werner whispered back.

"Why are you so . . ." Although he felt annoyed by Werner's behaviour, Ariel did not finish the sentence.

"It's not paranoia," Werner said. "Don't get me wrong, Ariel. It's prudence. Listen, you're too innocent, but let me tell you that we're all sardines in here, sardines surrounded by sharks. They can swallow us in a second. I have to be careful for you and me."

Indeed, Werner's mistrust reached everybody in the city and the country. He suspected that all eyes and ears were for the government. Everybody had a voice, but people used it to praise the government, which was its program of peace, progress, and social welfare under Alfredo Stroessner's iron hand. Under Stroessner's iron fist, nobody could ever alter that peace, stop the progress, or be indifferent to the people's enjoyment. Yet, Ariel was indifferent to Werner's ruminations. He did not care who was who at all.

"María Rosa told me a little about you, Werner," Ariel said, deciding to change the subject.

"Good or bad?"

"She told me you're a former Nazi."

"Sins of youth, Ariel."

"An attempt to justify yourself, I presume."

"Should I justify what I did in my younger days? I don't know, and you don't know, Ariel. Maybe someone will judge you in the far future for things you do now."

"No one shall judge me but God, Werner."

"Aha! Shouldn't you know what a sin pride is? Let me tell you that I was in this very same spirit when I was your age. Proud and brave. 'No one shall judge me but God.' A phrase for the bronze. But then, we were all believers."

"Believers of the wrong cause."

"Every cause is right if you believe in it, Ariel."

Ariel did not respond. Pensively, he cut a piece of the *schnitzel* and one asparagus and took them to his mouth.

"What else did Rosa María tell you about me?"

"She said that she believes in you," Ariel said, chewing the food.

"That's good, Ariel. It's nice to hear that."

"She did not answer my question." Ariel left the fork and the knife on the table and cleaned his mouth with a napkin.

"Which is?"

"How come you got involved in this project?"

"I was working in a laboratory in Berlin."

"When was that?"

"Throughout World War II, back in 1943. The war ended in 1945."

"Can you elaborate on this?"

"I don't think so, Ariel. Past is past, and I don't like to recall my life."

"Not all your life, Werner. Only about what brought you here."

Werner again relaxed in his chair, stretched his legs, and looked around for Dariusz. Dariusz came promptly with two new frothing beer jars, took the plates, the empty jars, and left. Werner drank and relaxed again and closed his eyes.

"I will start as a Charles Dicken's kind of *David Copperfield*," Werner said, smiling as if having to talk about a time no longer at his reach gave him joy. "I was born at the dawn of November 26, 1922, the same day and year that Howard Carter discovered the tomb of Tutankhamen, in an industrial suburb of Bremen . . ."

***

At the beginning of WWII, Werner Mann was a university student in a program in geology. He was a young, enthusiastic follower of Adolf Hitler, and he was active in the National Socialist Party. Because of his loyalty to the party, his bosses assigned him to work in a secret laboratory located a few blocks from the heart of Berlin. In this laboratory, Werner became a member of a unique research team whose objective was to find nontraditional ways to finance the Third Reich wars, campaigns, and programs, in addition to the confiscated assets in the occupied countries.

Werner knew nothing about the political and financial strategy that kept the laboratory running. He only knew about his specific duties, and of course, he could not and should not adventure to inquire further. He was the last hair on the tail of a hungry lion, continually hunting. His teammates were explorers, jewellers, geologists, and chemists. Werner's role was to classify, register on a ledger, and store samples of precious stones and precious metals that arrived at the laboratory in intervals.

His work demanded secrecy, and this exigence made it impossible for him to live the years of his youth as an ordinary citizen. Yet, he was proud of the new regime's triumphs, so Werner accepted the rules imposed on him in a good mood. Outside, in the city, he had no family and no friends. His only known relative was a disabled old aunt from whom he had some memories from his childhood. The old lady suffered a freak misfortune and died; she fell from her wheelchair and rolled down the hospital's marble stairs where she was a patient. The police archived the case without further investigation. The government took charge of her funeral. Werner received the brief, dry condolences through a card emblazoned with the symbol of the *Nationalsozialistische Deutsche Arbeiterpartei*, the NAZI party, and this was the only message he ever got in regards to his fading family.

Thus, the laboratory was all of what Werner Mann knew of the world—it became his home, and his teammates, his family, the only family he knew, until the end of the world. And so, among those walls, he spent the best years of his life.

The work schedule was intense, and the rules were strict. *Arbeit Macht Frei*, the diabolic cynicism of the motto was in the air as a virus. And so, the young Werner Mann continued his work, which for him was more than well-deserved freedom. Still, Werner's work was but another link in an interminable bureaucratic chain.

Before entering his laboratory section, Werner had to take his clothes off, take a cold shower, and wear the laboratory's dull uniform. At the end of his daily schedule, he had to take another shower, but this time in a transparent glass cage surrounded by eyes that followed every one of his movements. After the shower, a guard performed an invasive exam, and once he was free of this test, he would get dressed in his regular clothes and leave the laboratory. Werner never objected to these humiliations, finding them understandable given the nature of his work.

He dressed, and without any resentment, went to his apartment, listened to classical music, read books, or enjoyed long walks in the enclosed garden. The garden was part of a park surrounded by high walls with doors guarded by armed guards, accompanied by vicious dogs. The barking of dogs, the hysterical orders, the murmur of lost conversations, cries, and other sounds that reached his ears were constant. The building had windows that opened to blackened brick walls. God only knew what happened behind those walls. Perhaps they belonged to factories, prisons, or other laboratories, Werner never knew.

His employers provided him a small furnished apartment with a private bathroom and no kitchen, all within the laboratory's limits where he worked. He took his meals in the cafeteria, which was also a point of encounter and where one could meet new people and make friends, although this was not encouraged by the administration. Three or four times per month, a young woman knocked on his door. These visits were a courtesy from his employers, and although it was never the same woman, Werner waited for her visit as if the woman were the bride he never had.

Some of the high-ranked team members received sophisticated gifts within the restrictions imposed by the war. Although within a curfew, some of these gifts allowed some privileged employees to get out and visit Berlin. Others could go out on specific missions abroad. They were the ones who brought the samples for analysis. At times, one of these privileged characters brought a personal souvenir for some of the staff, and Werner, throughout the years, treasured a collection of artistic items whose origins were in faraway, exotic lands.

In this way, Werner overheard about an intriguing exploration trip that a group of military and geologists, under direct orders from the Third Reich, made to Paraguay, the beautiful landlocked country located in the heart of South America, and so, he recorded all the information he received from every expedition, especially from the one that went to Paraguay.

Some months before the Russians broke down Berlin's defences at the end of the war, the army destroyed the laboratory and dispersed the staff. In the chaos that ensued, the samples that the laboratory's employees had so meticulously stored vanished forever. Ultimately, Werner's eyes, ears, and hands were on the diaries, maps, and any other papers that referred to Paraguay's diamond field.

And for the first time in his life, Werner Mann found himself face to face with the reality of the last episodes of WWII—the destruction and defeat.

Despite being a civilian all of his life and never accused or suspect of a crime, for the two following years after the capitulation, Werner Mann found himself a prisoner in Stalag 344. It was a concentration camp built by the Germans, first to keep the allied prisoners and then used by the Soviets to hold Germany's prisoners. After Stalag 344, the Soviets transferred him and other prisoners to Danzig (now Gdansk, in Poland) and forced him to work in the harbour's construction.

"It must have been very hard on you, Werner," Ariel interrupted, shocked by the narrative.

"Indeed, Ariel. I tell you that that period of forced labour was one of the bitterest chapters of my life."

During the winter of 1953, he escaped from Poland and returned to Berlin. Berlin was a divided city among the Soviets, the Americans, the French, and the British. German refugees from Eastern Europe, evicted by the Soviets, crowded the streets and occupied most services.

And the years went by, and things improved. Werner completed his education, obtained a Ph.D. in Chemistry, and accepted a teaching position in a postsecondary institution in Bremen. He focused on his work as a professor and kept himself a bachelor.

And although he loved what he was doing, Werner had a plan for his life. He retired early and dedicated the following years to travel to Paraguay where, he thought, life had for him a prize to collect.

By the time he made Ariel Gimmel's acquaintance, Werner Mann had already passed his 61st birthday. Still, he was energetic and robust, a blue-eyed, tall man with stern Nordic features and long silvered hair. Nevertheless, Werner's physique remained strong, and his mind was lucid as he played chess with a younger man's mental agility and enthusiasm.

ASUNCIÓN SLEPT the siesta. Just a few vehicles in the streets. Stores, as usual, closed for the midday rest. The AC devices were working at their maximum. The rain had just stopped, and the humidity was unbearable.

Sitting in his favourite place on the terrace of cafeteria *Yasy Retá*, at a corner of the Hotel Guaraní, Werner Mann read a book. He was but one more tourist in the warm city. Werner waited for María Rosa. He knew that it would take at least a half-hour more for her to arrive.

He left the book aside and thought of María Rosa, the woman he loved without much of love. He also took some time to think of Ariel Gimmel, who may become his partner in his life's adventure. *Ariel is a promising young man,* thought Werner—and Werner would add, *Ariel is an innocent young man,* as he considered himself a good reader of human character, had broad international experience, and plenty of time to analyze people and behaviour. He was a psychologist by intuition. And he kept this interest in human behaviour since he considered himself a malleable instrument in the hands of destiny.

And because of a strange coincidence, Werner Mann, an ex-Nazi himself and admirer of the Hitler government, had installed himself temporarily in the south cone of Latin America, wherein Chile, Argentina, Paraguay, Bolivia, and Brazil had a sincere sympathy for the German military discipline. And besides, Werner knew that before and after World War II, these four countries had received many German expatriates. Most of them were simple citizens who had immigrated to South America, escaping the misery and the postwar chaos. Yet, among them, some war criminals intensely sought by the justice of many countries had encountered shelter here too. Many of these murderers found redemption and prospered under friendly Latin American military governments.

Not a day goes by, Werner thought to himself, *without our innocence validating barbarism.* And as if synchronicity, at Karl Jung's best, wanted to show its purest face, a man passed by him and sat at a table just a few places from where Werner enjoyed his draft beer. Werner saw him talking to one of the waitresses, and a minute later, the man had a foaming beer tumbler on his table.

Joseph Schwammberger! Werner said to himself, recognizing the man's face immediately, older for sure, but still holding the look of the vicious criminal he was while wearing the SS uniform. Werner had only read stories about this man. Regretfully, he was his countryman and a war criminal indeed. He had been the executioner of hundreds of Jewish people in ghettos in Poland, and until that moment, he was still living free in Argentina, and then perhaps going on a business trip or sightseeing in Asunción, despite the many charges laid against him by different governments and organizations.

And so, in front of Werner's astonished eyes, there he was—this despicable assassin, enjoying a beer in the calmness of a beautiful afternoon at the end of August 1983, exploring Asunción del Paraguay.

WERNER MANN lived in an apartment which he rented in a downtown four-star hotel. Like every day, he woke up early and thirsty, went to the washroom, took a quick shower, went to the refrigerator, grabbed one bottle of beer, opened it, placed the chess pieces on the chessboard, and drank his first beer of the day. Then, he went to the closet, took the clothes for the day, put them on, went back to the refrigerator, took another beer, and sat again, for this was from some time now, his routine. One or two beers and a couple of painkillers were his breakfast. He sipped his beer and meditated on the next move while waiting for Ariel, who promised he would be there within the hour. They had work to do. Werner knew, however, that as soon as Ariel arrived, he, Ariel, would ask for a real breakfast. And the same would happen with María Rosa.

Yet, as soon as Ariel arrived, Werner, almost drunk, signaled him his place in front of the chessboard. Although Ariel sat obediently and made his first move in response to Werner's challenge, he still could not control his eyes, which went through the door left ajar, beyond which he could see María Rosa, apparently profoundly asleep on the bed.

Ariel focused on the chessboard while Werner, in a guttural desultory presentation, introduced the subject of his concern. Ariel tried to make something from what he was listening to when movements in the next room distracted him and raising his eyes, he turned his head toward the open door and saw María Rosa, who had turned on the bed. Not conscious of her nakedness yet, the woman showed her body in all its splendidness. She had placed her hands behind her head. Her eyes fixed her unabashed gaze on some point upon the door frame as a smile danced on her face. And in that so sensual posture, she looked like *La Maja Desnuda,* an artwork by Spanish artist Francisco Goya. The view achieved to disconcert Ariel, whose pupils anchored on the golden body. *Woman, a mixture of a goddess and a panther*, as Mauricio Cardoso Ocampo, a nationally renowned Paraguayan poet and songwriter, expressed so well.

Driven by his innocence, Ariel wanted to stand up, go to the bedroom, and cover the woman's body with a blanket, but then he refrained from doing so because either María Rosa or Werner, or both, could misinterpret his purpose. Anyhow, the incident achieved to distract him, and he moved his queen to the wrong square. Werner smiled, took the queen, and replaced it with one of his knights. And yet, Ariel was not even as interested in the chess game as he seemed to be. Indeed, his attention focused on digesting the strange story Werner mumbled while moving a pawn here, a knight there, a bishop moving away from a pawn, and a checkmate. All done while sipping his beer.

A diamond field that lies hidden somewhere in the rainforest!

"It doesn't make sense!" Ariel said aloud—the thought was his first upon the revelation.

And he recalled the moment María Rosa talked to him about the treasure, which Ariel imagined was about a coffer with gold coins left forgotten in the jungle by the Spaniards who were fleeing the attacks of Natives. It was more plausible. It would make more sense for Ariel. Between the years 1500 and 1700, there was a lot of Spaniard and Portuguese traffic, the

Catholic Church included, whose subjects transported diverse treasures through and from the New World to Europe while expanding their influence.

They had not had breakfast yet, and although it did not appear to affect Werner, Ariel worried because he knew that Werner's refrigerator contained nothing but beer bottles.

And Ariel knew that María Rosa was also apprehensive about Werner's diet, for she once commented something along the lines, but swiftly, on the passing, as if she was not sure or afraid to recognize that Werner was becoming an alcoholic. Anyhow, the beer bottles in the refrigerator reminded Ariel that they both, and of course María Rosa too, needed something more substantial in their stomachs. Scrambled eggs and bacon would be okay, but Werner didn't seem to be hungry. He only focused on his beer, the chess game, and the fantastic story he was feeding to Ariel. And this story had the younger man walking on hot coals.

"Check again," Werner said, always smiling. "We have to be alert, Ariel. Always. We must focus. Nothing can distract us from our objective. It is the only way to achieve all of what we wish from this life."

"Can we have breakfast now?" Ariel said.

"Of course, my friend. I will order some breakfast right now." Werner stood, went to the telephone, dialed a number, and ordered. "Good," he said, placing the phone back in its cradle. "Breakfast will be here in just a few minutes."

At that moment, María Rosa sat on the bed, covered her breasts with one arm, gave herself an impulse, and walked, her long black hair flowing free while she sashayed to and through the washroom door. Yet this time, none of the men raised their heads from the chessboard.

***

María Rosa dropped by the car dealer in the mechanic section where Ariel worked. Ariel was not surprised to see her, as she occasionally serviced her car and often loaded gas there.

"I just wanted to give you this," María Rosa said, delivering Ariel a piece of paper.

Ariel saw a telephone number and a name written on the paper. They were alone for one moment in the service area.

"In case I don't answer the telephone," María Rosa said as a response to Ariel's surprised look. "Memorize and destroy it, Ariel."

"Are you playing Tania Bunke's role?"

"Don't be silly, Ariel. And it's not a play. I assure you."

"It's okay, María Rosa. I hope I never have to call this number."

"You may not, Ariel, but who knows?"

And after that conversation, they changed the topic and talked about mundane things, and five minutes later, she left the service area and went to her car.

THEIR CONVERSATION over the diamonds and the way to reach them had extended for several hours now. Werner opened another beer and offered one to Ariel. Ariel rejected it without lifting his eyes from the maps on the table with a gesture of his hand.

"I have written down for you the shopping list of all the things we will need, Ariel," Werner said, almost in a whisper, even though they were alone in Werner's apartment. "You must buy them one by one, each one of them in a separate store and at different times."

Although Werner's paranoia irritated Ariel, he accepted it as another habit of his old friend, for by then, Ariel had already considered Werner to be his friend.

"I don't want anything that can trace this shopping list to us."

"I understand," Ariel said. And this time, he did. He did understand the dangers to which Werner referred to and insisted about. Yet, now, Ariel could see the whole picture. And what if it was all true?

Werner's demeanor focused in that direction. Crazy or not, alcoholic or not, cynical or not, Werner knew what he was doing.

"Food and water go in the first place. If needed, we can get water from the rain. I'm telling you that it's the best. And then the equipment. Then clothes. As I said to you before, and I must insist on it, you must buy them in stores during the rush hour. I don't want to know about an alert employee who could remember your presence there. That would be bad for us. If they catch us in the first stage of our plan, it will be all finished, and I would have lost forty years of my life. Perhaps you could make it better. You could deny you know something.

María Rosa could vouch for you and move you away from danger. The government may evict me from the country, which would be too bad, but that would be the best outcome. Now, if they catch us in the process of extraction, then we are dead meat. I tell you, it will be worse than if they catch us plotting against the president. María Rosa knows the risks, and she agrees that they are worthy."

Ariel bit his lips. He was scared now but accepted it all as if it were a game. Or a joke. A joke from destiny.

How this strange subject weaved their lives together, uniting these three lives in such a fantastic project!

Ariel knew that Werner invested so much in this project—emotionally, financially, and in time, his hopes and dreams. And only he, Werner, knew the exact location of the diamond deposit if it ever existed. Ariel now hoped it was genuine and not a legend. Although, it was still hard for Ariel to comprehend how no one had yet uncovered such a treasure even with the modern techniques available even with the government's vast resources. But Ariel trusted Werner, and he was curious about how this whole venture would end.

"Not all," Werner said as if reading Ariel's mind. "On this Earth of ours, very little has already been discovered, Ariel. I'm telling you that humanity is still at the gates of its greatest findings."

"Yes, Werner, but aren't we bringing the frontier between fiction and reality too close?"

"Therefore," Werner continued, skipping Ariel's comment, "we can rent a car. That would be fine. A van or a station wagon, whichever is available. I'm a tourist, so that will be fine. A vehicle with four-wheel drive would be ideal, but I don't want to risk anything. I don't want people asking me where I'm going. Anyhow, we'll have to leave the vehicle hidden somewhere near this road." He signaled it on the map. "And then we'll have to walk. Remember that this is not an official map and that it is old. Perhaps the road doesn't exist anymore. And on walking, it is now easier for me to say than to do because I read in a book that walking in the jungle is not a joke. I don't want you to carry me half of the way."

"Horses? Mules?" suggested Ariel.

"That is out of the question, my dear friend. We cannot bring that type of animal into the rainforest. Yes, in a different scenario, they would be a solution. Not there. Better to go and do things the most quietly possible. Besides, I don't want to meet more people. You, María Rosa, and I are already too much. And I'm telling you that it's not because of a lack of resources or because I don't want to share. In this kind of business, the less, the better. Believe me. This venture carries more risks than robbing a bank or a train carrying gold ingots."

Ariel nodded.

THEY HAD already finished their dinner, and as it was now sadly usual, Werner exceeded his alcohol intake, had trouble coordinating his speech, and María Rosa struggled with his behaviour. Ariel followed the scene with the utmost attention. He felt sorry for the man who ruined his health with alcohol. But, there was no way to convince him to stop drinking. Werner always cut them short when both María Rosa and Ariel criticized his drinking habit.

"It's my health, guys, and it's my money," Werner said.

However, Werner must learn he was not acting alone anymore. Indeed, Werner must respond to Ariel and María Rosa for his actions. Apart from being partners, they were a family. The only family Werner ever had. Besides, Werner must be in good shape to accomplish his dreams. And the goals of his two partners as well. It must be his priority.

And so, both Ariel and María Rosa confronted Werner. If Werner continued drinking at this pace, the entire project would fail, and none of them—Werner, Ariel, or María Rosa— would benefit from the diamond deposit. Others would. Others would take over. Werner promised to listen and change his attitude, but his actions contradicted his words.

"I read that the opposition in Chile against General Pinochet is growing exponentially," Werner said as if the Latin American political map was something that interested him.

"I think that we should, must start something similar here," María Rosa said, but with such an intensity, that it startled both her friends.

Yet her passionate discharge provoked Werner's reaction. "Don't even think about that, María Rosa," he said. "You know where these revolutions begin, but you never know where they end."

"Would you be worried about your family if something happens in Chile, Ariel?" María Rosa asked to deviate the tension her venting produced, but she did it with a genuine interest for her youngest friend.

They all had seen on TV and read in the papers about the Chilean people's protests against Pinochet's dictatorship.

"No way!" Werner said. He had already drunk too much. Still, he jumped to answer before Ariel could say a word, his speech already slurred. "Whatever happens, the Jews will never be affected. They have nine lives, like cats."

María Rosa kicked Werner's knee under the table.

"My family is in business, Werner," Ariel said candidly. "Small business. They have no influence. They are not politicians."

"What I'm trying to say . . ." Werner's speech was incoherent.

"Don't say another word, Werner Mann, please," María Rosa said. "There are times that I would rather see you drinking than hear you speaking."

"Ahem!" Ariel intervened. After all, they were talking about his people, about him, a person, not a thing.

There was a long pause. María Rosa looked furious while Werner smiled stupidly and winked at her.

"They . . . the Jews never . . . raised their voices . . ." Werner started again, and he stopped there as if it were painful for him to gather the appropriate words, the non-offending words, for he knew, because of his experience in teaching, that the new generation grows even more sensitive than the precedent. "Indifference is the root of many evils." Finally, Werner completed his thought.

"Well, I give you a point in that, Werner," María Rosa said. And then, turning to Ariel, she said, "You must remember that this is exactly the way Hitler came to power. It was not because he had too many followers. On the contrary, it was because there were too many people who were indifferent to his rhetoric."

"They were different people," Ariel said as a conclusion as if he were still trying to calm down the spirits. "Different times," he repeated, as in the hope that those 'different people' and 'different times' would never return.

"Nothing has changed, Ariel," Werner stubbornly retorted. "Nothing will ever change. See this guy here in Paraguay, Stroessner. See that other guy over there in Chile, Pinochet."

"Hitler?" María Rosa said, the name burning like a thorn in her tongue.

"At least Hitler raised the country from its ruins," Werner said.

"And left it in ruins," María Rosa retorted.

"Because of the Communists and the Jews," Werner said.

"That's enough, Werner!"

Despite being drunk, Werner understood that he had to apologize, at least to Ariel, for his remark, although Ariel didn't take Werner's expletive as an insult to him.

"Okay, okay, I apologize," Werner said and burped.

María Rosa crossed her arms and looked away.

"Pardon, pardon!" Werner repeated.

"Stop, Werner, please!" María Rosa said. "It's over now, okay?"

The past belongs to the older guys, thought Ariel, yet he said nothing. To him, the past was a remote, wild, exotic destination he would never visit because he had set his whole life on future mode, running on just a one-way road with no U-turns.

"I meant," Werner said, totally out of time and moment, as it often happens with drunk people, "Jews are people who have survived through everything since ancient times."

María Rosa extended her leg under the table and forcibly kicked Werner's knee again. Finally, Werner understood, bit his lips, and covered his mouth with his hands.

Ariel was absent from these games and distracted himself with his thoughts. He thought of the orchard he would buy with his share of the diamonds, far away from all noise, far away from hate, a place with fresh water and land enough to grow all kinds of vegetables and fruits, according to his need because he was not thinking of harvesting to sell his produce in any market. No. He wanted to be away from any market or financial transaction. And in those seconds, sitting right there while María Rosa and Werner fought a battle on principles, Ariel built a world for himself. A world that he had already made many times before. A good world. *I don't like this human assembly,* he thought. *I would instead go and live in a cave or a cabin deep in the forest like a hermit, perhaps castaway on an unknown, desolate island.*

What a contradiction because all he dreamed could be possible for him if the diamond business came to fruition. For then, he insisted, he would have the money to go, find, and build that reclusive place he imagined. But then, he thought, there was—always present—the phantom of their plans of finding the diamond deposit being made public or discovered by the regime's secret police, and then he would have to say goodbye to his dreams, and most possibly, to his life. He knew well that his weight on the social scale was less than a feather. He was nobody. *It's true,* he thought, *I'm nobody. And if something goes wrong, I could end up in the Kafkaesque prison system of the regime.* He felt a knot in his stomach.

"I have to go to the washroom," Werner said, the words now hardly audible from his slurred speech. He stood up and staggered in the direction of the washroom.

"I'm sorry, again, Ariel," María Rosa said, patting Ariel's shoulder.

"Aw!" Ariel said. "Don't mind him much, María Rosa. Drunkards are like little boys. They always tell the truth. It's a good thing I don't drink that much because I don't know what would I say."

Once in the washroom, Werner washed his face with cold water, and his thoughts clarified somehow. He worried that Ariel might have to carry him through the rainforest if he fell ill, as he knew that young Ariel already had too much on his plate. Still, Werner did not feel that his health was yet that bad, but he couldn't exclude the possibility that it may occur.

On top of everything were the dangers that awaited them once they were on their way to the diamond deposit. First, there were those from the rainforest with all its surprises, the natural ones that were wild, dangerous animals, poisonous insects, vegetation, treacherous geography, massive torrents, and swamps full of deadly traps, and it was the weather, unpredictable most of the time. But then, there was the danger coming from the Aboriginal dwellers too, for he, Werner—and Ariel and María Rosa too, of course—had also to consider the wild, hostile Indigenous of whom he had already read about in some books—although, these references were unknown yet to Ariel.

And to add up to this picture, there they were, the drug dealers and the smugglers. And Werner knew about them because of the constant news and other mentions in police reports and information he had gathered. And he knew that these people—drug dealers and smugglers—were even more dangerous and violent than the savages. Worse, even than venomous snakes. And what else to add to this ruthless scenario than the guerrilla fighting their hopeless battles against the national army, whose fighters may kidnap them to exchange prisoners. And the military as well. They might wonder what these people—Werner and Ariel—were doing in such a place, so far away from civilization. And that would be like jumping from the pan onto the fire.

If Ariel knew, what Werner thought, the young man would abandon everything with no further thought, and he, Werner, would be alone. María Rosa would never accompany him to the jungle, and he would have no chance at all to start the search for a new partner again.

And although Werner tried to appear healthier, his drinking habit made things worse. For he knew well about his condition, which according to him, was not severe, although he knew not how to end it. Werner hoped things would go better for him once in the jungle, away from the alcohol and closer to fulfilling his dream. He did not want to see a doctor, for he suspected what the physician would tell him. Therefore, Werner did not want to hear about seeing a doctor because there was a force that propelled him to go blindly through the depth of night, not minding the abyss that may open at your next step. And it was what he did. He went blindly into the night, but he did not want to take his friends into his fall. And this was his dilemma.

On the other hand, Werner knew that young Ariel had put all the weight of the operation on Werner's shoulders. Ariel trusted Werner so much because Werner initiated him into this venture. And Ariel knew that Werner was the only one who could foresee the variables that might hinder the project's feasibility. And Ariel trusted that Werner would find the solution to any possible obstacle. To Ariel, the failure of Werner's plan would be disastrous. Werner had invested too much emotional capital in the project that, at this point, was unrecoverable. Therefore, a failure would mean the end of Werner's life.

And there was only one way their experience would come to fruition, one way only—to move ahead with the venture as planned, regardless of the outcome, *to go blindly into the night,* which indicated that Werner was right. And while the challenges were many, like tentacles of a horrifying beast, they had to beat it and cut its tentacles, one by one.

And if they failed, it would mean Ariel to confirm his beliefs that society had nothing to deliver to him. A young soul who wanted to live his life in contemplation of the miracles of nature. An individual who wants to live his life free of pressure, rights, and responsibilities. Away from the conflicts of modern human society. He had read about the ancient prophets who dedicated their lives to their God, although he had no prophecies to share. He knew about those Aztecs who lived away from any human contact. And although Ariel knew little about meditation, he would have liked to become one of those monks who lived in a monastery, for Ariel cheered this kind of life, a life dedicated to studying the human soul, nature, and the stars. Indeed, Ariel suffered, immersed in a world of ambition and all the evil behind it, something he saw daily in what people called civilization.

And what about María Rosa? She would continue doing what she had been doing for years, coming every day to her office, carrying on in her everyday life, and nothing would ever happen to her, for she was a good citizen. And that was what Werner thought. Yet, it was but the tip of the iceberg. Indeed, the truth was that, because of her political activities, María Rosa walked every day with a rope around her neck that may get tight at any moment, and she knew it. She knew that her underground activities might take her at any moment to the police headquarters, which was a place she had nightmares about.

But it was not because she might fail. Someone else may break down, compromise the entire operation, and blow her facade. Every chain had a weak link, and although María Rosa knew that she was not it, there was a chance someone else in her organization was. And the police and the secret service knew too—in fact, they were thoroughly seeking this weak link, too. So, it was just a matter of time for them to find it— time and timing.

And if there were no diamonds, she would continue struggling for a change of government that may bring—in a post-Stroessner era—new opportunities to herself as an individual and to her country as a whole. And it was at this point, Ariel disagreed, for to Ariel, human nature was ever-changing, and everything would continue the same, to one and the others, only that with a different name.

"I was worried about you, Werner," María Rosa said when Werner returned to join his friends after his unusually long visit to the washroom. "I was going to send Ariel to check up on you."

"María Rosa was ready to call an ambulance," Ariel said.

Werner smiled beatifically, said nothing, and just sat there. A waiter came.

"Just the bill, please," María Rosa said.

The waiter came back with the bill. Werner took out his wallet, but María Rosa grabbed it, counted the money, gave it to the waiter, and returned the wallet to Werner. Then she helped Werner onto his feet. She took Werner from his arm, they went out into the street and the fresco of the night, and Ariel followed them some steps behind, wrapped in the silence of his thoughts.

CAPRICIOUS RIVER

ONE NIGHT in July of 1943, a caravan of five black limousines left in secrecy a garage located at the *Leipzigerstrasse* in downtown Berlin. Hidden behind one of the limousines' dark windows, Dr. Berndt Zweig travelled in the back seat. When the caravan reached a point within the city limits, each car took a different direction—

Six weeks later, Dr. Zweig and his group gathered again, but this time in a remote site in South America, near an area known as *Tres Fronteras*, where the borders of Paraguay, Brazil, and Argentina meet.

The reunion's place was a *fazenda*, a ranch that belonged to a German citizen, naturalized Brazilian, a Mr. Gilberto Grünberg, by name. A German Junkers Ju 52 transport's frame sat under the bright sun not far from the main house. The airplane had brought Dr. Zweig and his party to this remote place of the South American subcontinent.

Gilberto Grünberg was a German expatriate. He was an industrious man. Don Gilberto built a cattle empire and one of the finest farms in the area, starting from nothing. He only married once and had no children. His wife, a Paraguayan beauty from Asunción, died young. The poison of a *yararacusú*, one of the most poisonous snakes in the region, took not only his wife but also what could have been Don Gilberto's first son.

After that sorrowful incident, Don Gilberto never married again. Instead, he found consolation to his solitude in expanding his ranch, raising cattle, and breeding horses. The horses were more loyal to the *gaúchos* who trained them in the corrals than Don Gilberto, who treated them like his children. On the other hand, the Natives whispered behind

Don Gilberto's back that the older man had a pact with *añá*, the devil, although Don Gilberto ignored both the Natives and their comments.

During the last years of his life, Don Gilberto became a fan of his horses and the new regime, the Third Reich, that had taken over in his Fatherland. From the borders of the rainforest, Don Gilberto envisioned the rebirth of a newly powerful Germany.

Don Gilberto was eighty years old when he met Dr. Berndt Zweig and his group. The group leader was Dr. Berndt Zweig, a fifty-five-year-old man, energetic, thin, and muscular. Apart from Dr. Zweig, the group comprised three geologists, one pilot, one mechanic, and one professional soldier. The pilot and the mechanic's mission was to transport the group to the *fazenda,* wait in the *fazenda* until the group returned from the expedition, and then take the group back to Germany. Therefore, the pilot and the mechanic had to remain guests in *Herr* Grünberg's home. The only professional soldier in the mission was forty-year-old Baron von Bohlen, the sole heir of a wealthy, aristocratic German family. His responsibility was the safety of the members of the expedition. However, the place where they were gathering seemed so peaceful and safe that he wondered if there would ever be the chance to test his skills.

At that time of the night, the ranch workers were long gone back to their cabins, the mosquitoes had stopped their annoying buzzing, and a pale moon was hanging high in a blue sky. The landscape seemed white under the moonlight as mice and snakes searched for food, and often both species coincided. Hidden by the pink flowers of the *lapachos* that surrounded the house, the round attentive eyes of owls followed both mice and snakes. The women of the house, as usual, gathered in the living room to play piano, knit, read, or talk about the day's events. Even in that remote corner of the world, decent European tradition prevailed. As Don Gilberto used to say, "If not for the heat, humidity, bugs, and snakes, the place would be a paradise."

"*Man kan nicht alles haben,*" Dr. Zweig said.

He was leaning on one of the pillars in the gallery that bordered the house. The rest of the men nodded as if Dr. Zweig had said a holy truth. They all sighed. The rest of the group, Don Gilberto among them, rested in comfortable leathered armchairs. Baron von Bohlen stood upright and watched the night with intense eyes. The host, Don Gilberto, drank *yerba mate*—the traditional warm drink in that part of the world—from an ox's horn. He sipped the infusion through a metal straw and offered the horn to his guests, but none of them dared to try it.

They talked about legends of the jungle and hidden golden cities in the depth of the forest.

"I wanted to explore the forest when I was younger," Don Gilberto said. "Twice I attempted it. However, even with the resources I had, I couldn't do so. Years later, I convinced myself that the woods were impenetrable to white folks. The Indigenous people move there like fish in the water. Anyhow, you know that I'm here to give you whatever you need, and this is my commitment to Berlin. To help you with whatever I can. I have no problem with that. And of course, I hope you will find what you are looking for, although I have no idea what it is. Never mind, I'm not going to inquire further."

No one spoke. The warm breeze accentuated the silence.

"Anyway," Don Gilberto continued, dismissing the fact he had been scorned by his guests, "I have two men who know the forest, and they can reach the place you talked me about, Herr Doktor. I have already convinced these people to accompany you, but we must understand them. These people are superstitious, and they believe that evil reigns in the forest. One of them is not so young but still is very strong. The other man is not a problem. He is a Native of this land, and he knows the forest well. These people have this gift, *und wie sie wiesen, Doktor*, these people are like animals. They orient themselves by the wind, without a compass. They go through the jungle from one side to the other, and they are never lost.

"But I'm telling you, *Herr Doktor,* that the area you showed me on your map is something entirely different because from the *fazenda* here, and to the point signaled in your chart, is very far. And there are no roads. And then there are the chaparral, the swamps that go for miles, and then the unending forest. I asked my men, and they confirmed this information. They said that most of the way is to go up and up, which is very dangerous. I beg your pardon. What river are you talking about, *Doktor* Zweig? No, *Doktor* Zweig. I'm sorry. I never heard of a river in that area. But, of course, I know that the *gaúchos* and the peasants talk about these things, but why they do it is to repeat what they heard from their parents like parrots, and so on, which in turn repeat what they hear from the Aboriginal dwellers who are liars. I know they are liars. Anyhow, over there, believe me, it is a difficult place to be.

You cannot expect anything good from there. Besides, there are snakes, the spiders, and even the other bugs, which are the worst."

"Which bugs you are referring to, *Herr* Grünberg?" the Baron von Bohlen asked.

Before answering, Don Gilberto poured more boiling water from a kettle into the bull's horn and sipped the *yerba mate* infusion through the metal straw. Satisfied, he turned toward Baron von Bohlen and said,

"The Aborigines, the Native people, is what I am talking about, *Herr* Baron von Bohlen. *Bixos do monte*—bugs from the forest—that's how the Brazilians call the Indigenous dwellers of this area."

"Are they dangerous?" someone else asked.

"Yes, if you confront them," Don Gilberto said. "Now, if you prepare well to face them, it is little they can do. Besides, Indigenous people avoid white people. But if they notice that you are invading their territory, they are pitiless. They hate white people who corner them and steal their land to transform it into cattle ranches. Poor people, I guess. I think that before the arrival of the Europeans, they were happier here."

"Nonsense," another voice said. "The aboriginals killed each other, and they still enjoy doing that."

"Don't we do the same thing?" Baron von Bohlen rebutted with the authority of one who has faced death many times in his life.

No one said anything.

"Yes," Baron von Bohlen insisted from the shadows. "We do that, and we're not happy because of what we do, are we?"

There was a tense pause, but none of the men rebutted Baron von Bohlen's words.

"The Aborigines have lost everything," Don Gilberto said, trying to lighten the atmosphere that had suddenly become heavier. "There are no treaties that order us to return to them what we took from them."

They were all silent as if mulling over these last words on the injustices committed by humankind. Yet, they also thought about their own lives on what was at stake for each one of them.

"Just to let you know," Don Gilberto's voice interrupted their thoughts, "not long ago, there was a war between Bolivians and Paraguayans, the Chaco War, they called it. The war ended about six years ago, in 1935, far from here, the Chaco Boreal they call that region, *el Infierno Verde*, the green hell. That's what they called the Chaco War. Both governments forced the Natives to fight that war, an alien war for the poor Aborigines. Both armies took them to the front like cattle. With little training, they gave them a *piripipi,* dressed them in uniforms, shoeless, of course, and to die for what, perhaps they never knew."

"Poor guys," someone said.

"That's so," Don Gilberto continued. "They pushed the Native dwellers to go to the battlefront, and those that could do so deserted and went back to the forest. The others remained there, left to die. According to Christianity, some of them received a sepulture, but most didn't have this privilege. Until they received the Holy Sacrament of Baptism by the Catholic Church, the Native dwellers were like animals, without a soul. Anyhow, as I said, most of them were food to the voracious ants and the animals. Here, in this climate, nothing lasts long. Imagine over there, in the green hell, it is green, and it is a hell of a landscape. It must have been hell for the soldiers of both countries in conflict. They never knew of a better life, anyway. And as I said, in the jungle, everything disappears in hours. Bones and skin vanish as butter on the stove. Nothing is left. This red soil eats all."

"What is *piripipí?*" Dr. Berndt Zweig asked, who was thinking of a kind of blowgun with poisoned darts, or perhaps a javelin.

"*Die Maschinenpistolen 28,*" Don Gilberto said.
"Submachine gun 28. Bolivian soldiers used them. Paraguayan soldiers baptized them *piripipí* during the war. I guess it was because of the characteristic sound when fired."

There was total silence. The visitors were all involved in their thoughts. Then, out there, far in the corrals, the horses neighed. The men stood upright and readied, their eyes alert. Don Gilberto smiled.

"The females are in heat," Don Gilberto explained, smiling, sipping from his mate.

The men relaxed.

"The neighing you heard comes from their jubilant squeaks."

Some of the men watched the moon high and white above in the sky.

"And talking about females," Don Gilberto said, "the Aboriginal people are very creative with their legends. For example, *Doktor* Zweig, a Native couple, man and wife, told me once about a tradition among the Natives. They said that in their tribe, it is the woman who proposes to the man."

The singing of the insects cooing the night.

"Well," Dr. Berndt Zweig said, "something peculiar, but nothing out of the ordinary, *Her* Grünberg."

No one from the group made another comment. The stillness of the night, the warm breeze, and their thoughts in the faraway country were all involved in what seemed to be an endless war.

"The woman proposes to her man by placing a diamond in his hand," Don Gilberto said, making another effort to keep alive the, until then, insubstantial conversation.

An explosion would have caused a lesser effect. So now, all men turned toward Don Gilberto.

"*Was haben Sie gesagt, Herr Grünberg?*" Dr. Zweig said.

Don Gilberto almost jumped from his comfortable leathered armchair.

"What, what did I say?" He was scared, suddenly scared.

"About the woman proposing the man," Dr. Zweig said, bending toward Don Gilberto.

"Ah!" Don Gilberto breathed again. "What about that?"

"She puts a diamond in the man's hand," Baron von Bohlen intervened.

"Oh, yes," Don Gilberto relaxed, "A diamond! Can you believe that? The Natives, as I said, are very imaginative with their legends."

"Where did they get that?" Dr. Zweig said, his voice toneless, spectral, and dry.

"I don't know, *Doktor* Zweig," Don Gilberto said. *Fuck, why did I talk?* He thought to himself, for he was commencing to feel the pressure. He knew these men were all expert torturers. A dry sweat ran down his spine. He would feel happy when these people left his home. "It's just a legend, *Doktor* Zweig. There are dozens of them. Nobody I knew has ever witnessed a Native's wedding."

The men, expecting an epiphany, relaxed yet turned around disappointed and went back to their thoughts.

"*Interessant. Sehr interessant, Herr Grünberg,*" Dr. Zweig said, almost to himself, scratching his chin.

The warm breeze continued blowing softly, suavely, the singing of the cicadas, the starred night—

"*Was einer Verld ist das!*" sighed Baron von Bohlen.

He was perhaps feeling as if he was living on another planet. So peaceful. So enchanting. So remote from the war that was consuming Europe. *What world is this* was perhaps the phrase that all of these men gathered there were thinking about.

"How would it have been in those times?" said a voice. "With the means they had, I mean, in this geography, without roads—?"

"There has not been much advancement," said another voice.

"Indeed," Don Gilberto said. "We haven't had much development, but development for what? I hope this place never develops. Progress, as you may know, is not always a good thing."

"Do they have a religion?" someone asked.

"The Natives?" Don Gilberto said. "I guess, although I'm not sure. It could be a natural religion. When the Spaniards and the Portuguese came to this land, they demanded that everybody embrace Christianity. The Jesuits, who were the ones that came here, had excellent techniques for converting the Aboriginal people. Yet, it's a known fact that they, the Aboriginals, hated the new teachings. So, in their wrath against the colonizers, sometimes the Natives put everything related to the Catholic Church into a canoe. Icons and crosses, visual depictions of Jesus and the Virgin, clothing used in the church—and send everything down the river with the hope that the river whitewater would take away all of the evils brought to them by the church. They wanted the river to take all of their demons away."

After these words, they all kept silent for a long while. A soft, nocturnal breeze came from the fields. The horses were now quiet. Indifferent to the snakes, the frogs sang in the pond. Indifferent to the owls, the snakes were getting closer to the frogs. And indifferent to all that surrounded them, the men thought of their families so far away. The moon lighted everything. And far, far away in the middle of the jungle, a promise awaited them all, a pledge hidden among the millenary roots of the rainforest.

Don Gilberto's harsh German mixed with soft Brazilian nuances removed the men from their reveries.

"Many stories are going around," Don Gilberto said. "Some are fictitious, and some are real. *Es steht in den Sternen geschrieben.* Yeah, you may accept that as the Natives say, these stories came from the stars. But anybody can think about what he or she want. However, I believe that many of these stories the white folks invented created a negative image of the Natives. For instance, one story goes that when Native women gave birth to twins, the tribe killed the second one because they believed it was an evil spirit following the first one, who was the good one, of course."

The wind blew softly on the fronds.

"What worries me, *Herr* Grünberg," said Dr. Berndt Zweig, "is the Paraguayan army border patrols. You know that our focus of interest is on the Paraguayan side."

"Yes, Doctor, so it is," Don Gilberto said. "Everything lies on the Paraguay side of the border, but what are you afraid of? Around here, I mean, in this region, the limits are still not clear. No soldiers are patrolling the border yet. The rainforest takes care of itself. Once you are on the way to your destination, you will better understand what I'm saying now. Besides, in the direction you are heading, the most probable thing is that you will never have to face a Native, and least of all a person from the civilization."

"But someone could see us, and he could go to denounce us to the authorities, *Herr* Grünberg," Baron von Bohlen said. "Perhaps they can send a reconnaissance plane."

"A reconnaissance plane?" Don Gilberto gave out a hearty laugh; he almost dropped the mate on the floor. "Please, *Reichfreiherr* von Bohlen. Here does not exist such a thing. Around here, you can see some airplanes. I don't know if they are either Argentinian or Brazilian. They are not even military planes, and they never go deep into the forest. It's not their territory. And by the way, have you ever seen the jungle from the air? A couple of years ago, I flew once in a small plane with a Belgian pilot who brought me some merchandise from a Brazilian city called Ponta Porá. The flight is the scariest thing you may ever experience. And the fog that covers the jungle is a wall. And when it's clear," Don Gilberto made a pause to add more intensity to his narrative. "When it is clear," he continued, "you see things where there is nothing. The forest tricks the human eye. You see roads where there is none. And for miles and miles, it is all green. But from the air, you don't see people, or the swamps, the cliffs, and the deep ravines."

"You know we must reach our destination in the allotted time, *Herr* Grünberg," Dr. Berndt Zweig said. "The program must go on, and it is up to us now to achieve our goal. But first, we have to confirm what is written on those letters."

"Letters?" Don Gilberto could not stop himself from asking. "What letters do you refer to, *Herr Doktor?*"

"*Entschuldigen Sie, Herr Grünberg,*" Dr. Berndt Zweig said. "I cannot expand on this subject."

"*Ich verstehe, Herr Doktor,*" Don Gilberto said. "*Bitte. Fahren Sie fort.*"

"Good," Dr. Berndt Zweig said. "We want no competitors. We need no help, least of all from any government officers, even though it could be a friendly one. It's not part of the project to attract attention to it. That's why we have to do it this way. We don't want to see ten thousand people devastating the jungle and digging holes all over the forest like maniacs. We know that the Brazilian have been exploring the Mato Grosso region in the Pantanal area, but not in that particular place. And I don't think that they would like to venture toward the Paraguayan side of the border."

They are exploring for gold, Don Gilberto thought, *or precious stones. But up there in the rainforest? I think these people are wrong.*

"I don't think so, either, *Herr Doktor,*" Don Gilberto said with an enthusiasm that hid his thoughts. "Unless there are agreements between both states."

"I see," Dr. Berndt Zweig said. "But those possible agreements are of no interest to us. On the contrary, they will be a serious inconvenience to our interests. That is why everything we do has to be in secrecy."

There was an uncomfortable pause. In the silence that followed, the singing of crickets reached clearly into their ears.

"However," Don Gilberto said, "we all have to be alert. This land is like a magician's hat, full of tricks. It promises a lot and delivers nothing. If you want to obtain something from it, we have to work harder. On the other hand, who knows? Maybe somewhere from here to the Andes, there is a fortune sleeping."

"And it will be us who will wake it up, gentlemen," Dr. Berndt Zweig said, addressing his comrades. "And to achieve this goal, the best we can do is to have a good night's sleep so tomorrow we can start afresh. A long day awaits. *Gute Nacht, Herr Grünberg. Gute Nacht, meine Kameraden. Heil Hitler!*"

"THIS is the area where the diamond field lies," Werner said and went back to making another circle in the already scratched map he had unfolded on the table.

The document contained a detailed view of the geography that Werner highlighted with passion. There were other circles on this map, yet they belonged not to Werner's markings but to the marks of the bottom of beer bottles that Werner drank one after the other.

"The purest diamonds ever found await us, Ariel," Werner continued, energized by the illusion of soon being able to have those precious stones in his hands. "Anyhow, this information would have never reached us, I mean, up there in Berlin, in the laboratory, if it were not for an individual who had the idea of sending it to us. This individual was Mr. Bartels, a covert agent of the National Socialist Party in this part of the world."

Werner reflected on the subject after a long silence, admiring the map in front of his eyes.

"Jesuit priests were the first ones with information on this diamond field," he said after a long pause. "The priests got the information and kept it to themselves. I don't know if they did some exploration, but I'm certain they didn't because I have the papers that confirm that they shared this information with no one."

"The Jesuits built Indigenous reductions in Paraguay, the north of Argentina, and the south of Brazil," María Rosa intervened.

Werner nodded and continued his presentation.

"According to the information, I gathered piece by piece throughout the years, of which, I have to warn you, may not be exactly as the official records claim. Thus, for example, on *November 16, of the year of our Lord, 1938*," Werner began to read from a document, "a woman working as an administrative employee of a non-governmental organization called Christian Missions, Mme. de L'Aarrot by name, found by accident a bunch of letters among the archives. These letters were part of a regular epistolary exchange between Jesuit priests. Christian Missions was excavating the Jesuit ruins in Trinidad's zone near Encarnación, in Paraguay. Mme. de L'Aarrot was in charge of recording, cataloging, and archiving the findings.

"Among the many letters, there was one dated *December 5, of the year of our Lord, 1767*. In this letter, one of the priests commented on a story that the Natives of his flock told him. Most of these Natives were Guaraní Aborigines converted to Christianity by the missioners. Apart from describing domestic issues, the said letter expanded about a peculiar Aboriginal tradition: the woman from the tribe of marriageable age proposes to her chosen man by placing one diamond in the man's hand. It's a peculiar tradition because, in our world, it is the man who proposes to the woman, and to celebrate such an event, the man is the one who gives a diamond ring to his chosen wife-to-be, isn't it fascinating?

"So, the primary question would be, where did the Aboriginal women get this tradition from? However, the important question should be, where did the Native bride-to-be get the diamond? Henceforward, this tradition gave birth to a legend about a deposit of precious stones that lay hidden deep in the jungle, at the shore of a hallucinatory river, in a specific point of a vast region of the southwestern Amazonian rainforest dominated by savage Aboriginals. A tip of that land that covers hundreds of miles of rainforest belongs now to the Republic of Paraguay."

Werner made a pause, grabbed a beer, gobbled it down, sighed, looked blankly around him, remembered where he was, and resumed his talking.

"Well," he said, "the Jesuit missioners had their ways with the Natives. The priests had their tactics to make the Natives talk. After all, the priests were their coaches, counselors, and protectors against the slave merchants. The priests were their 'Fathers.' It is possible that one or two, or maybe more Natives, approached their confessors and revealed the diamond field's existence. For sure, they cajoled them with promises of salvation, and so on. However, for some unknown reason, there are no records of exploration in this region. Neither the priests nor other Europeans ever set foot in the area, and if so, the Jesuits may have dismissed the information, either because it was a simple rumour or because they deemed it a legend. I guess the priests considered it too fantastic of a deal to take it seriously, a part of the Native people's mythology with no base in reality.

"Guaraní Natives explained to the Jesuit priests the location of the field at the shores of a monster river. *The trees melted and transformed in water,* wrote one priest rephrasing upon his interview with a Native. But this proved nothing. Another priest stated that the Natives spoke about *clouds that become a river*. The river comes from the sky. The rain forms the river. The river comes from hell like a monster and devours everything in its place. There you go," Werner said with a smile on his face.

"From hell. The river comes from hell. Sure, why not? The Natives were mixing Christian teaching with their symbolism—and if so," Werner said, "and it is as the Natives said it was, then it must be true. The river comes from somewhere, covers that part of the jungle, and disappears, leaving behind, as a reward, the fields covered with shining stones. Indeed, in the voices of the Natives, it could have sounded somehow cryptic. Think of it as the River Nile," Werner continued. "In every flood, it left the land covered with nutrient-rich soil the ancient Egyptians took advantage of for their agricultural purposes. This river, instead, leaves diamonds with every flooding. The point is, Mme. de L'Aarrot understood the importance of this document, yet she didn't take it to her superiors. Instead, she took it to her boyfriend, who by mere coincidence," Werner chuckled, "was Mr. Bartels."

Werner made a long pause, felt thirsty, and despite María Rosa's unfriendly stare, opened a beer and drank straight from the bottle and dried it without even stopping to breathe, even though María Rosa extended her hand and pushed his arm down to slow his drinking.

"Ah!" Werner was glowing. "I feel better now." He placed the empty bottle on the table and proceeded with the story. "Well. According to the news in the local newspaper, an accident happened in the Paraná River. A boat sank, which is a common misfortune, and one person drowned. In a column in the said newspaper, one of the accident witnesses, a fisherman, explained how he saved a drowning man. There were a man and a woman on the sinking boat, the fisherman said. Despite the desperation in the woman's cry for help, he could not save the woman, and she sank with the boat. There was no further investigation of the accident. The only notable line in this story is that the man who the fisherman saved was our Mr. Bartels, and the woman who drowned was Mme. de L'Aarrot."

Werner chuckled again at such an opportunistic turn of fate and looked to find another beer, but María Rosa stopped him. Werner sighed.

Ariel's expression showed how horrified he was as he followed how the drama unfolded.

"One of the conclusions of my inquiry," Werner continued, "is that the said Mr. Bartels used his influence to place Mme. de l'Aarrot in such a strategic position during the archeological studies carried on by Christian Missions."

"What a soulless criminal," Ariel said, disgusted. "Ambition kills, indeed."

Werner didn't answer. They both mulled over the criminal roots of the business they were thinking to accomplish.

"And so," Ariel said, "this guy, Bartels, sent the Jesuit letters to the Germans—"

Werner nodded.

"Then, it's a secret no more," Ariel said. "There must be a lot of people around that know about this deposit."

"Not so," Werner replied. "Remember that all the information on this subject centers on assumptions, which in turn base on myths. Several persons had access to these letters, that's true, but this does not mean that they took action. Why? I guess because there was never concrete proof of the existence of the diamond deposit, and all the information lies on an exchange of gossip between two priests living in a faraway mission three hundred years ago.

"It looks something similar to El Dorado, the golden city that the Spaniards searched for, or the Fountain of Youth in Florida. I guess those places indeed exist. I'm not joking. I'm telling you that the Natives gave the coordinates of their location using their cosmological viewpoint. Fortunately, for us, no one until now has been able to understand those codes. Listen. If I'm able to decipher that 'cosmological viewpoint,' then I assure you, Ariel, that we could find anything that until now remains hidden."

Ariel shook his head. *This idea is going too far,* he thought.

"Okay, I agree with you," Werner said as if he once again had read Ariel's thoughts. "Although you must remember that until Heinrich Schliemann discovered it, Troy was but a story of fiction. And the tomb of Tutankhamen, hidden for more than two thousand years, and no one ever knew about all that wealth buried there, in front of everybody."

"I understand that," Ariel said, "but you are taking this thing beyond that. It is as if you are looking for *Treasure Island*. No matter what action you take, it's, of course, fictional. It doesn't exist."

"*Treasure Island* is a fictional tale, Ariel. I agree with you. But what about the mines of King Solomon? It is also a legend that has gone on for so long. A legend is a legend is a legend. But, is it fiction, or does it have something real in it?"

"Okay," Ariel said, "but in regards to this diamond deposit hidden in the rainforest—"

"In regards to the diamond deposit hidden in the rainforest, Ariel, let me assure you that during the withdrawal phase and following rendition of the Germans, all documentation disappeared like magic from the laboratory. Nothing remained.

And on what attains to our particular business, there is nothing left, except that the dossier that contains the records on the diamond venture, and," Werner chuckled and made a long pause, as to create momentum, as if he were expecting to hear the sound of drums rolling, "the original letters the Jesuit priests exchanged," he finally said and sighed.

"But it is still a tale, Werner. It's still a legend," María Rosa said. Yet, she also felt that the resources she hoped could finance her revolutions were flying away toward a Hollywood sunset.

"C'mon, guys!"

"The said river doesn't exist, Werner."

"It does, Ariel. I will show you."

"Show me now."

"I can't. We must be in the jungle."

"What I think, Werner," Ariel said, "is that if it's true that the diamonds are there, someone must have already had access to such a deposit. Someone must have found the river, at least. But then, in your own words, no one until now has reached such a place. Even an aerial survey of the area showed no river flowing through."

"And this is good news, Ariel, the good news that no one has found the place. So we will be the first ones."

"You are pursuing a dream, Werner."

"It might as well be a dream, Ariel. But it's a dream worth pursuing. I'm not going to abandon it now. I cannot betray it. Besides, no one finding it until now does not mean it doesn't exist. On the contrary, it opens a door for us to adventure over there, and we could see it with our own eyes. If no one has ever found it, it only means that until now, no one has found it, that's all. For years and years, I have thought about it. I have studied the entire region, and I have concluded that the diamonds are waiting for us. I'm sure I have the answer to this mystery. That's why I'm here."

"So, we will be the first to adventure over there, won't we?" Ariel said.

Werner didn't answer, and his silence made Ariel think further about the adventure offered to him. Because Werner's argument did not entirely convince Ariel, it was difficult to believe that such a marvel was still undiscovered. The government, through its many tentacles, should have already closed the entire zone. Even the military, acting on their own, would have done the same. They would punish whoever entered the forbidden area. Therefore, something more could be there, and Werner was not telling him.

On the other hand, if such a large number of persons knew about this secret, why was there no news? Why were they not exploiting the land, destroying the rainforest, uprooting every tree? It was also probable that the cost of the operation could have made the project unrealizable. Still, to Ariel, it didn't make sense. In the Germans' case, it was somehow possible that they didn't follow up because of the war. And when the war ended, those who were aware of the secret passed away. It could be so, because as it seemed, Werner was the only one who knew about it—the only man left alive from all of those who worked in the laboratory. *Only that here in Paraguay,* Ariel thought, *there are so many big shots. Werner should be more careful with these people. People with a lot of influence in the government. Opportunistic politicians. Sycophants.*

Police. Unethical entrepreneurs. They are the elephants in this narrow path, thought Ariel, *and we are the frogs on the course of the elephants.*

However, despite his gloomy thoughts, Ariel saw himself exploring the rainforest, tracking through the dry leaves, digging the ground with his bare hands, and finding diamonds and diamonds and diamonds, and it would be as if his world had turned into a bright, giant gem.

"In here," Werner Mann's voice interrupted Ariel's thoughts. His index finger signaled a point in the map, "We will have to take a road which unfortunately does not appear on this map. Although this map is correct, it has not been updated for obvious reasons. So no one ever has been there yet."

Werner took another map from the pile of papers he had on the bed. "In this other map," he said, "you cannot see it, either, although this is a satellite map. We have to be thankful that the satellite is not recording this specific point of the jungle. Henceforth, we must guide ourselves only by the information we have. Even so, as I said, it's not updated. But you should not worry about this, Ariel."

"As you already know, the most important thing is not to attract attention to us. That's why I want to rent a simple vehicle, not a fancy one with double traction, which would be ideal for our venture. Now, I know that when rain falls, every rural road becomes a trap. Then, we will have no other way but to wait until the rain stops and the road is dry again. From this road, we have at least forty miles of bad road. Then, we will have to stop here," he made another circle on the map, "and leave the vehicle hidden among the shrubs and take whatever we may need. And then, walk."

"Sounds easy," Ariel said.

"Not so," Werner said. "This is the most challenging part. From here, we have to walk through the forest. And I'm worried about this portion of the adventure. There will at least be eight hours of a forced march through the jungle. There are no paths. We have to walk always following the north-northwest. We may have to stop and protect ourselves in case of rain, which I know is frequent and intense. And a swamp is there, a vast swamp we'll have to cross, and I'm thinking of that, too. Besides that, we will have to take care of the mosquitoes and the snakes, the aquatic ones are very venomous, and the spiders and other poisonous insects. And the humidity. And once we reach the river, we have to walk following its course, and that means going uphill, at least for five more hours, my best guess, until we find the river."

"A capricious river that comes from the clouds and disappears at will and uncovers a field of diamonds! What is this, Werner, a fairy tale?"

"A capricious river! That's what it is, Ariel. I'm sure it is. I once read a book on the Amazonian Native's cosmogony. That river exists. It's true. It comes and goes, but it does not come from the clouds. I'm ready to prove it, but only to one audience—you."

Werner rested and finished another bottle of beer, and then he sat with his eyes closed. Ariel sipped his beer and said nothing. Then, suddenly, Werner opened his eyes and stared at the map for a long time as if wanting to immerse himself in it, as if the capricious river showed itself as per magic in the middle of the rainforest.

"Here," Werner said. He had suddenly come back to life, and his reaction startled Ariel. Werner may have thought or remembered something. "This is on no map yet, Ariel, but I have a good copy of all the notes taken by Dr. Berndt Zweig . . ." Werner stopped. He knew he had committed a slip of the tongue.

Ariel just stared at him.

"I didn't tell you about this before," Werner said, "but certainly, there was a group that came to investigate this area back in 1941. It was a very secretive task, and the fact is that they found nothing, and that was the end of their attempts in this part of the world."

"Are you sure they found nothing, Werner?" Ariel said. "This is turning like those Russian dolls. One thing inside the other. One surprise after the other. Is there any bottom in this sea of half-truths?"

"You know they found nothing, Ariel. C'mon. If they had started something, we wouldn't be talking, right? There would be no secret to discuss. Yes, the Germans carried out their exploration in secret, but this issue would be public if they had found diamonds in the area. The number of people working there would have called everybody's attention. The group's objective, led by Dr. Zweig, was to confirm the legend to validate a theory. They didn't. They could not reach the deposit. Why? I don't know. I managed myself at significant risk even to my life to get a copy of the notes and some of the maps, and afterward, I thoroughly studied them. I was there in the laboratory when they came back, and I guess that they went around and around in the rainforest until they decided to return empty-handed to Germany."

"Okay," Ariel said, "but what tells you that it will not be the same with us. We may come back empty-handed too. If we ever come back."

"It won't happen, Ariel. I have had more time than they ever had to study all the parameters and geography. Now, I know better than they did in their time. Let me show you here on this map." Werner leaned again on the map. "Here," he said. "It shows clearly where the river makes a curve. Indeed, it makes a complete U. Over there, the stream's force must be powerful. I say this because of the geography of the region. And this is good for us because it is a known fact that the Native dwellers keep away from places where they cannot swim, use their canoes, or fish. So, I'm sure we won't see them over there. And around that U, I assure you, Ariel, there must lie the most incredible diamantiferous deposit as no other anywhere in the world."

The three of them dined in a downtown restaurant. By the end of dinner, Werner was drunk, and María Rosa intervened with authority. As a result, Werner had to exchange his beer bottle for one of mineral water. Werner complained to her that it was an excessive punishment to his body and that the sudden change would affect him.

"I will risk oxidizing," he said.

Anyhow, despite Werner's protests, there were no alcohol-related incidents, and the rest of the gathering flowed in harmony. After dinner, the three of them walked arm in arm to Werner's hotel. Asunción was usually a quiet city, and this evening was not the exception. The bell tolling from La Iglesia de la Encarnación marked the rhythm of their steps.

"Tonight is so quiet," María Rosa said.

Ariel smiled, enjoying the moment. Werner also smiled, but his smile lacked the authenticity of Ariel's.

"It's quiet by a decree," Werner said. And as it always happened, his character betrayed him, and he could not avoid making one of his sour comments. "The peace of a sleeping herd of sheep with the world on guard."

"Would you rather prefer a bath of blood, dear Werner?" María Rosa said.

"I said nothing. *Ich spreche nicht viel Spanisch,*" Werner said swift as a wasp.

"Werner would rather prefer that the Pope becomes a revolutionary, like Che Guevara," Ariel said in good humour.

"A revolutionary is not always necessary," Werner answered. "A true person is what we need. A person whose principles bring us all together toward a common goal."

"That sounds good to me," Ariel said.

SEATED ON Werner's bed, María Rosa watched an old movie on TV while both men talked in the living room. Ariel listened patiently, although he had heard the same explanation many times before. However, the young man needed to learn them by heart. There should be, as per Werner's words, the triumph of persistence. Those were the words that Werner struggled to instill in the young man's mind and heart—never, never give up!

"As I have already explained to you, Ariel," Werner said, "we're going to recollect whatever we can find in the least possible time. It's the opportunity of one's life. As we will spend at least two nights there in the open, in the middle of the rainforest, we will have enough time to explore the beach, the place where the river makes a U-turn. And after that, on our return, I foresee that we can make it faster, as we will come back more light, of course carrying the diamonds, and these, as you may feel already, will be our precious cargo."

"However, you have to consider that twelve or more hours walking in a hostile territory can be harsh. But we are already in the critical phase, and we cannot go back to ground zero."

"I insist on horses," Ariel said.

"Don't be silly, Ariel," Werner said. "That's only for bad movies about explorers in Africa. Horses are useless in the rainforest. I know that Dr. Zweig and his group used horses to cover part of their journey, but they had to abandon them when the rainforest became deeper. Besides, I already talked to you about the dangers. So let's forget about horses and donkeys. Don't even think of that."

"Yes," Ariel insisted, "but how come the pioneers, Spaniards, and Portuguese did it, with horses and all? How did they go through the Amazon with horses and all their paraphernalia?"

"They didn't know what kind of territory they were entering. Anyhow, I know the horses didn't last long. They ate them. That's for sure."

Ariel remained silent for several seconds. His concern, although he couldn't share it with Werner, was Werner's health. Ariel thought that Werner would feel ill once they were well into the rainforest, and it would be him, Ariel, who would have to carry Werner throughout the swamps and forest. But, of course, Ariel didn't want this to happen. That's why he, being a city man who had never seen the rainforest up close, insisted on bringing horses.

"Anyhow, Ariel," Werner said after waiting for Ariel's reaction, and as there was none, he continued, "What we are doing now is tossing a coin and hoping."

Tossing a coin with no tail, but two heads instead, a marked coin, thought Ariel, but he held his thought. He just listened. And in his mind, he began to picture the rainforest and the creatures of the jungle and the river flooding everything, and there was no ford to cross it. And on one side of the river, the military waited for them, their guns ready, while behind the trees, the Natives hid, standing by to finish the job, and the guerilla was active—and then, the drug dealers, and the smugglers, and the police, and the government officers—*Lord, pity us!*

"According to this map," Werner continued, speaking despite the visible apprehensions of his young associate, "this route ends here at this farm, although I don't know if either of them still exists, I mean either the road or the cattle ranch, the *fazenda*. The ranchers, you must remember, Ariel, burn portions of the rainforest to gain land to raise beef, and so we should avoid those people too."

So, no one to trust but God thought Ariel.

"In any case," Werner continued as if he had read Ariel's thoughts, "we could trust the poor peasants who suffer injustices from everybody, so the most probable is that if they see us, they will ignore us. And from here onward, we will find a road that will take us to this highway, and from here," he made an X on the map, "to the Paraguayan city of Q —. From here," he signaled the X again, "it will take us two or three hours to reach this city."

Ariel wondered about Werner's optimism. *Is it healthy?*

"We will leave the vehicle in Q —, at a place I have references of, so your boss can recover it," Werner continued, oblivious of Ariel's somber mood, "near the Brazilian border, and we will cross the border on foot. On the Brazilian side, we will take a flight to one of the main cities in the area, or perhaps further, to Foz do Iguaçu, and from there, I will call María Rosa. We will wait there until she meets us. I know she'd like to relax for some days in the resort city of Buzios. Anyhow, from there on, you are free to do whatever you decide."

Werner envisioned the future. No. He didn't foresee it. He touched it. If everything worked well, that should be the outcome. Werner's maxim: "It's the impossible that has made man what he is" was the engine of his life. Never give up on your dreams. Repeat this one and a thousand times.

Berlin. April 13, 1943.

WHILE ON every front, the war expanded, inside Werner's laboratory, the day's event was the arrival of Dr. Zweig's expedition to South America. As it was mandatory, the young Werner Mann, third assistant to Professor Ludwig Matheus, chief of the Department of Geology, joined the other team members to welcome the newly arrived travellers. Dr. Zweig and his associates looked tanned and thinner. However, the welcome party was brief and sorrowful this time, for there was not much to celebrate. The expedition didn't reach its objective, and the worst that happened to them was the loss of *Kameraden Reichfreiherr,* Ehrbert von Bohlen, who died in the jungle as a victim of a poisoned arrow during an encounter with savage Aboriginals. The expedition endured constant harassment from the Native people. According to the expedition members who volunteered to testify about the incident, *Reichfreiherr,* Ehrbert von Bohlen, protected the group's withdrawal. He had kept himself in the rearguard, oblivious of the great danger that surrounded him. A hero! *Kameraden Reichfreiherr,* Ehrbert von Bohlen, died as a hero. He sacrificed himself so that the members of the expedition could return to their families.

However, they never found the Count's body. Bodies in the rainforest disappear in a matter of hours. It is nature's deep cleaning. Therefore, it is impossible to recover a body from the rainforest. The settlers of that inhospitable land have this truth clear in their minds.

The Führer himself had appointed *Reichfreiherr*, Ehrbert von Bohlen. The Baron's mission was to accompany and protect the scientists throughout their essential mission to South America. There was nothing extraordinary in this appointment. It was customary that elite soldiers escorted the missions whose objective was to obtain financial benefit for the regime. But, *Reichfreiherr,* Ehrbert von Bohlen, was more than an elite soldier. He was a member of one of the most aristocratic families from Berlin and Germany's most immense fortunes. His father was a wealthy industrialist. Baron von Bohlen was engaged to the daughter of another millionaire, and the union of both families and wealth was one of the subjects in the daily gossip of society. Even the wedding list was not a secret, as among the guests at the wedding party was supposed to be the Führer himself and Joseph Goebbels, Martin Bormann, and General Hans Krebs.

Nevertheless, his powerful family had ordered an exhaustive investigation into the causes of the Baron's death. They had enough when they learned that they could not recover this body. *In the rainforest, bodies dissolve like salt in hot water,* expressed a certain *Herr* Gilberto Grünberg in his report, in cooperation with the Gestapo. The private family investigation produced no new elements, and aside from those already known facts, the Baron's death resulted from one, or several, poisoned arrows. Upon suffering a savage attack by the Aboriginals, the wounded Baron fell into a deep ravine, which made the recovery of his body an impossible mission. To the government, and the laboratory, *Reichfreiherr,* Ehrbert von Bohlen, was already a hero. And because of his many sacrifices defending the Fatherland, the military awarded him with the Iron Cross. He was indeed a gentleman. An aristocrat. A soldier.

Of course, the information delivered to the media and the public was different. The Baron von Bohlen had died from a heroic action during a secret mission on the Eastern front. The Third Reich demanded this sacrifice.

Afterward, everything came back to normalcy. There was no time for mourning or lavish celebrations. *Arbeit Macht Frei.* And as it is for everybody, work healed his or her sorrow.

Five days later

ARIEL HAD kept himself busy by shopping for the necessary articles that Werner had suggested. He had also made some time to wash and repair his old knapsack, a blue, white, and red striped canvas bag with several pockets—the American flag's knapsack that provoked scornful looks from the leftist students at the university—and which he had bought years ago from a secondhand outdoors supplier in Valparaiso. Ariel didn't use it much, for there was no reason to use it in the city. However, he had it almost forgotten inside a suitcase, and when he rediscovered it, he decided that it would make an excellent addition to his adventure.

Ariel added a ten-inch, transparent plastic hose and a thirty-litre jerry can container to his shopping list. The container was for extra gasoline, as Werner insisted. He didn't want them to find themselves trapped in the middle of the nothingness because of an empty fuel tank. The jerry can fit in the back of the station Falcon Station Wagon Ariel had already chosen to rent.

Also, as per Werner's specific shopping list, Ariel bought various items that included a series of instruments proper of a jeweller. Most of these instruments were unknown to him, and so he stored them in their original package. These items were: a jeweller's eye loupe magnifier of the type that attaches to spectacles, a microscope, calipers, a spectroscope, and a refractometer, two glass vials of the kind of those to collect samples in laboratories, and a scale of a type he even didn't know existed. Werner insisted on the extra care Ariel should have in the packaging and storage of these instruments as they were fragile.

Ariel also bought two picks, two shovels, two machetes, a pair of soft hand towels, and a couple of large food storage containers with sealable lids. Ariel never questioned Werner about any items from Werner's shopping list, but the two glass vials puzzled him even more than the other articles.

"They are for the diamonds," Werner had explained to him. "Once we have them cleaned, weighed, measured, and counted, we will put them in here. The vials are made of special glass and won't break easily, Ariel. Trust me."

And because Ariel accepted this explanation without further questioning, Werner felt pushed to go further in detail.

"You know, Ariel," Werner said, "in the diamond mines in South Africa, some of the workers used to steal diamonds using these types of vessels."

"How?" Ariel asked.

"Well, they filled the vessel with diamonds and introduced it up to their ass. This way, they passed the control point until the mine's administrator discovered the trick. Afterward, each worker had to suffer an invasive digital inspection of their colon." Werner chuckled upon this explanation as if it were something funny.

Ariel, on the contrary, was horrified.

SEVERAL DAYS went by, and because he had been busy with all the trip details, Ariel had not seen Werner or María Rosa. Ariel had already safely stored most of the items as per Werner's shopping list. However, something unexpected happened, which put Ariel's expectations of the venture on standby. María Rosa informed him that Werner was sick. Three days ago, she had to rush Werner to a hospital.

María Rosa explained to Ariel that she found Werner in his hotel apartment, suffering acute pain in his stomach. She called an ambulance and used her influence so Werner could have prompt medical care and a private room in the hospital. The doctor that took care of him diagnosed a severe stomach infection and prescribed antibiotics.

"He will be okay," the doctor said, "but no more alcohol."

This notice upset Werner so much, and he wanted to leave the hospital right away.

"This doctor knows nothing," Werner said to a concerned María Rosa. "I need rest. Look, I slept, and I feel well now. I need no antibiotics."

María Rosa made all that was possible for her to soothe him. She thought of the diamond venture and wondered how Ariel would react to news of a sick Werner. The truth was that María Rosa didn't have the strength to deal with both men.

"I'm not sick," Werner said as if he had read María Rosa's thoughts. "It's just a small inconvenience."

"Yeah, Werner. But this will mean a lot to Ariel. How do you think he will react?"

"I'll talk to him," Werner said.

María Rosa knew that the young man trusted Werner's knowledge and planning skills, as per her conversations with Ariel. She knew that her young friend would take any risk to achieve the objective. But now, Werner's bad health would demand to postpone the plan, perhaps indefinitely, and it could be possible to cancel it. Ariel was so enthusiastic about the project that he would be severely disappointed if the project didn't work. María Rosa was deeply concerned about this. She knew that everything depended on Werner's health, an issue none of them considered before.

"Werner wants to talk to you, Ariel," said María Rosa.

She knew about Ariel's sweet character, but she also knew the rare occasions when he exploded because of injustice or something similarly upsetting to the young man, and it was in such a way that he seemed to be a different person.

"How is he?"

"He is okay," María Rosa said. "He slept well, and today he is in better spirits. The good news is that he may be released from the hospital, if not today, for sure tomorrow in the morning."

"Well," Ariel said, "at least that's something."

"Please go now and talk to him. I cannot go with you because I have things to do. But I will call you later. If you want, we can have dinner together tonight, would you agree?"

"I will hear what he has to say first," Ariel said.

Werner received him in his room in the hospital. Ariel sat on a chair by the side of the bed. He looked at him with curiosity. Werner smiled. Ariel didn't.

"You gave me a big scare," Ariel said.

"I know, I know. Bad luck, though," Werner said. "But the important thing is what I have to tell you. This crisis in my health and the general political situation in the country demand that I change my plans—"

"I see," Ariel said, interrupting him. "I guess we will have to cancel everything."

"Demand that I change my plans," Werner continued, ignoring Ariel's asseveration, "and for a change, I mean to speed them up, Ariel, and this means that we must be prepared to go ahead with our exploration plans within a week, at least. Let's see, what day is it today?" Without waiting for Ariel to answer, he turned around and looked at his notes from the night table. "Ah! It's perfect. Say that we must be ready to go on September 4th, which is a Sunday, and that's perfect. Few people on the streets, few cars on the roads."

Ariel said no word, just stood up from the chair and went to the window. It was raining. One of those torrential rains so proper in the tropics, showers that refresh the air for some minutes, and afterward, the sun comes up again with much force. There was a thunderstorm. *The sky is falling,* he said to himself.

"That will be okay for me," Ariel said. He sounded absentminded. "Then I will be ready to start a new life by Rosh Hashanah, at home when we come back."

Ariel was referring to the Jewish New Year celebration.

"When is that?" Werner said.

"This year is set on September 7th to the 9th."

There was a long pause.

"We cannot postpone the trip," Werner said as if once again he were reading the thoughts of his young friend. "Rain or shine."

"But this is not possible," Ariel said, returning from his dreamy state of mind. "It can't be. You're sick. I won't be able to carry you once we are deep in the rainforest. It would be suicidal for us both."

"Silence!" Werner commanded in such a new tone of voice that Ariel was startled. It mainly was a military command he had never heard from Werner before. "We have to control ourselves, Ariel. To have dominion over oneself is vital to success. Emotions are okay, but we must hold them in tight reins at all times."

And then, Werner changed his tone of voice back to the way he usually talked.

"First," he said, "I'm not that sick, Ariel. You can go and ask the doctor. He confirmed it. I can go home today, but it is even better to be here one more day under medical observation, and this is good. Second thing, even if I'm sick, it would be an urgent reason to move faster. Third, and this is a gift to you, if something happens to me once we are in the jungle, you won't have to carry me. The rainforest will take care of me. The only thing I ask from you is, please don't ever abandon María Rosa. She is okay now, and perhaps she does not need us, but the government is showing some fragility, which may mean changes soon. If this happens, she may lose everything. I have seen this before. If the government changes, friends switch sides faster than thoughts. Henceforward, we have to move and move more quickly. Let's make from this our commitment. Do you agree?"

"I don't know," Ariel said. "The way things are—"

"The way things are, they are okay," again Werner interrupted him. "There is nothing else we could do. I waited already too long, although I don't blame it on anybody. It's my fault. I could have done this ten or twenty years ago, but the project was not yet mature. Now is the time to do it. And believe me, a belly infection will not stop me from what I wanted my entire life to achieve. Are you in, or are you out?"

"What happens if I withdraw?" Ariel said.

"Nothing," Werner said, "It's just that everything ends here. I will eventually die, and the forest will keep its secret. However, if someone discovers it, well, good luck to that person or persons, but nothing of it will be yours. The most probable is that the government will intervene. In any case, the rainforest, or whatever remains of it, will soon disappear. They will leave but a hole."

The vision of a rainforest devastated by the ambition of a few shook Ariel's beliefs.

"I'm in," Ariel said. "I will take a two-week vacation. Anyway, no one will miss me at work. So I have that clear."

"Good," Werner said. "Five days of action is the maximum I foresee, and after that, each one to their own."

"So, when will I see you again, I mean, away from the hospital?"

"I have to leave here tomorrow in the morning."

"Then, I will be here tomorrow in the morning to help you."

"That won't be necessary, Ariel. Thank you. María Rosa will be here. She will take care of everything. Better for you to meet me tomorrow at eight in the evening at my apartment at the hotel."

"I'll be there then."

Two days later, at twilight, María Rosa took both her friends for a walk around the neighbourhood. Werner felt a lot better, although he often complained about the lack of alcohol in his blood. Ariel was happy to stroll along with his friends.

María Rosa insisted that Werner's ideal recovery therapy was a good walk and keeping him away from alcoholic drinks. The day was beautiful, and the aroma of well-kept gardens reached their nostrils. Neighbours outside their homes shared their traditional tereré, an infusion made of yerba mate, herbs, and cold water that people enjoy through a sipping metal tube. Neighbours shared this drink, passing the container, usually made from an ox horn, from one hand to the other as a sign of friendship, and all of them sipped from the same tube. The same popular drink, but hot, is the *yerba mate*, or *mate*, although *tereré* is the preferred refreshing drink for the Paraguayans. And other neighbours prepared their habitual *parrillada*. The sound of melancholic songs called *Guaranías* interpreted in harp and guitar reached them from windows and doors ajar. Asunción entirely enjoyed the evening with the sound of *Guaranías*, tereré, and beef at the banks of the Paraguay River.

They had dinner at a fancy restaurant, and although Werner had to drink bottled water instead of beer, he didn't have a complaint, and even the experience put him in good humour. The three of them shared stories and anecdotes. Werner talked about his dream to find a field of diamonds hidden somewhere in the deep jungle, Ariel shared his dreams of living the life of a hermit, and María Rosa shared some of the latest gossips from her office in the government.

After dinner, the three of them mounted one of the old tramways still in service in the city and went sightseeing downtown. In a slip of the tongue, Werner recounted that the tramway brought him memories of a love he had in his younger days, far away in time and distance, in a prewar Europe, now gone forever. However, Werner managed to upset María Rosa with his story, who wanted to know more about that love still alive in Werner's memories as she was already jealous of that woman who dared to take place in Werner's heart. As always, Ariel was lost in his thoughts, his mind away from the city's rumble. María Rosa's moment of memories and jealousy passed as soon as they got off the tramway. Ariel walked ahead of them in the river's direction, and Werner and María Rosa, holding hands, followed behind. They stopped by the belvedere facing the river and enjoyed the scenic view of the river flowing peacefully down there, and above it, a bright moon on a starred night.

The breeze brought them the typical aroma of *pacholí* and oranges. Two young girls came by to sell the traditional chipa, a cornbread pastry that the girls carried in a basket covered with a white cloth. The smell of fresh warm chipa was appetizing, but they had already dined and were not hungry. The girls left them, singing and swinging their baskets, walking toward the busy streets of downtown Asunción.

And as if they were coming back to reality, they heard the loud cries of many children. Curious about the commotion's motive, they walked faster toward the street corner and saw a group of children walking behind a man who was dragging a heavy pig from a rope tied to the animal's thick neck. This scene happened in the middle of a street that opened to a poor neighbourhood. The man and the pig moved, surrounded by the children—boys and girls of all ages—who followed with attention every step man and pig gave as if it was a kind of carnival. Sometimes, the pig stopped, and the man struggled to move the animal from its stubborn position. When this happened, the bustle of the children increased. The beast's squealing shocked María Rosa, and above all, Ariel, for whom the spectacle disgusted profoundly. Instead, Werner observed the scene with interest.

The pig squealed, the children screamed, and the man pulled the rope with much force, while the children followed the sad spectacle as if the man dragging the pig was a show put there for them to enjoy. And the pig squealed, the children screamed, the river roared, and the moon, white and bright, reflected on the dark, magnetic water of the river, while a man with a guitar sang a song dedicated to a faraway lover, perhaps already in someone else's arms. The singing of the insects added life to the surrealist view.

The neighbours had set a large brazier, and on top of it, they placed a cauldron with boiling water. At a given time, as if on cue, the people waiting around the brazier stood up, moved forwards, grabbed the pig, lifted it, put the animal on a sturdy table, and tied the pig's feet. The swiftness of the action startled even the pig who stopped squealing, but soon after, perhaps realizing his fate, the brute shook his body with such strength that the table creaked. It seemed that the pig would cut the rope that immobilized it at any moment, and the animal would jump and run through the narrow streets.

The boiling water seemed to escape from the cauldron. Yet, nothing happened because the animal continued to struggle for its life, and the water kept boiling. The children circled the table as if they were performing a ceremony of some ancient religion.

The man that brought the pig was now stooping down over a stone, and he was sharpening an enormous knife. Consciously, or somewhat unconsciously, the man gave his movement a sexual connotation. Women who surrounded the man laughed aloud to his roguish insinuation. The sparkles that came out of the knife's metal hypnotized the children, who followed all with wide-open eyes.

Ariel wanted to march toward the crowd and free the pig, but María Rosa held him by his arm, and at the same time, her eyes pledged Werner to move away from there. Still, Werner seemed comfortable observing the scene with eyes that watched beyond the tragedy in progress.

The man finished his sharpening of the knife and tried it in a feather he grabbed from the ground. At the touch of the knife's edge, the feather flew away, cut in two. The children, mesmerized by the man's deftness, followed with wide-open eyes both parts of the feather as they glided for some time and then disappeared in the darkness toward the river.

The man with the sharpened knife in his hand came closer to the pig. By then, the beast was pushing and squealing so hard that neither María Rosa nor Ariel could bear it anymore. A cloud covered the moon, and the singer finished his song, the stream of the river continued imperturbable, the knife got closer to the pig's throat, the pig closed his eyes, there was a deep silence, the children's eyes reflected in the steel of the blade, and—

"Let's go," María Rosa said as if she had woken up from a bad dream, and she grabbed both her friends by their hands.

Her sudden reaction pushed Werner away from his hypnotic trance. And they walked down the streets of Asunción del Paraguay, breathing the aroma of the blue, white, and rose *lapacho* trees in bloom.

On another evening, and because of a social commitment, María Rosa Martinez asked Werner to accompany her to the church of La Encarnación. A top-ranked member of the government and a leader of the dominant political party had passed away. She explained that it was vital for her to be there because all the government staff was present at that sorrowful event. Attending the event was then mandatory. Werner reluctantly agreed to go with her. He avoided as much as he could that kind of commitment.

"To a funeral?" Werner said.

"To a funeral service in a church, Werner," María Rosa corrected him.

"In a Catholic church? Negative, María Rosa. By principle, I don't go to funeral services. Not in any Catholic church. Not even I will be present at my funeral. They will have to bury me *in absentia*."

"Do it for me, please, Werner," María Rosa said.

She had first asked this favour of Ariel, but there was no way to convince her young friend to do it.

"I would never go inside a Catholic temple," Ariel had said.

And so, she used all her charm to coax Werner instead. She knew that with a bit of coaxing, Werner would give in. And he did. The tricky part of her role in this drama would be that she would have to swallow all of Werner's sarcasm and criticism on whatever occurred during the ceremony. It was something akin to Werner's character.

On that afternoon, at the end of August 1983, María Rosa Martinez, supporting herself on Werner's arm, walked into the temple's central nave. As per the occasion, she was formally dressed, and despite his protests, she had dressed Werner more than appropriately. Werner asked a photographer parked there to take a picture of both of them, and María Rosa withdrew despite Werner's protest that it would be the only time in their ordinary life that María Rosa could see him dressed so decently. He needed the photo to perpetuate the unique opportunity to feel pleased with such handsome company.

The central nave of the church of La Encarnación looked packed to the last corner. The pew where they sat offered a strategic view of the entire altar and the front rows. There were people of a diverse society; however, those considered upper class occupied the front seats. María Rosa, who was a connoisseur of the elite, whispered some names in Werner's ear.

"Of course," Werner said, "God must feel flattered to host such a bunch of illustrious citizens in His house."

María Rosa shushed him, and as people were kneeling, María Rosa did so too and demanded that Werner kneel. However, Werner decided to sit, and from his position, he followed all the actions with attentive eyes. With curiosity, he observed the crowd, all of General Stroessner's devotees, whose regime bloomed thanks to his followers' loyalty.

The coffin that contained the departed benefactor's body laid in-state under the sorrowful stare of a crucified Christ. Several wreaths of different sizes and importance surrounded the casket. Flower bouquets in elegant vases covered every corner of the altar, and the atmosphere was heavy. It seemed that there was a silent contest among every one of the floral arrangements deposited there. A show of devotion toward the deceased. A conflict between the artistic and the mortuary, as ancient as the same humanity. *The offering of power,* the scathing Werner thought.

The ceremony took time to begin, and Werner felt annoyed. Gladly for him, at that very instant, whispering grew intense, all heads turned, and there was the Commander in Chief, surrounded by a set of sycophants. Alfredo Stroessner sauntered, nodding to everybody, acknowledging his flock as a Pope would do. There was some clapping, which was even timid enough to break the harmony in the temple. Despite being a tall man, Werner had to make an effort to look at the legendary *mburuvichá guazú,* the "great boss," as people called him in the sweet Guaraní tongue.

The mighty man reached the altar and humbly leaned over in front of the coffin. It was his way to say goodbye to his collaborator and friend, the promoter of many enterprises—a friend who departed after serving his nation in public and private service for a lifetime. Once the president accomplished his farewell, he sat in his assigned place, and the ceremony began.

Werner shook his head. He felt terrible with such an unnecessary protocol. *But, it's what we indeed are,* Werner thought, m*onkeys that are performing in a circus arena. It is easier to have the cross hanging from the neck as a necklace than follow Christ's steps.*

And he, as desperate as he was starting to feel, sought María Rosa's eyes, who, as if she were reading Werner's mind, put her index finger on her lips.

To celebrate Werner's quick recovery and a farewell to her two friends who were ready to begin the great adventure searching for the diamond deposit, María Rosa invited both of them for dinner to a restaurant, with the show included. Their spirits were high, and though Werner had only mineral water, he drank it with joy to see himself so close to the end of a venture he planned forty years ago. Their table was round and decorated with a vase of white carnations, a request of María Rosa to add another touch of beauty to their celebration.

As usual, the show, food, and service aimed to please the taste of the massive audience of tourists that filled the place. Ariel, however happy to be with his friends, was uncomfortable with such a boisterous audience. His character was akin to a peaceful patio night in a private house with just a few friends. He called those large gatherings "canned joy." Thus, he avoided such places as much as possible. On the other hand, Werner was a cosmopolitan, extroverted man, a researcher of human nature, who felt at home in such massive gatherings. María Rosa enjoyed the moment. She appreciated her friends' company, the show she had seen many times before, and the food, which was not the best, but she didn't care.

There was a large group of tourists at the brink of drunkenness at the table to their left. These people talked among themselves in loud voices and gesticulated vividly. *It's a stimulating group,* Werner thought. María Rosa proposed them a toast, and then she cajoled them into watching the show and participating in the old game of guessing what nationality this group and that group were over there.

Indeed, the whole world was there in that enormous function room. There were Americans, Argentinians, Brazilians, Spaniards, Europeans from diverse countries, and some Asians. However, Brazilians and Argentinians were the majority. María Rosa failed in her attempt to keep the interest of her friends on what was essential for her, so she contented herself with applauding every presentation, while a meditative Werner and an indifferent Ariel ate their dinner without even lifting their heads.

"The show is terrific," María Rosa, said clapping with enthusiasm.

"The show may be good," Werner said, "but the food is so-so."

"Either be the show or the food," Ariel intervened. "Werner is never happy."

"The food is not that important here, Werner," María Rosa said. "People here come to have a good time with drinks and a show."

"I have no drinks to enjoy," Werner said, "and I don't like the show. On the other hand, I've seen the same thing many times before."

"Oh c'mon, Werner," María Rosa said smiling.

As on cue, people crowded the dancing floor. The orchestra played polka, and while María Rosa seemed enthusiastic with the music, Werner chuckled, and Ariel yawned.

"Okay, guys," she said. "Come dance with me so that you won't fall asleep."

She grabbed both men, took them to the dance floor, and danced with one and the other. Ariel proved to be the most graceful, and thus, Werner remained aside as an observer while María Rosa and Ariel danced nonstop for a long time. The public was euphoric with the music. All tragedies were already past. The problems that affected the country stopped at the door.

After the orchestra, a stand-up comedian made everybody laugh, but Werner could not understand the jokes—most of them alluding to national events and culture still alien to him. And the night closed to the compass of *Galopera*, a folkloric dance performed by a group of graceful young women dressed in colourful blouses and skirts.

They made their way back to Werner's hotel in silence, each one mulling on their thoughts. Werner looked tired. Their taxi left them at the entrance of Werner's hotel.

"I would rather have a night in the jungle than another night like this one," Werner said, once in the hotel lobby.

"And I would rather have a minute of solitude than have to participate in that canned joy," Ariel said.

"You guys belong together," María Rosa said, and she grabbed both men by the arm and escorted them to the elevators.

Part Two

SAL GODOIJ

THREE DAYS after that last event, at the dawn of Sunday, September 4, 1983, Werner Mann and Ariel Gimmel left the city of Asunción in pursuit of their dream.

Ariel, at the wheel, thought of the road ahead, his route, the road he was opening with his tenacity in accepting the odds of the strange adventure he began when he met Werner.

Pensive, sitting by Ariel's side, Werner chewed a pill against the stomach acid, cursing not to be able to drink at least one bottle of beer. As much as he struggled to pass as a Native, Werner looked even more like a tourist. He wore shorts, black socks, heavy boots, and a handwoven palm explorer hat. From his neck hung his Nikon camera, and from his shoulder, a set of Zeiss binoculars in a leathered pocket. He had also given Ariel a similar pair as a gift.

Ariel had rented the vehicle to his name, a Ford Falcon station wagon. Nothing luxurious, not even with air conditioning, but a robust, practical car, nonetheless. He had taken personal care of loading the necessary items and covered it all with an impermeable canvas cloth.

They followed a secondary road and soon were rolling through rural fields patched among the wild vegetation. By his side, Ariel carried a container with cassettes, which formed his musical collection. From time to time, he selected one of the cassettes, placed it into the cassette deck, and filled the vehicle with music. Werner would be the navigator. He put the road maps on his knees and guided Ariel. This way, miles and hours went by.

They faced a crossroads, and Ariel stopped the vehicle. He waited for Werner's reaction. Werner chuckled.

"When facing a crossroads, the smart thing to do is to toss a coin," Werner said.

"Toss a coin and hope? You said that before, Werner."

Werner didn't answer. He seemed puzzled.

"Seriously, Werner. What do we do?" Ariel insisted. "Do we toss a coin?"

"No!" Werner said. "No coin-tossing here, Ariel. Follow the road to your right."

"Whatever you say, Werner."

The road was little more than a dirt route, narrower even, with shrubs growing at each side. The landscape became wilder as they moved through, always going north-northwest, and then, after a curb, they faced another crossroads.

"Here we are," Werner said with enthusiasm. "This road is the one the map shows. Go to the one to the left, please, Ariel. It's a more direct road, I know now. This route will take us faster. But, of course, things have changed a lot over the years, since the description of this road I have here tells about abundant forests."

"They cut the trees to make room for the cattle farms," Ariel said dryly.

Ariel got onto the road to the left. The dirt road was bumpy and made the riding uncomfortable.

"Well, I hope we won't have a storm," Ariel said. "If not, we will have to return. There is no way to travel this road if it rains."

"No, Ariel. No return. We can wait in the vehicle until the rains pass. You don't ever turn around at the first obstacle."

Ariel said nothing and continued driving, sorting out the uneven road's obstacles and the overgrown shrubs by the side of the road that hit the vehicle rhythmically. Werner was also silent. Some negative aspects of Ariel's character annoyed him, although he understood well the expectations of his young friend, which were the same as his own. On the other hand, Werner's health crisis recently suffered had helped him clarify his expectations. He now had a clearer mental picture of the chances he had to achieve his plan. And the odds, he thought, were in his favour. The crisis he'd had was a way for him to pay an installment of what he owed to life. Henceforward, there should not be more troubles. It's like paying any retail installment, he said to himself. Once you have paid, you are free. The payment could be a health issue, an accident, or a moment of bad luck, but once this happened in your life, you were free to continue forth. Great, thought Werner, this is great! He had explained his philosophy to the skeptical Ariel, although he did not get a good reception from his young friend.

"Life is a logical condition," Werner said aloud as if the thought escaped from his mouth.

Ariel just turned his head and smiled. He was already aware of his older friend's philosophical outbursts.

A 'logical condition' is complex for one to understand while living the moment, but when the moment passes, one can look back and breathe as to how lucky one has been. Thus, Werner thought, we must learn how to face the waves of life and react accordingly. Ariel, however, believed that life was either white or black. For him, there were no other shades. If it was yes, it was yes. No, it was a no. That was it. For him, there existed no half-truths or half-lies. "He is still a pure young man," María Rosa had told Werner when she introduced Ariel to him. "Anything wrong can hurt him."

The landscape changed, and they could see a green expanse dotted with tiny houses and surrounded by orchards. The tranquility of the landscape numbed Werner, who decided to take a nap.

He was already beginning to dream something about a snowy mountain when the thunder woke him up. He opened his eyes and saw that the entire view had darkened. I hope it does not rain, Werner thought. The flashes of lightning uncovered extraordinary scenery. Everything became surreal, and Werner felt that he was indeed dreaming. It didn't rain, though, yet the thunder became deafening. And while all of this happened, the world turned, turned, and Werner and Ariel travelled through that intense expanse of land, searching for their destiny while the lightning blinded them. And as the lightning sparkled, they both felt like time travellers journeying their moment through the Paraguayan landscape.

The dry electric storm ended. The road was not as hard-baked as initially seemed; it became softer, and the ride became pleasant. The tires crushed a serpent crossing, and Ariel wanted to stop and see it but decided against it and continued. The landscape gave way to a small village, then to another, and then to several cattle ranches where mongrels came out barking viciously.

They didn't stop at any of the villages. Werner said it was not prudent, so they continued their journey with the persistent signs of rain coming from black clouds on the horizon.

The ranches became sparse, and the road turned muddy and slippery, making driving difficult. The van skidded a couple of times, and Ariel made a great effort to keep the vehicle on the road. It is like driving on a wet bar of soap, Ariel thought. He prayed that no rain fell. The air was sticky. The rain clouds were still far west, but the humidity was higher. The sun was well over their heads, and the heat was unbearable.

They had to stop to rest, however. Ariel looked for a place to park and found it under two large palms. Both friends set everything to eat and ate and relaxed in the shadows of the palms. After their meal, Werner decided to walk, and he did for a while and arrived at a small house with an orchard enclosed in barbed wires. It must be for the animals, thought Werner. The barbed wire view brought him bad memories from the war. He walked toward the house. There was a man who seemed to be older than Werner was. The man was removing the shell of an armadillo, a tatú guazú as people in Paraguay called this animal, whose carcass hung from the lower branch of a blooming quebracho, while two small boys turned around and around, celebrating their grandfather's skill with the knife. The old man had in his mouth a handmade, black, strongly-scented cigar.

Werner came to join the old man. Ariel followed him.

"¿Mbae'chapá, dotor?"—How are you, doctor?—the grandfather said, greeting Werner in the sweet, languid nasal accent of the land people.

"I'poránte, Taita. ¿Ha'ndé?"—Very well, grandpa, and you?—Ariel said and bit his lips because he felt like the ventriloquist's doll, Werner being the ventriloquist.

"Espectacular, dotor," said the old man, ignoring Ariel and responding as if it had been Werner who had answered him. Werner didn't speak Guaraní, but he knew enough about the countrymen to gather that the title of "dotor"—doctor— with which the old man was addressing him was the most respectful way the humble ones had to refer to someone whom they believed was from a higher rank than they were. Thus, based solely on their physical appearance, when addressing a man, people were called either "Mi coronel" if the person of authority happened to be a man in uniform or "dotor" if he was a civilian. However, Ariel didn't enjoy this relevance because of his olive skin colour and black, curly hair.

Werner got closer, and with scientific curiosity, observed the older fellow's work. The man didn't object to Werner's presence; instead, he welcomed it. He seemed to feel stimulated by having someone other than the children admire his skills. However, for the children, the curious thing was now Werner. The children stopped playing and came by Werner's side. Perhaps the little ones considered Werner a most interesting trophy than what their grandfather had caught. Werner searched his pocket, wishing to find something to give the children, and his hands came out empty. The children looked at each other as disillusion painted on their faces. The karaí dotor was as poor as they were. Ariel turned around and walked away from there; he had decided to return to their vehicle.

At that moment, the grandfather finished removing the animal's skin, and with a great fuss, he gave the skin to the children. The children received it with exclamations of joy and pushing and jumping the way children do, while the old man began to open the belly of the tatú guazú to extract the innards, which he tossed in a plastic container. After that, the children and the grandfather forgot Werner.

A honk broke the still of the evening. Ariel was making signals to Werner to come back to the vehicle. Werner strolled back slowly with his hands in the pockets of his pants, pensively climbed into the car, and they proceeded with their journey.

"If it ever happens that someone asks these people if they have seen us," Werner said as if he were dictating a class to a broad audience, "they will never denounce you. They will never sell you to any authority, regardless of threats, torture, or a reward."

"I know that ch'amigo," Ariel said. "I was born here. I belong here."

"Aw!" Werner dismissed him with a gesture. "Jewish people belong everywhere. Jerusalem travels in their blood."

"There is always someone who reminds us about it," Ariel said.

"There is nothing wrong with that, Ariel."

"Indeed, Werner. I would feel proud if I was accepted everywhere, which I'm not."

"That does not have anything to do with race or beliefs, Ariel. I guess it goes with the individual's character."

"Not true, Werner. People discriminate as soon as they see you. You know that. See how that guy over there in that rancho reacted? He just ignored me."

"Yes, Ariel, and I'm sorry for I felt in the same trap, and again I apologize for that. However, the truth is that nobody wants to be equal to his neighbour, not even to their brothers."

"It is strange to hear this from a former Nazi."

"As I'm telling you," Werner said, ignoring Ariel's comment, "the higher the class people belong to, because people want to split into classes, the higher the wall they build to separate them from their neighbours."

"What kind of life did you have in that laboratory, I wonder?"

"Well, I was locked in. I assure you that I knew nothing about the country's politics and the barbaric actions the Nazis committed, which I learned about after the war. The laboratory bosses deprived me of any information about the front and results. The information I received was mostly about gems, precious metals, and chemistry. I didn't know a thing about crimes committed against such and such people. As I said, what surprised me is that the people who supported these crimes were people from the elite. They were not ignorant people, which is why I say that we humans discriminate against our neighbour no matter what. You can see this even in children."

"Yeah. It's painful."

They remained in silence, involved in their thoughts for a long while. The car was now through a cornfield, it was cornfields until the horizon, and a small town lying just there at the horizon line, and soon they went through the main street full of people. It was a religious procession in honour of their Patrona. They had no chance but to wait until the procession reached the Plaza de Los Héroes—for in each city, or town, or village, there is always a Plaza de Los Héroes—and turned toward the church.

"A good hour lost," Ariel said, speeding through the empty road.

Werner said nothing. He entertained himself, taking pictures of whatever he saw. A long time passed, and the monotony of the landscape was numbing Ariel.

"Well," Werner said as if he suddenly remembered something. "The good thing in all of that is that it was from there I got the information that will change our lives, Ariel. If not for that, I may have been somewhere in Germany, enjoying my retirement. And if we find what we are looking for, I will be a satisfied man. Satisfied with my life."

"We still have nothing," Ariel said.

But, again, the skeptical side of Ariel's character drove Werner uneasy. "Don't say that, Ariel," Werner said. "We have a lot. I have a lot. You have to trust me, so María Rosa and I thank you both. I know that to María Rosa, and perhaps to you too, I'm an old man full of weird ideas and hopes, and I have the conviction that we will succeed, so never give up, Ariel. Never. And I feel happy to share it with you, a young man with a healthy mind and body, and ambitious too."

"Listen," Werner continued after a pause, "neither you nor I asked to come to this life the way it was arranged for us, so then whatever comes out of our encounter, it will be welcome."

Ariel didn't follow the train of thought of his friend and remained silent. At the bottom of Ariel's heart, he felt comforted by the quick recovering of Werner's health. And with this thought, Ariel consoled himself that he would not need to carry Werner through the rainforest as Ariel thought when María Rosa broke the news. Yet, on the other hand, he knew that he would never abandon Werner to the forest's animals and insects.

Ariel quoted to himself an old saying he heard in his childhood: "Until now, everything was going well," the sailor said, walking on the plank toward the abyss while prodded by the pirate's sword.

"I hope everything goes well," Ariel said in a loud voice as if he was emerging from a deep dream.

"All will go well, Ariel," Werner said as if he was answering Ariel's prayers.

And Werner closed his eyes, slept, and dreamed he was young again, working in the laboratory in downtown Berlin. And in front of him, there was a table on which there was a minuscule scale, and he was weighing diamonds, an incredible amount of diamonds, and he felt so tired because there was no way he could ever finish, considering the amount which multiplied and multiplied.

WERNER WOKE up with a slight headache. He looked in the glove compartment and found the box with medicines. He grabbed a painkiller and swallowed it dry. After that, he looked at the landscape, abstracted in his thoughts. Something made him react, though. Ariel had been listening to music. He was changing cassettes, and then as if he had enough with it, he turned the radio on and switched the dial when Werner stopped him.

"Oh," Ariel said, "I'm sorry I woke you." He continued playing with the dial. "You slept like an angel."

Werner watched his wristwatch as if he had an appointment somewhere, and he was running late. Then he reached for his canteen and drank in long sips, his nape jumping as he gurgled the liquid. From the radio now came paused sounds and voices—paused accents—comments in Guaraní, music, *Guraranias*, and then transmission of a soccer game. Bored, Ariel switched the dial again, and now a woman was speaking in a soft, sensual, rhythmical Brazilian Portuguese; perhaps she was talking about her love life in a provincial city and then more soccer. Another switch of the dial, and this time a politician seemed to have swallowed the microphone and could not stop talking. Exasperated, Ariel turned the switch to another radio station, a man speaking something unintelligible in Guaraní, and then, Roberto Carlos singing *Detalhes* on a radio show—the music came strong, the voice clear, and then disappeared, taken by the waves. Ariel continued switching the dial and most radio stations broadcasted in Brazilian Portuguese. Werner fell asleep again, his head nodding, but something suddenly made him awake.

"Ariel," Werner said, "stop there. The radio you were listening to. Switch it back."

Reluctantly, Ariel began to play with the dial again, as Werner had said.

On the radio, the Brazilian speaker was giving an extensive account about . . . *Boeing coreano 747, vôo 007, com 269 passajeiros mais a tripulação que foi abatido na Sibéria por um avião de guerra Soviético* . . .

Werner urged himself to understand what the radio presenter was saying. Finally, he understood some keywords, but then the radio whirred intermittently, the voice faded, and Werner was upset.

"We are in the middle of nowhere, Werner." Ariel was somehow upset about his older friend's interest in news, which Ariel found morbid. "And who, by the way, wants to know what happens in the civilized criminal world? I don't."

"I guess it's important, Ariel. We are away from civilization, yet only for a short time. Hence, we should not break the contact."

"I don't care. I have no contacts to return. So for me, I would rather stay around here. I would build my cabin over there, exactly above that little hill. And I would become a hermit. That's my dream."

"And what about the diamonds, then?"

"I would rather have this view every day than a bunch of money, Werner."

"You are a romantic, crazy young man," Werner said, smiling.

Finally, there was nothing on the radio—only the whirring sound.

"We are climbing down a ravine," Ariel said. "That's why there is too much static. Besides, this is a cheap radio, Werner."
"It's true, Ariel. It's not a *Telefunken*."
After Werner's last word, Ariel fell into deep thought, and Werner wondered if something, he had said offended Ariel somehow.

But then, as if he'd just had a connection with a memory, Ariel, his eyes brightened, said, "There you are, Werner! You are right! We had one of those at home. A large *Telefunken* radio box. Not so elegant, but very operative."

The word *Telefunken* had awakened memories of Ariel's childhood, hence his reaction, which Werner took erroneously.

The journey continued.

"You don't care much about politics, eh, Ariel?" Werner retook his favourite subject. He could not hold it.

"I'm a man with no interest in the so-called public service, Werner. It's all so corrupt. Nothing is true. I don't care much about the economy. See? I'm not interested in becoming a millionaire, either. I wouldn't know what to do if I ever reached that status. However, I do follow the laws of Leviticus as much as I can. And I would share my fortune with everybody. Believe me, Werner, I have good intentions, although I shouldn't say that because in a human being, although good intentions may mean a good thing to someone, they may also mean disaster to another."

"Ah!" Werner said, startled by his friend's sudden philosophical outburst.

After a while, Ariel stopped the vehicle and went for a pee. In the meantime, Werner was curious to see the work of caterpillars that rolled over a leaf of corn.

Two hours on the road passed somberly for both friends. It was well past noontime when the rain began to fall, tiny drops at the beginning, then a deluge that lasted no more than fifteen minutes, and then the sun came out vigorous as ever. The car rolled through cornfields and then slowed to a complete stop.

"I think we have a flat tire," Ariel said.

He opened the door and walked around the front of the car. Then, upset, he kicked the right front tire with his right foot.

"It's this one," he said.

Werner got out and squatted over to check the damaged tire. Ariel went to the back door, opened it, and removed the cover to get the spare tire and the tools. He was doing this when he heard Werner talking to someone. Intrigued, Ariel looked about and saw two women heavily armed who were standing by Werner's side. And without Ariel noticing it, a third woman came behind him and helped him remove the spare tire. Ariel was startled.

"María Rosa worries about you guys," the woman said to Ariel almost whispering, and speaking fast.

Ariel looked at the woman with his eyes wide open. The verification that María Rosa had nexus with the guerrilla movement shocked Ariel, but he managed to keep his cool. *Of course,* he thought, *María Rosa knows our itinerary or at least part of it.*

"Are we in a dangerous zone?" Ariel asked.

"Not here, but by the river." The woman extended her arm and signaled to a place northwest, somewhere beyond the cornfield.

"Tell María Rosa we will be okay," Ariel said. "And thanks to her for looking after us."

"I will," the woman said.

"And thank you too, of course," Ariel repeated, yet, without a smile, the woman turned around and walked away, wheeling the spare tire with her hands.

María Rosa gave them our description, thought Ariel, *and they spotted us right away. Here, in this part of the country, a foreigner to pass unnoticed is impossible. And a guy like Werner is noticeable from miles ahead.*

The women were neither young nor old, nor friendly. And after the first one made that swift comment to Ariel, they all kept remote and cold. And although they were making themselves useful, they kept distant, as if they would not risk getting too involved with the strange men. The women knew who the two men were, and they knew that the two men needed help, and they—the three women—were there, offering their aid openly, efficiently, and emotionless. Werner, of course, did not suspect of María Rosa's involvement in the '*casual encounter.*' Still, he looked as startled as Ariel did.

Two of the three women went to work on the damaged tire, and in a matter of minutes, and without a word, they removed it, replaced it with the new one, tightened the lug nuts, and took the damaged tire, the jack, and the tool kit back to their place in the vehicle.

The third woman stood on guard by the side of the road, scouting the fields with binoculars. In Ariel's eyes, the woman looked like a crouching-down tigress ready to pounce on prey. From her right shoulder, a machine gun hung.

"That's a *Kalashnikov* rifle," confirmed Werner.

Ariel did not comment. Instead, he looked beyond the cornfield.

"I held once one exactly as this one, in my very hands," Werner insisted, whispering and showing his open palms to stress the experience he'd had as if, for him, it had happened just yesterday.

"Yeah, Werner," Ariel said casually, and then he grinned and added, "For sure, it was a picture in one of those weapons magazines."

Werner was going to answer, but then, one of the women came to meet them. The other one, who had already finished with the spare tire, joined the woman standing on guard by the road.

"Clarisa," the woman said, extending her hand.

Werner and Ariel shook it. It was a hard feminine hand.

"Thank you very much, Clarisa," Werner said and then turned around to wave to the other women, too. "Thank you," he said.

The women waved back and continued their vigilance.

"Don't mention it," Clarisa said. She did not smile.

"Is there something I can do for you . . . I mean . . . to pay for what you have done?" Werner asked.

"You never changed a tire, and that will be more than enough for us," Clarisa said, and then she turned around, went to join her partners, and in a blink of the eye, they disappeared among the cornfield.

"That Communist woman was patronizing us," Werner said.

"C'mon, Werner. She meant we never saw them, in case someone asks us."

Werner said something else that Ariel did not follow, for perhaps Werner expressed himself in his native German, so Ariel ignored him and went around the vehicle, confirming the tire pressure with a thump of his fist.

"They helped us, Werner. They may become our guardian angels, after all." Ariel was trying to appease the warrior in Werner.

"Dangerous people they are, Ariel. Don't be carried upon by their quietness."

Ariel did not answer, immersed as he was in his thoughts. He was thinking of María Rosa, and if since she became his friend, he could have once called her a 'dangerous' woman. She was not. María Rosa was sweet and caring. The brutal injustice may have hardened her, but her heart remained pure.

"For sure, they belong to one of the guerrilla groups," insisted Werner. "I read they are operative, but not in this area. Maybe they are an advance party. I don't know. I'm just guessing."

Ariel climbed in, started the engine, and patiently waited for Werner, who was now taking a leak standing by the side of the road. Finally, Werner came in, and the car moved forwards on the road through the cornfield.

THE ROAD was now flat, and yellowish vegetation sparsely covered the landscape. Some metres ahead, a man was standing by the road, holding out his right thumb. Ariel looked at Werner for approval, but Werner took his time to answer, and they drove past the man. In the rearview mirror, Ariel saw, among the dust, the figure of the man lifting his hands as he was protesting. Ariel pressed the brakes, and Werner frowned but said nothing. Ariel changed gears, and the vehicle slowly moved in reverse and stopped by the side of a man in his thirties wearing a blue NY cap, a red tie on a sweated but otherwise clean white shirt, black pants, and blue jute shoes, of the kind known as *alpargatas*, and probably crafted by himself. The man had a pleasant smile—a candid face.

"*Gracias, ch'amigo,*" said the man, opening the back door, climbing in, and making himself comfortable among the parcels on the seat.

"Where are you heading, my friend?" Ariel asked.

"Are you heading east or west?" the man said instead.

"West," Werner said.

"Northwest," Ariel candidly said, and Werner gave him the stink eye.

"Good," the man said. "Then drop me at the next crossroads if you will, please. It is about ten miles from here."

The man's speech was articulate and educated.

"Suits me well," Werner said.

"I'm Carlos, by the way. Carlos Santana, like the musician, which I'm not."

If you're not a musician, they did not ask, what are you, instead?

"Werner."

"Ariel."

They shook hands, and after that, they rode in silence until Ariel broke it with a question.

"What is at the next crossroads, Carlos?"

"*Jah! Das ist eine gute Frage, Ariel!*" Werner suddenly said and then, realizing he had spoken in German, reversed into his broken Spanish. "It seems to me that there is nothing around here."

"Empty it is, sir!"

They all looked around the empty, flat, yellowish landscape.

"And let me tell you," Carlos proceeded, "that not long ago, about thirty years ago or less, this area was populated by trees. And yet, this is what remains of the rainforest, at least in this part of the country. And there is a village down there." Then, with his hand, Carlos signaled somewhere beyond the horizon.

Among the tall grass, they could see now the silhouettes of houses far east. Perhaps a small community.

"Is that where you live?" Ariel asked.

"Not in the village. From the crossroads, I walk two more miles going west and reach my home, which is the school."

"What school?" Ariel said, looking at Carlos' face through the rearview mirror.

"My school. I'm a teacher."

"A rural teacher?" Ariel said.

"That's me," Carlos said and smiled widely. A smile of satisfaction.

A humble and proud man. *An unusual combination* thought Werner.

"I have a variable class number, though. Boys and girls, sometimes twelve, sometimes twenty. They all come from the neighbouring communities."

"Why is the number a variation?" Werner said.

"It's not easy. Different reasons. It's never the same."

Again, the two friends remained silent. Neither dared to question Carlos why it was not easy. What those different reasons were and why it was never the same, although both of them suspected that the circumstances, although varied, would not relate to the children's interest in schooling.

They arrived at the crossroads.

"Thank you very much, my friends," the teacher said and prepared to get out of the vehicle.

"We can take you to the school, Carlos," Ariel said in an impulse. "We are within the schedule so that it won't affect us much."

Werner swallowed yet reluctantly nodded in approval.

"That's very kind of you, my friends," Carlos said and accommodated himself again in the seat.

Ariel turned west, and the landscape did not change. The vehicle rolled on a reddish, dusty road until they arrived at a couple of rundown buildings set on a place where no grass grew. The site had a sad look to it.

"It looks sad without the children," Carlos said as if reading Ariel's thoughts. "On Sundays, it's like this. Tomorrow will be another story."

Following Carlos' directions, Ariel stopped in front of one of the buildings.

"This is the school," Carlos said as if he were introducing an old friend to his two newly made acquaintances.

At the entrance, an arch with a fading sign read, *Escuela Básica N° 1.1 . . . Lydia Y..ro..s,* and a flagpole with the Paraguayan flag was waving high, welcoming the visitors.

"The house over there is the school workshop," continued Carlos. "In there, the students learn some handwork, the boys, and some cooking, the girls. Then yonder, there is an orchard, part of the curriculum, too. Most kids here come from peasant families, you know. It's the way it is. Behind the school are the washrooms, the showers, and a dirt soccer field. Boys mostly play soccer, and I keep the ball. I'm the referee. The girls stay inside. They cook or work on handcrafting, and that's all for sports and recreation during recess time. And over there is the well from where we get the water. So, let's come inside, my friends, and if you are not in a hurry, I will treat you with a refreshing tereré."

Werner and Ariel exchanged looks.

"Thank you, Carlos," Ariel said, "but we will skip the tereré. It will be a short visit, anyway. It was most of all my curiosity, you know. I always wanted to become a rural teacher."

"Come, Ariel," Carlos said, and then to Werner, "Please, sir, come on in. I will show you the school."

They came into a large room with mud-brick walls covered with a lousy finishing of whitewash, a deteriorated wooden floor, naked wood beams in the ceiling, and large windows with some of the glass missing in them, and rows of small wooden desks and benches. And at the front, a desk with a chair for the teacher, and a blackboard, and on the wall for everybody to view it, there was the most luxurious object in the entire classroom, a large portrait of His Excellency, Alfredo Stroessner, looking as he probably did in his younger days. On the walls, there were also fading, old, unframed photographs cut from newspapers and magazines stuck to the walls, presumably to remind the children of moments and events of vague worthiness in their country's history. The blackboard had something written on it. Beside it, there was one bookshelf with ten or more books and handicrafts that the children had made and two empty clay flowerpots.

The simplicity of the place shocked Ariel. Instead, Werner was indifferent, biting his nails and ogling his wristwatch most of the time.

Ariel walked about the room, touching with certain tenderness the small wooden desks where the children took their daily lessons and imagined them with their heads down, their little hands at work, handwriting with shaking calligraphy what the teacher was dictating, and felt moved by the scene he created in his mind.

Then, he saw that there was another door there, by the side of the blackboard.

"It goes to the kitchen and into my bedroom," Carlos said, following Ariel's eyesight. "It's a small room, like the cell of a monk, but that's what I am, after all, a monk preaching here to the children's souls."

Carlos's words struck a chord in Ariel's heart, and he turned to read what was on the blackboard. It was a quotation from somewhere, a passage from some book, or perhaps it was a psalm.

"*Lord, take my hand and guide me blindly into the children's souls, you who taught us as we were children.*"

"I would love to do this, Carlos," Ariel said. "To have a job like this one you have."

"You must be strong, my friend," Carlos said. "You do what you love to do, but your work depends on others. You cannot provide the children with your word only."

Ariel turned to peruse the books on the bookshelf.

"A couple of years ago," Carlos said, "the president came to the town, about one mile down the road. The very same '*mburuvicha guazú*' came with all those big shots, politicians and all. What did the president come for? To inaugurate the town's first public library. Speeches, promises, embraces, flags, the National Anthem, and the little children from this school in their clean white aprons went there to perform for His Excellency. They cut the tape, and the library was open and full of books. The books are still there, only that the library is now closed. They fear that the children can learn something from those books."

"Let's go, Ariel," Werner commanded. "It's getting late."

"We have to go, Carlos," Ariel said as if excusing himself.

"Go with God, my friend. I'm here if someday you decide to pass by and say hi."

Already comfortably seated in the car, Werner waved goodbye. Ariel climbed in, turned the engine on, and the station wagon gradually gained speed. He looked in the rearview mirror, but the thin red dust rising—or was it his tears?—had already covered his vision.

The purring of the engine numbed Werner. They had been for hours on the road now, and he felt exhausted. He fell asleep and dreamed of something about a hand. The hand hit his face, and he could not avoid it. He passed out in his dream, but then the hand that struck him extended toward him again when he was falling, and he grasped it and woke up, and then he realized that Ariel was trying to wake him up. Werner opened his eyes, and he came back to reality and recovered.

It was well past noontime, and the monotony of the view made them feel languid—grassland after grassland, not a tree on site. And then northwest, the scenery changed. There were rolling hills and forests and creeks, and over the treetops, the blue sky. Electric blue. And a breeze. A storm was lurking somewhere.

"Down there is the river," Ariel said. "And a bridge. There is police control further down. I saw them from uphill when we passed the curve. They saw us too, for sure."

Ariel recalled what the woman guerrilla told him about the action being somewhere beyond the cornfield, but he did not know if it was coming toward them or if they were going toward it. Now, from where they were, he knew it was the latter.

"It will be okay, Ariel. I will talk to them," Werner said in a paternalistic tone that upset Ariel.

"They may ask us to go back from where we came. Maybe we have to look for another road."

"We don't know that yet, Ariel. Relax."

There was a pronounced curve, and Ariel reduced the speed to a minimum. Two soldiers hidden in the bushes spied on their movements. Perhaps they did so for a long time, without Ariel or Werner realizing it. They were not police but soldiers. The soldiers startled Ariel when they showed unnoticed at the car windows.

"Keep moving!" one of the soldiers said. It was an order.

The car kept moving.

"There must be more soldiers hiding in the bushes, Werner said. "They must be playing one of their war games."

"We cannot go back now," Ariel said somberly. "They will not allow us to back up."

Werner said nothing. The car continued advancing, Ariel managing the curves at minimum speed until they saw the river, the bridge, and a contingent of soldiers. It was impossible to know how many there were. They had spread in a large area on both sides of the bridge and into the fields ahead. One officer signaled Ariel not to stop. There were several military vehicles, small and large. Two big trucks were sitting in the clearing near the bridge. They were empty. Perhaps the soldiers were doing exercises in the vicinity.

"They are looking for guerrillas," Werner sentenced.

"Maybe they know about those women we met down there, Werner. The soldiers may think we are a part of their group."

"Nonsense, Ariel. Don't worry about that. Just relax."

"It will be better for us if we can turn around," Ariel said.

"It's too late now, Ariel. They are going to check what we are carrying."

"We are in a hot spot, Werner."

"I didn't know there were soldiers in this area, Ariel."

"You didn't know that there were also guerrillas here."

"I cannot know everything that is happening in this country, Ariel."

"The guerrilla is okay because they hide, but at least we should be aware of the military control, shouldn't we?"

"Oh c'mon, Ariel. Military men are all over the country. There is no way to avoid them. We just have to follow our plan. Play it cool, okay?"

Steered by Ariel's firm hand, the vehicle slowly rolled until it stopped. There was another truck in front of them, but it wasn't a military truck. It was a private one. On the bed of this truck, a group of people wearing formal clothes was on their way to a religious feast—peasants celebrating some church feast. A religious festivity, perhaps honouring the Virgin. Werner knew about popular traditions. A lot of fervor. A lot of prayers. And a lot of drinks, food, and beautiful young ladies seeking husbands.

A couple of privates came toward the van. There was no sympathy in their icy, alert eyes. As they got closer to the vehicle, Werner opened the door and climbed down.

"*No se baje del auto, dotor,*" the private said with the languorous, characteristic nasal accent of the people of that region of the world. "Wait until you're told to do so."

Werner climbed back into the van as instructed and closed the door. Ariel made a friendly sign to the soldier, yet, stone-faced, the private only stared at him.

"They never taught these people to smile," Ariel said.

Werner shushed Ariel.

"These people have to face tough situations," Werner said. "They are trained to deal with death."

Ariel put his index finger on his temple, the universal sign which means they are all crazy. And he wanted to scream. Instead, he stretched and relaxed in the driver's seat. And so, they sat there for a long time. Lastly, the truck in front of them rolled slowly toward the bridge, and the privates in front moved to let it pass. People onboard the vehicle made warm signals to Werner and Ariel, and both friends waved back. Werner lifted the camera that he held from his neck and pointed the lens toward the soldiers. Ariel noticed Werner's action, and in a quick movement, slapped him on the arm. Werner dropped the camera to his chest.

"Are you crazy?" Ariel whispered, pronouncing every word carefully. "We can go to jail for taking pictures of the soldiers."

"C'mon, Ariel. They look so handsome in their uniforms."

Ariel did not answer but shook his head side to side. At that moment, another group of privates trotted in front of the vehicle. Firm. Tough people. Weapons at the ready. Both friends focused on watching the soldiers' parade and overlooked the officer—a captain—who knocked on Ariel's door. Another private, this one by Werner's side, appeared on the other side, pointing at Werner with a submachine gun. Werner looked the soldier in his eyes.

"Is this necessary?" Werner mumbled.

"You!" the captain said, pointing at Ariel, who was sitting at the wheel. "Get out of the car! Have your documentation in your hand. Yours and the car's documentation too!"

Ariel promptly followed the instructions. Werner, instead, remained seated and observed the scene with interest. The captain turned toward Werner and looked at him with suspicion.

"You, sir," the captain said. "Do you need an invitation?"

Werner got out of the car, showing his empty hands.

"*Ape, la che documento*,"—These are my documents— Werner said, trying to make a quip using Guaraní language, which of course flopped given the circumstances.

Embarrassed because of his friend's childish behaviour at such a dreadful moment, Ariel covered his face with his hands.

"Papers!" the captain barked again. It was a dry, cutting voice—no sympathy, no courtesy.

Werner handed him his German passport. Without looking at it, the captain passed it over to another soldier along with Ariel's papers. The soldier went to a tent and gave the documents to another officer sitting behind a table. The officer at the table checked Werner's passport and tried to match his name to other names in a notebook.

Werner thought he had just had a *déjà vu*. His mind went back to the months after the war. At every place, Soviet soldiers were controlling the population. And wherever he went, more soldiers were asking for papers. And while he waited in the cold, he observed one of the soldiers comparing his documents to the list he had in a notebook, the same scene presented now before his eyes. The date, the weather, and the geography changed. They, the Soviet soldiers, like this soldier now in front of his eyes, were looking for signs, any sign, to prove he was carrying *die Geisterpapiere*—fake papers.

The voice of the captain removed him from his memories. "What is in the trunk?" the captain asked.

"Sir! Food, souvenirs, tools, and a container with gasoline, sir!" Werner had acquired the same tone of voice and stance that the marines do when talking to a superior, as seen in the movies, but Werner's performance sounded weak and phony, bordering on ridicule.

Ariel looked toward the river and covered his face with his hand.

The captain looked at Werner with curiosity. "Where are you heading?"

"Sir! We are taking these things to people of scarce resources, sir. Poor peasants, sir."

The captain stared into Werner's eyes.

"Am I an idiot?" the captain asked.

This time, Ariel looked as if he were praying.

"Sir, no, sir!" Werner answered. His innocent blue eyes held the captain's cold stare without blinking. "I don't think so, sir!"

One of the soldiers was peering over the station wagon window and signaled something to the captain. The captain stepped forwards toward the vehicle and saw Ariel's American flag coloured backpack sitting on the back seat as Carlos left it when he climbed out of the car.

"You are an American!" the captain said.

"No, sir, I am not, sir!" Werner said, almost as an outburst.

"You're from the Peace Corps," the captain said. He neither asked nor averred. Perhaps he was answering a question he had made himself a few minutes ago.

Werner was going to answer, but the captain interrupted him. "No! You are a Mennonite!" the captain said after the pause.

Perhaps the captain answered another question he had made to himself—his observation based on Werner's Nordic type. Most Mennonites came to Paraguay from Eastern Europe as well as from Canada. Mennonites founded colonies in a very rough country, resulting from hard work and order, becoming examples of economic success.

"No, sir!" Werner said. "I'm not a religious man, sir!"

"*¿No creés vos en la virgencita, pikó?*"—You don't believe in the Virgin, do you?

The captain stared at Werner as if he was indeed a strange animal feeding on the captain's patience. Werner stood there and said nothing. Finally, the captain turned to Ariel, who was following the scene with wide-open eyes.

"*Vos ch'raa, vos sí que crees en la virgencita,*"—You, my friend! Of course, you believe in the Virgin, don't you?

The captain emphasized his statement and felt well. He was proud of himself for having found Ariel, a believer like himself. However, Ariel's delayed response to his inquiry upset him. The army captain couldn't find anyone—between these two foreigners—who shared his belief, and this, for him, was an impossible thing to happen. It was unthinkable for him to find someone who didn't believe in the Virgin, in this case, in the Virgin of Caacupé, the nation's religious symbol. Now, to find one person who was not a believer was indeed a reprehensible thing, but to find two men who didn't believe in the Virgin and who were travelling together was indeed a tragedy. Demons were taking over the world. For the captain, these two men either were Martians or, worse even, Communists.

Communists supported the guerrillas, and the guerrillas were terrorists; terrorists killed soldiers, but the worst thing was that they—the Communists—didn't believe in the Virgin. And that was their actual crime.

Ariel swallowed hard. The captain, the man with the power, the judge, the master of their lives, or freedom, the ranked officer invested with such authority, stood there, inflexibly waiting for Ariel's answer.

"I . . ." Ariel didn't know what to say. "I'm a Jew, captain," he said after a moment of vacillation as if he were excusing himself because of his faith. "Jewish people respect other religions . . ."

"You don't believe in the Virgin!" the captain said. Then, horrified, he looked around as if seeking support against these two peculiar people but found nothing of what he was searching for in the empty stares of the privates who surrounded him.

"I pray to my Lord to give you wisdom," Ariel said. He was pale but didn't flinch.

"Let's go on to check what these people are carrying," the captain said, feeling already defeated.

Ariel rushed to the station wagon and opened the back door. One soldier lifted the canvas and peered inside the small cargo. There were nothing dangerous in there, and no firearms either. The soldiers opened the American flag knapsack, scattered the content on the grass. Ariel blushed but could do nothing to stop the humiliation. From some steps behind, he and Werner followed the soldiers' activity. The captain came back to them, a private following him closely behind. The soldier held the box that contained Werner's jewelry instruments.

"What is this?" the captain said, pointing at the box with instruments.

"It's a scientific kit for children, sir!" Werner said. "This is to help them with their experiments in sciences, sir!"

Again, Ariel covered his face.

"Am I an idiot?" the captain asked.

"No, sir, you are not, sir!"

"Are you pulling my knee?"

"Yes, sir! No, sir! I mean, yes, sir!"

"Tell me the truth," the captain said.

"Yes, sir, it's the truth, sir!" Werner said. "It's a scientific kit for children, sir!"

"It's true, sir," Ariel intervened. "It's for the kids of a poor school. We're sure they will appreciate this gift."

"And where is that?" the captain asked, always staring at Werner without even bothering to turn to face Ariel.

"It is a rural school, sir!" Werner answered. "We don't know the name of the school, sir!"

"It's *Escuela Básica Nº 1117*," Ariel said, making up the number of what he remembered from Carlos's school name.

"And where is that?" the captain said, still addressing Werner only.

"To the east, sir," Werner said.

"You are not going east," the captain said.

"I knew it, sir," Werner said. "But we have taken this road because it has a better view. We are not in a hurry, anyway. We are enjoying the landscape, sir."

The captain stared at Werner. He was again going to ask, 'Am I an idiot?' but refrained from doing so. Still, he sensed something was wrong, although he didn't know what to make of it all. He had never heard of it before: two non-believers carrying unusual gifts for children of a poor school, situated in the wrong cardinal direction. Werner stood his ground. His blue eyes fixed on the captain's, not blinking. After twelve long seconds, the captain scratched his head, faced the soldier who returned the stare with a blank face, turned around, and walked away.

After a while, a lieutenant and another soldier holding Werner's box with instruments approached the station wagon. The soldier placed the box on the ground and went on to check thoroughly every corner of the vehicle: Werner and Ariel's stuff, food boxes, shovels, picks, machetes, clothes—everything. Their action attracted the curiosity of other soldiers who came to witness what was going on. One of the soldiers noticed the jerry can holding about thirty litres of gasoline. He had it in his hands, unscrewed the cap, sniffed the content, and screwed the cap again, but then other soldiers came and did the same, held the jerry can, unscrewed the cap, sniffed it, and screwed it back, and so they did, as many times as soldiers approached the car to do so. Then, the soldiers felt free to search the glove compartment and took everything from there as well. They checked under the seats, under the vehicle, the tires, and even the engine they searched clean.

Werner and Ariel moved some yards away and sat under a tree's shadow, called *palo santo*.

"I will take some leaves of this tree," Werner said. "As soon as we can, I will make tea for both of us. I read that the leaves of this tree are the best remedy against stomach aches."

Ariel said nothing. He focused his attention on the activity of the soldiers and the traffic—more trucks came and parked behind the van, and more people gathered by the roadside. Sitting in the tree's shadow, Werner and Ariel heard orders barked here and there and down there on the bridge.

"*I'vaí, la situación, ch'amigo,*"—The situation doesn't look good, my friend—Ariel said. Perhaps he was thinking, and the thought escaped through his voice.

"What?" Werner said.

Ariel didn't answer. One minute passed in silence. *We are at the mercy of a religious zealot,* Ariel thought to himself.

"What are you thinking, Ariel?" Werner said as if he could read Ariel's thoughts. "Ah! I bet it is about the captain. Don't worry about that guy. He just needs to keep himself busy to be happy. You know. When a man of power has nothing to do, it is dangerous to himself and others. That's why in most armies, they are never idle."

"I think the guy is crazy and dangerous," Ariel said. "I would rather be away from here. The sooner, the better."

Beyond the lines of cars, on the other side of the road, a group had improvised a soccer game. Despite the heat, the players, most peasants, ran behind a make-up ball, kicking it at will—shouts, laughter, noise, and dust, and the blessed innocence of childlike people.

More cars were coming.

"This is good for us," Werner said. "They will soon be so busy, they will forget us."

Ariel didn't answer. Werner got up and went to have a closer view of what was happening to fight his boredom.

A group of soldiers was checking a recently arrived vehicle with peasants travelling in the freight bed. The soldiers ordered everybody to get out, and the peasants climbed down and gathered at the truck's side.

"Is this necessary?" Werner said, but to himself, a question pestering him for a long time now, yet he could not hold it anymore, and so he spoke his mind out, and one of the soldiers heard him.

The soldier denounced Werner's attitude to a sergeant. Ariel, who was following the scene, wanted the earth to swallow him. The sergeant approached Werner.

"Go back to your place!" Then, commanded the sergeant, "If you come by here once again, I will hold you for interfering with army procedures."

An embarrassed Werner came back to sit under the *palo santo* by Ariel's side. After a while, both friends were impatient.

"This is taking too long," Werner said.

At that moment, the captain, the religious zealot as Ariel had described him, came back accompanied by his assistant. The captain summoned both friends.

"You two, follow me," the captain said.

Werner and Ariel followed the captain to a tent, and they went inside. A lieutenant sitting at a table stood up and militarily saluted the captain. Over the table laid a closed photo album of about twenty pages thick. The captain opened the book on one page and shoved it to a corner of the table.

"Sit over there," he said, signaling to the empty chairs.

"Look at these photographs. See if you recognize one or two."

Werner and Ariel did as the captain told them. The captain sat in the remaining chair in front of them while the lieutenant stood behind the captain's chair. Werner and Ariel perused the photos on that page, four photos of men and women taken in different contexts. None of them was familiar to them. Werner turned the page.

"Did I say that you can turn the page?" the captain asked.

Werner looked embarrassed. "Sir. No, sir," Werner said. "I'm sorry."

"You should be," the captain said. "Keep looking."

"I'm sorry again, sir," Werner said and closed the album. "I don't know any of these people, sir."

"Why did you close the book?" the captain asked. "Did I tell you to close it?"

"No, sir," Werner said.

Ariel was shaking by his side.

"Why are you so nervous?" the lieutenant asked Ariel.

"He is just nervous," Werner said.

"Are you his ventriloquist?" the captain asked, and Ariel was startled because he'd had the same thought earlier in the morning when they met the old man down there in that *rancho*.

Werner said nothing. The lieutenant pointed to one of the photographs—a group of men and women of undefined ages. The lieutenant looked at the captain, and the captain took over.

"These men, and their women," the captain said—*their women*, he said, as if women were accessories to men, "passed through this area not long ago. Peasants saw them and denounced them to the authorities, as they must do so, as decent anti-Communist citizens should do. Now, are you, or are you not, decent anti-Communist citizens?"

Werner was going to answer, but the captain interrupted him. "These people are terrorists. If you were on the road, the chances are that you may have seen them. Did you?"

"We found many men and women on the road, sir," Ariel said, "but it's difficult to recognize them in these pictures." And then, he added, "You know? You see faces, but not hearts."

The captain stared at Ariel for at least ten seconds. Ten seconds is a lot of time, should someone happen to be in that situation.

The captain gave the book back to the lieutenant.

"Let's go to your vehicle," the captain said.

They followed the captain to the station wagon. The captain's assistant followed some steps behind, his weapon at the ready. Werner ignored him and felt lighter, yet Ariel felt oppressed. And then, a soldier informed the captain of the search's outcome and showed him two shovels and two large machetes.

"*Usted*," the captain barked to Werner. "*Apersónese para acá.*"—You! Come over here!

Werner came closer to the captain. "Yes, sir!" Werner said.

Ariel was praying for Werner not to attempt a military salute, but Werner did it anyway. Yet, Werner's salutation failed to impress the captain. Ariel blushed and again covered his face with his hands.

"What do you intend to do with these things?" the captain said.

"Sir, I repeat to you, sir, that these are gifts, sir. There are many poor people around who need these things, sir."

The captain stared at him for about five seconds without a definable expression, then turned around and approached the van. He noticed the jerry can. He unscrewed it, sniffed it, and screwed the cap back on.

"So, you are going far."

Neither Werner nor Ariel answered.

Finally, exasperated by their silence, the captain unscrewed the cap again, but as if he had suddenly remembered that he had done that already, he stood there, caressing his chin, absorbed in his thoughts.

"Listen, *kara'i*," the captain said after a minute or so, and as if he had reached an important conclusion. "You may think that I'm an idiot, but I assure you, I'm not!"

Werner was going to answer, but Ariel nudged him. The captain turned his back on them and walked away, followed by his assistant.

The two friends were alone.

"What now, Werner?"

"I don't know, Ariel. We just have to wait."

"And pray . . ." Ariel said, feeling desolate.

Ten more minutes went by, and it seemed an eternity to both friends who were witnessing as other cars—and people—came and went, and none of them stayed there as long as they had been.

The captain came back to them; his assistant had their documents in his hands.

"You can continue," the captain said and turned his back to them before any of them could say a word.

The assistant delivered the documents to Werner's hand, turned around, and rushed behind the captain. Ariel and Werner stood there, staring at the captain's back, who most probably had forgotten them already.

They went back to their van and checked their belongings as the soldiers had left them piling up on the ground by the side of the vehicle, in disarray, although everything was there. Werner's main concern was the box with instruments; he checked it and found everything okay. Ariel did his best to rearrange the goods as he had them before, covered everything back with the canvas, and closed the door. He then went back to the driver's seat and started the engine. Werner climbed in, closed the door, and the car rolled toward the bridge. The soldiers ignored them.

"It is a rigorous control," Ariel said.

"It is a stupid control," Werner said. "As if the criminals don't have documents."

"*Guerrilleros*," Ariel corrected Werner. "These soldiers are looking for guerrilla. It's a good thing that neither of us looks like guerrilla men, Werner."

"Anybody can look like a guerrilla man, Ariel."

"No, of course not, Werner. Not just anybody. Remember those women over there?"

"They were not among the people in the photographs in the book," Werner said.

"They may as well have been, Werner, only that their appearances were different. And neither you nor I recognized neither. And that was good for us. And you can say that they are *guerrilleras*. All those women down there looked like guerrilla women because they were acting on their beliefs.

Only people who act on their beliefs look like what they say they are. And this applies to all of us in society. And on the guerrilla, only the true guerrilla people are what they look like. The others are but revolutionaries from their mouth out; they grow a beard and take pictures of themselves wearing a beret, like Che Guevara. And this is because all those idealistic people want to look like Che Guevara; to look like the static Che Guevara in the photography, of course, not like the rebel one in action."

Werner thought about this conclusive logic of his young friend. Then, for a long while, they travelled in silence.

"Perhaps they will be here when we return," Ariel said.

"The soldiers?" Werner said, startled by his friend's sudden comment. "I don't think so. But if they happen to be here, we will not know that, for sure. And I won't care, either."

"I agree," Ariel said. "Of course, if this dream comes true—"

"It will, Ariel. It will. And you know why? It is not because we are smart or because we know what to do or how to do it or plan it. Sometimes the best plans fail. We will succeed. After all, we keep trying it because we are persistent. We never give up. That is the only key to success, Ariel: persistence is key to every success."

"You can tell me that you read about that in a bestseller, Werner, but I don't believe in it. Persistence is okay, but I'm not going to crash my head against a wall hoping that the wall will break. See? The odds are that my head will break. And so, it's all God's will. If God wants to help you, then everything comes easy for you, which is what people, in their ignorance, call good luck."

Werner stared at his young friend for a while but decided to hold his thoughts. Finally, he closed his eyes and seemed to sleep.

AFTER HOURS of driving through bumpy, dusty roads carved into the vegetation, hundreds of colourful wildflowers, birds, and leaves came to their encounter as if they were penetrating a rainbow world which the incredible noise made alive.

Ariel steered the vehicle onto a path that cut as a scar through the most incredible view they ever imagined existed. The greenery grew with such force that the trail could disappear at any time, swallowed by the rainforest. It was night already, an incredible colourful night with different black, mysterious tones. And with the night, the rain came, and they felt like they were under a waterfall. Ariel stopped the vehicle because to continue driving in those conditions would be suicidal. Inside the car, they ate a delicious cold dinner, and Werner even dared to open a bottle of red wine he had carefully packed, although, in their frantic search, the soldiers had removed the package.

"*L'Chaim*," Ariel toasted, holding in his hand a paper cup. "I wish this wine doesn't make you ill, Werner."

"To our health," Werner toasted back. "I don't think the wine will be bad for me, Ariel. I read that it is like a tonic."

And they both drank, although Werner was careful and had only two or three sips. After their meal, they relaxed and slept, dreaming of gifts, like children dream of Santa Claus.

When they woke up, they discovered that the jungle's noise had by then increased, and it was as varied as the view. And above, the sky was as blue as ever, and the sun's rays seemed to dance over the treetops.

And they continued their journey.

Soon, Ariel found another path that followed through the bushes. And then another crossroads, a trail that was almost invisible under the tangled greenery. Finally, indecisive about continuing, Ariel stopped the vehicle.

"Don't stop!" Werner said, coming suddenly alive from the somnolence he had fallen. "We have to go that way."

"How do you know it is the right way, Werner?" Ariel asked. "I don't think the car can go there."

"I know, Ariel, trust me."

I have trusted you too much already, Ariel thought to himself. He didn't say, and the car pushed on through the greenery.

"I have been counting the crossroads," Werner said as if Ariel needed an explanation. "This is the one."

Then it came to Ariel that somehow, Werner knew about something he didn't share with him in the past. So, perhaps, Werner, a younger Werner, came by himself to this very same spot to study the terrain, and that's how he knew, for Ariel knew well by then that this road was in no printed map.

"Have you been here before, Werner?" Ariel said. "Tell me the truth."

"There is no truth but the truth," Werner said. "No, Ariel, I haven't been here before. How could I? All I've done is fill the dotted line left since the Jesuits' time, the German expedition, the information I gathered while in the laboratory, and the maps I have. Besides, my dear Ariel, this is a kind of Sherlock Holmes' type of work, where you have to follow all the hidden clues to arrive at your destination. In this case, the clues are clear in front of us all of the time. For example, the sun's position, geological clues, soil type, and vegetation, can you see? It is detective work, and it's simple. It will help to remember that the ancient sailors used the stars to guide them to their destination. I do the same, and it's nothing but, as I said, filling the dotted line."

Ariel had no response to this strange logic and continued driving through a denser, fantastic, wondrous world that overwhelmed him at every turn of the wheel, the vehicle moving through the cacophony of the rainforest. The tangled shrubbery extended in front of them for miles and miles. Ariel steered the car with dexterity, managing the narrow road full of wild vegetation on both sides, steeped curves, never-ending ascents, and fallen branches as he kept a constant watch on the deep ravines that bordered the narrow road where the width of the vehicle barely fit.

And it seemed to them they were in a kind of forgotten world. The infinite shades of the rainforest were far-fetched, and the noise was deafening. The jungle colours were everywhere: the multicoloured birds and the colourful snakes and the leaves, the wild orchids and crotons. And thousands of butterflies of different sizes and colours, with flashy drawings on their wings that adhered themselves to the glass of the windshield, and thus travelled with Werner and Ariel, escorting them toward the dark depth of the rainforest.

And to the liveliness of the vegetation added the vibrancy of every animal, bird, and insect that expressed themselves in their language in the loudest and most varied way possible. It was the feast of sound and noise, a carnival of expressions, birds of thousands of species, monkeys, oversized frogs, crickets, caterpillars, flying cockroaches, and even more giant spiders. And to all of this noise added the buzzing of mosquitoes and colourful, voracious flies. And from time to time, sometimes further, sometimes nearer, the roaring of a jaguar. A honking coming from a vehicle would have sounded there so trifling, so ridiculous.

And through all this thriving territory, the car moved slowly, very slowly. Up there, through the ceibo's foliage, they could see pieces of the bright blue sky, which from down there, where they felt so small, the sky was indeed a door to nothingness.

"Oh, my goodness!" Ariel exclaimed. "If something happens to us here, nobody will ever find us."

Werner was not in a talkative mood, so he just nodded, and from time to time, he cursed the fact he could not have access to a sparkling cold Schopp beer. Instead, he focused on what he considered his main task, checking the map he had placed on his knees. This particular document was not a printed map but an old sketch, perhaps a copy of a copy made by an ancient cartographer from a remote village in Germany, far away in his Native Bavaria. The details on the map were somehow confusing, but Werner seemed to understand them well.

The road narrowed and became a painful red scar in the intense greenery through and beyond.

"It's clay," Werner said. "The best kind. Here is a paradise for a ceramist."

"Here is a paradise that should never be disturbed by the presence of man," Ariel said, his eyes always fixed on the road. "Least of all, 'civilized,' ambitious men."

Werner chuckled.

Ariel had difficulties steering the vehicle that was now rolling over the shrubs. It was a scary situation, and he prayed not to find a tree growing in the middle of the road. The branches of the trees and shrubs scratched the painting of the station wagon.

"I reckon," Werner said, "that at this speed, it will take us more than half a day to reach the place signaled here." Werner showed the map to Ariel, who, of course, could not turn to see it as he had his attention focused on the road.

There was a curve, almost a straight angle ahead, Ariel slowed even more and managed the turn well, and after that, the road went downhill.

"Who the heck designed this road?" Ariel said.

"I think it was the drug dealers, Ariel. They use those all-terrain vehicles, so for them, it is not a problem. The drug dealers use this road as a way to avoid border controls."

"Well, I hope we don't find any drug dealers here. I don't think they will welcome us."

"Well, you can see that no one has used this road for a long time, so it's improbable we will find a human being for miles around."

Ariel said nothing, his eyes and hands focused ahead. Two or three more hours later, the situation and the landscape were the same. It seemed they had stopped hours ago in the same place. However, Werner was attentive to the marks on his map and the road.

"We must be close to the place where we should leave the vehicle," Werner said.

And then came a steep descent, and Ariel again slowed the vehicle to the minimum. The path ahead was hardly visible because of the vegetation; should that peculiar red dust not have been there, Ariel would not have had a sign to follow through, like a beacon beaming through the fog.

"This clay here," Werner said as he was always ready to give a lecture on any subject. "It's the result of erosion, and it shows that when people remove the trees—to build a road, for example—the land turns into a desert."

"Farms," Ariel said. "That's the evil that makes people cut trees. Farms-and-cattle-plus-ambition-plus-irresponsibility-equals-destruction-of-the-rainforest."

Werner remained silent, involved in his thoughts.

"I hope it doesn't rain," Ariel said. "If it rains now, we will have to stay here until tomorrow. And that's if the torrent does not drag us, I don't know where."

"There are no signs of rain, Ariel," Werner said, and through the treetops, studied the pieces of bright blue sky. "I guess, at least on that point, we must relax."

Half an hour passed, and the windshield wiper could not cope with so much rain. There was such a rainfall that neither Werner nor Ariel could believe it. Ariel stopped the car, turned the wheel so that the tires moved toward the trees instead of following the road, and sighed. It was impossible to drive through with such a storm. Moreover, the noise of the rain falling on the vegetation was deafening.

"Now I know that the weather forecast only works within the city limits," Ariel said.

Werner did not answer. He worried that the stream's force forming on the road would move the car as he had predicted. However, despite the stream's strength that grew wild, the station wagon remained strong, but it would not last if the rain continued. Ariel hoped that the rain would pass soon. But instead, the van shook so much that it seemed they were rolling on pebbles. Werner put the seat back and closed his eyes. Ariel instead continued trying to see something through the windshield covered by a mass of water, as if they had submerged in the torrent. But then, forty minutes later, the rain stopped, the day surged bright again, and as by an act of magic, the cacophony of the jungle came back to its highest level, replacing the sound of the rain. The soil absorbed the water, and it was all about as normal as if the torrential rain had never happened.

Ariel put the vehicle in motion. It was a slow march, though. The road was full of branches and other vegetation dragged by the storm. The sun was still high, but they both knew that soon it would be the night. A characteristic of the tropics. No lengthy sunsets to enjoy. Just day and then night.

WERNER HAD fallen asleep again and was gently snoring. Ariel smiled, relaxed, put a cassette into the cassette case, and listened to music at a low volume. The road was better now. The ground became thicker, although the red cloud of dust that the tires raised always followed them. Then, suddenly, there was a sharp turn coming. Ariel managed the curve, and once he passed it, he abruptly pushed the brake pedal. An abyss of terrifying depth opened just a few feet in front of him. He shook Werner's shoulders to wake him up. Werner almost jumped up in his seat.

Toward their right, the path continued through the jungle's unperturbed wall, but toward the left, the entire jungle fell into a vertical depth of several hundred feet. It was a hallucinatory view—the spectacle was as scary as it was fascinating. A cold sweat ran through Ariel's spine. He had stopped the vehicle just about ten feet from the treacherous border of a giant sinkhole, a bottomless precipice. If he had come at a higher speed, he would not have had time to brake, and because of the loose terrain, they would have disappeared, swallowed by the monstrous crater. Around it, the rainforest extended unmeasurable and indifferent.

Barely holding himself to his soul at the high suspense he was, Ariel shifted the engine in reverse, and the station wagon pulled backward in slow motion. After a few yards moving in reverse, Ariel finally grounded the car to a halt, ensuring it was safely away from the abyss. He opened the door, got out, stretched his arms, and went slowly about the road to face the awe-inspiring crater. Werner followed him. The sinkhole had smooth stone walls, almost polished, a neat circumference of about one complete football stadium. It was but a miracle that the road still stood. For nearly four yards, the trail narrowed even more, just the width of a small vehicle and too close to the abyss. Dangerously close. Ariel looked at Werner with a mute question in his eyes. *What do we do now?*

"We have to cross on to the other side," Werner said, answering Ariel's mute question.

"Are you sure, Werner?" Ariel said. "This is suicidal."

"You can do it, Ariel."

"No, Werner. The road is falling to pieces. We will end up at the bottom of this abyss."

"I don't think so," Werner said.

"It will be better if we turn around and go back."

"No way, Ariel. Besides, there is no room for the vehicle to turn around. So we have only one way to go. The other alternative is to remain here until our bodies rot."

"We could go back on foot, following the road, Werner."

"And abandon here all that we have brought? No way, Ariel."

"Ah! These are only material things, Werner."

"They are NOT material things, Ariel. They are part of my dream. To go back means to give up on my dreams," Werner said. "I cannot do that. At my age, I cannot. I should not do that. You may have other dreams, Ariel, but not me. The diamond field has been the dream of my life, and I'm not going to abandon it because of an event."

"An event?"

"This is what this hole is, Ariel. A natural geographical event."

"It looks like a sinkhole to me."

Werner didn't answer. He stepped forwards, walked about one hundred yards, stopped, measured the road's width, returned to the vehicle, and measured the car's width from its tires. Then again, Werner stepped forwards and stopped in the very place where the road seemed gnawed by the sinkhole walls. Then he began jumping as a child would on a bed with an agility that Ariel never imagined or had seen Werner do before. Ariel was speechless, but then his voice came back to him, and he screamed.

"Stop it, Werner! Are you crazy? This whole place will collapse!"

Werner stopped jumping. He understood that he had overdone it.

"Calm down, Ariel. There is no danger of collapse here."

"How can you be so sure? I can hardly watch this thing."

"As I said, Ariel, this is a natural geographical event. An extreme one, indeed. A subterranean river perhaps created cavities that, in time, collapsed, causing this large sinkhole. It could have also been gas. Whatever it was that caused this sinkhole, it already happened. The ground along the road is firm. I have to say we are lucky that the sinkhole didn't swallow the road."

"It can swallow us instead."

"C'mon, Ariel. Don't exaggerate. The only thing you have to do is to drive the car very slowly. This part is wide enough for the width of the vehicle."

"No, it's not, Werner. I won't go there, even if you offer me a load of diamonds."

"Then, I will do it, Ariel, although my sight is not as good as it used to be, and neither is my pulse. The chances are that I cannot steer the vehicle straight, but then, at least, I will die trying. You can go ahead and sit by the side of the road and watch. Or you can stay here to watch me how I cross and then join me there on the other side. If not, if something happens, you can go, on foot, of course, all the way back to civilization and live there happily ever after, even against your principles."

"Oh, stop it, Werner! Let's go!" Ariel said, walking toward the vehicle. "Don't tell me tragic stories."

"Virtuous reflex," Werner said. "Your reaction is called virtuous reflex, Ariel. You don't want to feel guilty, so you go against any odds. The hero's impulse urges the hero to give his or her life for a cause he or she believes is noble."

"Was it virtuous reflex that you were saying the Nazis, your fellow Nazis, by the way, used in the concentration camps? Ah, no! That was applied psychology, eh Werner?"

Werner didn't follow the comment. Instead, he seemed to be worried about the weather as he was watching the sky.

"Better we have to make a decision now, Ariel, because if we stay here talking about things from the past that we all hope will never return, the rain may catch us, and this time it will be a problem, as we are so close to this sinkhole."

Ariel didn't answer. He climbed into the vehicle, turned the engine on, and began moving slowly. Werner watched and directed him with his hands.

"Get in, Werner. I think I can manage without your silly gestures."

Werner jumped in, closed the door carefully, fastened the seat belt, and watched Ariel steering the vehicle, rolling slowly over the treacherous road.

"You don't have your seat belt on, Ariel."

"It won't do as much good if we plunge, Werner."

Werner swallowed his words. As they moved, there were no more comments. Inch by inch, the tires grasped that horrifying stretch of the road. The tires clung to the dust as if they wanted to be a part of that red soil. Ariel looked suspiciously to his side of the road. The tires bit the road, causing small landslides that fell down the bottomless chasm. The border of the road seemed to melt as salt in water under the pressure of the tires. The bushes to the right crashed violently against the car's frame and appeared to push the vehicle toward the abyss. Inch by inch, the car moved—

Finally, the abyss was behind them.

"Ooff!" both friends sighed.

Ariel pushed the gas pedal as if wanting to run away from there. And then he stopped the car and dried the sweat on his forehead. The path of fear was behind them now. Werner climbed out of the vehicle, went behind the bushes, and returned after a while.

When Werner returned, Ariel had set some food and drinks on the seat, and they relaxed and enjoyed the meal. Then, with their stomachs satisfied, they felt better, and now Werner focused on his maps.

"This event," Werner said, "Must be recent because it does not show here on this map, and it has been pretty accurate until now. And it does not show in Dr. Zweig's notes, too, so, something does not match."

"Perhaps they came through a different road," Ariel said, his hands again clenched to the steering wheel, his eyes fixed on the road ahead. He didn't want more geological surprises.

"I don't think so, Ariel. Until we met the geological event, the map and the notes described the road pretty well."

"What do you think, Werner?"

"I think this event is something recent. The fact that there is no information about it is not a surprise. This place is fairly away from civilization. Most natural events that happen in isolated places are never recorded."

"Natural events? C'mon, Werner. That is a fancy name for a disaster. We were coming from a deluge and then the sinkhole. Think about it."

"Interestingly enough, Ariel, all these disasters, as you call them, only matter if they affect humans. If there are no humans affected, then there are no records, and if there are no records, who care?"

"Only nature is destroyed, but what about the Natives? Aren't they humans too?"

"Nature is never destroyed, Ariel, only changed. It transforms itself. And of course, the Native dwellers are humans, but they don't record these disasters because these events are natural things for them, so it is probable that they have a register of these events in their songs and their legends."

"But this is recent, Werner. Someone must have noticed. The sinkhole is too big."

"It's nothing if we compare it to the extension of this territory, which also may mean that this geological area is still experiencing changes."

Ariel listened with attention.

"The Earth expels gases and minerals from its centre. Therefore, there must be an incredible unexplored richness under the rainforest. Gas and minerals. Also, there must be constant volcanic activity, which would explain that theory about the diamonds that we are about to validate."

Gas, minerals, and diamonds that sooner or later will cause this paradise to disappear, thought Ariel, but said nothing because Werner would have said he always had negative thoughts. And so he remained silent. Werner, too, was involved in his thoughts.

After a while, they decided to proceed with their journey among the jungle's cacophony and colours. They were in a space without time. Indeed, time seemed a strange element in that landscape, odd as them and their vehicle.

They came to a stretch of the road that was somewhat better than the one they had travelled on until now, so Ariel felt he could speed up, and again a cloud of red dust followed the vehicle.

And then they followed a sharp curve, and after that, the road continued straight until it seemed to go into three tall conic peaks covered by the most incredible vegetation and flowers of every imaginable colour and shape.

"There it is! There it is!" Werner screamed, almost jumping on his seat. "We made it, Ariel. Here is where we have to leave the car."

He had the map in one hand and showed it to Ariel, who could not turn his head to look at it because he focused his attention on the road. Werner touched him on the shoulder, so Ariel reduced the vehicle's speed until it stopped entirely but kept the engine idling.

"Here," Werner said, leaning on the map with enthusiasm. "See? Three peaks like cones in succession. They are the door to a small range of low altitude mountains covered by vegetation."

"Perhaps they are pyramids from an unknown ancient civilization not yet discovered nor explored," Ariel said.

"Perhaps," Werner said. "But we're not archeologists. Our objective is quite different."

Ariel said nothing, shifted the vehicle into first gear, and rolled slowly, looking for a place to park. Finally, he found a place that looked appropriate and went off the road.

"Farther down, Ariel," Werner said. "We have to hide the van, but we want to find it when we return. I wouldn't like any drug dealer stealing our vehicle and leaving us here at the mercy of the jungle."

"Or the guerrilla," Ariel said somberly. "Remember those were guerrilla guys who the soldiers were chasing."

"Yeah, but that is far from here, Ariel. Guerrilla needs support from the population to survive, and here they have nothing."

"Still, better to be safe than sorry."

"I agree with that, Ariel. Better safe than sorry."

"See, Werner? That's the benefit of our 'civilization.' Smugglers, terrorists, *guerrilleros*, criminals, robbers, drug dealers, corrupt politicians, you name it. Pandora's Box at its best."

"That's not civilization, Ariel. That's the dregs of society."

"They are criminals anyway, Werner. We should never justify crime with philosophy or because there is a lapse in the law. A judge should never be a coward. Coward judges are the reason why the world is upside down. That's why we are the way we are."

"Quite drastic, aren't you, eh, Ariel?"

"Better focus on the task at hand, Werner. I feel that even though we are deeper in the rainforest, we still must protect ourselves from civilization."

Ariel passed through a barrier of bushes and kept driving further forwards until he found a clearing ahead of him. He steered the car there, and satisfied, killed the engine. Werner climbed out of the vehicle and stretched. Then he walked back to the road. Ariel followed him. Werner signaled toward where Ariel just parked the van. Ariel could not see it. Both men smiled. Incredible as it seemed, the bush through which the tires had crashed a minute or so ago was now back standing, hiding the vehicle completely.

Around them, the branches of the *yvyrayú* covered their view of the sky. The leaves of the *carová, lapachos,* and *quebrachos,* the flowers' aroma, and their multi colourful blooming and shapes made them believe they were at the core of that giant rainbow Ariel had envisioned at the beginning of his journey. The mosquitoes' buzzing and flies added to the cacophony of a million sounds carried by the breeze. Just above their heads, hanging from the branches of a *yvyra pytá*, a family of *kaí* monkeys frantically jumped from one tree branch to the other. Werner and Ariel felt they were between the whole and the nothingness.

Werner consulted with his wristwatch, a trivial human action, a reminder of civilization, yet in that atmosphere, the gesture was so alien that even Werner himself smirked, ashamed of himself.

They went back to the station wagon and began unloading it. They filled their backpacks with the necessary items, and this task kept them busy for several minutes. Ariel's tricoloured knapsack with the colours of the American flag stood out amongst the greenery.

Werner finished loading his backpack, and then with a leather belt, he tied a small shovel, a pick, and his canteen. Then, he tried to lift the bag, put it on his back, and found it heavier than he had thought. Werner knew that walking through the rainforest carrying this heavy pack on his back would be challenging at his age, in his physical shape, and as sick as he was just a few days ago, for the symptoms of his stomach infection, which debilitated him, might come back. Yet, he didn't comment on his apprehension with Ariel but placed the knapsack on the ground, and despite its weight, he added a sleeping bag and a roll of impermeable fabric. Then he changed his running shoes for a pair of boots the kind of military wear, and despite the humidity, covered himself with a light impermeable jacket of the type called windbreaker. Finally, he hung a lamp to batteries from his neck, and he was ready to pursue his lifelong dream. Ariel, by his side, did likewise.

The sun was still high over the treetops. Through the clearing in the treetops, they could see several *taguató* that were circling the area. Still, it could be only a coincidence to see those birds of prey circling just in where they were, but the view of them gave Ariel an uneasy feeling.

"We have to hurry," Werner said. "Night will catch up halfway."

"I see," Ariel said.

He checked the vehicle for the last time and then helped Werner with his backpack. Then, Ariel also hung a lamp from his neck, loaded his knapsack on his back, and they were ready to go. Both friends were in good humour.

"Let's go," Werner said.

"Let's go," Ariel answered.

BUTTERFLIES, SPIDERS, snakes, and the entire greenery moved along at their every step. The echo of the rainforest nestled in their ears. The ground was soft, covered by a carpet of moss, leaves, and roots. There was a chance that they were the first non-Native humans in decades to step on that carpet, for according to Werner, they were walking on the same path that Dr. Berndt Zweig and his group had stepped on forty years ago.

On the branch of a *yvyraró*, a *curiyú* gently rocked. Probably, the serpent was digesting its last meal. On the tree branches above, the chattering of birds of a hundred species, shapes, sizes, and colours pursued them, the *chajá,* always kissing their partner; and there were many toucans, other birds, their names in Guaraní, *gua'a hovy*, *kanindé*, and the *gua'a pyta.* And the *tuyuyú cuarteleros,* the *charatas* and hundreds of other incredible species of birds unknown to all those who live in cities, and of course, preying on the birds' eggs there were the snakes, and a curious *ñacurutú* stuck out its head among the pink flowers of a black *lapacho.*

Ariel's biggest concern was precisely the snakes—those *yarará* were at the top of his worries. Werner put him at ease by giving him a lecture on the behaviour of poisonous snakes in that area of the world. However, Werner's explanation did not satisfy Ariel, who was always in doubt of Werner's theoretical knowledge.

"One thing is to read a book about a subject, Werner," Ariel said, challenging Werner's thesis. "And another one is walking in the rainforest as we are doing."

"Those books you dismiss so lightly," Werner answered, "Were written by subject matter experts, Ariel, so, please don't belittle their knowledge."

"Yeah," Ariel said. "Whatever you say, Werner. But you know that looking at an illustration of a poisonous snake in the pages of a book in the comfort of a library is quite different from finding a real one sticking out their forked tongue at you, just inches away from your eyes."

"It's not quite different, Ariel," Werner answered. "What the books achieve is to put into your hand what otherwise would be impossible for an ordinary person to experience."

"Whatever, Werner," Ariel rebutted again. "Theory or practice, the rainforest follows wise laws we humans are yet unable to understand."

"The books help us to understand it better, Ariel."

"I don't know, Werner," Ariel said. "It seems to me that we humans will never understand nature's laws. This entire wonderful world follows an extraordinary divine plan where all, including the Native dwellers, animals, plants, insects, and the whole of nature, adjusts to its rhythm."

"So, what you are saying is that it is all human's fault. It's not so, Ariel. Nature knows how to defend itself."

"No, Werner, it doesn't. It's lost. With us, nature doesn't know how to act or react. I tell you that those who mess with nature's rhythm are we, the so-called civilized humans. In the natural world, they, the trees, the vegetation, the animals, birds, fish, arachnids, insects all follow strict laws. We, humans, obey no rules. What we do, we do it by impulse. In the natural world, there are no impulses. Everything has a plan.

There is an objective for every creature in the universe. That's what my father taught me. We owe respect and love to every creature on the Earth, beginning with ourselves."

Werner listened with utmost attention to his young friend's philosophical speech, and in his inner self, he decided that Ariel was right. Despite his reading on nature, he hoped that they were never within the range of a *yaguareté* or a *ñaniná*.

On the other hand, Ariel also thought of his old friend's words and hoped that jaguars and snakes had read Werner's *Manual of Survival in the Jungle*, the book Werner seemed to have written at some point in his life, away from a jungle, though. Ariel, however, was prudent enough not to express his thoughts in a loud voice. His theoretical friend could be hurt.

ALONG THREE hours passed. They walked one behind the other at a quick pace whenever the terrain allowed them to do so, surrounded by the ever-present cacophony of the rainforest; indeed, this festival of sounds pushed them to continue despite how tired they felt. And so, they walked briskly and alert.

Werner ahead had found a path, perhaps made by the Natives. The track ran through the trees and on firmer ground, which helped them to keep their pace. In his gloved hand, Werner held a machete. He had not used it properly, but he thought that the opportunity to use it would come soon.

A light that sparkled here and there surrounded them as if they were walking in a fantastic forest. It was the effect of the sunrays on the wet leaves, but this effect ended all of a sudden, and it was all dark. And with darkness, it seemed that the sound of the rainforest had increased in volume. In the forest and the big cities, it is evident that the night gives life to another kind of life—a more aggressive one, closer to death. Ariel stepped on faster.

"It always called my attention," Werner said without stopping, "How night comes so fast in the tropics. In just a minute, without pauses."

Very close to them, they heard a feline roar.

"Yaguareté," Werner said.

Another roar followed immediately, this time even closer. It sounded indeed scary.

"Yaguareté," Ariel said. "We better get back."

Werner said nothing and lit his lamp. Ariel followed suit. The effect of the light penetrating the darkness was incredible. A cloud of mosquitoes and all kinds of flying insects came to gather around the lamp. Werner, however, focused his attention on the sounds. The yaguareté's roaring continued, but it was evident that the animal had moved away from them, and the roaring had now attenuated by other sounds. But what Werner wanted to hear was the sound of the stream of the river. That was the only sound that mattered to him.

The light of the lamps continued to show them a phantasmagoric spectacle. Giant thorny vines fell from the tall trees that delayed every step of the two friends. To these vines added the enormous spiderwebs that were like curtains between one tree and the next. And the roots that grew oversized and that blocked their way and the fallen leaves that hid treacherous holes in the uneven ground—

But none of this defeated Werner, who attacked every obstacle with obstinacy as if he were a modern Don Quixote. And so, he continued opening a path with his machete held high, and in this way, he cut the vines, the bushes, the spider webs, the branches, and everything that threatened to stop him, or that which could hinder his march toward his dream of diamonds.

THE FIRM ground gave way to a swampy one where their boots sank, and they were challenging to remove because it was as if the ground sucked them down. However, many hours of this strenuous exercise exhausted them both. Besides, it was dangerous. The topography was full of poisonous creatures.

The swamp continued. It seemed infinite. Ariel was afraid to fall into a deep hole from where he could not escape. It would be a slow and painful death. And then, another even more nightmarish landscape came into view. There, everything was surreal. The swamp was now more liquid, their boots filled with water, and it was very uncomfortable. They stopped for a moment because they were too tired to observe the extraterrestrial landscape that surrounded them.

Around them, the green rainforest had turned into a phantasmagoric view, filled with white trees with naked branches, and they all looked like corpses, like zombies that were to move at any moment. The scenery impacted both friends. The trees had black cavities that looked like empty eye sockets and toothless mouths opened in an eternal silent cry for help. The scene was hair-raising. This sad spectacle continued for miles and miles. Werner put off the light of his lamp, and Ariel did likewise.

Ariel was curious about what kind of experiment his friend wanted to perform on that ground. The scenery increased in its phantasmagoric intensity. The dead-like tree bark had a strange glow as a vegetal aura. The phantasmagoric reflection of those glowing wooden skeletons on the water's surface was something they never imagined possible, as if the trees were indeed living monsters that followed Werner and Ariel with their dead eyes, this time from under the water. They lit the lamps again, and this time, as if to complete the scene, the lamps' beam highlighted the big eyes of giant multicoloured frogs that played hide-and-seek with the water snakes of transparent bodies.

"It should be better if we get back, Werner," Ariel said. "We are lost."

"We are not lost, Ariel. It's the correct way. We have to continue."

"This place is full of *ñacaninás* and a lot of other poisonous things, Werner. So we better go back and start again."

"No way, Ariel. There is no way to return. We have to keep going until we reach the river. Henceforward, we must overcome our fears and every obstacle after that."

Perhaps because of the environment, Werner and Ariel's voices had acquired a strange tone. *What a weird thing,* Ariel thought. He got goosebumps. Werner continued walking in the water, and by then, he had advanced about three yards ahead of Ariel. Ariel had no more options but to follow him. He lifted his foot high above the water and then put it back, making sure the ground he was stepping on was solid, and this way, he continued for a long time, but this method proved to be tiring and slow. He screamed several times for Werner to stop and wait for him, but either Werner didn't listen, or his voice was not coming out because the water began to boil around him. And then, several movements in the shadows scared him even more. By then, Werner had stopped and returned to meet Ariel, who seemed greatly relieved to see his friend.

Werner directed his lamp's beam toward the water. Ariel followed suit. The profile of a prehistoric animal camouflaged among the fallen trunks came to view. The beast's teeth shone in the beam of the lamps; in its jaws, a prey convulsed rhythmically, still struggling for its life.

"*Yacaré,*" Werner said.

"*Yacaré,*" Ariel said.

"Dinner time," Werner said.

"We could be next, Werner. Better we get back."

"I don't think they will attack us, Ariel. The *yacaré* surround us and would have done it already if they wanted."

And to bear out Werner's words, the beams of light showed a group of *yacaré* that swam at a short distance from where they were. Dark, solid, prehistorical masses swiftly moved around them, their primitive bodies hitting their tails on the water as if they were playing or if the animals wanted to scare them. The movement of the *yacarés* in the darkness gave Werner and Ariel the idea that the water was alive. Ariel moved ahead, but his lamp showed him two more *yacarés* in front of him with an attitude as if the animals were proposedly closing their only exit.

Werner came by Ariel's side, and neither the men nor the *yacarés* moved, and then Werner realized what an exciting situation it was. As fear paralyzed Ariel, Werner discovered that the beams of their lights also paralyzed the *yacarés*. There was no doubt that it was the first time in their lives that the *yacarés* were seeing the artificial light. One of the animals had its jaws wide open and moved as if it were rocking in the water. Werner touched Ariel's arm, and Ariel reacted, lifting the machete as if he were ready to fight for his life.

"Easy, Ariel," Werner said. "They won't attack us. We are too big for them."

"Better we get back, Werner. It's the most prudent idea."

"No, Ariel. We're already closer to our objective than ever. I'm not going to go back empty-handed."

"Empty-handed, but alive, Werner."

"Let's move forwards slowly, Ariel."

"I'm afraid that these animals will cut us both in half if we move."

"That happens only in the movies, Ariel. These animals are shy and avoid humans. It's the light that attracted them."

"I'm sure you read about that in a book, Werner, but I don't believe any of that."

"Let's move, Ariel. We have to keep moving. It's dangerous to stay here because the *yacarés* also attract the *yaguaretés*. The jaguars feed on *yacarés*, so better get out of here fast."

They moved through the water, advancing step after step and always keeping the lamps' light on the eyes of the *yacarés*. Around them, darkness was intense, which accented the white trees' extraordinary macabre spectacle whose naked branches were like hands praying to the blackness above.

The *yacarés* increased in number. Perhaps they were curious about the strangers. Werner concluded that they were indeed in great danger and expected a miracle, which happened just a second after his thought because two of the animals began a fight that attracted the others, thus breaking the spell of the light from the lamps. The two friends could see the prehistoric profile of the *yacarés* moving away from them.

Both friends kept moving through that interminable swamp. They moved faster now because they were away from the threats of the *yacarés*. Still, Werner thought they could meet some jaguars that may have used the swamp as their hunting ground, and Werner knew that the jaguars would be as forgiving with them as the *yacarés* were. A pair of giant snails had adhered to Ariel's pants, and at Ariel's screams, Werner had removed them with the point of his machete. The snails fell into the water.

"These snails are also part of the menu of the *yacarés*," Werner said.

"Yeah," Ariel said. "The little ones are always the meal of the bigger ones, and this happens at all levels. It happens in nature as well as in humanity."

"The scare has turned you into a philosopher, eh, Ariel? And this is good. It means you have recovered your energy. You know now how fear activates the brain. Indeed, fear is the best remedy to keep the brain alert."

"Perhaps you don't care about your life, Werner, but I'm still young, and I guess there is still something useful I can do with my life."

"You're wrong, Ariel. I care for my life and yours. And I do because I have this dream to fulfill. When I have no more dreams to fulfill, it will be then that I will die."

THREE HOURS had passed, the swamp continued, and the ground had turned muddy again. They could barely walk. To remove their boots that had stuck fast in the mud was a tiring task.

"What we had done," Werner said to answer Ariel's mute question, "was to wade the swamp. Then, as I read in Dr. Zweig's notes, the Native guides took the group through the swamp. I'm sure this is the safest and fastest way."

They advanced little in their constant struggle with the swamp, but their efforts came to fruition when they found firm ground again, and soon they found a clearing and moved toward it. The solid terrain allowed them to step faster, but as soon they reached the clearing and dropped to the floor, exhausted as they were, they froze in terror.

A few steps from where they were, a *yaguareté* was feeding on a *yacaré*. The *yaguareté* had hunted the *yacaré* in the swamp and dragged it to this site. It still had its powerful canines incrusted in the *yacaré*'s head. As the feline moved his head, its eyes came to meet those of Werner. The expression in the animal's eyes showed the hunt's excitement, but at the same time, its annoyance because of the interruption of its meal. Ariel had already started to step back slowly and then turned around, and abandoning all his equipment, ran through the bushes in a crazed frenzy of a run. Werner walked a few steps backward, keeping his eyes fixed on the massive feline, and then, as Ariel had done, dropped his backpack and started as well a crazed run. The roar of the enormous jaguar followed him as if it had its claws opened and was extending toward him.

Werner didn't know how long he had been running when his legs gave up. He stopped moving, and exhausted, fell to the ground and rested for what seemed to him just a while. His heart was beating so hard that he thought he was going to have a heart attack. Then, after a time had passed, Werner recovered his strength, and his mind became clear. *Where is Ariel?* Werner wondered. *Oh, my God, where is Ariel?*

Werner retraced his footsteps, calling Ariel at a great voice, but the chance that another human being heard him in the middle of that cacophony was nil. Upon realizing that there was no way to contact Ariel in that way, Werner decided to go back to where they had dropped their equipment because without it, Werner wouldn't survive in the jungle, and it was probable that Ariel would do the same.

And although, as per his wristwatch, a good two hours had elapsed since they encountered the *yaguareté,* Werner was surprised to find the place where they saw the feline eating the *yacaré* too soon. Indeed, he was at a short distance from the site where he started his crazy run through the forest, although Werner thought he had been running for hours. *Oh, my God,* he thought with horror, *I have been running in circles.* If the jaguar had decided to hunt for them, the animal would have just taken a minute to catch any one of them. And for the first time in his life, Werner felt so ridiculously defenceless that he cried bitterly. Then, in the clearing of the forest, he found the abandoned half-eaten carcass of the *yacaré*. Werner was leery that the large cat would still be around and could ambush him. Deeply afraid, he gathered his things and those of Ariel, and this simple task proved to be difficult because of his state of mind. He felt so tired, and his stomach pained.

Werner sat on a protruding root and mulled on the facts of nature, wondering about the incredible strength of the jaws of the jaguar that effortlessly dragged the moribund body of a large *yacaré* for several yards until the jaguar found a quiet place to eat it. Absorbed in his thoughts, Werner overlooked Ariel, who had returned and was now in front of him, and still, he didn't react, but Ariel's voice startled him. Both friends embraced, and after that, they gathered their belongings, loaded the backpacks, and resumed their way toward the mythical diamond deposit.

But the night's emotions and the tiredness they felt in their muscles impeded them from walking as fast as they intended to, so after two hours of a forced march, both felt that they could not continue unless they took a break to drink and eat. And so they did. And as soon as they found what they believed was an appropriate dry place, they dropped their backpacks on the ground, searched for their drinks and food, and ate it cold, and it was delicious. After their meal, Ariel fell asleep, and although Werner thought that they were not in a safe place, after all, he too fell asleep nonetheless, albeit he had a disturbing dream, and he woke up.

Werner woke up. In the beginning, Werner didn't know where he was, and he stood up like an automaton, looked around him, got his bearings, realized where he was, and went to shake Ariel, who was deeply asleep.

"Ariel, wake up," Werner said. "Get up. We cannot stay here. This place is not safe."

Werner's lamp's beam focused on Ariel's face, that's why Ariel could hardly see anything, but Werner saw a *mbopi pepé* that crept smoothly around Ariel's backpack. Werner screamed in terror, grabbed a stick, and with it, removed the snake that at an incredible speed coiled its body, turned its head, and flicked its forked tongue in the direction of Werner's hand. Werner reacted and threw away the stick and the snake with it.

"There was no need to do that, Werner. We must remember these animals are at home. We are their home invaders here."

"The bite of that landlord could have killed you in less than two minutes, Ariel."

"It's not true, Werner. If that *mbopi pepé* had wanted to attack me, it would have done already while I was asleep. It had no intention to do so. Unless it feels there is a threat, the snake is a shy animal that only minds its own business."

"C'mon, Ariel. As it just happened with the *yaguareté* down there, with any living creature in this rainforest for that matter, if we give them the opportunity, they will kill us."

"You're confusing things here, Werner. With all my respect, you confuse animals' behaviour with that of humans. It's not the same, of course. We're not in our living room at home here. We were the ones who interrupted the *yaguareté*'s lunch, and we are in its territory. In the case of the snake, she is not invading our home. In our world, when someone invades our property, we solve the problem with gunshots, isn't it true? But these animals, what can they do but show themselves, because it's the only way they have to tell us we are trespassing on their home. The little we have left for them."

"Yes, Ariel, but—"

"But nothing," Ariel interrupted. "You know, Werner," Ariel, implacable, continued, "cruelty in the natural world could never match brutality in the human world. Why? Because cruelty in nature aims to balance the survival of the species.

And because cruelty in nature constricts itself to satisfy immediate needs. Therefore, it acts only on what is necessary to maintain this balance. Ergo, when nature achieves the balance, cruelty stops. Instead, in humans, cruelty runs on fear and ambition, and no balance exists in either condition; hence, cruelty in humans is limitless."

"Yes, but—"

"I said that there are no 'buts' here, Werner. We have plenty of examples here. See? The *yaguareté* is hungry, kills the *yacaré*, and feeds on it. The *yaguareté* is satisfied and goes to sleep while the other *yacaré* in the swamp swim unbothered until the cycle repeats. In the *yaguareté*'s place, a human kills the *yacaré* and kills all the other *yacaré* as well. He even dries the swamp if there is something of value in it. And a human is never satisfied; even with his stomach full, he ogles other animals to kill for sport, eat, for pleasure, or tame the animal for work, diversion, or both, and destroys it just for the sake of destroying life or many. In our civilization, animals will always lose."

Werner didn't answer. He was busy trying to put his belongings in his backpack. And while arranging his effects, Werner mulled over Ariel's words. *Ariel,* Werner thought to himself, *seems to hate humankind. 'Our civilization,' Ariel had said.* Indeed, Ariel was revealing himself as a different person. Definitively, this new Ariel was not the tender one who Werner had met in Asunción. Perhaps now that they were away from civilization, Ariel's true nature was showing up, opening to him like a new book. *It's an interesting mutation of the soul,* Werner thought while he lifted his backpack.

This action signaled to Ariel that it was time to resume the march, so he got ready to walk. Werner had already moved some steps ahead and was walking faster. Ariel felt touched by Werner's willingness, heading forward at full speed despite his age and discomfort, even though he looked exhausted.

The terrain became more challenging to walk on as they moved on, the humidity increased, and the evergreen became more luxuriant as the cacophony increased. The trees showed long, strong buttresses that grew from their trunks and expanded, making every step even more difficult.

"Maybe there are Native people around here," Ariel said.

"It's probable," Werner said. "I'm crossing my fingers. I don't like to meet them, yet in Dr. Zweig's chronicles, he said they met the Aboriginal dwellers."

"For sure, the Germans had a close encounter with the Natives. I do not doubt it, and they said nothing, not wanting to discourage the ones who could be coming after them. The future expeditions."

"It's possible," Werner said.

"You know something you are not telling me, Werner. That's not fair."

"Well," Werner said, "the information I got says that they are savages. Very dangerous. That's all."

"That's not comforting," Ariel said, almost to himself.

The swamp and the phantasmagoric forest were far behind now. Both friends walked, distracted by the pulsing noise from which they could not escape as if they were in a cage. *An evergreen cage* thought Ariel. But to their amazement, there was some shifting in the noise's nuances, and then they understood that it was not night anymore but daytime.

They could see the clarity of a new day through the foliage, although darkness in most places still prevailed. And wherever some sunrays crossed the crocket, the rainforest renovated its energy. Exhausted as they felt, the new day gave them some vitality, and they found some strength to speed the march, although the terrain was now going uphill, muddy and slippery, and consequently, they had to slow their pace. Sometimes, they had to stop to get their bearings and to seek a path to continue. In this part, the jungle was so inextricable, they had to use their machetes willy-nilly and at full strength to open a trail, and this task exhausted them even more.

Ariel shouted for Werner to stop for a rest, but either Werner didn't hear him or didn't want to stop. They were now going upward as it was very tiring; it was as if they were climbing up a steep forested mountain, which added to the difficulties. At some point, they had to crawl, their hands holding from the buttress roots and using them as steps as in a stepladder. Then, there was a strange tremor. It sounded like thunder that was echoing through the entire rainforest, approaching fast. It was a peculiar sound. Both friends stopped their climbing and listened for a moment. In a moment, the thunder seemed to surround them.

"Thunder!" Ariel said. "Soon, we will have a storm, Werner. Better, hurry up. We have to find a shelter."

Werner didn't answer. He was listening. His ears were trying to pass through the incredible cacophony of the rainforest and filter that sound.

"It's not thunder, Ariel," Werner said after a while. "It's the river. We must be close."

Werner's speech was faltering. He was gasping and near complete exhaustion. The climbing of this part of the forest had claimed all his energy but not his enthusiasm.

The thunder came again, this time stronger. Powerful. The echo of it hit every tree, every trunk, and every leaf.

"The river?" Ariel said. "So, the river exists after all. I wonder why no one until now has found it. That's strange."

"It's not strange, Ariel. The only thing is that the river comes and goes."

"What? What do you mean, Werner?"

"You will see, Ariel. You will see."

"If this is the noise of its stream, it must be a giant river, Werner."

"It is, Ariel. It's huge. I guess we must be close to it."

Ariel said nothing. He had already learned that in the rainforest, it was all relative. Nothing they knew from 'civilization' applied there. Concepts of distance, for example. Near could as well means hours and hours of walking.

The thunder came clear-cut to their ears now, like loud explosions. A spectacular battle was taking place just on the other side of the trees. Werner and Ariel hurried their climbing, their hands holding the protruding buttresses, the bindweeds hanging over their heads as a green rain.

"That's not a river stream, Werner," Ariel said, stopping for some seconds to listen. "That's thunder, pure and simple. For sure, it is going to rain soon."

"It's the river, Ariel. Still, we try to reach the top of this hill—or whatever we are climbing—fast and find a place to rest. It must be flat up there, I guess. I feel I cannot give another step, and I'm hungry, thirsty, and tired. I want to rest."

"Same here," Ariel said. "I'm so tired, physically and mentally."

"It's true," Werner said. "This thing—to walk blindly in a place like this—exhausts the stronger ones. However, there is no other way, Ariel. I have been following the exact references the Native guides gave to Dr. Zweig. I guess any other way must be even more dangerous. If you think of it, after all, the way we have come has not been bad at all."

"We should find a place to cover us from the rain," Ariel said, avoiding Werner's point that the walking had been without incidents, like a walk in the park. "Whatever you say, Werner," he mumbled.

The thunder now shook the trees, and a cloud of bats flew over their heads. Both friends dove to the ground and kept their bodies stuck to the soil despite the soil's humidity; however, Werner stood upright with a jump despite his tiredness and moved away from where they laid.

"Move, Ariel, quick!" Werner exclaimed.

"What's wrong, Werner?" Ariel was now moving closer to the shocked Werner.

"Move away fast from there," Werner mumbled. And he signaled to a place where several disgusting-looking creatures crept feverishly.

"What are those?" Ariel said.

"*Cienpies*," Werner mumbled, almost out of breath for the effort he had made walking, climbing, and now jumping away from the danger. "Look, Ariel, they are everywhere. This is a hunting field for them." He looked around. "Aha! It's because of the bats. These creatures feed on the bats."

"Oh my, oh my!" Ariel exclaimed.

"They are Scolopendra centipedes, Ariel. Voracious, carnivorous creatures that feed on whatever prey they can catch: mice, snakes, frogs, spiders, and so on. They have a lot of food here with the bats." Werner grabbed a stick and removed the dry leaves, and some larger Scolopendra moved away fast toward the darkness under the roots. "See?" Werner said, showing Ariel one of the larger ones, some even seven inches long. "With these claws, which are also called *forcipules*, the Scolopendra sizes its prey even if it is bigger than them. The Scolopendra then injects a venom that paralyzes its victim and then eats it completely. So we have to be careful. Their bite, though not fatal, is quite a problem for a human."

Ariel checked Werner's clothes, and then he checked his own and tried to clean his back, just in case he had one of the little monsters adhered to his body.

"You are clean," Werner reassured him.

Ariel, curious about the strange, repellent creatures, turned around to look at them creeping around.

"What a wonder our planet is, isn't it, Werner? Will we ever learn about it before we destroy it?"

Werner didn't answer as he had continued climbing up, constantly crawling up, holding on to the roots and bushes, moving slowly. Ariel followed him, but soon he surpassed Werner. More thunder shook the trees.

"It seems that it is going to rain any moment now, Werner," Ariel said.

Werner didn't answer, yet he quickened his steps.

ARIEL HAD again gained some distance ahead of Werner, but he missed a root to grab and fell back in his hurriedness. In a moment, Werner was by his side and helped him to recover.

"I'm fine," Ariel said, embarrassed at having to depend on his older friend. "But better keep moving, Werner. Rain will be here soon, and the force of the gale may take us downhill. We may lose everything. Hurry up."

"The thunder comes from the river, Ariel. We have been listening to it for quite a while now. If it were thunder that announced rain, we would be soaked already."

The thunder was now deafening.

"Indeed, I don't think it is going to rain now, Ariel. You must know that in the rainforest because you cannot see the sky, the same rainforest tells you if a storm is coming. You can read about it in any book."

"Any book would be already wet, Werner. For a long time now, what we have been doing is just breathing—"

A deafening thunder canceled Ariel's words, and then lightning reflected on the higher leaves. It was a hallucinating spectacle.

Ariel unfolded the waterproof canvas, covered himself entirely with it, and then tied it at his waist. Dressed in this way, Ariel looked like a medieval monk. Werner could not avoid a smile and continued climbing up, oblivious to Ariel's concern.

There was a sequence of thunder and more lightning. A warm wind moved the treetops and reached them softly, and the rain came so powerfully they stood there for a moment as if the raindrops had knocked them out. And the forest was full of shining here and there, through the leaves, and the falling water, and there was rain everywhere. The thundering surrounded them as if they were in the middle of a battlefield.

Ariel thought they had, by a magic trick, returned to prehistoric times. This thought made him feel good. A place without cities. Not so many people. Good people. A place with unexplored valleys. Virgin jungles. Virgin mountains. Rivers of pure water. *Ah,* thought Ariel, *this is life. Life away from civilization is the only life a person deserves to live.* Accompanied by these thoughts, Ariel continued climbing. The terrain had changed, and it was now less inclined so that they could walk faster now despite the rain.

Werner instead thought only to find a shelter to escape the rain. His stomach bothered him for quite a while, but he didn't want to tell this to Ariel so as not to worry his young friend. Werner was mad at himself too. He should have listened to the young man. Sometimes the years don't bring wisdom, but obstinacy, like in his case. He had grown to become an obstinate man, a trait that María Rosa had always criticized him for. Stubborn and proud, he knew that these negative qualities would not help him in the rainforest.

Werner grabbed what he believed was a branch, but it was the tail of a dead *kaí*, a victim of a hungry beast. Part of its rear and the column attached to the head was what the attacker left of the little monkey. The fate of the small animal moved Werner. He took the remains in his hands—the dead yellowish eyes fixed on him. Werner's hands shook, and the head dropped from his hand.

THE TERRAIN turned into a cliff, and again they moved upward, holding from the roots and bushes as they did before, only that now they were moving on a ground that also moved. What a strange sensation. The land was indeed moving as the water poured down. Werner thought about the time. He could not see his wristwatch, so he calculated the time to be about ten in the morning, although it was pitch dark. Indeed, down there, the light was a privilege.

Ariel had stopped well ahead of Werner, and now he was screaming and waving his arms frantically, trying to call Werner's attention. The rain continued pouring, and the thunder was deafening. With a lot of effort, Werner rushed up to his encounter. The landscape around him had changed. It was again phantasmagoric but nothing like the effect the dead forest in the swamp produced in them. The scenery was different, with no dead trees but instead phosphorescent rocks. All around them sparkled with a strange phosphorescence, which caused the most extraordinary effect along with the rainfall.

"It's because of the metals," Werner said. "Oh my God."

Suddenly, Werner forgot his exhaustion, the rain, and the thunder and focused on the waterproof bag that contained some instruments. He went around the rock while the rain continued falling at full force. Perplexed, Ariel followed his activity.

"Gold!" Werner said. "Ariel, we're sitting on a geological deposit of fantastic wealth. This rock here is gold. Oh my God! For thousands of years, the rainwater has been dragging this wealth toward the bottom. Down there, the swamp must be the richest alluvia ever. The bottom of the swamp we passed through must be full of gold nuggets."

"And if you could, you would bring heavy machinery and dry the swamp, as I said to you not long ago in this very swamp, wouldn't you, Werner?"

"All the Earth was given to man by God, Ariel, to enjoy and live from it. You should know that."

"You have said it, Werner, and you are right, TO ENJOY, not to destroy, and God didn't say to live FROM it, but to live IN it. God loves all HIS creatures, and so should we."

Werner didn't answer. Ariel's comment irritated Werner, and so he abstained from responding.

His thoughts then went in a different direction. That of his yet unfulfilled dream to become a rich man. And so, mulling over, he walked toward another massive rock which sat there as a mute witness of some geological phenomena in prehistoric times. Always indifferent to the rainfall that poured nonstop, Werner contemplated the enormous stone for a long time.

"I bet a dinosaur came here once upon a time to scratch its back on this very same rock," he said and then began hitting the rock to take samples.

Then, at some point, Ariel focused his lamp on Werner's body and saw how his friend's clothes were full of luminous dots.

"Look at yourself, Werner. What is that?"

Werner looked at his arms and legs and saw what had marveled Ariel. They were standing at the foot of a gigantic rock, which seemed to signal the top of a hill, and from where they were, they could see the black sky and a dense fog that covered a significant portion of the rainforest. The rumble of a great volume of water moving nearby gave both friends goosebumps. Everything there was grandiose. Ariel again directed the lamp toward the rock, which seemed to sparkle at the touch of light.

"It is quartz, Ariel. Crystals of quartz," Werner said. "I knew already that there was an incalculable wealth in this area. This rock, for example." He extended his arms as if he were able to cover the entire giant rock in his embrace. "It must have erupted from the centre of the Earth thousands of years ago, or perhaps just recently. I would need more time to study it. It must have been an impressive eruption. There must have been extraordinary events happening in this part of the world, and no one in the civilized world has ever noticed. Remember the event we saw when we were coming, the sinkhole? That is a portent. And now this. We are on the right track, Ariel. An interesting day awaits us ahead. In the meantime, I guess a good idea will be to climb onto this rock to rest. Above, we will be safer."

And so both men gave themselves to the task of finding an access point to climb the rock. Ariel found a strange rock formation, a vertical line of small holes, which reminded him of a stepladder carved in the stone. Ariel studied the peculiar construction with attention while Werner directed the lamp's beam toward one of the small holes; sharp shrieks came from it.

"Rodents," Werner concluded. "These are their nests. Here they protect themselves from their enemies."

Ariel studied the terrain with the curiosity of a child exploring new grounds for his antics.

"For some reason," Werner continued, "the rodents do not fear this rock, although all other creatures do. Therefore, it would be fascinating to perform a petrological study of this area. The findings would amaze all of humanity."

"Amazing how all of humanity has already cost too much of Mother Earth, Werner. And it's even more unbelievable how it will mean the destruction of this rainforest. So thank you very much, Werner, but no thanks."

Werner didn't answer. Instead, he focused his attention on stepping in the rodents' holes and climbing up. Ariel followed him.

They reached the top of the rock. Its surface was flat and wide enough for both friends to sit, stretch, and sleep safely. Standing on the rock, Ariel looked around, but he could see nothing because of the rain and the fog. But the sound was incredible up there. It came to him in full, as if he were standing by an enormous loudspeaker of the best quality. Werner was soaked to his bones, but not so for Ariel, who had been more cautious; he had covered himself with the waterproof canvas before the rainfall. Werner unfolded his waterproof canvass and extended it in full over him until he felt protected from the downpour.

"The good thing is there is no wind," Ariel commented.

Werner searched his knapsack, took dry clothes, socks, underwear, an undershirt, and a shirt, and tightly folded the clothes, making a small package. He then, under his canvas, changed his clothes and felt better. Then, Werner arranged the wet clothes and put them in an empty plastic bag brought for that purpose. Satisfied, he then, from the same backpack, took some food and shared it with Ariel. Then Werner grabbed his canteen, unscrewed it, and took a long gulp. Ariel noticed the change in his friend's mood, felt better, rummaged into his knapsack, took two sandwiches, and both friends ate their meal surrounded by the ceaseless cacophony of the jungle. And then came the thunder, and again the rain, and listening to the rain, they slept.

The roar of a nearby jaguar woke them up.

"I hope this rock also repels the *yaguareté*," Ariel said.

"I don't think it will ever come up here," Werner said.

There was no rain anymore, and the piece of the sky they could see was of an intense blue, and in sharp contrast, at the treetops, the fog was dense and covered the rainforest as a giant stain. Yet, the air was warm.

The jaguar's roar seemed to be approaching. Ariel wanted to stand up and run, but Werner held him by his arm.

"Easy, Ariel, I told you. I'm sure they cannot climb this rock."

Ariel didn't calm; his chest felt agitated. They heard another roar, almost over their heads. Despite Werner's opposition, Ariel stood up, his heart beating hard. Werner continued lying down as if he were in a five-star hotel's best bed. The feline's roar seemed to be now by their side, and it was so powerful that Ariel thought that he could also feel the breathing of the jaguar on his neck. Werner smiled.

"How dare you smile and be so quiet in a moment like this, Werner. Are you crazy?"

"It's okay, Ariel, relax. No jaguar can come up here. We are too high. Besides, the walls of this rock are so vertical and smooth that no jaguar will ever be able to climb it. We are safe."

"But, the roar is too close—"

"That's the effect of the rainforest, Ariel, and it's magic, isn't it? Magic. This rock acts as a microphone, and as such, amplifies the sound. I'm sure the jaguar is somewhere down there, but not too close, and that we are not its objective. I'm sure it has not even smelled us yet."

Werner's explanation did not convince Ariel. He stood upright, walked around, examined every corner of the rock, and found that Werner was right. There were several rocks. The one where they were sitting was quite large and emplaced in a clearing, so there were no trees for a jaguar to climb and then jump to the rock. But, on the other hand, the rock offered no support for the jaguar to ascend, and for sure, the animal was not that intelligent as to climb up using the holes carved in the rock, which mice used as nests. So, they were safe. Ariel came back to where Werner was getting ready to resume the march. A hawk circled over their heads, its wings fully extended and its claws open, prepared to grab prey.

"What a beautiful bird!" Ariel exclaimed.

"Majestic, isn't it?" Werner said.

They both followed the flying of the hawk that went through the trees and disappeared into the woods. They heard twice the roaring of the jaguar again, but this time it sounded further away.

"It's gone," Werner said. He watched the sky that was clean, blue, and bright after the storm. He looked at his watch. "It's already past noon, Ariel. So we must hurry."

They were walking for a long time now. The thunder of the river accompanied them now but suddenly became thunderous. It was a rumble like a train approaching fast.

"It seems we are going straight to the river," Werner said.

"Or the river is coming to us," Ariel said. "Better we climb one of these trees."

"There is no time—"

The earth shook with great force. Both men could not stay standing and fell to the ground.

"It's an earthquake!" Werner said.

The rumble passed. The movement lasted at least thirty seconds. They seemed to be the only living creatures for miles around to have noticed the earthquake. The jungle continued its carnival of colours and cacophony as if nothing had ever happened. The two friends recovered and continued their march through.

"I told you there is a lot of geological activity in this area," Werner said to conclude a conversation that never started.

The terrain changed. The rocky area changed to another, flatter but populated with tall bushes and gigantic trees. The landscape confirmed Ariel's idea that they were in a lost world, a prehistoric universe. Ariel daydreamed that he would never find civilization again. That he would remain in that prehistorical region, lost forever to the civilized world he had always disagreed with.

Instead, Werner thought of the former expedition that forty years ago came, using perhaps the same path, they were on now. But they, the members of that expedition, trusted their every step to the Natives that guided them. But of course, the Native guides didn't know what the white men were looking for, because the white men always asked them general questions about such and such geological formation, which the Natives knew existed, like, the rocky area, for example, and the river, and the U-turn in the river, of course. But this information was also contradictory because the guides were unsure about the river. One said it existed; however, the other said he had never seen such a river in that area.

Still, following the priests' vague illustrations in their letter exchanges, the Germans opted to visit the site and confirm the information. Yet, in the priests' drawings, the river existed, and it was huge as the Natives described it, but such pictures, the Jesuit priests recognized, were drawn when listening to the Natives' talking. Yet, the Natives changed their version depending on who the speaker and the listener were.

Anyhow, this was the hint the Germans followed, the same lead that Werner pursued too tenaciously. The river's description was the same Werner mentioned to Ariel and María Rosa at the beginning of the adventure. For what Werner was doing was but to complete the dotted line.

On the other hand, although Dr. Zweig and his associates had covered the same distance in the same time Werner and Ariel had done, Werner and Ariel had done so without the Native guides and the logistics the Germans brought into the jungle. And the Germans were many to support each other if something happened, besides the fact that they had weapons, even machine guns. And they made the entire trip during daylight.

However, Dr. Zweig's notes revealed that the guides made a mistake and guided the group through the swamp, which had cost the expedition time and loss of equipment. Werner had learned from that error and had come wading the swamp and thus reached the firm ground in less time. Had this information not been missing from Dr. Zweig's notes, Werner and Ariel would have made the same error, but because of their lack of equipment and experience, it would have been a fatal mistake for the two friends.

Werner was happy to have held to this information, which increased his confidence, but he didn't share this feeling with Ariel. If he had done so, Ariel would have reacted, saying that he, Werner, had hidden information from Ariel, and it would have been a motive for a fight. *In some cases, the least information one receives, the better it is,* Werner said to himself.

The rainforest sounds reached their ears as if they were the voice of a giant claiming their attention, and from where they were, the rumble of the river stream came to them with such force that they could feel they were at the riverside. They were still miles of a rough march away from it. The two friends were now having a comfortable break under a gigantic *wimba* tree. To the rumble of the river, the stream joined the rumble of thunder again. They could see through the *wimba* tree branches, and the sparks of lightning reflected on its leaves.

"The roar of that *yaguareté* kept me sleeping with one eye open," Ariel said. "I thought it was on the rock with us."

Werner was going to answer him, but a thunderous explosion muted him. The thunder came as a powerful whip, and to the noise followed a lightning festival that expanded through the day, tearing it off as a delicate fabric. And then the rain came again, so strong this time the trees crunched under its weight. It was a brutal demonstration of nature's power. Werner and Ariel had just seconds to shelter themselves under the canopy of branches and cover themselves with their waterproof canvases, and slept because there was nothing they could do until that incredible vitality diminished.

Side by side, under the *wimba* tree, they were a sculpture of filial love, while a prehistoric storm engulfed the rainforest as it did millions of years ago.

The storm passed, and the fog, the thunder, the lightning, and the rainfall gave way back to the jungle's unique colours and cacophony. And the rumble of the river's rolling water surpassed every other noise. For the river were the monster and the God that reigned over all of the rainforest's living creatures.

They were standing over a fallen tree, with a clear view of what they had in front of them. There was a wide valley, and through this valley, the river ran, and both friends could not believe what their eyes were showing them. The valley was the work of the river, year after year carving through the rock. The mass of water ran along cliffs with vertical stone walls, then the valley opened wide, and the river seemed to expand for as long as the view could reach. A stormy sea that hurried forwards, unstoppable. The foam and the fog that came from the river made the spectacle a surrealist one. There was a contest of the greatest whirlpools ever; vortexes that swallowed everything that came near them. And the water crashed against the rock with such an impressive force in a demonstration of natural power that both friends never believed it could exist.

The river moved at such speed that it seemed that the water was not moving at all, but they were. And along with them, the entire landscape was rolling away, and the river was the engine sitting there, energizing the trees, the weather, and the whole jungle.

"This is incredible!" Ariel exclaimed. "This is amazing. But why could no one find it before? It is strange—"

"The reason is simple, Ariel," Werner said. "If you read the notes of the Jesuit Fathers again, you will see that the answer is right there. Neither the priests nor anyone else, for that matter, understood what the Natives meant. The trees melted, they used to say, and then the forest became water. They also noted that the water comes from the clouds, and they didn't mean rain but the river, the water coming through the fog. It's a subterranean river, Ariel. It emerges seasonally. It comes with force from under the earth, covers some miles, and turns around, making the U-turn as the Jesuit records explain, and then disappears again underground. That's all the mystery. The Aboriginals explained it in their way, in their own words."

Ariel was speechless, fascinated by the spectacle.

"This has remained unchanged since the first man stepped on Earth!" Werner screamed as if he understood that his young friend was under a spell. He even cupped his hands and got closer to Ariel's ear to make himself heard.

"What a wonder!" Ariel said. "I wish God in His wisdom illuminates humankind, so no one ever comes here to destroy this place. I wish there were an Eleventh Commandment that said: don't disturb nature."

"We won't, Ariel. What we will do is just collect the fruits that emerge from the depth of the earth, likewise how a peasant harvests the ripe fruits that fall from the tree."

Werner checked his knapsack, got his binoculars, looked through them, adjusted them, looked again, and scouted the landscape. Ariel also got his lenses and explored the site for a long time. After a while, they both sat on the massive trunk and mulled on the marvel lying in front of their eyes. A gust of wind brought the thunder of the river even closer with the force of an eruption. Even the giant trunk where they were sitting seemed to shake, and the earth was rocking, although Werner and Ariel took time to understand that it was another earthquake.

The tremor came so strong that they had to lie down and hold themselves to the tree trunk to avoid the force of the quake throwing them away. Such was the shaking that even trees were falling, uprooted by the strength of the tremor. Then, finally, the earthquake passed, or it was a permanent one. They could not say. Such was the pulsating vigor of the earth.

"Earth is indeed alive as you say, Ariel," Werner said, and he was still shaking by the motion of so many incredible events.

Ariel checked his belongings and was pleased to notice nothing was missing. Meanwhile, Werner stood on the tree trunk and again studied the landscape. He looked like a Viking conqueror standing on the prow of his ship. His long silvered hair, still with some golden curls, sparkled in the daylight. Then, after a long moment of reflection, he turned to Ariel.

"The problem is," he said as if he were weighing every word on a scale, "the river attracts not only the animals but also the Aboriginals."

"Then we can get back, Werner. The Native dwellers may cut our heads off. In that condition, the diamonds won't help us. Just go back and forget about this business."

"Well," Werner said carefully, "after we went through all of what we have been through, I wouldn't favour such a possibility. However, it's probable that because of the river's neighbourhood, the Natives may come. Yet, I know that the few tribes that still inhabit the rainforest are still hunters and collectors. They travel great distances to hunt, and so, eventually, their hunting may bring them here."

"They may not be friendly, but we must remember that we are the ones who are invading their territory," Ariel said and went through the bushes to investigate further.

Werner stood there alone among the hubbub of the rainforest.

"I thought it could be a passage that could take us down to the river," Ariel said once he returned. "However, from this end, it looks like an impossible thing to do."

"I guess we must continue walking west, Ariel. This will takes us at least three more hours of walking."

"Okay then," Ariel said with resignation. "We should not waste more time. Better let's go, Werner."

After two more hours of an exhausting march through, the jungle didn't show signs of opening as Werner had predicted. On the contrary, the terrain had turned wilder, hence challenging to go through. They found a deep ravine. They had to move step by step to descend, dragging down and holding onto the branches and bushes. Their feet could hardly find firm ground. It was all slippery, and every step down was an achievement. They knew that a fall would be mortal. *It's worse than walking on thin ice,* thought Werner.

Ariel thought they had taken the wrong road by chance because they could no longer hear the river. Perhaps they should go back to the fallen tree from where they could see the river, but then he thought to go back would be impossible. To climb back the ravine they were now descending would be a nightmare that would undermine all their strength, and it wasn't a good idea. Perhaps, on the return of their adventure, they could take another way. Or, there would not be rain.

Werner, on the other hand, felt weak. He had constant back pain that had worsened. And on top of all, his stomach ached. He had to stop several times, thus losing sight of Ariel, who was going down faster and already seemed to reach the bottom of the interminable ravine. So, Werner sat to rest for a moment, and while sitting there, he watched a family of red bald *uakari* primates that looked at him with curious round eyes and cadaveric expressions.

Indeed, the furry monkeys had never seen a human being before, or nobody like Werner, and were not afraid of the white man. One of the *uakari* primates was mean-looking and robust, and Werner was worried about it. The animal opened its mouth, showing a pair of powerful lower incisors, but it was more yawning than threatening to attack. Ariel's voice calling him awoke him from his observation, and he moved down faster. The *uakari* monkeys followed him, jumping from branch to branch with remarkable precision, without ever losing their balance. Finally, Werner reached the place where Ariel was waiting for him. Ariel looked worried.

"Are you okay, Werner?"

Werner dismissed him with a signal of his hand. He was trying to regain his breathing after the effort.

"I'm okay, Ariel. Just my old bones are complaining. But I feel okay."

Around them, the *uakari* monkeys gathered again, this time in a more significant number.

"Have you made new acquaintances, Werner?" Ariel said, looking around him. "It seems that they like you, somehow."

The red-faced primates were shrieking and jumping and seemed inoffensive.

"We better keep moving, Ariel. We already know how unpredictable the animals are in the wilderness."

"Are you sure we are on the right track?"

"Yes and no, Ariel. Well, we should be walking now on flat terrain, but Dr. Zweig's notes don't describe this ravine, which is strange because I know he was a meticulous man."

"Perhaps this ravine is the result of earthquakes. Recent earthquakes, like the crater we passed on our way here."

"It's possible, Ariel, it's possible." Werner scratched his head and studied the terrain.

"It's interesting, though," Ariel said after a while, "that we, living in the city, never wonder about what happens in other parts of the world unless it's a tragedy that brings some revenue to people in the news business or politicians."

"Yeah," Werner said, still looking around the ravine. "An earthquake is the explanation. A recent one."

"Nobody seems to understand that the Earth is alive, Werner."

Werner was now getting his bearings. He was looking at his compass and made some notes in his pocket notebook. Ariel showed his impatience. After a while, Werner decided on the course of action.

"Let's go down to the left, westbound, Ariel," he said.

"Are you sure, Werner?"

"It's better than staying here, giving these friends more fun to see two lost city slickers who have no idea where to go."

Werner signaled the gathering of *uakari* monkeys, which, with their round eyes, followed their every move. But, for Ariel, it was a disturbing scene, too. What if they became suddenly wild and ripped them to pieces?

"They are inoffensive, Ariel," Werner said as if he were reading Ariel's thoughts. "They only eat nuts and leaves."

"Just let's get out of here, Werner. I bet you these monkeys have never read an encyclopedia."

"Keep moving then, Ariel. Down and to the left."

"But to the left, we will face the cliff that falls on the river, Werner. Better to go to the right."

"We know already in what direction is the river, Ariel. To the right, we will be moving away from it."

"Yes, but it is possible we find a better passage, and in the end, we could save time and energy."

"Okay, Ariel. We will go to the right as you say, but I'm sure we will waste time and energy instead."

They continued their descent. The *uakari* lost interest and went away, jumping on the tree trunks, shrieking, and playing hide-and-seek. The terrain to the right was slippery and treacherous, but the descent was not as steep as before. Despite Werner's efforts to hide his discomfort, it became evident to Ariel that he must stop paying attention to Werner's health. The backache and stomach discomfort added to the pain in his knee. Werner had stopped and was putting some cream on it.

"I think that the problem in your knee is not new, eh, Werner?"

"Indeed, it's not that old either, one of these things that comes with age, I guess. Part of the aging package, Ariel."

Ariel set his waterproof blanket on the ground and helped Werner to rest in a comfortable position. He even used his knapsack to support Werner's head. Then Ariel gathered some small pieces of dry wood and leaves and kindled a fire. Ariel placed a steel mug on the fire, and from his canteen, poured water into it. When it boiled, he tossed a tea bag into it, covered the mug with a sleeve of his jacket, removed it from the fire, and left it to cool. Then, he gave Werner the mug, who had followed Ariel's every movement with open interest.

"What a boy scout you are," Werner said, sipping the hot tea, and he felt reborn.

He searched among his medicines, took a pill, and swallowed it with another sip of the tea. *The best tea I've ever had,* he thought. In the meantime, Ariel had put a pan on the fire, dropped canned beef stew on the pan, stirred it, and sat by Werner's side. The familiar smell coming from the heated pan filled their nostrils.

And they ate, drank, and departed like old pals. The stress and discomfort seemed to have gone with a cup of tea and a hot meal in friendship.

And after the break, they continued walking, for just at the turn of the ravine, their dream awaited them, or if it were not the next, then it would be the next or the next—

They moved again through the irregular terrain. The humidity was so intense that the trees seemed to ooze water. They had to make great efforts coming down step by step on that slippery vegetation. This way, they reached the bottom of another incredible ravine. They followed through the bottom ground until they found an impassable forest of thorny shrubs. A colony of enormous rodents with sharp teeth and red eyes carved in their faces came to welcome them with their curiosity, and then the rodents ran to hide among the thorns.

"I hope we won't have to choose between the thorns and the rats," Ariel said.

They tried to go around this strange forest, but the landscape was the same wherever they went. Finally, Werner stopped and scrutinized the terrain in front of his eyes. Then again took his instruments and started making measurements in his notebook.

"Listen, Ariel," he said after a while, although Ariel had moved far up, trying to escape from the field of thorns. "We are moving away from the river. We must return to our last camp and, from there, walk to the left, westbound."

Ariel said nothing because he knew Werner was right this time, so he just turned around and began the descent again. Soon both friends were moving faster, leaving behind the thorny bushes and the rats. *We did lose time and energy*, Werner thought to himself. He regretted having now to move at a fast pace, well ahead of Ariel. Ariel seemed to read Werner's thoughts and felt embarrassed for having taken the wrong way. He wanted to apologize to Werner but decided to keep quiet instead. In the end, everything fell on Werner. Werner embarked Ariel on this venture, and it was his obligation to know the road better. But then, Ariel repented for his thoughts because he knew that his friend couldn't possibly know everything, especially to learn ahead of time about the geological changes the rainforest so often experienced.

A swarm of butterflies with intense blue and black circles on their wings startled Ariel, who never imagined that this kind of creature existed. There were hundreds, thousands of them! They came straight to him, encircled him a couple of times, and then stood there, fluttering their wings in front of his astonished eyes as if they were dancing. It was an incredible combination of colour and flowing mystery. The dance of the butterflies hypnotized Ariel. Several minutes went by. All activities seemed to have halted, and even the rainforest's sounds paused in those minutes. Only the dancing of the butterflies was on. It was beautiful. It was touching! The butterflies came in waves of coordinated fluttering and then, in the same way, went back as if following the rhythm of, for Ariel, imperceptible music.

Werner, who by then was several yards ahead, noticed that Ariel was not following him, turned around, and retraced his steps until he saw Ariel standing there amidst the vegetation, yet because of the dense leaves, Werner could not see the butterflies that had bewitched Ariel.

"Hurry up, Ariel!" Werner shouted from afar.

Werner's sharp command broke the enchantment Ariel had fallen into, and the butterflies camouflaged amongst the flowers and leaves.

"Coming!" Ariel screamed back, and in quick steps, he reached Werner, who had resumed the march with reanimated vigor.

Ariel decided not to tell Werner about the magical moment he had experienced, but he was too agitated; still, he wanted to say something, and he couldn't find the words.

"Werner," he said after a while, "those butterflies down there—they wanted to deliver us a message—"

Werner chuckled and said nothing, and Ariel didn't insist—

They paced in silence for a long time, each one involved in their thoughts.

After hours of steady climbing, the ravine on whose border they were walking became a cliff of immeasurable depth.

"I think we are at the top of a mountain," Werner said. "A mountain covered by the forest."

From where they were, they could see all over the magnificent spectacle of the rainforest and a large, foggy, mysterious area that looked like an enlarged, white, gaseous island. Ariel was breathing hard. He felt tired but did not want to tell Werner, who seemed energetic and more vigorous instead. Ariel admired Werner's tenacity. They were now walking through a narrow path barely wide enough for one person. A dense forest of *guatambúes* covered their way to their right, so they walked between a green wall and the cliff whose border looked gnawed by either erosion or earthquakes. Bushes and trees were growing along the cliff's verge, making the path treacherous because one could not see where the cliff edge was. From time to time, hundreds of large, noisy, colourful birds emerged from the fog, flew over under the sun, made a great curve, and dived back into the mist.

The fog is there because of the river, thought Werner with a jump in his heart. *The river's water must be cold, almost freezing, and the hot air above is an excellent combination for the fog. So, I'm right about the sources of the river. And the mist makes the river invisible from above.* In this mindset, Werner turned back to tell Ariel the excellent news, but the one thousand noises from the rainforest had increased to unsupportable decibels, and he lost track of his thoughts.

The noise was as powerful, and at times, it seemed that they were inside a giant musical instrument that played thousands of diverse melodies simultaneously but at different volumes and rhythms. Indeed, the noise amplified and reduced as if a colossal symphonic orchestra played those thousands of melodies. It was a fantastic acoustic sensation. But the heat and humidity turned it all so unbearable that Werner felt he was swimming in his sweat. His stomach discomfort returned, and he took a painkiller from his first-aid kit and chewed it. Then he drank a long sip of water from his canteen and resumed the march.

Ariel was some steps ahead of Werner, cutting shrubs and vines, opening his way through the vegetation, swinging his machete left and right like a madman, hacking his way through. Werner followed suit, and he charged the foliage like a modern Don Quixote would do charging the windmills. But then, a pronounced slope came to view, and they began descending it carefully, and thus, Werner could not use his machete anymore, so he focused on the path he was stepping on.

The terrain became slippery, and both friends held onto the branches so as not to fall. Moving through that kind of surface at inches of the abyss border was a thriller of nightmarish proportions. Besides, they were facing a surreal world roofed by a dark, intensely green canopy and dense layers of fog, multicoloured flowers in bloom, polychromatic butterflies, rainbow-coloured birds, and gold-yellow bees buzzing all over. Ariel stood behind, fascinated by the stunning view as always, and Werner passed by him and marched ahead, fighting his way through the vegetation, a man with a mission.

But then, just a few yards down the path, Werner suddenly stopped, and Ariel saw him falling on his knees. Ariel sprinted forwards to see what it was that had called Werner's attention, but his foot caught on a protruding root, and he tripped over and fell on his hands. The force of the fall made his body roll over toward the abyss, and he would have fallen down the cliff if it were not for his American flag coloured knapsack—its belts entangled in the branch of a tree that grew at the cliff border.

Although hanging as he was in such an uncomfortable position, Ariel had to accept that he did not die because of an extraordinary feat of good luck. With his legs dangling in the abyss, Ariel cried in desperation while trying to hold on to something. Finally, he managed to grasp some shrubs, but the terrain started to crumble down under his weight.

Upon hearing the cry, Werner turned around and came back as fast as he could. He dropped to his knees, grabbed Ariel's hand, and pulled him up, but he couldn't do much because Ariel's knapsack remained entangled in the overhanging branch in the cliff's wall, which because of Ariel's weight, was already bending dangerously and could break at any moment. So Werner directed Ariel's right hand to another root that seemed sturdy enough. And in the nick of time, Ariel grasped this root with all his strength, for then the branch broke. The sudden loss of support made Ariel's body swing, still with his knapsack on his back, but he fought for his life, holding his grip tight on the protruding root. His left hand grabbed another shrub that supported his weight for just a second, and then the shrub came out roots and all.

Now Ariel was hanging from his right hand, which began to bleed, and the pain was excruciating, but he didn't give in. Drops of blood fell into his eyes and blinded him. He screamed. Werner took his leather belt, dropped it on his belly, tied the strap to Ariel's left hand, and pulled with all his force.

The effort was fruitful, and Ariel released the protruding root and grasped another visible one some inches above his head. His feet found a place to stand, and soon he was on the path. He took off his knapsack, dropped it on the ground, lay on his back, and breathed heavily. Werner took his canteen, unscrewed it, and gave it to Ariel. Ariel sipped the water and coughed. Werner grabbed him by his armpits and dragged him to a *guatambú*, where he rested in a seating position with his back against the tree. Ariel was still gasping and scared, and his hand was bleeding. Werner rushed to his knapsack, got his first-aid kit and a small container with oxygenated water, and poured some of the liquid on Ariel's shaking hand. Then he applied some antibiotic cream and bandaged the hand. Ariel left him to do this with a smile. Once Werner finished dressing Ariel's hand, he got a little box of pills, chose one, and gave it to Ariel along with his canteen.

"Swallow it, and drink as much water as you can," Werner said, "Don't worry about the water. We can get more from the falling rain

Ariel smiled and swallowed the pill and the water as per Werner's instructions, and then he rested again.

"Wow! That was a scare," Ariel said, his heart still pumping hard.

"Definitively. Ariel, your bones won't rest here,"

"Oh, I don't know about that, Werner. We still have a long way to go, and yet, I may become a good souvenir for the rainforest."

"It was good I was not too far,"

They sat there for a while, recovering their bodies and spirits.

"What a strange situation," Ariel said. "I never thought of a Nazi risking his life to save that of a Jew."

"It doesn't matter now, Ariel. The important thing is we are together because we have a common goal. We have new things to worry about."

"True. We need each other."

"That's so, Ariel. No philosophy should hurt the soul. No philosophy should separate one from the other. And I'm not saying to love each other. Respect for each other is more than enough."

After a while, Ariel felt better and decided to continue their march.

"What were you looking at, Werner? It was why I tripped over. I wanted to see what called your attention."

"Of course, Ariel," Werner said as if he remembered something of utmost importance. "Come to see this; it's so interesting."

They both went to where Werner had stopped just a few minutes before. One cross stood at the trunk of an enormous *cancharana* tree trunk whose roots grew toward the abyss. The cross was but two simple wood pieces, crudely worked by machete from branches of the same *cancharana* tree and united by a cloth with fading colours. One could still see the black, the red, and the yellow. Another cross made of black metal, tied to a tricoloured ribbon, hung from the humble cross. The ribbon's colours, white, red, and black, were also fading. Visibly moved by the modest homage, Werner fell on his knees and touched the cross. He was startled, shocked. Ariel called upon him.

"What's it, Werner?"

"This is incredible," Werner said.

"What is incredible?

"I've found the place where Baron von Bohlen died."

"Who? You never told me about someone left dead here."

"*Reichfreiherr,* Ehrbert von Bohlen, most known as Baron von Bohlen, Ariel. He was part of the guard who escorted scientists on the first and last expedition to this land, and they all came back to Germany, except him."

"What happened to him?"

"He died during an attack by the Aboriginal savages. A poisoned arrow sent from a blowpipe killed him, and his body fell down the cliff. It was then impossible for the group to recover his body."

"An attack by savages, poisoned arrows, and people murdered—what are you talking about, Werner? You never said a word about this before—"

"Well, Ariel. The truth is I never thought that we could find something. So there was no need to give explanations in advance."

"Natives who send poisoned arrows—okay, Werner, we better get back. No use for the diamonds. If the Natives find us, they will kill us, and we will accompany the late Baron down there. Yes. It's better if we turn around and get back home. I have already lost interest in this business."

"C'mon, don't make a mountain out of a molehill, Ariel, because this happened a long time ago."

"Who was this man, Werner?"

"He was an aristocrat, Ariel, a famous soldier. A man of fortune."

"Aristocrat, he could have been, Werner, a soldier, yes, he was, but a man of fortune? I doubt it. Look where he is now."

"I mean money, Ariel. His family was wealthy. Very rich. They owned industries and businesses in Hamburg and Bremen."

"Did you know him?"

"No. Those people frequented different social levels."

"And what is this?" Ariel was pointing at the medal that hung from the rustic wooden cross.

"This is the Iron Cross, Ariel," Werner said, and then he remained silent for several seconds, his eyes fixed on the small object, partially deteriorated by time and weather.

"I see," Ariel said. "That was the cross the Nazis used. Therefore, that man who died here was a Nazi. He was a member of the team in the laboratory where you worked. Therefore, you are a Nazi too. Mystery solved."

"Indeed, there is a mystery, Ariel, and it's not yet solved. The man who died here was not a member of the team in the laboratory. He was not a scientist and indeed not a politician. He was a soldier, but he was not an ordinary soldier. On the contrary, he was a member of the elite. The thing is, why they assigned him to this task, I will never find out." Once he finished this sentence, Werner went back to his respectful silence.

"For sure, he was a guard," Ariel said. "One of the bodyguards of the group. I guess he was one of the custodians, so the scientists would not desert the regime. It would be appropriate considering how the regime worked. Controlling every movement of its subjects."

"I would favour your analysis, Ariel," Werner said, "if it were not for this detail." He leaned over, and with care, he took the cross in his hand and showed it to Ariel.

"This is the Iron Cross, Ariel. This symbol had nothing to do with the National Socialist Party. It was a reward for demonstrated courage in action. No civilian ever deserved this cross. No member of the National Socialist Party got it. The Iron Cross was a military award. It was only for those who demonstrated courage, only for those who won prestige on the battlefront. And by the way, many high-ranking officers of the armed forces never agreed with the Third Reich's politics."

Ariel didn't answer. His eyes swept through the surroundings apprehensively. Meanwhile, Werner was deeply involved in looking around for hints on the death of Baron von Bohlen.

"Of course," Werner said after a while as if Ariel had said something, which he hadn't. "After forty years in the middle of the jungle, how could I think that nothing would change?"

"I thought you would have known more about this business."

"I knew little, Ariel. I knew but little. Now, I know a little more. There was a lot of censorship in the news we received. I only knew that Baron von Bohlen had died. On the circumstance of his death, I already told you what happened."

Ariel leaned over and observed the cross with curiosity. Then again, he looked around, expecting to see Native dwellers with their bows and poisoned arrows and their javelins, but he saw nothing. The trees impeded him from seeing the forest, and it was a real thing, not the cliché sentence meaning something different.

"They all returned home, Ariel," Werner was saying. "I mean, all the members of the expedition. Two were chemists, one a geologist, the other two were gemologists, and one was a physician, a specialist in tropical sickness. Indeed, any one of them within the team was a specialist in his field. There were no females on this team and no military personnel either. Dr. Zweig, the group leader, had some military training, but he was not a soldier. The only professional soldier on the team was Baron von Bohlen." Werner made a pause. He was pondering to linger or not on his revelation. Then he decided to continue ahead with the truth, and so he said, "Besides the death of Baron von Bohlen, and according to the notes I had, there were two other people who died."

"What!?" Ariel exclaimed. "The Natives killed two other members of the expedition?"

"No. The two other dead people were the guides."

"Oh, the Natives killed them too?"

"No. The Natives didn't kill them."

"What? Who killed them then?"

Werner's answer sounded lugubrious. "Well, the guides knew too much. It was not convenient to leave them alive."

"The Germans killed them?"

"Yes, Ariel. The Germans did."

"That is so awful, Werner!" Ariel said. "Your people had respect for nobody."

Werner didn't answer. He was thinking about Baron von Bohlen. A rich, famous young man, ready to marry one of the most beautiful women of the aristocracy. The Baron's obituary was extensive and highlighted the Baron's life, achievements, family, and future wife. However, there were no details regarding the place and circumstances of his death. Some newspapers speculated that the Baron had died completing a secret suicidal mission somewhere on the Eastern front. The government delivered the condolences to the family, gave no further information, and closed the case. Baron von Bohlen died as a hero, and that was what would remain in the collective mind.

"At that time," Werner said after mulling on Baron von Bohlen's life and death, and as if more explanation was necessary to placate Ariel's reaction, "there was a German-born Brazilian citizen, a cattle rancher living on the Argentina-Brazil border. *Herr* Grünberg, a.k.a. Gilberto, his Brazilian name, was an admirer of Hitler and a fan of the National Socialist Party's achievements. This man helped Dr. Zweig and his men reach this area in search of the diamond deposit. Much of the information regarding the death of Baron von Bohlen came to us through *Herr* Grünberg. But of course, all these people are dead now. *Herr* Grünberg, or Don Gilberto, as Dr. Zweig stated, was an old man already. I think he was over eighty. And at the time, neither Baron von Bohlen nor I reached yet thirty. I know the farm does not exist either. Don

Gilberto was the one who put two Native guides from his staff to guide the Germans through the rainforest. I also know that out of an act of contrition, perhaps, he helped their families."

"How cruel!" Ariel said, horrified. "And as revenge, the Natives ambushed the group and killed this aristocrat who gave his life to defend his comrades."

Werner didn't answer. Instead, as if he were a sleuth whose mission was to solve the mystery of the Baron, he went through the entire scene, checking every inch around the humble cross. Then he mulled on its findings.

"Why is only the cross here?" Ariel was circling the site and examining the cliff with his binoculars. But, unfortunately, he could see nothing because, by this hour, a dense fog covered most of the area.

"I think," Werner said, "that given the situation he faced, he knew he was going to die. The arrows may have hit him already, and the poison was making its effect in his body. We cannot know how many he received. I suspect that when the Natives attacked, he kept himself in the rearguard to cover the group's escape. So he was alone there. He held the Natives at bay as much as he could. But then, weakened by the poison, he gave a step backward—"

Werner acted his part and did as Baron von Bohlen could have done, going back toward the cliff. And he was too much into his role that he again was nearing the edge of the precipice, and Ariel had to jump ahead and hold him by his arm and move him back to a safer place. However, as absorbed as Werner was with his relation, he barely noticed Ariel's action and continued outpouring his version of the tragic event.

"—and fell into the abyss but didn't fall at once. With the bit of strength Baron von Bohlen had, held himself with his hands onto a root or a bush, as you did, Ariel. And I guess that the Natives may have ignored him and collected their dead and disappeared in the jungle. So there he was, Baron von Bohlen, alone in this last supreme second of his life, almost dying, hanging from a root with no one to help him. I'm speculating here, but I knew of the spirit of those people. And it is easier to deduce that in that supreme instant, he reacted and took off from his neck the Iron Cross and tossed it toward this pass, and then he fell into the abyss. His comrades returned to look for him and found the cross lying here on this path."

Again, Ariel focused his binoculars on the cliff's bottom and held it there for a long time, studying the terrain. The fog had been clearing, and it was now a transparent silk fabric covering the treetops of the enormous *virapitá* and black *lapachos*, whose roots were at the bottom of the cliff, almost three hundred yards down from where they were standing.

"Poor guy," Ariel said, thoughtful after a while of exploring the area. "Because of his ignorance, he died the way he did. He came here to attempt against the sacred nature and the life of the Natives. Yet, when victory is present for the white man, the Natives don't exist. An unequal situation by all means, if you think it over, Werner. Fragile blowpipes and arrows against war professionals carrying machine guns. A professional elite soldier against naked primitive men."

"Primitive men who had the jungle in their favour," Werner rebuked, just to stress the advantage the Native warriors had against a cornered, lonely, scared European whose only fault was to hold his right to defend himself against the savages.

Ariel didn't answer. He squatted in front of the cross and focused on the ribbon piece that held the two wooden sticks that formed the sacred symbol.

"Baron Herbert von Bohlen, you said, Werner?"

"Why, what is it?"

"He is not the one. It's another person, Werner. Someone died here, but it was not Baron von Bohlen. Look here."

Ariel was pointing at a handwritten inscription on the fabric of the ribbon.

"Look, Werner, the name written here is not Herbert von Bohlen, but Friede Seiner Asche. The man who died here is not the Baron, but another man with the name of Friederick, not Herbert. Still, I guess that Mr. Friederick Seiner Asche was as well a soldier of the Third Reich."

Speechless, Werner approached the cross, fell on his knees, and examined the ribbon. Intrigued, Ariel followed his every movement with attention.

"No, Ariel," Werner said after a while, involved in deep meditation. Indeed, the finding of this humble monument affected him heavily. "It's not another person," he continued, "This is not his name. *Friede seiner Asche* is equivalent to, *Que en Paz Descance,* in Spanish.

Ariel stood upright. His eyes travelled from the cross to the bottom of the cliff. *Rest in Peace*, he thought.

"This man," Werner said, interrupting Ariel's thought, "Had everything in the world to be a happy man. He made enormous sacrifices on the battlefront to deserve this decoration. Yet, look where everything ended: at the bottom of a cliff, without a tomb, in a remote jungle at the end of the world."

"This man chose his death," Ariel said.

"You're wrong, Ariel," Werner said, "You can choose your life but never your death, for no one knows when his or her time is."

"You're the one who is wrong, Werner," Ariel said. 'We are all slaves of beginnings, for we cannot free ourselves from how a thing started. But we can be masters of the endings, for it's in one's decision to end what somehow started. No one can choose his birthday, but anybody can choose his death. Suicidal people, for example, choose their death."

Werner said nothing after Ariel's remark.

"See how ungrateful life can be?" Ariel said, "You can say it with much authority because you have had a longer life, Werner. And back to this particular case, is it, or is it not, the end this man chose?"

Werner didn't follow Ariel's train of thought.

"I'm sure the body of the Baron must still be down at the bottom of the cliff," Werner said.

"I think that there is nothing at the bottom of the cliff," Ariel said.

"I don't think so. There must be the Baron's skeleton still wearing his uniform, and the uniform must still be recognizable despite the time and the weather. And the weaponry, and equipment, all of it was of the best quality, so it must still be there."

"Well, if you say so," Ariel said. "Would you like to go down and confirm your theory, Werner?"

Werner missed the sarcasm in Ariel's words.

"It's not a bad idea, Ariel," Werner said with a naïveté not yet expected from a man as old and experienced as Werner Mann.

"Ah!" Ariel said. "And if we find his remains, we could repatriate them."

Werner looked at him and finally understood Ariel's sarcasm, but he was not hurt.

"Let's go," Werner said, loading his backpack on his back and collecting the other items left scattered on the ground.

Ariel gave a last long look at the humble monument and followed Werner, who had already turned around the massive trunk of a *guabiyú*.

They marched steadily, but the direction they followed didn't bring them to the river as Werner had predicted. Instead, the landscape continued unchanged for two more hours, and then the terrain turned muddy and slippery and began a problematic descent where they were at risk of falling at every step. Going through this terrain took them more time than expected, and they were worried because soon it would be night, and the rain was again falling hard. And when the landscape stopped its descent, they faced a valley of thorny bushes that blocked their way. They could see how the mass of thorny bushes extended for at least half a mile from the height they were. The options they had were to go back or climb the ravine up again and try to find a way to walk on its borders, thus giving a detour around the bushy field.

"Or cutting through the bushes with our machetes," an exasperated Ariel said.

The rain didn't stop. Despite the rain, the most rational move was to climb back up the ravine and seek a path on its borders, but the question was which side to mount, the east or the west. Werner consulted his compass and opted for the west side. Ariel guessed that it was not a rational decision but a hunch from Werner. However, Ariel agreed because he also had the feeling that going to the west side of the ravine would take them faster to the river.

They had already discovered that the ravines usually opened after a few miles, and if they chose the wrong side, they would end up far from their objective and in a most challenging situation. And they were fighting against time and the rainforest. They were not wrong, though, to have chosen the west side. They found several clearings that allowed them to move faster, and they even decided to rest, eat, and drink something when the rain diminished and transformed into a dense fog.

At the bottom of the ravine, the thorny jungle turned more and more scarce and changed again to the trees, ivy, and bushes with flowers in bloom. The cacophony, the singing of birds, the cries of the monkeys, and the buzzing of insects were so deafening they had to cover their ears, although they thought they were already getting used to the noise. They walked in the middle of dense fog. The humidity, as throughout their journey, was unbearable. Nevertheless, the river's rumble became clearer in their ears, and they felt happy to be so close to their first objective.

They came onto a flat terrain formed by a carpet of leaves and roots that soon changed into a carpet of pebbles. Werner stopped and stooped down to grab one of the pebbles and examined it with a critical eye.

"These pebbles," Werner said, "Are normally found in river beds. It means that the river floods this area seasonally. Like the Nile does."

"Well, I hope the period of flooding will not start now," Ariel said.

"It's a land full of precious sediments," Werner ignored Ariel's comments and continued as if he were lecturing to an attentive audience.

From where they were, they could hear the constant rumble of the river. It sounded like bolts of thunder, one after the other. *Oh my God,* thought Ariel, *the stream of that river must be mighty.*

But as they walked for one more hour and were exhausted, they still could not see the river, but they found a path covered with black dust that was winding through the tall bushes.

"Coke," Werner said, bending down to collect a sample of the dust, "It's amazing, Ariel. An incalculable fortune lies here."

"You're right, Werner!" Ariel said. "The incalculable fortune that lies here is beauty and peace, freshwater, the rain, the vegetation, the butterflies, the bees, the animals—all holy nature. It's priceless, indeed. So I'm ready to offer my life against the greediness of civilization."

"But, that's why we are here, Ariel."

"Hold on, Werner. We haven't come here to create expectations for more than what we already planned. You said that whatever we obtained would be more than enough for us, but it's a known fact that to any 'civilized person,' enough is never enough. So I want to make sure that this landscape will never be affected."

"I understand your point, Ariel. But not even God can stop the destruction of this land. So sooner or later, explorers will come, and they will uncover this richness and all life as we are seeing it will end, and the Aboriginals will end up as workers for the new owners of the land."

"But the Native dwellers are the true owners of the land, Werner."

"Yes, Ariel, we know that. But we also know that they don't have the force to sustain their rights. The Native people have neither a voice nor a vote in this matter. Obscure brains in lighted salons located way far from here manage this land. The Native people couldn't do anything. You well know that human rights are only valid if you have the force to validate them. Moreover, the Natives live on land that is not even theirs as you think. For the land belongs to the state, and if the state is generous enough, it may keep a portion of it for the Natives, and if not, the Aborigine's culture, their history, their traditions will all be gone in smoke as happened in the Caribbean and so many other places of the world."

Ariel sighed. He didn't wonder if the rumble of the machines would silence the thunder of the river. Instead, he wondered when this disgrace would happen.

"It will, Ariel," Werner said again as if he had read Ariel's thoughts. "The rainforest will be no match for the bulldozers."

I cannot believe that one day soon, civilization will silence the river, and the butterflies will stop their dancing. Ariel thought.

ERNER HAD been studying the terrain for a long time now.

"Ariel," Werner said, "someone used this path recently."

Ariel paid attention to Werner's words.

"And I think it's a path with regular traffic," Werner said.

"People?" Ariel said.

"It's possible. Native dwellers, maybe."

"Native dwellers?"

"Hard to know. It could be the Natives; it could be animals. See how it winds around here? But this path goes to the river, so I don't think the Native people come down this path. Must be animals coming to drink at the river."

"One may come to drink, and others may come to eat those that drink," Ariel said.

"It's possible," Werner said. "Jaguars, maybe."

"Uh oh! I hope we don't ever encounter face to face any *yaguareté* again."

"We just have to be alert," Werner said.

Werner remembered how easy it was for the feline to dominate that enormous *caiman* and drag it through until the jaguar found a quiet place to eat its prey. *Indeed, he thought, the machete would be useless if the feline decided to attack because jaguars choose their game carefully and then stalk them, ambush them and jump on their back, nailing their powerful fangs into the prey's head, thus destroying the prey's brain.*

And taken by his thought, Werner lifted his machete as if it would be enough to subdue an attacking jaguar, and then he turned violently with the machete high in his arm as if indeed he were a Samurai and a jaguar were in the middle of its jump on its way to catch him and bite his brain. Werner's sudden movement put Ariel on alert.

"What is it, Werner? What is happening?"

Werner was embarrassed, but he was not going to let his young friend see it.

"I heard noises and reacted. I don't like surprises."

"For sure, it's a jaguar that is following our smell, Werner. So it's good you are prepared."

"We should be, we should be, Ariel."

A couple of yards ahead and on a curve of the path, they found the dispersed remains of one animal.

A mammiferous, Werner thought.

"*Capybara,*" Ariel said.

"This carcass is fresh," Werner said.

And then he thought of the omen he'd had some minutes ago when he turned suddenly because he almost felt a beast was jumping on his back. *Perhaps I was not wrong,* Werner thought. And so, he went on and knelt to examine the remains.

"Yes, Ariel," he said, "they are the remains of a *capybara*. It's for sure the work of a *yaguareté*. It must be a huge cat. I guess the jaguar dragged it here as the one we saw did with that *caiman*. These are mighty animals. Their jaws are powerful."

"A *yaguareté*—" Ariel looked with suspicion around every bush, his machete high in his arm, ready to hit the ambushing beast.

"This one is already satisfied, Ariel," Werner said. "He for sure caught the *capybara* at night. Jaguars are nocturnal. We shouldn't worry."

"Perhaps this one doesn't know this, Werner."

"Doesn't know what, Ariel?"

"He doesn't know he is nocturnal. Perhaps he didn't read the same book you read. Remember that the one that was eating the *yacaré* was doing it in plain daylight."

Werner didn't answer. Annoyed, he moved ahead in silence. Ariel followed him.

THE RIVER was just there, at a distance no longer than sixty yards. The wind was blowing more forcefully, and the rumble from the river came to them deafening, but the wind brought something more than the thunder of the river into Ariel's ears. Werner was going to say something, but Ariel shushed him with his hand on Werner's mouth. Werner was startled. Ariel put his index finger on his mouth and signaled to Werner to get down. They both squatted.

"What's wrong?" Werner whispered.

"Listen."

The wind brought them the smell of a thousand fruits, the river's rumble, and the cacophony from the jungle, but also a different sound, like the tweeting of birds. And then they heard laughter, the vibrant, clear sound of the laughter one hears from a child's lips. Werner and Ariel stood there static as if they had frozen. Yes, the sound of laughing came clear to them now. Who were these people? White explorers? Smugglers? Soldiers? Native dwellers? Whatever the answer, they knew their dream had just evaporated. Gone with a laugh.

"They are Native people," Ariel said.

"They are children," Werner said. "It's a group of children."

Werner squatted with the binoculars in his hands and listened with an attentive ear. It was hard to discriminate any sound from the many that filled their ears, but then the voices became more explicit with another wind blow. Werner made a decision. He removed the bushes, made a clearing, and scanned the site with his binoculars.

"They are young girls, Ariel," he said. "Teenagers. All girls."

Ariel searched for his binoculars and removed the bushes by his side, making room to observe.

"Oh, my goodness!" Ariel said after a while. "That means that their parents must be around."

"It's possible," an apprehensive Werner said. He was thinking of how bad it would be for them to face the Native inhabitants. And if this were not bad enough news, nesting in his mind was what could happen to them if the Native warriors happened to catch them spying on their younger ones.

"*Ayoreos,*" Ariel said. "I don't know. Perhaps they are *Tobaty*."

"I don't know, Ariel. I guess, because of the geographic zone, they must be *Aché Guayakí*."

"But what about the men of the tribe? They must be around."

"I think they feel safe here. The men must be in another part. We are lucky to be against the wind. If not, they would have noticed us already."

Ariel kept focusing his binoculars on the group of girls. The girls, a group of six, perhaps between sixteen to twenty years old, wore their hair cut as a circular crown around their head, and interlaced among their hair were the diamonds that so much had called Werner's attention. Thin handcrafted vegetal ribbons adorned their cinnamon skin. These natural ornaments fell from their shoulders to their back and then twisted around their hips and thighs. They wore no clothes.

"They are all pretty," Ariel said after a while.

"That means you saw one that you like more than the others, eh, Ariel?"

"Aw, c'mon, Werner, you must be kidding!"

"Nothing wrong with that, Ariel. It's called love at first sight."

Ariel didn't answer. Instead, he focused his binoculars on the group of young Native girls.

"Yeah," he said aloud, but to himself. "That girl is indeed pretty." Ariel sighed.

Werner chuckled. "Ariel is in love with an Aboriginal girl; now, this is news. Love at first sight!"

Ariel blushed and didn't answer. Instead, he took his camera and pointed the lens toward the girls' group but lowered the camera without taking any photos. Ariel smiled. His eyes were bright, and again he blushed and sighed. Werner gave him tender pats on his back.

THE SITUATION did not change. It seemed that the girls would not leave the area soon, so Werner and Ariel decided to move. They moved as the military did as they had seen in the movies. They crawled and moved behind the bush in front of them and then to another one. Along with their bodies, they dragged their knapsacks and their equipment. The girls' singing voices came and went, crushed by the river's rumble and many other sounds coming from everywhere. Perhaps there was a beach across from where they stood, but they could not see it yet. The force of the stream seemed to be uncontrollable. And amidst all that thunder, the cheerful voices of the girls reached them clearer now.

The two friends realized they had stopped in an uncomfortable place, for in front of them, there were no more bushes to protect them from the sight of the girls. It was indeed dangerous. The wind could change its course, and the girls would notice them. They could see or hear them. It was a risky situation. Indeed, anybody passing by could see them crawling, spying on those girls. The girls' voices came closer now, almost to their side. Their tone had a musical tinge, as if instead of talking, they were singing.

"They are singing!" Ariel whispered.

"Sounds like that, eh, Ariel? Perhaps it is the way their language is."

Ariel continued studying the girls with attention. For him, the girls were authentic diamonds. Diamonds—

"Werner," he said, interrupting his thoughts. "Have you noticed their ornaments?"

Werner didn't answer.

Ariel insisted, "Brilliant dots—"

"They are diamonds, Ariel," Werner responded with a shake in his voice. "Diamonds in their hair."

"Diamonds?" Ariel could not believe what he was hearing.

"They are not cut nor polished yet, Ariel. They are in their natural state. Wow! It's fascinating. I'm sure they are of the purest quality. Each one of them carries on their heads more richness than a queen ever thought of."

"They may deserve those diamonds more than any queen," was Ariel's curt response.

Werner chuckled. *The genuine Ariel in body and soul is emerging in the rainforest,* Werner thought. He again focused the binoculars on the group and beyond, toward the beach and the river. And then to the jungle. Once again, he had the feeling that he was floating in a cloud. *It is like being in a reverie,* he thought. He seemed to flow while the rich, lovely tone of the Native girls' singing voices reached his ears vivacious and beautiful. This sensation of floating away along the landscape came to him when he saw the river for the first time. When Ariel confessed to him that he had the same sensation, Werner felt relieved he was not delirious.

Indeed, the feeling of standing there with the river in full view was stunning. It was indeed, as if one were travelling along, everything moving, which was the impression the river stream provoked. The whole place seemed truly moving ahead with the river. And then, Werner again turned the binoculars to the group of Native girls.

"I think they are all about the same age, seventeen the youngest, twenty the oldest one," Werner whispered.

Ariel didn't answer. He was in awe of everything he was seeing and hearing.

Werner complained of cramping in his thighs and sat on the ground. Ariel was on guard, scanning the scene with his binoculars. The bush hid them both entirely, and they felt safe there. But, unfortunately, the situation didn't improve, and it got on Werner's nerves. They sat there for the longest time, listening to the Native girls' melodic voices and mulling on what to do next if the situation extended because they—the girls—seemed unwilling to leave the place.

"I wonder where their chaperone is," Ariel whispered.

Despite the complicated situation, Ariel's candid comment caused Werner to shake with a burst of laughter he could barely contain, yet Ariel didn't notice the effect his comments had on his old friend and continued observing the girls.

"I guess we should get moving, Werner," Ariel said in a low voice after a while. "We cannot stay here longer. Perhaps they are waiting for the rest of the tribe to come here to pick them up."

"I think you are right, Ariel," Werner said. "But there is no way to move. They could see us."

"We could crawl backward as we came here," Ariel said.

"I don't know, Ariel," Werner said, feeling that he was not in form to practice forced military exercises. Further to that, his back was hurting badly now.

He searched in his knapsack, took his medicines, selected a pill, and swallowed it with a sip of water. He put everything back and waited for Ariel's comments. There was none. Ariel turned his head and went back to scan the scene in front of him with his binoculars. Then he moved the binoculars all about the place to where his range of vision allowed him. Ariel turned around to see where they had come. He could see the group of Native girls, part of the beach, some of the river, and the jungle's borders. The treetops were bright with sunlight; the rest was in shadows. *Soon will be night,* he thought. *We have to get out of here.*

"Werner," Ariel said, "I think that these girls may be a bait set here by the males of the tribe."

"Nonsense, Ariel. The Native people need no bait to catch us. If they were around, we would be in their hands already."

Ariel had goosebumps but said nothing. Werner squatted, grabbed his binoculars, observed the scene, and almost jumped. As if on cue, Ariel grabbed his binoculars. The girls were on their feet, alert and looking around. Werner could see the tense muscles of their long legs, ready to start a run. The breeze toyed with their long black hair, and the diamonds on their heads sparkled with fury.

"They are indeed gorgeous," Ariel said once again, his frivolous observation totally out of context with the stressful moment they were in as if he had found his comment in a magician's box.

"Okay, Ariel," Werner said. "Confess to me. Which one of those girls has touched your heart?"

Ariel blushed and didn't answer. Werner grunted. *It's okay,* Werner said to himself. *Ariel is a young man, and the situation here proves that physical attraction defeats fear.*

Both friends continued observing the girls, following their every move. A long time passed. Five minutes perhaps. Eight minutes. Werner's stomach grumbled, and as if it was a response from nature, a solitary thunder crossed the air. The sound of the thunder ruffled the hair of both friends. The girls continued to be alert, watching around them as if they were seeking something. Ariel and Werner's thoughts were the same: *did they see us? Have they smelled us? Have they heard us?*

The chirping of their voices reached them sweet and strong as the wind was blowing harder. But they were still there, giving no signals of moving away. Ariel sat now and was searching in his knapsack. He took out the box with his rations, opened it, found a cold chicken leg, and began munching on it. Werner looked at him reprovingly, but he understood that he, too, was starving. Ariel offered him a piece of chicken. Werner looked around, worried. Then he stretched his arm and grabbed the offering. The wind continued to come from the east, so it was not probable that the girls could notice any strange smell, but the wind also brought more rumble, and dark clouds covered the sky.

Busy as they were munching their food with great appetite, they hardly noticed the shadows that now covered the site, but another wind strike brought the girls' singing voices closer to them. They dropped the food and squatted again to peep through the bush leaves. The girls were now trotting away from them. They trotted, talked, and played amongst themselves. They were graceful, agile, and slender, moving toward the other side of the beach. They ran fast, and in a matter of minutes, disappeared in the distance. A professional athlete would have taken much time to cover the same length, not even considering the rough terrain. Both friends were startled. *Wow! We are so limited physically against everything and everybody here,* Werner thought.

Ariel followed them with his binoculars until they disappeared into the distance.

"They are indeed charming," he said once more. Everything related to those young women, their bodies, their physical beauty, their physical prowess, the surroundings where they lived, the diamonds on their heads, their singing voices, and their grace and swiftness in their movements all impressed him. Ariel sighed.

"Can you imagine, Ariel," Werner said, understanding the emotional state his young friend was in, "how these women did turn crazy the Europeans who arrived at this land, after months of sailing stormy seas and exploring hostile territories."

Ariel felt shocked by the emotion of the encounter.

"Yes, Werner," Ariel said almost to himself, even though he could not know whether Werner was listening to his words or not. "I do imagine. Yet, you may remember that the Native people were almost animals to the first explorers because they didn't have the Holy Sacrament of Baptism. In the Catholic Church's eyes, the Natives' behaviour was horrendous. In all senses, the Natives were foul creatures. But then, what they did was baptize them, dress them, educate them, and in the process, the Europeans did a lot of damage—lots of destruction. Irreversible damage, indeed, Werner, let me tell you that you and I have witnessed what a few privileged ones have witnessed—life in its most beautiful natural state. Very few people in the 'civilized world' know that the Native people suffered the most heinous, barbaric form of cultural uprooting by the European colonizers and their descendants ever known by any other human group.

"And this atrocious behaviour continues into our days, not only here in the Amazonian rainforest but also in Africa and any other places where their inhabitants are weak and too poor to complain and make their complaints known to the world. They have no money, nobody hears their cries, and they have no justice. And how the forefathers of the Native people of the Americas were subject to the ignorance of the conquerors, the sicknesses the Europeans brought to the New World, and the fanaticism of the Catholic Church.

"And, I know, Werner—don't shush me—in today's times, the Native dwellers continue to live at the edge of extinction, while powerful people who have never seen a rainforest in their entire lives gamble their fates in useless meetings. And these powerful people do this supported by corrupt politicians who wash their hands and look another way while the farmers and logging consortiums corner the Natives more and more until they are forever extinguished. I tell you, Werner, that the Native dwellers' struggle is a permanent holocaust."

"To me, Werner," Ariel continued his passionate speech, "to see these people in their natural habitat, living their lives as they have been living through thousands of years, without damaging nature, is a privilege, a blessing. This place is the last shelter of the innocence, Werner."

"Perhaps there will be ways to protect them, Ariel."

"Like how? What do you propose, Werner?"

"I don't know. Perhaps a park; a private park for them only."

"I see," Ariel said. "As a zoo for Native dwellers, or like the parks for animals that exist in Africa. And then people will pay to see them, and there will be signs all over that will say: Please, don't feed the Natives."

"Let's go, Ariel. Leave human misery aside. We have a lot to do for ourselves."

It was night already. Like that, a snapping, and it was deep dark. Both friends had walked for an hour wading the beach and had just lit their lamps when they faced a clay terrain surrounded by a wall of enormous rocks. A layer of multicoloured stones that sparkled when the light hit them covered the ground. It was a fascinating view. It was all darkness, but then those little stars were all over the terrain. Werner stooped down, grabbed one of the rocks, examined it, and then tossed it away.

"Basalt," Werner said. "And mica and quartz, as well. The samples that we found in those rocks are part of an eruption, a volcanic eruption. This geological material is the result of giant outbursts that happened millions of years ago. So I'm telling you, Ariel, every step here is a feast to a geologist."

Ariel focused his concern on another subject. "The Native dwellers may come anytime, Werner. The entire tribe may as well be here at sunrise."

"I don't think so, Ariel. I don't see a reason why they should hurry back here. The girls seemed to feel safe. They didn't see us. If they had seen us, we could have been in big trouble. If this is a place of relaxation for them, I'm sure that there must be hundreds of places as beautiful as this."

"They come here to obtain the stones for their hair, Werner."

"The diamonds? No. I don't think so. Must be other places where they got them. I'm sure that yonder the river must be an even larger deposit. I feel this place must be the most amazing geological field in the entire world. Wow! It's amazing, Ariel."

"The amazing thing will be if we get out of here alive, Werner."

Werner was going to answer when the entire jungle seemed to be in flames. The view around them was so breathtaking their hearts almost stopped. A round white moon had come up from the treetops and illuminated in the most fantastic, psychedelic way the entire landscape, and the shining was such an astonishing view that extended well beyond the riverside. There was no need for the lamps with such natural nocturnal light, so they put them off to save batteries and stood paralogized by the extraordinary beauty that surrounded them, each one in their own world. *Baruch Attah Adonai, Eloheynu Melech Ha-Olam. I thank you for Thy generosity.* Ariel prayed, thanking God for so much magnificence. And he requested God, His favour, to preserve this magnificent land, away forever from the hand of the civilized man. In the meantime, Werner made plans about how he could get rich without destroying the golden goose.

After a while, they moved away, Werner leading the way. The chain of rocks continued and took them to the beach. The rumble of the water was such they had to scream to make themselves heard what the one was saying to the other. They both were exhausted. So many emotions lived, so many expectations still ahead, so much new ground to explore. Werner began climbing a rock. By then, he could barely walk and was desperately looking for a safe place to camp for the night, and he was already moving toward a place among the rocks when he stopped, again amazed by the view, and called for Ariel.

They saw the perfect U that the river formed from where they were at the top of the rock's chain, as described in Werner's notes. The notes specified the diamond deposit field on the beach across from this accentuated curve in the river's course. A fortune was sitting there for them. A strong emotion overwhelmed them, and they both fell to the ground, Werner on his back with his arms open in a cross. It was indeed a stunning view. It was an extraordinary feeling. The river seemed to come to them swirling, cyclonic, roaring as an apocalyptic beast, its claws of foam ready to snatch them from the rocks, but then suddenly, as if controlled by a divine leash, the creature turned around and went onto the other side always roaring, constantly rumbling, reverberating through the jungle, leaving a great echo in their ears.

The moon was now high in the sky, and its white light made it so clear around them that it seemed a midnight sun was lighting the entire place.

"Wow!" Werner exclaimed as he stepped on the higher rock. "The force of these waters would be enough to provide electricity to an entire city for years and years with no need for a damn. It would just be enough to install the turbines and generators here directly, and the water force would do the work. Cheaper and economically feasible, without environmental impact, flooding the land, relocating the Aboriginals, or other nasty businesses."

"Your words are an insult to this place, Werner," Ariel said, visibly upset. "Let me remind you that before you build your hydroelectric leviathan, we have to get at least one diamond. Until now, I have seen none, despite all of our sacrifice coming here."

Werner didn't follow up on Ariel's train of thought. Instead, he said, "Ariel! You're unrecognizable."

Ariel looked at Werner as if it was the first time he had seen him in years. "My God!" Ariel said. "You look like a scarecrow!"

And then Ariel realized that he could as well look as bad as his old friend could, and thus he laughed heartedly at both of their sad appearances.

"Okay, okay," Werner said, sharing his young friend's sudden outburst of good humour. "We may camp here, Ariel. We can wash in one of the ponds by the beach, and then we will kindle a bonfire and cook something. I'm dying to have a hot meal."

Ariel collected himself and came back to his anxious mood.

"A bonfire, here?" Ariel said. "Are you sure, Werner?"

"We will kindle it between those stones. Just a small bonfire enough for us. I don't think it will call the attention of anybody."

"But the Natives—"

"That only happens in the movies, Ariel," Werner interrupted. "The girls went that way, we came this way and found nobody, and so we are safe."

"*Be'ezrat Hashem!*" Ariel said, opening his arms to the heavens as his forefathers had done, reminding himself that the will of God was above all!

THEY ATE a hot meal, and satisfied, they slept under the moonlight, lulled by the river and the cacophony from the rainforest.

Ariel dreamed. A girl came to visit him in his dream. She was one of the Native girls, coming toward him from the river. Her feet did not reach the floor. She was floating in the air. At first, she was a blue butterfly fluttering her way over through his dream. Then the butterfly metamorphosed into the Native girl. She was beautiful! More beautiful than even the way he had seen her by the river with her friends. Her silky black hair adorned with diamonds waved in the dream, her almond-shaped amber eyes sparkled bright, and her lips were the colour of a blooming wild rose. She blinked deliciously, and her eyes became intense.

She smiled and extended her right hand closed in a fist toward him. He did the same, raised his hand, and she opened her fist, and there was in the palm of her hand a stone that shone under the moonlight! The girl held the stone for a second or two and then deposited it into Ariel's open palm. She then placed her hand on Ariel's, thus covering the stone with her hand, so the diamond—for it was a diamond!—lay trapped between both hands, like a pearl in between the oyster's shell. And thus there they were, both with their hands interlaced in the dream. It seemed so physical that Ariel felt her breath warming his skin as she came closer, but then, she became a butterfly again and fluttered away.

Ariel tossed and turned and then sat startled and already fully awake. He discovered he had the diamond in his hand and was puzzled, breathless, but then he reacted and looked at the small stone shining in the moonlight. Then, Ariel stood upright, put the diamond in his shirt pocket, went up to the rock, and sat there. He was pensive, contemplating the river, the never-sleeping rainforest, the moon, the entire universe beating within him.

A few steps away, Werner snored. He was also dreaming— he dreamed he was sliding down a slope, practicing extreme skiing in Chamonix-Mont-Blanc when a roaring woke him up. The roaring brought both friends back to the reality of the rainforest.

"It's a *yaguareté*," Werner said. He was already upright, standing there with his machete in his hand.

"Yeah," Ariel said, just recovering from his dream. "It's a *yaguareté*."

Ariel walked to the fire, which by then was but a few embers still burning, put some more sticks on it, and blew on it until the fire rekindled.

The feline's roaring reached them in critical waves. The jaguar was prowling over somewhere closer. They could even hear the purring coming from its powerful throat, but the animal was not getting closer for some reason. Something held it back.

"Can you see it, Ariel?"

"No. It must be behind those rocks."

The sound of rolling pebbles came neatly into their ears.

"It's down there to the right, Werner. Perhaps we are too high for it."

"It's only one," Werner said.

They heard another similar roaring from the opposite side.

"It's a couple," Ariel said.

"The one closer is the female then," Werner said. "In nature, it is the female who is the one who always leads the hunt."

The roaring stopped all of a sudden and then resumed stronger.

"They have surrounded us," Ariel said in a panic.

"Calm down, Ariel. Perhaps we are not their target," Werner said. "They could have attacked us while we slept."

Ariel had goosebumps.

"Perhaps the fire kept them away," Ariel said. "They may have waited until the fire died."

The roaring came stronger and shook them to their bones, and like an echo, another roaring resounded some steps further.

"They must be exchanging coordinates," Ariel said.

From then on, the roaring changed to a continuous purring, and it was then that Ariel saw one of the animals in the moonlight. The feline was crouching on a large stone and yawned, showing off its splendid fangs. Werner and Ariel both had cold shivers in their spines. It was terrifying. What a beautiful beast it was! Its eyes shined like the diamonds that shined in the hair of the Native girls.

The eyes of the jaguar appeared fixed on them, but the animal was not looking at them. Something else seemed to have distracted it. In a moment, the other jaguar came behind the first one, and another pair of shining eyes focused on something that caught the interest of both felines. Easier prey, maybe. Or a bigger one of which the jaguars were scared. However, the big cats didn't seem afraid. They just stood there some twenty or so yards away, ostensibly ignoring their human prey. For a while, the purring continued, and then, like if something, or someone, had broken the spell, the jaguars stood upward from their crouching position, turned around, and moved away, their bodies swaying softly under the moonlight.

"Strange thing," Werner said.

"Extraordinary," Ariel said. "A miracle. Indeed, an extraordinary thing."

"We were not their target. Something must be down there that distracted the jaguars."

Ariel moved some steps down as if to investigate, but Werner stopped him.

"Hold on, Ariel. Whatever it was must also be gone by now. Perhaps it was a bigger animal, and we don't want that kind of encounter anymore. So instead, we should take advantage of being awake to go and work down the beach to see what we can find. That will be productive."

Warner looked at his wristwatch.

"It's six-fifteen in the morning," Werner said. "We have slept almost nine hours. If the *yaguaretés* didn't wake us up, we could have been sleeping all day."

But then, Ariel remembered the diamond. He palped his shirt pocket as he was sure that he put it there, and there it was! He grew pale.

"What's wrong, Ariel?" Werner said. "Did you lose something?"

Suddenly, Ariel realized that he should not tell about his dream or the stone that shone under the moonlight to Werner. It was something too fantastic to share, and this fantasy belonged to him and him only. And he decided it would be his secret. *That is strange. It was part of the dream, and it is here!* Ariel said to himself.

"Nothing, Werner," Ariel answered. "It's nothing."

Werner started arranging his belongings, and a pensive Ariel went to sit on the rock.

Sitting on the rock, Ariel contemplated the new day. He had his eyes fixed on the immensity from where the day was coming, and then his eyes went toward the river that thundered. And he remembered that part of the Native legend he heard the first time from Werner's lips about a peculiar Aboriginal tradition among the Aboriginal women: the woman from the tribe of marriageable age proposes to her chosen man by placing one diamond in the man's hand. And it happened to him, in a dream. No. It was not a dream. He searched again for the small stone in his shirt pocket, and it was there, shining this time under the sunlight. *It cannot be! It's incredible!* Ariel thought. Indeed, the most beautiful young woman he saw on the river shore had proposed to him. And he did not even know her, not even her name. Why! And then, this meant—if he accepted—would he marry her and the entire rainforest with her? Ariel fell on his knees. He was praying. He was seeking advice from his Creator.

Werner saw him and shook his head. *The Native girl must have affected his heart, if not his brain,* Werner thought to himself.

Yet, in the tranquility of the morning, Werner also fell into a meditation mode. He thought about his life and the strange events that brought him to this place in the middle of the rainforest in the heart of South America. And he thought of María Rosa Martinez as well, and in all of what his life had been until that moment.

"There is something here that protects us, Werner," Ariel said, interrupting Werner's mulling on his life. "No doubt that it is the Lord or some of His messengers. Perhaps the stones, perhaps the Lord himself. And I know that the Lord brought me here. And nothing bad will ever happen either to you or to me. For you, Werner, you as well are a messenger of the Lord."

"Very poetic," Werner said. "Very prophetic and touching. But now, this messenger of God says that it's time for work. So better, get ready. But first, we will have breakfast, and then we will go on exploring for the best place to start our work on the riverside."

On their way to the beach, they followed a passage carved through a narrow gorge. The sun of a new day was coming fast and bright, and the sunlight crashed against the walls, sending sparks all over. It was a hallucinatory spectacle. Werner stooped down and grabbed a hexagonal-shaped stone.

"It's quartz," he said. "As I told you many times before, Ariel, this region is completely mineral. All the rocks and the sand is alluvial sands. Here there is an incalculable fortune in gold, iron, coke, and diamonds. What a pity not having at our disposal a piece of proper mining equipment. With a mid-sized excavator, we could become millionaires, Ariel."

"Blaspheme!" Ariel said. "You cannot stop talking blaspheme, Werner, hurting with your every word this holy place. You offend the Almighty."

"It is okay, Ariel. Calm down. It impresses me the amount of mineral wealth that lies here. I understand now that Dr. Zweig and his men never reached this place physically."

"So," Ariel said, "the notes are not entirely telling the truth?"

"Someone is lying, Ariel. That's why Dr. Zweig's notes, although specific regarding this place's location, are vague regarding the findings. The guides led the Germans, but the Native guides may not have trusted the white men. Indeed, Ariel, I'm telling you that if they had reached this place, the Germans would have done anything within their reach to set a camp here. They would have negotiated with any government, and then a mining city would have grown here."

"It would be a repeated history nonetheless," Ariel said, "Like so many cities that once upon a time were the centre of the world and then vanished into oblivion. I heard about such places in northern Chile, in a place called Chañarcillo, a silver mine. And then, Potosi in Bolivia, also silver."

"And Manaus in Brazil," Werner added. "We must remember when Manaus was the city centre of the world for the rubber business. But here, this city would have been a mythical city built on diamonds in the middle of the rainforest."

"Dr. Zweig lied," Ariel said. "Yes, he did, and we must thank him after all. He lied to save face and to keep his rank and privileges, and with that, he unknowingly saved this place."

"How strange." Werner was mulling over this puzzle. "But then, what is the truth? In his notes, Dr. Zweig said that the Germans killed the Native guides so they would not reveal the location of this place to anyone."

"The evidence shows that the guides deserted the Germans and left them alone in the middle of the forest," Ariel said as if he were a lawyer presenting his case to an invisible court. "That's clear. Then the Germans had no other option but to return to where they came from, for if they had not done so, they would have been wandering through the rainforest for the rest of their lives. And then either the animals or the Natives would have killed them."

"That's to thread it too fine, Ariel. Oh, I think that we will never solve this puzzle."

Werner stood there, mulling it over and scratching his head.

"Well," Werner said after a while, "what is past is past, Ariel. So let's go on with our business."

"Okay, Werner, but we should never forget: what is past to some is present to others."

"Where did you get that, Ariel?"

"It's a psalm in the scriptures, Werner."

Werner didn't feel like pressing Ariel to reveal in what chapter of the scriptures, such a psalm appears or if it was another of Ariel's astray ideas. Anyhow, Werner didn't understand its meaning, so he didn't answer, turned around, searched his knapsack, set up his equipment, selected a place, and with great enthusiasm began to work removing the soil with his shovel.

Since the first moment they arrived at that place, Werner knew they were in a diamond field of incredible wealth, and he knew that the real treasure, which he could never exploit, was the one that lay underneath the surface of those sands, formed by hundreds of cataclysms during millions of years.

THEY HAD worked all day without a rest. Werner had set up his rudimentary but essential laboratory to clean, measure, and weigh the stones. The ground around them was full of tiny holes where they had tested the soil. Werner took some pictures of the place. He wanted to take a picture of Ariel, but Ariel declined. Ariel then took a picture of a smiling Werner holding a little shovel, with the diamond deposit as a background.

The sun was high in the sky, burning their backs. The humidity was as maddening as the buzzing and biting of the mosquitoes that had proclaimed themselves defenders of the area against those two strangers who dared to break the place's peace. Nevertheless, both friends continued painfully moving, driven by their vehemence in collecting the brilliant stones. A pair of small human shadows lost in the immensity of that belt of brown beach between the river's hurricane water and the eternal green of the rainforest.

"This is very interesting, Ariel," Werner said during a moment of rest. "I'm telling you how lucky we have been. At certain periods, perhaps not even yearly, the river floods this beach just as the Nile does. The water then covers this mineral deposit. When there is no water, the forest covers it all. That's why the Germans, and no one until now, have found it. I guess that even the Native dwellers knew nothing about this behaviour from the river. And even if their guides had brought them to the right place, they were in the wrong season. Thus, finding the deposit would have been impossible for them. So we have been lucky to find this open for us. For as the Nile withdraws, leaving the soil ready for sowing, this so capricious river also withdraws, leaving the diamonds to us."

It was nonstop work, and they were exhausted. Ariel followed every step Werner taught him. He worked with enthusiasm, digging the soil with his small shovel, and he shone when he saw the little irregular-shaped, crystallized, diminutive stones, the fruit of his work trapped in the metallic sieve. However, the heat was unbearable because of the humidity. At some point during his digging, Werner felt that someone was watching him, and he stopped to look around, yet he decided not to go to his knapsack to check for his binoculars because he concluded that looking through the haze formed by the heat would be useless. He only could distinguish the limits of the jungle that surrounded them like a crown, and at their back, the river and its never-ending thundering.

But then, in the sky appeared an enormous beast with fully extended wings, a dragon, yet it was not a dragon, it was but a black cloud in the form of a dragon with wings, and tail and fire, and the lightning began, and the thunder and the rain came in a blink of the eye. And it lasted no more than twenty minutes, though, but this time Werner had taken precautions, and so they were prepared for the rain. When they counted their treasure, Werner discovered that he already had twenty-five diamonds inside his vial, and Ariel had added one more to his treasure, so there were now twelve, one of them of great value, as Werner told Ariel when both examined the stone, and Werner weighed it in the unique portable scale he had brought.

"Indeed," Werner had said. "Roughly seven and a half carats, and then look at its clarity, its colour, and its shape. It's a rare gem, very appreciated in the market; the price must be good. You have done well, Ariel."

Werner had similar value stones in his "piggybank," as he called his glass container. When exposed to sunlight, the crystal stones shone with such intensity, Werner shed tears of joy.

"It's a dream, Ariel," Werner repeated at every moment. "A dream that came through after more than forty years of waiting."

"Well, I hope this dream does not become a nightmare."

"Please, Ariel. Refrain from being an ill-omen bird. You have the proof that all that I told you is the truth. Truth and reality, which are two conditions seldom converging."

"Oh c'mon, Werner, I'm not an ill-omen bird. I just say what I feel. All this beauty that surrounds us has for me more value than all the diamonds in the world." Ariel made a pause, then he continued, "When the idea of coming here and searching for the diamonds set in me, I got the jitters. You have to understand that the idea was hard to swallow. However, I believe in the chances that life gives, so I said to myself, why not? The worst thing I could do was not to try. And here I am. But this grandiosity, this gift from God, is well beyond any wealth you or anybody can accumulate in a lifetime. Compared to the life I live in the city, this is a paradise. Why then would I want to go back to the city? I will have the same life, only that with more money. And more money does not always mean wealth, Werner. That's why I said the dream might turn out into a nightmare. Pushed by greed, things may come, but not all of them are good things. I don't want my life to take the direction of greed. However, I knew nothing about what I was saying to you but until I came here."

"What do you want to do then, Ariel? Do you want to stay here? Is that what you want?"

"Why not, Werner? To stay here to live or to die. I have nobody who may miss me in the city—nobody. Here I could conquer myself; I could find myself a new person and build myself a new me. Here I have everything."

"But that will be like throwing your life out the window, Ariel. Nobody is so crazy as to do that. And remember that whatever diamonds you have plus mine, we will have a fortune. So why are you thinking about throwing this fortune away?"

"I'm sure that this—" he extended his arms and swirled around, "—is all I need. And tell me, Werner, how many diamonds did you say we had before?"

"Why, Ariel? You told me you got twelve diamonds, and I got twenty-five. Of course, we will get more. We will keep removing the earth for more. As I told you, this is just the beginning—"

"Well, twelve is more than enough for me. You said so. And it's interesting because twelve is a magic number, did you know that, Werner?"

"I don't know about that, Ariel. I know that twelve in Spanish equals sweet in Portuguese."

"Ah! That sweet could become bitter, Werner. Real bitter."

"You should not be so negative, Ariel," Werner said exasperatedly.

"I'm not negative, Werner. The truth is I would love to stay here forever."

"You are crazy, Ariel. Why would you like to do such a thing? Think about it. This place is unknown. I agree with that. However, at any moment, it can become a popular spot. Any satellite could discover the enormous mineral wealth it hides, and rich predators will negotiate with the government for a long-term contract to explore and exploit this region's minerals. Therefore, legions will come. Thousands will come. And people will cut every tree. They will bring heavy machinery and build camps for workers, highways, train tracks, and airports. And they will tame the river and build a dam. And they will not give a shit about the rainforest that by then will be just a few sparse trees and garbage all over, and who will cry 'stop!' No one because those who dare to defend the rainforest will be sequestered, incarcerated, and murdered. And behind the miners will come the speculators and the prostitutes, the merchants of all, and the preachers. And the birds, snakes, and every animal will have no place for this paradise will become hellish, for the rainforest will become the wane forest, and there will be no corner where the animals can go free."

"And those who will arrive will kill every Native dweller, or they will move them to new shacks around the city with the minimum service, and they will rape the women and steal the jewels on their heads. And who will cry 'genocide!' Nobody will. It's the *ñembotagüi* law. As Jesus said, 'forgive them, Father, for they know not what they are doing.' But there will be no Jesus to stop them here.

"The will to know about this place, or places as this one, doesn't exist in humans. There is no commitment to the Earth at all. And people close their ears and eyes because nobody wants problems. Everybody wants to earn their daily bread—the way they do it does not matter. And so, the Native dwellers will continue as helpless as when the first European stepped on this Holy Land. And you, Ariel. What will you do? Nothing. You will do nothing. You will be dead. The first people who come here will kill you for no reason, for this is the way of man. And all this beauty that makes you cry will become garbage. And human excrement and plastic will taint this natural beauty as it does as we speak with the oceans. And the smoke of the burning forest will fill the air, and no creature will be able to breathe. And this all will happen because we are humans, the Earth is round, and we are many and greedy because greed is no longer a sin but is now a way of life, which is out of control, and there is no other destiny, for this one destiny we all have reflects the misery of the human being."

"Well, well, well, Werner. And you are the one who told me that I'm pessimistic."

"I'm pessimistic, but I have earned the right to become this way because I'm old, and I have seen it all. You haven't yet started to live."

Ariel sat on the ground with his hands on his head as if covering himself. Werner felt pity for him, and he was mad at himself for being rude in explaining human cruelty to a young man.

"C'mon, Ariel," Werner said. "Some things will come to us as the wave of a tsunami, and we may have just to run away. But in the meantime, we have to take whatever comes to us and enjoy it for the time allotted to us. That's the mandate."

THEY WENT back by the river to fill their canteens and then moved to the forest border where they found a secure place that could keep them away from the beasts, although not from the mosquitoes that followed them with fury. There they spent the rest of the evening, and they talked and philosophized, and made peace between their ideas—so different—and made plans for a future, each one on his own. They dug a hole wide and deep enough to bury their tools, instruments, and garbage. And they ate cold leftovers, drank water from the river, and cleaned themselves, and afterward, they dropped all scraps and tools into the hole and covered it all with the red soil of the jungle. And with great effort, they rolled a rock and placed it where the spot had been, and Werner brought some bushes, which he planted there, and it was all left hidden as if it were the tomb of a lousy civilization.

"Within a few days," Werner said, "this spot will be jungle again."

And then, they prepared to sleep.

Werner fell asleep right away, exhausted as he was, but not Ariel. Even though Ariel was as tired as Werner, he could not sleep. He lay there for a long time with his eyes wide open, listening to the clamor of the rainforest, and as he was getting drowsy and falling into a trancelike state, he saw a group of strange people who crept toward their site, so light they seemed to be floating in the air—

But then he lost consciousness, and when he woke up, he had no memory of this dream. The sun was already high in the blue sky.

"If we want to beat the sun, we have to keep ourselves awake all night," Ariel said.

Werner consulted his wristwatch.

"True," he said. "It's already nine in the morning. We have fallen asleep again."

"There were no jaguars to awake us this time," Ariel said.

Werner fixed his photographic camera in its leather box and hung it from his neck. They made a last check of their belongings, buried the tools they had brought, and erased every hint of they ever being there

"We will walk lighter on our way back," Ariel said. "That's good. We will reach the van in less time."

Werner was looking into his knapsack.

"We have nothing left to eat," Werner said, feeling wretched. "I miss a good *bratwurst* and an iced Schopp German beer."

"We will not be short of food, Werner," Ariel said. "You know already that nature will provide for us."

Ariel was utterly sarcastic by repeating the exact words Werner had said to him at their arrival to the rainforest. *We will not be short of food, Ariel,* Werner had said, *you know already that nature will provide for us.* And to give Ariel an example, Werner had taken a fruit hanging on the lower branches of a tree, and Werner had said, *Look here, Ariel, this is a wild avocado, these fruits are delicious,* and he had opened the fruit, taken the pit out with his knife, and he had eaten the entire avocado. *It's delicious, Ariel. You should try it too.* Ariel had said, *No, Werner, I pass.* Werner had eaten the fruit with great appetite. Ariel had watched him and said nothing; his gut had told him not to follow Werner's dietary instructions. Next, they faced another tree hanging colourful, inviting fruits, and

Werner had said, *Wild guavas, Ariel, these are also delicious.* And then he had taken a bite of one or two. And as Werner had done with the wild avocados, he had selected three of the fruits, put them into his knapsack, and had continued walking.

But then, after a while, Werner had begun to feel stomach cramps, and he had wild diarrhea that attracted a nest of bright flies whose buzzing hurt the ears and had given Werner a headache. This incident had made them waste precious time, and although Ariel had been sorry for Werner, he had been mad at his friend for being so careless about what he brought into his stomach. *Diarrhea is not bad after all, Werner*, Ariel had said, pushing further into Werner's misery. *Once your stomach is clean from all those bratwursts you have eaten, you will be ready to digest these healthy fruits.*

"Let's go," Werner said, annoyed by Ariel's sarcasm.

They had an excellent walk through the sempiternal cacophony of the tropical forest.

Ariel was enjoying the moment, his present in paradise, as he felt it in his heart. Then on the walk back to civilization, his mind felt freer to pay more attention to the wonder that surrounded him, and something peculiar called his attention. He stood there, startled because he saw at his feet, crawling in front of him, a snail with a beautiful tiny rainbow-coloured shell.

The snail moved his tentacles as if saying hello to him. And Ariel smiled at the sight of the beautiful little animal and waved his hand, and then saw another, and another snail, coming from among the leaves, and they were hundreds and made a road in front of them, slowly moving, and Ariel could not walk, so he stood there, entranced by their behaviour. And the snails' bright rainbow-coloured shells seemed to play with him as if Ariel were a charming prince in an enchanted forest of some long-forgotten fairy tale. Then after a while, in the way they had come, one by one, the tiny snails melted into the vegetation, and again Ariel was there left alone, dazzled and marveled by so much beauty, wondering what had he done to deserve such miracles.

Not far ahead, Werner was instead thinking about what lay ahead in his future. He calculated that they should be back in the van by sunset. He was in good humour, having accomplished his objective, albeit partially, according to himself, although he would never share this feeling with Ariel. After more than forty years, the seed had germinated, and in what a way it had, indeed! With the diamonds he had, he could live a good life with no worries, at least for money, for the rest of his life. And he thought that one day, not long into the future, he would return to this place for more. And he would come back alone and at the right time, for he knew now about the river behaviour and the direction he should follow once in the jungle, and he knew about the place, the dangers, and the weather. *So*, he thought, *it will all depend on the planning, which I'm good at, and I need nobody. I will be free.*

Of course, he could not share his thoughts with Ariel. Werner already knew how apprehensive his young friend was regarding the things of nature. These were his most secret thoughts, and these thoughts didn't mean he was greedy, not at all, but he considered the wealth laying by the river shore to be too great to let it be there to rest in peace for centuries ahead. And he would take just enough for him to live like a king. No, no. Of course, he was not greedy. He had already in mind to share his entire newly acquired wealth with María Rosa Martinez, and upon his departure from this world, he would also leave a part to Ariel Gimmel, whether the young man liked it or not.

And, no, he would not destroy nature. He would never allow himself to destroy the beauty of the rainforest, above all because there were also the Native girls who, why not, had again awoken his appetite for a new sensual exotic adventure. He was not too old after all.

These thoughts carried him through the rainforest and made his every step lighter. His health had improved with the exercise. His body was obedient to every movement and the clean air, free of the contaminants in the city. Moreover, his steps were lighter as they moved, driven by the secret energy of the diamonds he carried.

Werner stopped some yards ahead and was now collecting some roots and leaves. Ariel hurried to see what he had.

"These," Werner said, "Are very good to contain hunger and stomach aches. Have one, Ariel. Just chew it."

Out of courtesy for his friend, Ariel accepted, but he didn't put the leaf in his mouth.

"What an irony," Ariel said, "We own a fortune in diamonds, and we have to eat roots and leaves and drink the water of the river. So what do you think, Werner? Is not this a warning from life? A message from God?"

"I don't know, Ariel. I don't know about this messenger God that sends us too many confusing messages. Indeed, God sends us many signals. I agree with you. Good for some, bad for others. That's maybe God's balance, but I'm sure that in the end, He gives a shit about us."

"That's not true, Werner. All come from God. We have to follow His guidance. We are His children!"

"What God, Ariel?" Werner raised his hands to the heavens. "We humans are orphans. Orphans are what we are." He turned around and walked ahead.

The rainforest had wrapped them again fully with its noise, its aromas, and its colours. Werner always kept ahead, chewing a root as if it were chewing gum. The march had taken them a significant part of the day, and they had rested just a moment and then continued at forced pace.

They followed back the same path they had come and noticed how the jungle had changed in just a couple of days—the jungle's response to the machete. So fast, the changes had occurred. Where there was a fallen trunk before now, there was another tree growing high and robust, populated by an entire universe of life, microorganisms, other plants, giant mushrooms, flowers, fruits, seeds, butterflies, birds, monkeys, snakes, spiders, ants, and a myriad of other insects, all living in a whirlpool of passion—which a tree is.

"There you are, Werner," Ariel said, taking a moment to contemplate a tree. "Here is a manifestation of life, which means God. If people don't know how much life a tree contains and don't believe in Him, it's not God's fault. The fault is in those who cut the tree."

Werner was getting his bearings, trying to find the place where the fallen comrade's monument was, close to the site where Ariel almost fell to death. From that distance, Ariel sensed that Werner appeared confused, searching eagerly for the humble memorial. It seems that he could not find it. Ariel saw Werner coming back and forth, bending here and there, and standing up, and placing his hands akimbo, his head moving, his eyes searching, probably with an interrogation sign in them. There was the cliff and the chain of palms, and the *ceibos, samuús, quebrachos, amambays,* and *lapachos,* but not the humble monument, for the bushes covered it all now. Of course, the rainforest had changed the entire place in just hours. Still, Werner paused his search for some seconds as an homage to the man fallen forever there in the invisible trenches of the rainforest.

Ariel, some steps behind, saw Werner's coming and going, and he also stopped, but not because of Werner but because a red feathered hummingbird started fluttering his tiny wings just as if he wanted to land on his nose. Ariel smiled and extended his hand as inviting the little bird to land there instead, but then, another hummingbird, this one covered with a bright orange feathered coat, distracted him.

And soon, to Ariel's astonished eyes, the hummingbirds multiplied, and they were now hundreds fluttering their wings in front of him. But what made the spectacle the most fantastic was that each of the little birds had a different colour. Some of them were red, others yellow, others pink, others orange, and others white, and so when they moved together, they looked as if they were flames, tongues of flames—fire alive, burning the trees around them. And the flames went up and down, right and left, according to the fluttering of their wings, and this spectacle was such a magnificent show of beauty that emotions filled Ariel's heart, and he cried. And he let his tears run loose, and he felt better and waved his hands to the tiny birds, and they started to fly away one by one like sparks of a fire blown by the wind. And then, when they were all gone, Ariel stood there alone amongst the wild vegetation, still weeping while admiring the flowers that fell in cascades from one tree to the other, and he felt that this magnificent garden was there for him and him only.

WERNER WANTED to reach where the massive rock was where they had rested on their way to the river, but it was also impossible to find. Although Werner's compass persisted in signaling the right direction, everything seemed like they had dreamed about it. *Indeed, we are going in the right direction,* Werner thought, *but somehow we took a different path.* He was thinking about a 'path' but to find a 'path' amidst that indescribable landscape was a kind of cruel joke. And they again confronted a sharp slope with a viscose ground, which turned into a tortured walk while they had to descend, holding from shrubs and roots as they had seen the monkeys do. Their clothes were full of mud, their boots heavier, and their arms were in pain because of so much effort. However, they both were thankful because it was not raining, for rain would have made going downhill impossible.

And thus, once they both were on the horizontal and firmer ground, they felt more at ease, for they knew they had accomplished a difficult task. Werner was ahead, walking now more energetically, feeling more motivated, and Ariel was almost running behind, risking falling, his feet tangled in those extraordinary roots that appeared to be alive, like serpents, children of the tree. But his fear was not just falling but also to lose sight of Werner, for he knew if that happened, it would be impossible to find him even if he screamed and screamed his name because to have someone make his voice heard in that stridency was unimaginable.

And then there was a clearing in the forest. Werner continued at a good pace, always alert, rising and lowering his machete to the right and then to the left, although sometimes his effort seemed fruitless, trying to open a path through, cutting shrubs, bushes, flowers, and fruits. Meanwhile, behind him, Ariel moved as in a dream, absent-minded, taken by the beauty that surrounded him. Therefore, it was odd that Ariel was the one who saw them first.

The Natives grouped themselves in a clearing of a small forest of young *quebrachos*. Werner walked through the Natives' group without seeing them as if the Native people were a branch of any of the *quebrachos*. The Natives let Werner walk through, but Ariel screamed, and his scream broke the spell. Werner stopped his walk, turned around toward Ariel to see what happened, saw the Native people, and came back fast to meet Ariel as if he wanted to protect his young friend from the aggressive Natives. And, on the other hand, the Natives studied the pair of strangers with open curiosity. There was no animosity in their gestures, just curiosity.

They were six male adults, four males and two females of an undefined age with pale skin, as they had seen in the girls by the river. Probably they belonged to the same family. They were tall, muscular, flexible, fit, and with curious eyes like children. One of them, the older one, it seemed, had a thick leather belt with a metal buckle hanging in a bandolier from his left shoulder—something carved on that buckle called Werner's attention, although whatever it was, weather, time, and use had almost erased it.

"It's a military belt," Werner whispered into Ariel's astounded ears.

Ariel thought that the Natives had a previous encounter with white men and that the belt was part of the booty, or if one wanted to give the Natives the benefit of the doubt, Ariel could have thought that the Natives may have found that object somewhere else. They all wore their hair cut following the contour of the head, covering their ears and forefront. They all carried ornaments, no diamonds, only vegetal ornaments in the hair, chest, waist, and legs, and had no tattoos, nor was their skin painted. Other than that, they were all naked. All of them carried bows and arrows as large as they were. They had the arrows wrapped in bunches under their armpits and tied to their shoulder with a vegetal rope. It was probable that there were more Natives around, but until that moment, whatever their number was, they were invisible.

And to break the ice as he had seen in the movies—the cavalry lieutenant addressing the chief—Werner stepped onward, raised one hand, his palm opened, and said, "Hi!"

The Natives looked at each other and then slapped amongst themselves as if what they had seen was something funny. Werner and Ariel relaxed, but the Natives were not laughing. It only seemed to the strangers' eyes that the Natives were having a great time. Werner and Ariel concurred that the Natives were not as ferocious as they imagined them to be.

The Native man who carried the leather belt came closer to Werner and looked him in the eye. Werner blinked several times at the calm stare of this man. Then, the Native man took his sight away from Werner and turned toward the group that followed the scene with interest. The group then restarted the same ceremony like at the beginning, slapping each other all over their bodies as if they were thrilled.

"What's going on?" Ariel asked, trying to comprehend the Aboriginals' strange behaviour.

"I don't know," Werner said.

"I guess," Ariel said, "for them, we are kind of comical fellows."

"For me, they are the comical fellows," Werner said as if somehow Ariel's words had offended him.

The older Native man with the leather belt again stepped in front of Werner and put his hand on Werner's head. Werner let him do so. The Natives then applauded and bent over as if making a reverence with both hands on their stomachs. Anybody from the civilized world could interpret his action as the Native man either having a sudden stomach ache or enjoying the time of his life, having an inner laugh. Neither was happening, though, and all the action transpired in silence. The others in his group did nothing this time. They just stood there looking at each other and then to both strangers with open, candid eyes. Werner and Ariel felt as if they were in a display window in the middle of the rainforest.

After making his odd gestures, the Native with the leather belt forgot Werner and came close to Ariel, but he didn't repeat the ceremony he had made with Werner. Instead, he passed his nose around Ariel's body as if he were sniffing Ariel. Although uncomfortable with this situation, Ariel resisted it calmly. The older Native repeated the gestures: the clapping, the bending over holding with his stomach, however, this time, the group slapped each other with energy, and after that, they all turned to look at the strangers with their open, transparent, candid eyes.

"I'm sure they have made a bet," Werner said.

"What?" Ariel said.

"Yes," Werner said, "I'm sure they have followed us since a long time ago, most probably since we left our camp over there by the river. I'm even sure now that they were spying on us in our camp."

"I cannot believe that they could have killed us if they wanted. What are the Natives going to do with us now?"

"I don't know," Werner said.

While Werner and Ariel spoke, the group of Native dwellers deliberated the same way the players of any sport do before the beginning of the game—they were all together, forming a circle. They had embraced together, each arm interlaced with the arm of the other, their heads together, and while they were busy with this ceremony, they ignored the two men who looked at what they were doing with startled eyes. The group remained embraced for a long time, and then, to both friends' astonished eyes, they disappeared into the vegetation. Werner and Ariel could not believe it. In front of their very eyes, the Native people had performed a trick no magician ever did. They melted into the leaves and bushes and the trees in a snap of the fingers. Both friends ran to where the Natives had been, and it was all but vegetation.

"The forest swallowed them," Ariel exclaimed, and his words were prophetic for what was to come, but it would not be him, but another who would repeat them.

They had yet to reach the place where they had left their vehicle. To achieve that, they had to walk the next twenty miles or so through the rainforest. For a long time, both friends stood there in silence, each analyzing the situation from their point of view until Werner decided.

"Let's go," Werner said. "I'm sure that there is nothing to worry about."

And they continued to march through that incredible prehistoric landscape, among giant trees loaded with fruits and flowers and butterflies and bees, a paradise for the collector of colours and sounds. Again, they moved through fields of bushes of incredible beauty. And again, they confronted the swamp, but it was several miles away from where they had crossed it the first time.

The friends made a detour because they witnessed a *yaguareté* that was hunting a kind of wild pig, and from a distance, they noticed how the *yaguareté* embedded its powerful jaws into the pig's head until the pig stopped squealing. And then, the feline tore off the pig's skin and muscle and scattered its innards, acting as if it was selecting the best parts, and all under the endless chatter of parrots and toucans with beaks and feathers so colourful that it looked like they were hand-painted. As if it were a child's mischief to paint them with strokes of colour here and there. And to all the sounds of the jungle joined the constant drumming of the rain. The *yatay* leaves received the rain and projected it to the ground in small cascades, and it was such a wonderful thing to view.

And some miles ahead, an avenue of palms opened for them, palms of such thin trunks that they seemed to be the work of a skilled sculptor, and on their branches hung the *gua'a hovy*, as it was their name in the expressive Guaraní language, beautiful birds flaunting an iridescent blue plumage. And on a fallen trunk, they witnessed two big birds of those called *king vultures* feeding on the remains of an unknown animal; their beaks red, although they could not say if the colour were for the blood from their victim or the natural red on their beaks.

As soon as they sensed the two strangers, the two birds adopted an impressive stance: stopped eating, stood upright with their chests expanded, extended wide their bicolour wings as a shield and a weapon, and cocked their heads as if they were challenging the strangers to make the first move. Werner and Ariel had learned that prudence was the best way to leave the rainforest alive, so they stepped back slowly, moving some yards away from the birds.

Werner decided to make another detour; however, this detour brought them back to the swamp. And they continued, this time soaked to the bones under an intense downpour through the incredible forest, trying to retake their way back to the line of *yatay* that seemed to be put there on purpose by God Himself, like a lighthouse to guide them through, and not be adrift in that endless, stormy, deep green ocean.

WERNER HAD stopped well ahead of Ariel and watched something with curiosity, but when Ariel got nearer, he turned around and stopped him.

"What is it?" Ariel said.

Werner shushed him and signaled a giant bright-coloured frog sitting by the water, enjoying the sunlight, and then, Werner signaled toward another point just a few inches away, where a giant centipede of the arthropod species called Scolopendra, twenty inches long, was creeping toward the frog. The Scolopendra climbed on the back of the frog. At the contact, the frog jumped and fell into the water and revolved, trying to get rid of the ravenous aggressor, but to no avail because the Scolopendra had already embedded its poisonous claws deeply into the frog's back. Yet, the water's motion attracted the curiosity of a *yacaré* that approached fast and cut both frog and Scolopendra in half with a single movement of its jaws. It was then that a swift shadow moved in front of Werner and Ariel's astonished eyes; it was a jaguar.

With an impressive roar, wide opened jaws, and extended claws, the feline jumped on the *yacaré*'s head, but because at that very moment the *yacaré* was turning to grab the other half of the frog that was still floating in the water, the jaguar missed its target and instead buried its fangs deeply into the *yacaré*'s snout. As a reaction to this attack, the *yacaré* shut its jaws, thus holding the jaguar from its jawbone, and in this way, both animals secured themselves in a mortal lock of which no one could escape. Yet, the commotion they caused attracted another *yacaré* that grabbed one of the feline's kicking hind legs, ripped it off from the thigh with great force, the water burst red, and the *yacaré* swam away with the jaguar's hind limb hanging from its jaws. Finally, the *yacaré* holding the bleeding jaguar submerged, and the surface of the swamp came back to be as calm as before as if a tragedy of such a consequence had never taken place.

    Werner and Ariel stood there overwhelmed by nature's show of cruelty, while on the tree branches above them, a family of howler monkeys mourned the incident with a long-lasting wailing cry that surpassed any decibel level ever endured by human ears.

They may have been walking for hours. Although Werner spoke, he seemed to be talking to himself, reflecting, yet aloud, on the past event.

"This is nature," Werner said as if he was trying to convince himself of something beyond his comprehension limits. "Nature is not only fragrant flowers and beautiful butterflies; it's also this constant struggle for survival, and over here, there are no middle terms; either one eats or is eaten."

He felt exhausted after the long forced walk, and he felt dizzy too. Although he had the drive to continue to persist, the effort had been too much for him. Indeed, the heat, humidity, the forced march, the pressure, and the hunger were taking their toll on his weakened body. And he was feeling dizzy because the landscape they were coming through seemed to move in circles. The trees were indeed turning around him. Werner stopped to focus on what was happening. Ariel, too, watched with open mouth how the trees moved, but no trees were moving. Instead, they were the Native dwellers who had returned and had surrounded them once again.

Ariel reacted and ran back to Werner to protect him or protect himself under Werner's wings. Albeit as in their first encounter, the Native people didn't seem to be aggressive. And as he had done the first time they met, the Native man with the belt across his chest came to Werner, and he performed the same ceremony. He smelled Werner and bent over as if he were laughing, a mute laugh, or perhaps it was reverence, a deep reverence, while the others also bowed and followed the movements of the belted Native. And it was at that moment that more Natives came into view. Males and females stood there as if they had come there to witness a miracle. Among the newly arrived people was an older male, thin with the skin of a different cinnamon tone than the others, weathered complexion, muscular, energetic looking, long white hair, and blue eyes.

As soon as this man emerged from the group, Werner stepped back and continued walking backward as if someone were pushing him from his chest until a tree stopped his movement, and his back rested on the trunk. Werner looked startled. The older Native man stared at Werner from head to toe, stepped forwards toward him, kept his gaze fixed on Werner's eyes, and so spoke to him in German:

"You will not talk about this to nobody. To remain here, to live here, was my decision. I wanted to get away from everything, and this is what I will tell you, and you will not repeat it."

And the older Native, who happened to be no other than Baron von Bohlen, alive and living a second life, confessed to Werner what he could not say to any other white man, albeit Werner was the first German expatriate he had spoken to in more than forty years.

While this meeting took place, the Natives embraced together as soccer teams do when penalties define a championship. There was a miracle floating in the air. With his eyes fixed on the scene, Ariel tried to grasp the wonder while Werner and the older Native man whispered to each other in German, and this scene lasted a long time, perhaps twenty minutes or more. Then, the older Native man left Werner, moved toward Ariel, stared him straight in his eyes, sniffed him, and talked to him briefly, again in German, a language Ariel didn't understand.

Ariel could not take his eyes away, as if the older Native man had hypnotized him. The older Native man took Ariel's hand and held it for a moment, and then he hugged Ariel. And Ariel felt peace in his heart and cried while keeping to the older Native man's embrace. The older man kissed Ariel's forehead as if he were his father, then turned toward the others to introduce Ariel to the group. And then again, the group disappeared in a whiff of greenery as if someone had closed a green curtain in a vegetal theatre, signaling the drama's end.

Werner and Ariel stood there alone, lonelier than they had ever felt before.

More hours passed, and it was dark, and the activity became more frantic and mortal, and the mosquitoes began their buzzing of blood, and the birds went to sleep, but not the monkeys, and the jaguars woke up, and the serpents went on to hunt, and both friends walked like sleepwalkers until dawn.

Part Three

It was well into the evening of the next day when Ariel, hungry, thirsty, and exhausted, arrived at the road they had travelled just three days before and near the place where they had left their vehicle. Werner was running late behind him.

Ariel took his coloured American flag striped knapsack, dropped it on the ground, knelt on the road's red clay, and prayed. But then, a large *yararacusú* came sidewinding its way toward him. Ariel saw the poisonous snake and stood up, but then the *yararacusú* stopped in the middle of the road, its forked tongue flickering toward Ariel as if curious of such unappetizing prey, then turned around and went back to the forest, leaving the young man alone in his wait.

"I'm sorry, my friend," Ariel said. "It was not in my plans to alter your trip."

And so it was that Ariel's first words on his way to civilization went to a *yararacusú*.

Time went by, and already Ariel was feeling worried for his friend when Werner came utterly exhausted, his body showing piece by piece from behind the trunk of a *quebracho*, and let himself drop on the red dust of the road before realizing that Ariel was by his side.

"Ah!" Werner exclaimed. And it was this one-syllable word that Werner proffered, his first word on his way to civilization.

The sun was but a blinding disk, and the humidity was unsupportable. A family of spider monkeys was celebrating something among the branches of a mango tree across the road.

And then, sitting in the middle of that road that cut the jungle as a scar, the words came out of Werner's mouth like water from a broken dam.

"That's all that remains of Baron von Bohlen," Werner said, still shaking because of the experience to have seen and spoken to a man he thought to be dead more than forty years ago.

"Nothing about his death was factual. And it was a decision he, Baron von Bohlen, took in a second of his life. He doesn't remember, doesn't want to remember his past life; he has no regrets. Now that I saw him, I can tell you what went through his mind, but I'm speculating on what I knew about him because his life was somehow a public one, a guy spoiled by the media. It was a unique opportunity. He wanted to be free, and he achieved that. To be free of any social ties. Above all, he wanted to be free from his father, an influential figure who molded his son to become his mirror image, notwithstanding the young man's feelings who wanted to pursue different interests. He wanted to be free from his mother, whom he hated because she demanded too much from him. He wanted to be free from the army and the politics attached to the military, and from the system that smothered him, and he wanted to be free of all those fake relationships, like that of his fiancée, whom he never loved but who was demanding a commitment because it was necessary to both families.

"He wanted to be free, and he achieved it. To be free and live a life that destiny put in his road for him to live and that he ended up accepting and enjoying, away from any artificiality that governed his life until the very moment he decided to break free."

Sometime later, the Natives told Baron von Bohlen that the German group found nothing of what they were looking for because during the season the Germans arrived, the river had gone into its subterranean phase and that by then, the shrubs already covered the river bed making it invisible to anybody. The Germans then wandered adrift in the jungle until they found their way back to civilization, returning to Germany to confirm that the diamond deposit information was indeed a legend. And so, they never came back. For the Germans were indeed looking for a river, as three hundred years ago, the Jesuits did without finding it either.

Although this theory had to wait for validation, such a capricious river was the primary reference for finding the diamond deposit. For it was not until Ariel and Werner came that it proved factual. For although the Germans at first considered the exchange of letters between the two Jesuit priests to be no more than gossip, at some point, they decided it was worthy of further investigation. Yet, as it turned out, Ariel and Werner were the lucky ones, only that Werner did not know that the river was a subterranean one that emerged during a specific period and then disappeared through never-explored tunnels underground the jungle. He suspected something like that, but he was not sure about this phenomenon until he arrived at the place.

"The Native dwellers of these territories," Werner continued his recount on the short but substantial conversation he had with Baron von Bohlen, or what remained from him, "followed the expedition since the Germans stepped on their territory. The Natives were the evil who constantly lay in wait for the expedition's every step throughout the jungle. The

Germans marched under the shadows of the trees, followed closely by the Aboriginals. Baron von Bohlen knew that there was a chance that the Native people could accept him, but for this to happen, he had to separate from his comrades. On the other hand, his comrades never suspected of his intentions. He knew how to control himself. Besides, a man of his caliber had to disappear with dignity. A glorious death was the most reasonable action to perform. And thus, to fake a glorious death was not difficult. To die protecting his people from an attack by the Natives could not have been a better idea.

"And so, when they arrived at the sector of the narrow path bordered by the cliff, Baron von Bohlen felt that his moment of glory had arrived. His moment to break the ties he despised. And so, he kept himself in the rearguard, and from that position, he urged his comrades to take shelter, for the Aboriginals were coming to kill them all. Invisible behind the vegetation, the Aboriginals followed the white man's strange behaviour; and they understood what von Bohlen wanted to do. The only thing that affected the Natives was when von Bohlen began to shoot his machine gun. He directed his machine gun to the sky and began shooting like a lunatic. The Natives had never seen a lunatic before. Lunacy is a thing of civilization. Thus, they knew not about the distance the human mind can move through, and so, without even proposing it, the Natives helped Baron von Bohlen, not even knowing why they were doing what they were doing.

"And so, when the gunfire began, they screamed at loud voices, cries that reached the ears of those escaping through the path. The scared German scientists ran faster without even seeing where they were stepping, which was also the moment

the Native guides took advantage to break ties and return
to their homes and kept away from Don Gilberto, of course.
The expedition members continued with their crazy escape,
always feeling the iced breath of death on their backs. And
the shooting stopped, and the cries stopped, but the members
of the expedition continued running, seizing from the shrubs
to stumble down, or seizing from the roots to climb up, and
never stopping to look behind them because none of them
wanted to fall into the Natives' hands."

"Meanwhile, Werner continued, "Baron von Bohlen threw
his weapon down the abyss, took off the Iron Cross, dropped
it at the border of the cliff—although, not in his last breathe
of life as I pictured the event—and went blindly into the
jungle. The Natives found him, of course, and he made
them understand what he wanted to do. Baron von Bohlen
then peeled off his clothes as the serpent shed its skin and
immersed himself in Aboriginal skin. He ceased being a white,
noble European soldier and became an Amazonian Native.
And in the skin of a Native, he lived the life that was in him to
live. And this happened because the Aboriginals adopted him.
And they adopted him because there is nothing more valuable
to a Native, a natural being from the land, than another being
who carries nature within. For what the rainforest does is to
teach us all a person's heart.

"I can see now," Werner pursued on with his relation, mixing
it with his thoughts and conclusions, "although democracy is
a better tool to administer the welfare of the people, it's not a
tool to model their lives. You know how, through propaganda,
those in power model people's thoughts, and in this way,
free expression ceases to exist. Baron von Bohlen disagreed

with those tactics, and they, those in power, knew about his disagreement. Hence, hard times expected him at his return. You may say he was selfish, but you have to consider also that he was seeking his happiness. If happiness is within you, looking for it in a stranger's passion is a mistake."

Werner repeated word by word the last of Baron von Bohlen's sentences, "*We followed you since the girls down there in the river told us that there were strangers in our land. We came back at night and saw the fire and then the jaguars. It was not prudent to come into view because we knew nothing about your intentions. However, I suspected your objective. Please, destroy all the photographs you have from this place. What you have, keep it, and say not a word where you got it. Don't come back here. No one should ever know about this place. And we can see that your friend has a good soul, so it will be a good thing if he can rescue himself. He can live with us in harmony with nature. One of ours has chosen him already, and it will be a great honour to bring him among us.*"

"What?" Ariel said, "Have I been chosen, by whom?"

"I don't know. The Natives are mysterious people, Ariel. Their words may have a different meaning than in our vocabulary."

Chosen by whom, Ariel kept thinking. He remembered the Native girl from the river, and he recalled seeing her coming to him in his dream. She had dropped a diamond in his hand! So it became clear in Ariel's mind that the girl had indeed given him the diamond and that it was a kind of ceremony. And following an impulse, he searched his clothes again, seeking for the lost stone, and there it was in his shirt pocket where he had left it, forgotten. So the shock of a meaning directed to him by nature came back to him in force but not yet well-defined.

And so they both continued sitting on the road's red clay, feeling in their skin the unrelenting, deafening cacophony of the rainforest, for the revelations had overwhelmed them, and now they both mulled on the strange turns of life—

ARIEL FIRSTLY heard the sound, and it came into him because it was different from all the other sounds his ears had become accustomed to already. A murmur seemed to advance through the red clay road, and it was not a natural sound. Neither was it one of the millions from the jungle. Ariel stood upright, visibly worried.

"What's wrong, Ariel?" Werner moved restlessly, trying to stand up, but he felt so tired he could not.

At that moment, as if cut from all other sounds, it came clear to Ariel's ears, the sound of a car engine, and then almost immediately, he saw the dust rising on the road, a signal evident that a vehicle was quickly approaching them. Gathering strength, Ariel grabbed Werner by the armpits and dragged him frantically to move him toward the dense vegetation that edged the road.

"Werner, please move! We have to get out of here, fast!"

Ariel trusted that the bushes would hide them from anybody standing on the road. He was recovering from his effort, dragging Werner away, when the vehicle passed by them at great speed. The driver of that car was, for sure, an expert connoisseur of that road. *Whoever these people are, an encounter with them would be dangerous for us,* thought Werner, but he didn't share his thought with Ariel, who was now on his stomach, his head down to avoid the dust the vehicle raised when it passed. And then it came to him as a strike, that he had left his coloured American flag striped knapsack by the roadside, worried as he was to move Werner away from sight, achieving to do it but in the nick of time as the car passed by the road. The knapsack was so noticeable that Ariel felt the pain in his heart as he knew that the vehicle's occupants could not have missed it. Still slithering like a snake, Ariel approached the road and extended his hand, grabbed the knapsack, and as fast as he could, he went back under the protection of the shrubs. But by then, the vehicle had made an abrupt stop, raised a cloud of red dust, and was reversing at great speed as it passed swiftly by the place where both friends were hiding. With sudden braking, the car stopped at less than a yard down the road from Werner and Ariel, and their hearts beat hard. Again, a large cloud of red dust exploded into the air at the vehicle's sharp braking. Hundreds of birds took flight, their sharp squawking adding to the commotion.

"Oh my, oh my!" Werner said. "I hope they don't have dogs."

The doors of the car opened. There was no barking but voices—voices of people from civilization. Masculine voices. They spoke in a local jargon as if they were rhythmically dragging the words. Their soft accent disturbed Werner, who related it to the regular communication of the worst criminals, those who masked their intentions with that sweet but terrifying modulation characteristic of the underworld from that region. The terror in Ariel and Werner's hearts made the voices of those men surpass the cacophony of the jungle. The men discussed something, which for sure was about Ariel's American flag coloured knapsack. Afterward, the men laughed aloud, and the doors of the vehicle closed—four muffled sounds that sounded ridiculous among the stridency of the rainforest—and the car was again in motion, but only backing up for at least another ten yards, and then, stopped once more.

Two men came out of the vehicle and walked ahead, inspecting the roadside. The car rolled closer behind at low speed. This search went on step by step until the men stopped almost in front of both friends. Ariel and Werner heard every word the men said, although they understood nothing. Ariel hardly recognized a few words; some were in Guaraní, others in Spanish, others in Portuguese. The meaning of whole sentences was obscure to Ariel. Indeed, to a new learner, a non-Native of the region, the lingo those men spoke, a made-up dialect, a random mixture of three languages, without rules, with words linked together at the whim of the speakers, was a difficult thing to understand; and to add to it all the cadences of the accent, it was almost an impossible task.

The doors closed again after some tense moments, and the car sped up, leaving behind the characteristically red cloud. Ariel and Werner remained with their faces close to the ground until a column of red ants reminded them where they were. At that very moment, night came. A night as red as the red dust rising off the road.

Overcoming their terror, both friends decided to come out of their hiding place, and step by step, they approached the road.

"This is the civilization you crave, Werner," Ariel whispered, and it was the voice of the *yararacusú* Ariel had found on the road, and that had turned away as the snake sensed the stranger sitting there.

"These guys must be smugglers," Werner said. "Of everything—people, weapons, liquor, drugs—"

Ariel did not answer. He was pale and hit his head with his fists several times.

"This road leads to another one that leads to the Brazilian border," Werner said, only to say something in his drive to calm Ariel down.

"What else do you know that you haven't told me, Werner? Please don't keep on lying to me."

Werner didn't follow Ariel's question. Instead, he answered his own question. "Yes," Werner said, "there must be a *fazenda* where these guys hide their merchandise. They may even have a clandestine airstrip."

"They may be as well drug dealers," Ariel said.

"It's possible, Ariel. There must be coca plantations around here, hence these guys' presence in this region. They use the rainforest to cover their plantations from vigilance from the air."

"This is absurd," Ariel said. "As soon as we taste civilization, we taste death."

"True!" Werner said. "These people are evil."

"What do we do now?" Ariel kept his voice low and soft, almost whispering.

They were now under the branches of a giant *samu'u*, covered with fragrant flowers.

"We should find the van and get out of here, fast," Werner said.

Shadows came fast. The place looked different now—phantasmagorical, cruel, and deadly. All around were deep shadows, noises, and aromas. Ariel found his lamp and wanted to light it, but Werner stopped him.

"Don't even think of that, Ariel. Light at night is visible from a long distance. Remember what happened down there with the Aboriginal people."

"We have to look for the van in the dark then," Ariel said.

Werner took a handkerchief from his pocket and covered Ariel's lamp.

"There," Werner said. "There will be no reflection now. I guess that you can light it up now, Ariel."

The lamp gave a mean pale light, but it was enough to see around, yet the soft shine attracted all kinds of flying insects that buzzed around them. Werner also lit his lamp, but he put his hat on it to cover it, and so the two friends walked, groping through the bushes as blind people would, grabbing every branch at eye level to check if they were the ones that they cut to cover the van.

"I guess it is to the other side," Ariel said.

"No, Ariel. It's here." But then Werner retracted. "I guess you are right."

They moved again, barely guided by the lamps' mean light whose task it seemed was but to emphasize the shadows. From time to time, they cocked their head toward the road, their ears alert to any abnormal noise, although discriminating any sound over there was an impossible task. Although they didn't talk about it, they both were afraid the bandits could return and see them. It was all black now. The reddish of the night had turned into a deep black. The road, however, seemed to glimmer with a phantasmagoric shining. There was a far roaring, and then another one closer.

"Every cat turns black at night, Ariel," Werner said.

"Not only cats, Werner. The entire geography. Better if we stay here and sleep. Tomorrow in daylight, we will continue."

Werner was chewing a piece of root.

"If we spend the night here, tomorrow there will only be our bones left, Ariel. The ants don't sleep. Besides, I have a horrible hunger. My stomach is consuming me. And I have no pills left to fight the acid."

"Too bad, Werner. In the van, we have food and water. I hope it is still intact."

"It is, Ariel. All the food is in sealed containers. Even with this temperature, it will hold well for two more days."

Ariel didn't answer. Instead, he was silent, standing there with his hand signaling something ahead. Werner got closer to him and looked toward where Ariel was signaling, but the mean light showed nothing.

"What is it, Ariel? C'mon, man. Don't scare me."

"It's here!" Ariel exclaimed. "This is the place where we left the van. Look!"

"I cannot believe it," Werner said.

Then, taking all precautions away, he took his hat from the lantern, and the beam of light came straight to the bushes where he saw parts of the hidden van. Ariel did the same, and both focused their lamps on the car. It seemed impossible for them that someone could be watching the jungle in the darkness for such a long time and from so far away. No. That was sensibly impossible!

THEY SHELTERED themselves inside the van and felt safer, as if the station wagon had turned into a cocoon, protecting them from adversity. And they ate a cold meal, drank cold drinks, and forgot the danger. And they were happy to escape from the mosquitoes and all kinds of other annoying insects, from tiny voracious flies, little beetles, and enormous nocturnal butterflies that covered the windshield and windows of the vehicle.

About these large butterflies, people call *uras*. Werner had heard stories from the Paraguayan folklore about the *uras* depositing their eggs on people's heads. Larvae then develop and feed on the scalp, mostly children. And adding up to the nocturnal show, giant yellow cockroaches crashed against the glass attracted by the lamps' light in the vehicle's interior.

Yet, so protected, Ariel and Werner devoured the salted dry meat, a delicious cold chicken stew, bread, oranges, and plenty of water, and this was their meal. And they enjoyed it because, after all, at sunrise, they would be on their way back to civilization, and so, they relaxed.

Following an impulse, Ariel searched for the vial where he held the diamonds and studied them under the weak light in the car.

But then, at that very moment, the van moved as if pushed by a great force. It was another earthquake. It was intense, forceful, even some large trees fell uprooted by the earthquake, and although the tremor lasted no less than twenty seconds, it didn't stop the deafening orgy of sounds of which they could not escape, as if they were prisoners in a thunderous, pulsating spider web. Once the tremor ended,

Ariel placed the vial on the floor by the clutch pedal in front of him, closed his eyes, and fell asleep, but his sleep was restless, and he woke up after a few minutes.

He was dreaming of a giant spider that was moving closer to him and was already climbing on his shoulder, and in terror, he discovered that it was not a dream, only that there was not a spider on his shoulder but in the windshield, and it was a massive spider! The oversized arachnid moved its hairy legs as if feeling every place before stepping firmly on it. Ariel jumped, scared, and woke up Werner. The spider explored the alien surface of the glass.

"It's a tarantula!" Ariel exclaimed, although his voice almost lost with the scare.

"No, it's not a tarantula, Ariel. It's a wandering spider!"

"It looks like a tarantula to me!"

"It's a wandering spider. This kind of spider is very poisonous," Werner said. "They are nocturnal. It's hunting!"

And so, both friends followed the movement of the spider that moved as if it were dancing. At some moment, the spider raised its frontal limbs and stood there, with its frontal limbs in high as it seemed to be the spider's natural response to a threat. As if the spider had noticed them, although it was, for them, the spider, the true menace. It was a terrifying sight but magnificent as well. Ariel blessed the protection the glass gave them. After a while, the wandering spider disappeared into the shadows. Werner put his lamp off, set the back of his seat in a flat position, and closed his eyes. Ariel followed his example, but yet again, startled, he woke. Werner was also awake. They heard a thump on the roof of the vehicle as if something heavy had fallen over the van. And they were curious about it, but none of them wanted to get out of the cabin, so they waited.

Not long after that, they saw an enormous boa constrictor slithering on the windshield. Werner and Ariel watched the giant serpent move slowly down as if they were sitting in a tri-dimensional theatre watching wild scenes from the front line. The long white belly of the snake moved at an exasperating slowness. Once the serpent went out of sight, they closed their eyes and slept.

And so, both friends rested, at least for a while, but it was not comfortable at all. Still, they were safe from the darkness and the dwellers of shadows. It was dark indeed, the landscape. The rainforest was still in shadows, but one could see some bright spots here and there, as the sunlight was already hitting the treetops, and the light was cascading down leaf by leaf. It was such a wonderful thing to see.

Then at a certain point already nearing sunrise, Werner, who could not sleep at all, heard a vehicle's noise coming on the road. He sat with his back erect, trying to identify the sound, but it was impossible. *It must be my imagination*, Werner thought. But because he was already fully awake, he decided to get ready for the return trip. To the light of his lamp, and for one more time, Werner contemplated and counted the diamonds. Then he put the vial back in a secret pocket inside his trousers by his crotch, and he sighed in relief, for he felt the diamonds would be safer there. Yet, his movements caused Ariel to wake up.

"I had had a bad dream," Ariel said.

"How bad?"

"A premonitory one. Like a warning."

"Oh c'mon, Ariel. Stop being so dark."

Without answering, Ariel opened the glove compartment, took a small copybook and a pen, opened it, wrote a number on a page, ripped it out, and gave Werner the piece of paper.

"What is it?" Werner asked, reading the number.

"This number is where we can reach María Rosa just in case she doesn't answer her telephone."

"I have her number."

"Just in case she doesn't answer the number you have, Werner! Say, in case of an emergency."

"Shouldn't be any, Ariel. Why?"

"What time is it?" Ariel said instead.

"It's already six, Ariel."

"So let's hit the road, Werner,"

"Okay. Let's go now," Werner put the paper in his shirt pocket.

"Okay. Just let me take a leak—"

Ariel opened the car door, and when he did, the point of his shoe touched the tube with diamonds, and it dropped onto the ground.

"Ah!" Ariel said. "Imagine if I lose my diamonds after all the sacrifice I went through!"

Ariel bent down to pick up the vial and wanted to drop it inside the car, but instead, he carried it, and because of the urgency, he left it leaning against the left front tire and hurried a couple of steps away to pee by a *yatay*.

Werner was getting ready for the journey back to Asunción as soon as Ariel returned, and so he had already secured the seat belt when he ogled a shadow standing outside the vehicle by his side. Startled, and as in an impulse, Werner opened the door, and there was in front of him a lanky, tall, unknown man elegantly dressed and wearing a black hat. Both men stared at each other with curiosity, but Werner was startled to find that strange man there. The man did not smile. Werner sensed the danger sitting in the man's cold eyes, turned his head to look for Ariel, and saw him coming toward the car accompanied by another man. A cold sweat ran through Werner's spine.

"*Vaya, vaya, vaya,*" The man with the black hat said, "*¿O qué coisa bonitinha é o que temos por aquí, che'raá? Dois mitacuñamí sozinhas.*"—Well, well, well. What a beautiful thing do we have here, eh, my friend? Two lonely virgin young girls.

The man spoke with a soft, languorous accent, uttering every word slowly as if he had a hard time pronouncing it. In his speech, he mixed words from Spanish, Portuguese, and Guaraní. He looked totally out of place there, dressed in elegantly expensive clothes. He wore a distinctive black felt hat, an extravagant accessory to wear in the rainforest, and to match it all, a heavy Rolex gold watch shone on his left wrist.

"*¿O karaí está perdido?*" The other man said with the same mellifluous tone of his partner.

This man was of athletic build. One could see that he was muscular and younger, at least Ariel's age, but obviously with a different upbringing. When this man spoke, he showed an upper and lower line of gold teeth. Werner looked at this man. *A boxer,* he thought, *a heavyweight boxer.* And he wondered how many of them were out there, waiting on the road. Possibly three or four. The other men were undoubtedly in the vehicle waiting for the news the two men would bring to them. *Are these men the same whose car we saw yesterday?* Werner asked himself. *Yes, it is probable. Very probable.*

"No," Werner said in Spanish after taking time to understand the meaning of the man's words. Even though, and given the circumstances, Werner spoke with a voice that was not his own. His accent became heavier. "We're not lost. We were resting. We spent the night here."

"*Vocé é un Americano,*" the man wearing the black hat said. He was stating a fact.

"No," Werner said, "I'm not American. I'm German."

"*Alemão,*" The man in the black hat said, as it was for him a difficult task to understand this.

"I'm from here!" Ariel intervened even though no one had asked him anything, but he was annoyed, feeling shunned from the conversation.

The man with the gold teeth looked at Ariel from head to toe, and then the man looked at his partner, and both men exploded in a loud laugh, but there was nothing warm in that laugh. Ariel and Werner's eyes met.

"*¿Mbaei'chapá, che'raa?*" The man with the gold teeth said.

Ariel looked at both unknown men with contempt. Werner remained silent, thinking of ways to escape that trap. He was worried.

"*¿Reñe'êkuaápa la guaraníme, chera'a?*"—Do you speak Guaraní, my friend?—the man with the black hat asked.

If Ariel responded in Guaraní, then it could be that the thugs would consider him a friend. But Ariel didn't answer. Instead, he just stood there and bit his lips.

"What can we do for you, gentlemen?" Werner intervened, even though no one asked him to intervene. It was a risky interruption.

Both men turned to look at Werner with attention. It was as if both men were acting on cue yet not deciding what to do next. Werner cursed himself. *How is it that we let ourselves fall into this trap?* He thought. Werner could not console himself for what Werner considered his fault. He knew they were in hostile territory. He had heard their voices and their words the day before when the bandits searched for Ariel's knapsack. Werner guessed right on their activities. They were soulless criminals of the worst kind.

"*¿E que é o seu negocio por aqui, karaí alemão?*" The man with the gold teeth said.

Werner took the time of his life to understand the meaning of the man's words.

"We're scientists," Werner finally said. "I'm a doctor. Mister Gimmel is my assistant. We are studying flora and fauna of the region."

"*¿O qué?*" The man with the black hat said.

"The plants and the animals," Ariel said.

The man with the gold teeth turned around and stared at Ariel as if Ariel was a kind of insect—a cricket singing a sad tune. Then he looked at the van.

"*¿E este o seu carrinho?*" He said, as if with revulsion, yet addressing no one in particular.

"No," Ariel said, "It's not our car. We rent it."

The man with the gold teeth again turned to stare at Ariel, as if each time Ariel mutated into a different kind of insect.

"It has an excellent engine," Ariel said again as if his innocence pushed him to barter their lives for the car.

The man with the gold teeth stared at Ariel. To him, Ariel, the insect, was now stuck in cardboard, his body pierced by a needle, his skinny legs moving frantically, trying to escape.

The man ignored Ariel. He had his hands extended on the van's hood and focused on a family of *kaí* disputing a blooming *quebracho* branch and spat. After some seconds of shrieking, the little monkeys disappeared among the leaves of the tree. The man with the black hat stared at Werner as if wondering what to do with him.

A horn resounded in the forest. As impossible as it was, the obnoxious artificial sound reverberated for a long time as if it were hitting every tree in the woods. Werner crossed his fingers and thought to ask for help, but from who?

"*Você dotor, venha conosco,*"—You doctor, come with us!—the man with the black hat said and stepped on toward Werner.

Werner attempted to step back, and he could not do it because, in just one movement, the thug held him from his right arm and twisted it. Werner was so bewildered that he could not defend himself. Ariel was moving forwards to help Werner, but the man with the gold teeth shoved him back with both his hands open and pressed against Ariel's chest. Ariel stepped back and decided to calm down. Having overpowered Werner, the man with the black hat took the camera and the binoculars from Werner's neck and threw them into the van.

"*Você não vai precissar desta porcaria, dotor!*"—You will not need this shit, doctor!—the thug said.

The man with the black hat pushed Werner toward the road. However, the reluctant Werner stopped and turned around to see if Ariel was still there but could not see anything because he had already walked around the trunk of a *yatay* and the enormous palm tree blocked his view. The man with the black hat gave him another push in his back, and Werner went on.

On the road sat a mid-gray painted Land Rover 110 Defender V8 County Station Wagon, the exact car they saw the night before, a well-appointed expensive off-road vehicle fit for twelve passengers, probably the last model of its series. Werner lost any hope and began sweating. There were four men inside the Land Rover. One was sitting at the wheel, the other by the driver's side, and the other two in the back seat. Behind them, two empty rows of seats faced each other.

Leaving Werner standing on the road, the man with the black hat climbed in and closed the door.

Standing there, his head down, his hands on his back, Werner felt like an accused man waiting for a verdict. Around him, the indifferent rainforest vibrated with the most incredible sounds. Finally, after a while, the jury seemed to have made a decision. One of the men sitting in the back seat jumped out of the vehicle and held the door open. The other men remained in their places inside the Land Rover.

"*Suba, dotor,*" the man holding the door open said. "*Vamos a precisar dos seus servicios.*"—Get in, doctor, we're going to need your help.

Werner turned his head to see if Ariel was coming, but all of what he could see was the road and the vegetation.

"*Suba, dotor.*" This time the man at the wheel spoke. The same accent. The same resigned calm in his manners.

"What do you need?" Werner said, showing his bad humour. It was enough for him. "If you have someone sick among your partners, I don't have any problem seeing him, although I could not be of much help. I have a doctorate, but I'm not a physician, if you see what I mean. Besides, I need my assistant—"

"*Suba, dotor,*" the man with the black hat said.

Werner watched at him and said nothing. The other men stared at Werner, but their gaze pierced through as if Werner were not there, as if he already did not exist. But Werner didn't want these men to see that he was afraid of them. After all, he was a representative of people famous for, among other many things, their arrogance. Yet, his innocence rather than his arrogance motivated the action he sought to impose on those men.

"I will go," Werner said. "But I want to be sure that my assistant will follow us in our vehicle."

"*Suba, dotor,*" the man holding the door said, and forgetting his manners, pushed Werner inside the vehicle and then sat by his side, sandwiching Werner between him and his partner.

The man closed the door, and the driver put the Land Rover in gear and accelerated, leaving behind the irreverent red cloud of dust. The man with the black hat stayed on the road until the red cloud dimmed over the treetops. Then he returned to the place where the man with the gold teeth kept watch of Ariel.

Ariel heard neither the sound of the doors closing nor the sound of the engine starting. At that moment, nothing overcame the sound of the forest and his heart. He was alone there with that strange man. A bandit, for sure. He didn't know who these men were nor what their intentions were. He suspected they were smugglers, but they could also be drug dealers. Criminals anyway.

It is a good thing they haven't found the diamonds, thought Ariel. He looked toward the vial that contained his diamonds. There it was, still reclined by the left front tire of the van as he had left it just minutes ago. Yet, at the exact moment of his thought, a curious ray of light hit the vial, and the stones sparkled. Ariel wanted to move and grab the vial and insert it in his body, the way Werner told him, once, the diamond miners in South Africa used to steal the stones. Either this information was true or false, or another of Werner's sarcastic comments.

Nevertheless, given the circumstances, he decided not to do so. But the vial with the diamonds was still there, scintillating under the sun rays. And then he wanted to cover the vial with his foot, but his watcher could see his movement and find the diamonds, and that would become a worse situation. Moreover, it had been by chance that the vial had fallen onto the ground just seconds before the strangers came.

The man with the black hat came back and talked to the man with the gold teeth. Both men conversed for a long while and ignored Ariel, who stood there, not knowing what to do. Then the man with the gold teeth went to the van. He opened the doors, started the engine, and checked the gas needle. Then he went to the back, saw the jerry can and the hose, unscrewed it, sniffed it, and shook it a little. Satisfied, he took the clear plastic hose, inserted it in the jerry can, took the other end to the gas tank, unscrewed the tank tap, blew into the hose, and placed the hose inside the gas tank. Gas from the jerry can flowed into the gas tank.

While the clear plastic hose did its work, both thugs began removing everything from the vehicle. They tossed away the knapsacks, the food containers with the food leftovers, the photo cameras, the canteens with water, the binoculars, and the garments. They didn't stop to check for valuables or something that could be valuable for them. Everything just went out and began piling up on the ground.

Their action reminded Ariel of that of the soldiers. However, the thugs were more careless. Ariel stood there watching them. He could have easily escaped if he wanted to do so because by just moving inside the forest a few steps, he would have lost them forever. Those men would have never followed him through the woods, but Ariel thought that the men could take revenge on Werner and kill him if Ariel escaped. Therefore, he stood there and hoped—he hoped as he who having betted all his savings to just one number hopes, while the roulette wheel turns and turns—

MEANWHILE IN Asunción, María Rosa Martinez worried for her friends. She had had no news from them since they began their adventure, and it had been already five days. María Rosa was attentive to Werner's messages, but the days had gone by, and she had no word from her friends. In the deep of her heart, she hoped that Werner had found the diamonds and that he was by now safe somewhere, ready to call her. But the call never came, and she was distraught.

María Rosa knew the place was dangerous as her attempts to contact the guerrilla, Clarisa among them, had gone unanswered. She knew that her comrades—full of activity as they were, with their own skirmishes against the military, yet not far from her friends' whereabouts—were not interested in looking for them. And María Rosa knew never to contact the police. She knew this well.

And so, her only support, paradoxically as per her revolutionary ideas, would be someone from the government, a higher-ranked politician, or military, perhaps. Still, she was reticent to raise the alarm, for she knew as well that Werner would oppose to her doing so. For she knew that Werner was a prudent man, although her concern also included Werner's health, and she trusted that Ariel would take care of him as Ariel himself promised her he would do. To María Rosa, Werner was a capable man whom any country would have been proud to have among its citizens so that Werner could enjoy citizenship and a pension, under the condition that he delivered his strategic knowledge, which could be of use in government programs for the country's advancement.

However, her efforts had been fruitless, mainly because Werner's opposition disliked the idea of María Rosa's involvement in his private affairs.

Albeit, the absence of news from Werner motivated her to request a private reunion with Senator Orozco, a professional politician—if such an animal ever existed—a man of influence, a Catholic, and a man she loathed. Anyhow, Senator Orozco had no scruples. He openly harassed women—a womanizer he would describe himself with pride. Yet, lately, as per his constant visit to the party headquarters, he had noticed María Rosa and had directed his flirting interest to her. And she had no defence but to smile, which had sent the wrong message to the man. Still, an influential chieftain, and a close friend to the president, was essential to María Rosa's clandestine activities. *In vino veritas*, the Romans said. *Wine brings the truth.* Yet, lust brings the facts faster. She thought she could obtain some vital information from the senator. She thought she could exploit the senator's sexual appetite, but she did not have the guts to proceed. It was all but her fantasy to submit a powerful man to her whims.

On the other hand, the senator, like any other high-ranked officer of the supreme government, felt his duty to hold audiences—not too often though—with low-ranked officers of his government. Senator Orozco wanted to know what the people's concerns were—not that he was, on the whole, interested in doing something to solve these concerns. But in doing so, Senator Orozco wanted to show his comrades in the party how human he was. Although in María Rosa's case, he knew as per her solitude open on his desk, it was a concern of a personal character. Still, because she was an attractive woman and a loyal party member with no red annotations on her dossier, he, Senator Orozco, acceded to receive her in his office.

"I appreciate you receiving me, Senator."

"What can I do for you, María Rosa?"

María Rosa explained the motive of her visit and her concern for both her friends.

"Mr. Werner, Senator," she explained, "is a friend of mine, a German citizen, a tourist, and a botanical scholar like Bertoni—Moisés Bertoni, the famous Swiss naturalist who devoted his life to the study of nature, mainly in Paraguay. He went on a trip of study to Amambay. On his trek, Mr. Werner took a young man named Ariel Gimmel with him as an assistant. Possibly, they went into the mountains to study the flora of the rainforest. But, lamentably, Senator, both men have failed to return on the agreed date."

The Senator scribbled some notes in his notepad. Impulsively, María Rosa leaned over the desk to see what he was writing. The Senator stopped his writing, and now there was a lascivious glow parked in his pupils, staring at her cleavage.

María Rosa blushed. She could see that the Senator thought her movement was intentionally inviting.

"I am afraid that an accident may have happened to them, Senator Orozco," María Rosa said as if excusing herself from her impertinence.

Her trembling, supplicating lips bewitched the Senator.

"That is a dangerous zone where your friends went, María Rosa," the Senator said, enjoying the spell. "Guerrilla Communists are operating in that area."

"I thought we already eradicated them, Senator."

"Still, some minor groups remain. But we are working on them."

"Well. We will succeed, Senator."

"We will, María Rosa. We will. There is no other way."

"And of my friends, Senator?"

"Ah! I will see to that, María Rosa. But I cannot promise you anything, you know? We have other priorities."

"I understand, Senator."

"People should be more responsible where they are going, don't you think so, María Rosa?"

"You are quite right, Senator . . ."

The Senator stood up, and María Rosa understood that the interview had finished. She also stood, and getting closer to the desk, extended her hand.

"Thank you, Senator. I appreciate your help."

Senator Orozco clasped María Rosa's hand, and the force in the man's hand—it was an intentional motion—made her bend over the desk, and so, Senator Orozco again ogled lasciviously into her cleavage, and although María Rosa felt a flush of panic, she managed to smile. General Orozco reciprocated the smile—the snake smiling to the mouse. And then he walked around the desk, put her right hand on her lower back, and softly pushed her to the door.

But before opening it, he placed himself behind her and, with his hands under her armpits, fondled her breasts, and at the same time, brought his mouth to her ear and whispered, "One problem has two solutions, my dear."

María Rosa felt humiliated, but for the love of her friends, again she managed to turn around, smiled—a pale smile—and then stepped out. Senator Orozco closed the door after her, and then he sat at his desk, caressed his chin with his right hand, smiled to a promise of a forthcoming satisfaction, inhaled the feminine scent still lingering in the room, leaned on the interphone, and pressed a button.

Disturbed, María Rosa went to her car. Inside, without starting the engine, she stood there in the visitor's parking area, breathing agitatedly. She wondered if there was an exit to her problem, for she knew that by trying to solve one problem, she had fallen into another, conclusively, a bigger one. And if no is no and yes is yes, what is then a pale smile as a response to the brutal sexual harassment she suffered? *Close your eyes and empty your thoughts, just for the duration of it. The pain will be sharp, but it will pass, and then there will be peace,* she was quoting Joan of Arc, sentenced to death by burning at the stake and later sanctified. But she was not such a saint. *Like in medieval times,* she said to herself but dismissed the thought and started the engine.

And yet, there will always be medieval times for some women. There will always be stakes burning, haunting fire seeking their bodies—

CAPRICIOUS RIVER

THE LAND Rover moved at great speed. The driver was an expert steering the vehicle with such haste on that narrow and deteriorated road. Werner wanted to turn his head to look if Ariel was following behind, but he could not do it, for the two men at each side of him barely allowed him to breathe, least of all to turn around and look. And even if he could have managed to turn around, he could have seen nothing because of the red dust hovering behind the vehicle. Werner wondered how the driver would have done so when he faced the giant sinkhole, the geological event, which was now miles away, and that had so much scared both Werner and Ariel. *I guess this guy never pushes the brakes,* thought Werner. It was possible. The Land Rover 110 was suitable for that kind of terrain, and the driver seemed to be a fearless master, driving through that impossible road.

"Where are we going?" Werner dared to ask.

None of the men answered. Werner thought that if they wanted him dead, he would be dead already. *They need me for something, perhaps ransom,* he thought. But that was crazy. There was no way those men would get some money in exchange for him from anybody anywhere. Werner thought of Ariel and wished fervently that the kid was okay. Ariel was his responsibility. Werner saw him so enthusiastic to accomplish anything possible. And Werner regretted to have motivated him to accompany him without alerting the young man about the real dangers, which were not in the jungle but the civilization. *What civilization?* Werner cursed himself. *These criminals are the product of evolution,* he thought. It's what we have accomplished in millions of years of development, the creation of criminals. And we are in their hands like goats in the hands of the slaughterer. The bandits were silent. The situation was surreal. *It must be a dream,* Werner said to himself. *Where is Ariel? Perhaps he is in another dream. A deeper one, maybe.* The journey was monotonous, and Werner began to doze, his head nodding.

There was a crossroads. The driver took the one road to his right, and nothing changed for some time. Yet, to change the mood, the driver put on the radio and listened to music. It was an excellent rhythmic selection. Then the music stopped, and there were some ads, and then the news. Werner was fully awake now. Because of the radio and the information, he knew what time it was. Eight in the morning already. He felt hungry. The thugs at his side moved and bent over toward the front of the vehicle. Something on the news called their attention. The broadcaster was speaking in clear Spanish, and Werner understood what was happening. There had been another skirmish between an army patrol and a column of *guerrilleros*. The guerrilla men seemed to be well-trained and armed. There were several casualties among the soldiers.

"*¡Ah, caralho!*" the driver said. "*¡Kurapepê guerrillero Comunista hina, canalhas de mierda vão a remover o nido de vespas!*"—Oh, fuck! Here they are, the Communist guerrilla men, fucking bandits, they are going to stir the wasps' nest!

His partners said nothing. They were, perhaps, thinking about the same thing. *What do these guys think?* Werner wondered. And if so, in what language do they do this?

Werner had mixed feelings; if he fell in the guerrilla men's hands, he could have more chances than if he continued in the bandits' hands. The guerrillas were, after all, leftist politicians who were trying to install a new order, a revolution. Their enemies were the soldiers, servants of the repressive apparatus of the state. The guerrilla men would not harm Werner, a member of the people, because it was for the people. They were fighting their war. But the guerrilla men could as well hold Werner and force him to work for the revolution or ask for a ransom for his freedom; for to the guerrilla men, Werner was a bourgeois, hence, an enemy of the guerrilla movement.

On the other hand, to the ruffians, everybody was their enemy. A bandit does not have a flag. Neither did they have a cause because it was all about their welfare. Money and that was it. And this was why the best allies of any revolution were the outlaws, and yet, although they could pass as children of the oppressed, they had no interest in any class struggle. Neither were they, Robin Hood, stealing from the rich to give to the poor. Instead, their goal lay in finding ways of getting rich fast without suffering any harm. And so, in this ludicrous *ménage à trois*, Werner's best option was the soldiers, and the soldiers only.

Beyond the clouds, a plane was turning high up in the sky. It was a shining silvered point in the luminous sky. Then, all of a sudden, the aircraft came near. It was a warplane, an impressively small, delicate, powerful, mortal contraption. It came very low and slow, as if the pilot had decided to land just there, but then accelerated and disappeared in the bright sky in a second. The sound of the engine remained for a long time echoing inside the vehicle. The thugs moved in their seats, trying to locate the warplane, exchanged looks, and said nothing. The journey continued.

The lack of a decent conversation, the sugary music on the radio, the road, the landscape, and his thoughts increased Werner's exhaustion. And it all became torture. He was hungry, thirsty, and wanted to pee. He moved restlessly in his seat. The two men who oppressed him turned their heads to watch him. One of them elbowed him. It was a nasty hit.

"*Tranquilo, dotor,*" the man said.

The driver looked by the rear mirror, and Werner could see the man's eyes. They were small, clear, and hardened like diamonds. *What a strange thing,* Werner thought.

"*¿Qué é o que acontece, dotor?*" The driver said.

"I want to pee," Werner said.

The driver steered the Land Rover to the roadside and pushed the brakes. The thug by Werner's side opened the door and stepped out. Werner got out behind him, and he went to pee on a bush. The urine flow upset a family of bluish rats of significant size that escaped from under the bush and crossed the road, uttering short shrieks of protest. Werner felt mortified. With his head down, he climbed back into the vehicle. The thug followed him, closed the door, and told his partners about Werner's experience with the rats with a broad smile. The bandits let out a loud hearty laugh. Werner understood they were laughing at him and felt more embarrassed. As a slight relief for him, the vehicle sped up.

"*¿Qué alívio, eh dotor?*"—Feeling better, doctor?—the driver said, smiling slyly.

Werner didn't answer and kept his head low. The rainforest opened and widened, changing to rolling hills, cattle farms, and plantation after plantation. Then the road ended in a crossroads, and to one side was another rural way, and to the other was a wider highway with more traffic. Werner felt better, although he knew not why. The sun was now on his right. *We are going to the Brazilian border,* he said to himself.

The highway began a steep descent, and after that, a sharp curve followed. Blooming natural gardens covered this part of the road on both sides. The driver managed the angle at full speed and then braked abruptly. And because of the inertia, the car tilted sideways, but the Land Rover, built to afford these types of demands, balanced and kept rolling strong. Yet, just passing a curve, there was a roadblock about twenty metres ahead. The soldiers had placed a military truck across the road. The driver changed gears, made a U-turn, the tires screeched, the Land Rover gained momentum, but then again, the driver slammed on the brakes. While the driver was maneuvring, the soldiers had thrown a spike strip across the road. Then, they approached the vehicle from behind the trees. One of them was pointing a machine gun at the driver's face.

"Negative!" the soldier holding the machine gun commanded. "Keep moving ahead!"

There was another soldier by the side of the road holding a radio device. Werner saw the uniforms and felt relieved. The soldier with the machine gun stood alert by the side road. With one hand, the soldier held the machine gun and, with the other, signaled ahead. No jokes, no games here. The driver switched to the rear gear, the vehicle pulled back, turned around, and moved forwards. The military truck's tires crushed flowers, snails, and frogs, backing up to make room for the Land Rover to pass, then moving back again, blocking the road.

"¡*Caralho! ¡Estamos jodidos!*"—Fuck! We're in a big shit!— the driver said, and no one else uttered a word.

The Land Rover rolled at low speed. They were now behind a line of automobiles and heavy trucks, and Werner felt even better. *The more people, the better*, he thought. The vehicles were gradually rolling. Three army trucks were visible, parked at the side of the road. A long line of all sorts of cars waited under the fierce sun. Then, up in the sky, the warplane came out in sight again, and the thunder of its engine followed it up close. The warplane made a long curve and passed through, almost skimming the treetops. The pilot seemed to be enjoying a great time. After this show, the warplane disappeared again.

The magic of war machines, Werner said to himself. The coming and going of the warplane caused a hypnotic effect, and it seemed to Werner that all—the bandits, the soldiers, the entire landscape—fell into a vacuum in space-time. He felt as if he was floating in space, and that time had stopped as if Werner had dissociated himself from his body, but soon he recovered. He understood that all those feelings were but a product of the pressure that he was in. And he thought of his recent experience with the soldiers. But by then, Ariel was at his side. He missed his young friend so much. *The best thing*, Werner thought, *is that the bandits are now in a trap.*

But of course, the bandits were no match for the soldiers. However, once again, his impulsive character betrayed him; it did as he could not contain a smile, a broad, scornful smile that relieved the pain in his heart and the pressure in his mind. The driver, though, noticed the smile through the rear mirror.

"*¿M'bae la vy'a che, dotor?*"—Are you feeling happy, doctor?—the man said.

Werner didn't understand what the man said but felt the diamond eyes' cold carats all over him. The man by Werner's side gave him another vicious elbowing, and Werner struggled to breathe. The pain in his chest was piercing, but as a relief to him, the vehicle came to a stop.

"No one gets out!" An officer with a megaphone was directing the line of cars. "Keep yourselves inside your vehicles!"

The soldiers were checking everybody's documents in the neighbourhood. In doing so, they were quickly moving forwards toward the Land Rover 110. A group of peasants was eating and drinking in the bed of one light pick-up, and Werner remembered how hungry and thirsty he was.

"*Estos mbore ainda procuram pelo Che Guevara.*"—These assholes are still looking for Che Guevara—one of the thugs said.

And upon hearing this sarcastic comment, the others thugs chuckled. The observation was sarcastic because it portrayed the military as idiots, seeking a man who had already been dead for sixteen years to the date.

The mix of languages and the accent continued to impress Werner, who sat there seized by deep sorrow, thinking of Ariel's destiny. Yet, still oblivious of Werner's mood, the man by Werner's left side bent over and said something in the driver's ear. The driver sought under his seat and gave Werner a well-worn, wide-brimmed straw hat of the peasants' type.

"*Akávo é para o senhor dotor, póngaselo, não fale, e quédese tranquilo.*"—This hat is for you, doctor. Put it on and keep quiet.

Werner didn't understand what the man said, but the gesture was enough. He took the hat and put it on. The men at each side of Werner moved to make room for the hat. They made no comments.

A soldier got closer to the Land Rover but kept his distance, his weapon at the ready. Then a young lieutenant approached, followed by three soldiers coming from the other side of the field. The soldiers had their guns trained at the occupants of all vehicles detained there. The young lieutenant checked the papers and consulted with two assistants. He was the one with the megaphone, and from time to time, he spoke through it with a commanding, stentorious voice.

"Listen, folks!" he said, addressing everybody. "Keep yourselves in your cars. Don't come out. Have your hands visible and your pieces of identification ready."

Some soldiers ran to one side where there was obvious trouble. The echo of gunshots increased the tension of the moment. People screamed. The young lieutenant stood there by the line of cars as if nothing happened. The shooting continued intermittently. The shooting seemed to be taking place a mile or so away in a nearby forest.

Then a military jeep came by, and a group of people got out. Werner saw two women who came with their hands tied behind their backs. *Oh, fuck!* Werner thought, *they got Clarisa!* He gulped. Two soldiers walked behind the two women. The group went to a tent that Werner had not noticed before. Getting closer, Werner saw with relief that they were not the women he thought they could be, but instead, two skinny men with long hair hanging onto their shoulders. Though they looked emaciated, skin and bones, they had a rough and dangerous aura.

Werner breathed, alleviated. None of the women they had found down the road who helped them change the flat tire were there. The group passed, and the driver in the Land Rover spat outside the window but said nothing because by then, a high-ranked army officer followed by his assistant was coming toward the vehicle. The driver's eyes followed the high-ranked army officer's every movement.

"*Emañamí, ch'amigo*," the driver said to his partners with a smirk. "*Ape um coronel está vindo oñangorekóta nde membykuéra*"—Look, my friends. A colonel is coming here to take care of his little ones.

No one commented on anything. Instead, the bandits followed the colonel's movements.

"Documents where I can see them. Hands too!" the colonel commanded.

"*¡Pé'ina nde tavyraí!*"—Here, idiot!—whispered the driver to himself and took his weapon from under the seat.

The thug sitting by the driver's side put his hand on the driver's wrist and pressed it down, holding it there. The driver looked at his partner. Both pairs of eyes locked in a silent battle of wills. Without breaking the gaze, his partner shook his head. The colonel was about ten steps away by then. His voice broke the spell, and the partner released the driver's hand holding the weapon.

"Open all doors!" the colonel commanded. "Keep seated! Don't get out! Keep your hands where I can see them! No sudden movements!"

The colonel, as the lieutenant with the megaphone, had a strong, commanding voice.

"*Mbareté la che coronel, hína,*"—My colonel is a fucking bully—the thug seated by the driver's side said as if he were spitting the words.

The driver looked through the rear mirrors and saw two more soldiers strategically positioned behind the vehicle with their weapons at the ready. He had not seen the soldiers there before. However, as if he wanted to test the colonel's authority, the man sitting by Werner's side opened the door and got out of the vehicle; the soldier stared at him and said nothing. The thug thought of the soldier's reaction as weakness and stepped forwards.

"*¿Mbae pikó' la nde'porte che sargento?*"—Hi, how are you, my sergeant?—said the thug, addressing the private as if he were a ranked sergeant.

The private ignored him.

"*Ñembotagüí la kuimba'e, hína,*"—Fucking stupid toy soldier—the thug said to his partners, turning back to the Land Rover 110 and climbing in.

They all laughed mockingly.

The colonel didn't notice the thug's action because, at that very moment, the warplane came back again, flying low. The colonel turned around and paid full attention to the warplane, and his eyes followed it until it disappeared into the shining sky. Perhaps the colonel thought that he had pursued the wrong career; that he should have graduated from the Air Force instead, and that he could have become that pilot over there, protected in his flying machine, amazing the viewers with his pirouettes, and enjoying the view from above—

BACK IN the rainforest, the thug with the gold teeth removed the clear plastic hose from the gas tank. He shook it, screwed the tap on the gas tank, tossed the hose back into the vehicle, and closed the lid on the jerry can. Then he closed the back door, sat at the wheel, turned the start key on, and the engine responded with a soft purring. A ray of light hit the mouth of the man, and the gold teeth shone. The man with the black hat raised his hand and gave him a thumb up. Satisfied, the thug with the gold teeth pressed the clutch pedal, moved the gear stick into reverse, and the car slowly rolled back, its tires crushing the snails, the leaves, the caterpillars, the flowers, the roots, and the entire rainforest. The car disappeared behind the same *yatay* that had hidden Ariel from Werner's eyes some minutes ago.

The thug with the black hat stood among the blooming *quebrachos,* his attention set on something shining in the grass in the space where the car was. The man reacted as if a stone had hit him. He slapped his forehead, moved forwards, leaned over, and grabbed the vial. He took it at eye level and shook it; the diamonds sparkled in the sunlight. Then the man turned around, took a revolver from his pocket, and aimed it at Ariel standing there frozen by panic.

"¡*Ay ch'rang'aa!*" the thug exclaimed. "¡*Añeteté a lenda había sido, caralho!*"—Aye, my dear, the fucking legend happens to be true!

And with loud cries, he summoned his partner back on the road, supposedly waiting for him inside the vehicle.

T HE COLONEL had not yet turned his sight toward the Land Rover. He was still watching the way the warplane had gone, and now he was talking on a radio held by his assistant.

"*I'vaí la situación, ch'amigo,*"—We are in a shitty situation, my friends—the driver said.

"*Não ten nada que temer, ch'amigo,*" the man sitting at the right of Werner said. "*Não é a nosotros aos que eles procuram. Ape kuimba'e están buscando Comunistas. Enemigo del gobierno, hína.*"—There is nothing to be afraid of, my friends. The soldiers here are looking for Communists—enemies of the government.

"So it is," Werner said, although no one had asked him anything. "Guerrilla guys."

"*Yahá, entonce lo yaguá, hína,*"—Let's move ahead then, my friends—said the same thug, as if Werner were his buddy. "*Nosotro não tenemo nada que ver.*"—We have nothing to do with this thing.

The conversation stopped as fast as it had begun, for the colonel was now coming directly toward them. From his uncomfortable position, Werner paid full attention to what was going on around him. His eyes, as well as his ears, were restless. He knew that a situation like this could not extend for long. Sooner or later, something was going to happen. The soldiers had, for sure, identified the bandits already. However, Werner also knew that the bandits were crazy enough not to hesitate to start a shootout, which might turn out to become a massacre to make a way to escape the situation. They almost did before, should the thug sitting by the side of the driver had not held the driver's wrist down while the driver was holding in his hand a gun, ready to shoot. Albeit, it was now improbable that the bandits could do something as cornered as they were.

I hope they surrender, thought Werner. And so, like many times before in his life, Werner hoped for an opportunity.

The soldiers were now taking the documents from the bandits. One of the soldiers asked Werner for his papers.

"I have no documents," Werner said.

The bandits looked at Werner. The soldier who asked Werner about his documents turned back toward the officer and explained the situation.

"Let's see!" the colonel said and snapped his fingers. "You all get out of the vehicle! Quick! Soldiers! Register them thoroughly! No sudden movements! Keep your hands where we can see them!"

"Get out!" one soldier standing by the front door said to the driver.

The soldier was almost a kid. The driver got out violently, intending to hit the soldier in the face with the door, but the soldier was quick enough and stepped back. He put one knee on the ground and pointed the barrel of his fusil to the driver's face. The other soldiers put one knee on the floor and pointed their weapons at the bandits as if on cue. The colonel saw the incident, and with two quick steps, came in front of the driver and hit him with a vicious punch to the face.

"I said no fucking sudden movements!" the officer said.

The thug fell on his back with his arms open, and his body hit the ground, his broken nose copiously bleeding.

"*Aichelláranga ch'kuimba'i, caralho si te pego,*"—I shall be so sorry for you if I get you, fucking toy soldier—mumbled the thug, trying to contain the bleeding by compressing his nose with his hand.

The thug who travelled by the driver's seat got a towel from the glove compartment and put the towel on his partner's face. All the other occupants, including Werner, got out of the Land Rover and stood by the vehicle's side. Taking advantage of the commotion, unnoticed, one of the thugs dropped his revolver on the grass and pushed it with his foot under the car. Werner attempted to step toward the soldiers, but the sly thug who had dropped the gun held him by his elbow.

"¡*Nao tão rápido assim, caralho dotor!*"—Not so fast, fucking doctor!—the thug mumbled.

With the help of his partner, the driver stood up, holding the towel on his face. He opened and closed his mouth as if trying to breathe and then slowly went to lean on the front of the vehicle, his left foot resting on the bumper. His face had swollen fast. His partner followed him and stood by his side. The driver's fingers drummed on the car's hood.

The soldiers checked the thugs and Werner thoroughly, yet none had guns on them. Conclusively, an assistant informed the colonel.

"There must be weapons in the Land Rover," the colonel said.

At that moment, as if Werner wanted to challenge his captors, he took his hat off and threw it away. His long blonde hair shone in the sunlight. The two thugs holding Werner by his elbows looked at him in the face. Werner smirked and smiled. One of the thugs holding Werner hit him hard between his ribs. Werner bent down, fell on his knees, and cried in pain. Some of the soldiers came to see Werner.

"*¡Está bem!*" one of the thugs said. "*O meu amigo está enfermo, isso e tudo.*"—It's okay! My friend is sick, that's all.

"*Assim,*" the other thug said. "*So quiere probocar.*"—That's right. He just wants to puke.

"I'm okay." Werner stood upright and gave a thumb up to the soldier.

The colonel came and looked at Werner, then turned toward the soldiers.

"You!" the officer said to the thugs who were holding Werner. "And you too," he addressed the driver with the broken nose and his partner. "Keep your hands on the car's hood! Keep your feet away from the car. Stretch as much as you can. Don't move. Don't talk. You know the drill!"

The thugs obeyed the order. The driver dropped the towel that covered his nose. By then, it was not bleeding anymore, although anybody could see that the man was still in great pain. He followed what his partners did. With his arms stretched, he let himself fall on the car's hood, put his hands there, and in this way kept in balance, dividing his weight between his hands and his toes. This kind of exercise was a common punishment used to immobilize an enemy. With the bulk of the body on hands and toes, the bandits could not move without a guard noticing it.

"You, come over here with me," the officer said to Werner.

However, while the thugs could not move their arms and legs and couldn't speak either, they could move their eyes. And their eyes talked.

Werner followed the colonel, and both men began to walk away from the scene. Yet, Werner's character once again betrayed him because he could not contain himself as he walked. He turned around, walked some steps backward, raised both his hands, and with a smirk on his face, he made a thrusting upright motion with both middle fingers, the obscene gesture directed to the thugs.

From then on, everything happened in seconds.

The soldiers who kept their eyes on the thugs turned their heads to look at Werner. The four thugs looked at Werner and then at the soldiers. Unaware of what was happening at his back, the colonel continued walking two steps ahead of Werner.

Somewhere, a drummer was drumming. Then, the warplane came back again, gliding over the treetops. The colonel's eyes followed the warplane's pirouette. And then, there was a bang on the cymbals.

The thug who had dropped his revolver under the vehicle let himself fall onto the ground, stretched his hand, grabbed the weapon, turned around, aimed, pulled the trigger, and his head exploded! Yet, there was no explosion, for the only explosion they all heard was but the engine of the warplane that by then was a twinkling point in the faraway sky. The bullet intended for Werner hit the colonel's back of his head, killing him instantly. The soldier who shot the thug was now pointing his rifle at the other three thugs who were still keeping their hands on the car's hood, but by then, they had their bodies sprayed with the blood, hair, skin, bone, and brain tissue of their partner's head.

And down the road, a school bus stopped, and the children inside were singing a popular, lively folkloric song. Their clear, well-tuned voices added an eerie musical background to the bloody drama taking place just about a couple of yards away from them.

THE MAN with the black hat stood in front of Ariel with the vial in one hand and a gun in the other, pointing the gun to Ariel's chest. The shrieking of monkeys was deafening. The entire jungle seemed to converge at that point. A warm breeze blew, and a restless sun shone beyond the treetops. Ariel stared at the vial with the diamonds, which the man with the black hat oscillated in his hand as if he wanted to hypnotize Ariel with it.

The man had turned his head several times and called his partner in a loud voice, but the man with the gold teeth never responded. The man with the black hat mulled over this event for a while and concluded that his obligation was to check up on his partner's welfare, but he had to kill Ariel before doing that. But then, the man with the black hat understood the dichotomy in which he was in because he couldn't kill Ariel, at least not before Ariel guided him and his partner to the diamond field. Then they could leave the young man's body to the rainforest, and they would be rich. It would be the jackpot of their criminal lives.

Yet, he could not do it all alone. He needed his partner as he never did before. Where the hell had his partner gone? He had not abandoned him there, of course. His partner would have never done that. That was unthinkable of him, given the lifetime friendship that united them both, for he knew his partner since the man with the gold teeth was a child. He didn't hear the car's engine either—the cacophony that surrounded him would have made it impossible for him to listen to that specific sound. If his partner had decided to leave him there, he could have done so the minute they separated, and he could have done nothing about it.

Again, to kill the young man and then try to reach the next *fazenda* on foot, about seventy miles away, following the road through the rainforest. No. That would be a crazy walk, and he knew it. And because he had to save bullets to protect himself, better go away and leave the young man alive and alone here in the jungle. Afterward, the same jungle would take care of him. But he didn't want to do that. To have to walk miles and miles on the red road and under the sun. And then there was the rain, the storm that transformed the road into a river. *No. Not that way,* he said to himself. He stretched his arms without taking his eyes off Ariel, not even for a second.

But then, he thought, *I could return later on, more prepared and with tools. I will explore the jungle and seek the place where the diamonds are!* But that would end up being a crazy move as well. *No,* the man with the black hat said to himself, *the best option is to torture this young man, and he will guide me to the diamonds. I can do this because I need nobody but my skills and weapon. And I will become a rich man. Very rich.* He bent over and put the glass container carefully on the grass, and then he switched the gun from one hand to the other.

"*Arrójese no chão, e coloque as suas mãos nas costas,*"— Lie on the floor and put your hands on your back—the man with the black hat said.

Ariel again thought to escape, but he knew that this time the thug, like a sinister shadow, had a reason to follow him. However, he knew as well that the thug would not kill him because he needed the information. For sure, the thug would kill Ariel afterward once Ariel had confessed to the location of the diamond deposit, and Ariel, under torture, of course, would have acceded to escort the bandit to the field. But to do it would be unthinkable as well—to go back to the river—as they both would have to walk through the jungle as he had done with Werner. *I cannot do that,* Ariel thought. The thug could not do that either. To walk through the rainforest with those fancy leather shoes, without food—

Yet, Ariel still hoped for a miracle, and as he was dropping onto the ground as the thug had commanded him to do so, he heard a gunshot. A dry, toneless crack that sounded so alien in that place that hundreds of birds of so many different kinds flew through the leaves and went up in panic toward the open sun. Ariel saw that the bullet had hit the vial where he held the diamonds, and the vial had exploded, scattering the diamonds all over the ground.

He wanted to stand up and comb the grass to recover the diamonds because the shining stones were still part of his dream, but he saw a swift shadow pass in front of his eyes when he was standing upright, and he was perplexed because it could not be the man wearing the black hat, but another. The man wearing the black hat was still there, the weapon in his hand, his mouth wide open as if uttering a cry, yet instead, blood blurted out.

And then, the man stepped forwards as if he were performing ridiculous dance steps, fell facedown, and hit the ground with an absurd thud. Yet, the dull sound silenced the entire jungle. His body shook, and then it was quiet; and it laid there on the grass, among the leaves, the flowers and the butterflies, and the eternity of maggots.

From his back jutted out the diamond point of a long arrow stained with fragments of bone, muscle, blood, and skin. The gunshot Ariel heard was not for him. The man, in postmortem spam—the arrow pierced the man's chest—pulled the trigger. And the bullet, which crashed against the vial dispersing the diamonds, was but a coincidence, a divine intervention, perhaps, yet a call to Ariel's future as well.

Ariel witnessed all of it, feeling that he was in a nightmare, or as if all this drama was but a projection in slow motion of an old movie he never wanted to watch. Then, horrified, he turned around and saw a Native man lying on his back with his legs separated, forming a perfect V, his feet resting on a large wooden bow, while with his hands, he stretched the vegetal string that contained another long arrow. Everything seemed surreal to Ariel.

He looked again at the site where he had seen the Native with the bow and arrow and saw nobody. Just the perennial vegetation was there surrounding him like a shroud of protection. Ariel closed his eyes and forced himself to think that what happened was but a thing of his imagination, but then he also pushed himself to open his eyes and saw the dead man's body. And he forced himself to open his eyes to remind himself that life may as well be a dream, but just a half of it because the other half is already here for us to live it, and either it satisfies us or not.

Ariel fell on his knees and cried with so much pain in his heart that the butterflies stopped their flight to console him, the monkeys paused their playing, the serpents surrounded him, the sun created no shadows, the wind felt so weak to move no leaves, the birds shook their wings, and a rainbow of feathers covered him. And so, he found comfort in the nature surrounding him, and so the rainforest bloomed up once again.

He stood upright, dried his face with his hands, and stepped toward the road. The van was there. The engine was running idle. He saw nobody there and wondered about the man with the gold teeth. He walked around the vehicle and saw the man who was lying on the road. The red road lay there with an even larger shade of red. With great care, Ariel got near the man and saw that he was dead. As his partner with the black hat, the man with the gold teeth had his eyes and mouth wide open. Something in his expression caught Ariel's attention. If not were for the fatal circumstances of his death, the man seemed to be laughing. His gold teeth shone in the sunlight. It was indeed the perfect frame for a cynical photographer to immortalize the image of joy, for if it were not because of the diamond-pointed arrow that pierced his chest, Ariel would have sworn that the man was alive.

Waiting in a room inside a military outpost, his stomach churning from anxiety and an ulcer, Werner awaited news from Ariel. However, the information that reached him was valueless, previously filtered to conform to the military and the government's censorship, due to the sensitive area where the search took place. Therefore, Werner concluded, the chances to find Ariel alive were nil. And this happened because he lied concerning the location where Ariel and the bandits were. Werner could not, and should not, open to the military and tell the truth. He was not going to show them on a map the exact spot where the car was.

The bandits were now prisoners of the military. They were associated with the assassination of an army colonel, which carried a severe punishment, including life imprisonment in a military prison. And the bandits knew that if to this charge the justice added the kidnapping of a person and the murder of another, then all chances they could get out of jail one time soon would be remote. And thus, they were uncooperative and liars too. On their declaration to the military, the thugs said they knew nothing about Dr. Werner Mann, a German citizen whose interest in studying the region's flora and fauna brought him to the area. Instead, according to the thugs, they favoured the German doctor whom they found walking alone and confused on the road.

"The heat must have affected his mind," the thugs said.

"The German doctor was hitchhiking alone when we found him," the bandits declared. "Yes, he seemed lost, and as we stopped to help him, he asked us to take him to the nearby village. That was what we were doing when the soldiers stopped us. We knew nothing about a van or a young man."

"No, we had no more partners on this trip. We were only four, so we didn't know anything about what the German doctor declared against us."

"No. We didn't kidnap the man. As anybody could see, the doctor was free to go anywhere when the soldiers stopped our vehicle."

Regarding their partner, the one who killed the army colonel and lost his life—and his head—the thugs stated that they knew little about this man.

"He was, of course, a complex man. He was crazy, and we all had problems containing him."

"No. We didn't know if the man had a family,"

"We knew him little,"

"He was a new addition to our team. His role was to protect our group from bandits who are a nuisance on those solitary roads."

On their occupation, they stated they were merchants, importers of electronic articles. Their place of residence was an address somewhere in the outskirts of the Brazilian city of Dourados.

On the other hand, Werner's lies fit well within the story's context that María Rosa Martinez had told General Orozco. María Rosa knew what she had to say, given the circumstances. They both had rehearsed this situation many times before. Werner had explained that it might become a necessary evil, although the chance of becoming involved in an incident with the military or with bandits was yet a remote one.

And although the military still had questions for him, the military released him, either because:

    A—There were no charges against him.
    B—He was an older man.
    C—He was an outsider, a citizen of another country.
    D—He was sick.
    E—One big shot out there in Asunción felt sorry for him.
    F—All of the above.

Aside from Ariel's welfare, Werner was worried about the diamonds. There was a high probability that the thugs who held Ariel may have discovered the diamonds, which would mean that the bandits would have forced Ariel to disclose the diamond deposit's location. However, Werner knew that Ariel would not give in, even though the thugs would have tortured him. This thought troubled Werner even more. While oppressed between the two thugs in the Land Rover, Werner didn't think of the diamonds but about Ariel's well-being. If the bandits discovered the diamond deposit, it could become a public issue, and then Werner and Ariel would fall from the pan to the fire. Werner's stressing moments affected his stomach and the pain returned in full. A long time had passed since he had chewed the last pain reliever pill he carried in his pocket.

On the other hand, Werner was grateful to María Rosa for her help and concern. She was indeed the will behind his freedom. But Werner would have preferred that things would not have taken the direction they did. *We fell into a paranormal chance vortex,* Werner thought. In his philosophy of life, there existed these gaps he called vortexes, either positive or negative. *Most people recognize only adverse events from where it is difficult to exit, and so some people live in a negative paranormal chance vortex all of their lives.* And this is what Werner used to tell María Rosa in moments of philosophical moods.

However, aside from chance vortexes or not, Werner thought that it was his fault to drop himself in the middle of that road and that Ariel risked all to move him from there, so as the occupants of the Land Rover could not see them. *Was my fault that Ariel distracted himself and forgot his backpack by the side of the road where the bandits saw it,* Werner thought. And worst of all was that they had to use the lamps to locate the vehicle. They have been candid enough to trust that the bandits had forgotten them and that they would not be there observing them from a distance. Indeed, the bandits possessed skills that were unknown to them. *Poor Ariel,* Werner thought. *How much he might be suffering in the hands of those criminals—*

THE DRIVER'S seat had a small pool of fresh blood in it. Ariel reckoned that the arrow entered the man's chest when he was sitting in the car, his feet on the road, the door wide open, facing the vegetation, waiting for his partner, thinking, perhaps reviewing his life.

He'd had time to start the engine, leaving it running in neutral. He didn't die instantly, though. The man was young and healthy, and the arrow didn't reach his heart. The pain, however, must have been unbearable. Yet, he had the strength to stand upright and move away from the car. Probably, he wanted to warn his partner, but he could not go any further. It was then that he fell on the road, and he laughed out loud, for it might have been his character to laugh at the jokes of destiny, although bleeding himself to death was indeed a bad joke.

Ariel found a rag in the glove compartment and cleaned the blood. Disgusted, holding the rag with a stick, he went to the side of the road, made a hole, and buried the rag. After that, Ariel returned to the van, turned the engine off, and sat there with both hands holding fiercely onto the wheel. He didn't know what to do. The Natives had killed these two men that were threatening his life. They came from the depth of the rainforest. Probably, they were following them, Werner and Ariel. And because of a strange chance of destiny, they became his custodian angels. They hid in the vegetation and saw what had happened. But, because the Natives knew well about the white men's criminal behaviour, they didn't intervene. Instead, they waited, and when they saw the other ones leaving, taking Werner with them, they saw their opportunity. And in the nick of time, for these thugs were ready to kill Ariel and steal the van, and the thugs would have left him there for the jungle's gastric juices to work on him. And so he would disappear forever, and no one ever would have known what happened to him.

Albeit, there could be another twist to this story when by mere chance, the man with the black hat discovered the vial with the diamonds, which also would have meant for them a change of plans; plans that would have been not in Ariel's best interest, either.

And Ariel thought of Werner and convinced himself that those criminals would not kill him. The thugs had for sure thought that Werner could be of some value for them, and that's why they took him. But they had no plans for Ariel, the young man was just a nuisance, and it was better to leave him in the jungle. And they almost achieved this objective if not but for the Native people's timely intervention.

What could he do now?

And so, feeling for the first time in his life that he could become the owner of his destiny, Ariel prayed the way he remembered doing when he was a boy, by his father's side at home, which was the temple, for in the city there was not yet a synagogue. He directed his prayer to Hashem, his Celestial Father, and his words overflowed from his memory and heart and surged vibrant and harmonious. He asked the intervention of Hashem, his Lord, to help him in the odd convergence life had put him into.

And his words were: *"Baruch Attah Adonai Eloheynu Melech Ha-Olam."*—Blessed be you, Lord, King of the Universe.

His words escaped from his heart to his mouth and the road. And from there to the entire rainforest, and rose to the sky. And while Ariel prayed, a man stood on the road. It was a rabbi, and he was smiling and waving at Ariel. Tears blinded Ariel, yet when his eyes became transparent, he saw no one on the road.

Ariel took this vision as a revelation from Hashem and understood what to do. For he understood that his entire life had been as if he were completing a dotted line, each event being a line between dots. And he understood that the rabbi was a signal he should follow. And the Native girls had been a signal as well. And then again, the Native dwellers of the rainforest who saved his life. And the European aristocrat turned an Aborigen. And even his first encounter with María Rosa had been a message from God. And Werner had for sure been a messenger from God.

And Ariel understood now how infinite God's ways are. And he sighed, and his heart calmed and felt better. And being so close to death, Ariel thought of his life.

And he returned where the body of the man with the black hat laid.

ARIEL CIRCUMVENTED the body of the man lying there with his mouth wide open. Despite his revulsion, Ariel could not avoid but watch the body. A hairy, fat caterpillar was creeping into the open mouth. The man had died with his eyes open. Although for an instant, Ariel's heart gave a start because he saw how the man's eyes blinked, then he realized it was but the effect of an ants' colony that had already set their nest in the deceased's corneas. Two feet away, a blue frog had taken the man's black hat as its permanent residence.

Ariel looked away and focused on collecting their belongings scattered among the vegetation by the thugs. Then decidedly, he stepped on the diamonds, and without looking at them, hid them with his feet under the carpet of dry leaves and carried their belongings to the station wagon.

Ariel made one more trip back to make sure that no item from the civilization remained there. Then, satisfied, he went back to the vehicle and saw the other body lying there. Holding his revulsion, Ariel took the body by the armpits, dragged it through the vegetation, and left it side by side with the other body. And he focused so much on this task that he did not notice that none of the bodies had arrows sticking out from them. Ariel had not realized how fast the day had gone and how dark it was all around him, and it was not until he felt the drops falling on his body that he realized that a great storm was already in progress.

Ariel went back to the van, started the engine, turned the lights on, made a U-turn, which was not easy to do because of the road's narrowness, and moved away in the direction of where he and Werner had come.

The storm was so violent that the windshield wipers barely coped with the rainfall. And from behind the water's curtain, several pairs of eyes witnessed his departure.

The three men who kidnapped Werner were now in a federal prison in Dourados, Brazil, where they claimed to be citizens. Albeit as the police investigated, they were not who they said they were. However, they all had pending trials for several crimes in various courts in different states, including probation violations. Paraguay's military police wanted no business with these criminals, so they wasted no time delivering them to their Brazilian counterparts.

Waiting for a judge to decide their fate, the three men wondered in their cell about their two friends' destiny lost in the rainforest. It was indeed strange that they still hadn't contacted their friends now in jail. The men sensed that something terrible had happened to their friends down there in the jungle. Otherwise, one way or another, the two men would have already found means to contact their friends, wherever they were. They had gone through dilemmas in the past, but this one was far beyond, in time and mystery.

"*Os bixos do monte os pegaron,*"—The Native people got them—said one of them.

"*O mato os engoliu,*"— The forest swallowed them—said another one.

"*O Luisão pegou a eles, hina,*"—The devilish spirit of the forest got them—added the third one.

Yet, whatever motivated their two fellow mates' disappearance, the bandits knew at the bottom of their hearts that they would never learn the truth.

ARIEL'S FATE was also a mystery to Werner. Because of his recent experience in the zone, he surmised that the Natives had something to do with it. The thugs had probably had an encounter with the Natives. The Natives must have followed Werner and Ariel throughout the rainforest until they reached the van. If this was the case, then the disappearance of the two thugs was no mystery. However, Werner reckoned, the Natives' encounter occurred in the same spot where he left Ariel, accompanied by those two miserable men. It had to be this way because if the thugs had the chance to escape in Ariel's vehicle, it would have been impossible for the Natives to get them.

And although Werner knew that among the Natives there was a white man with an extraordinary story, Werner knew as well that the soul of the white man had given way to the soul of a Native, and so, Werner knew that the white Native was but the ghost of the European man he once was.

And he, Baron von Bohlen, was for sure as wild and savage in defence of his territory as those who had adopted him. Indeed, the Native had shown them his most friendly face. However, Werner knew, because he had read about it in several books, how savagely the Native dwellers react if attacked. Their first encounter, fortuitous or not, was their first real experience facing the rainforest's Aboriginal people. Then, it was possible that the vanishing of the two thugs, and Ariel, resulted from an encounter with the Native people of the rainforest, and a fight ensued, given the high power of the weapons of the bandits. But the Natives outsmarted the bandits, and Ariel died trapped between both sides. By now, his body could be lying on the vegetation, left to the work of the jungle's gastric juices.

Werner mulled on this and other possibilities for several hours, yet all of them led him to the sorrowful conclusion of Ariel's demise, and he could do nothing about it.

He had been let free by the military, and he could not go back to tell them a different story. That would be a crazy thing to do. And in case that the thugs had managed to make Ariel confess about the location of the deposit of diamonds, and despite the obstacles, they still decided to go through the jungle, they, the thugs, would keep this secret anyway, although the most probable thing was that they would kill themselves, which would be the natural order of ambition.

In the silence of his rumination, Werner cursed the diamonds.

But it was not until listening to the news that confirmed the end of the search that Werner had the certainty of Ariel's death.

And alone in that room in a faraway military outpost, Werner cried, and for the first time in a long time in his life, he begged God to illuminate forever with a Star of David, the place where his young friend lost his life.

THE RAINFALL persisted strong, and the road was now slippery and muddy. Ariel steered the machine with the drive of a man on a mission. A holy mission. His objective was not so far. Despite the rain, he was approaching it fast and remembered how afraid he was when he drove through this same road five days ago in Werner's company. Yes, he recalled, Werner was there to encourage him. And he wondered if the action he was ready to accomplish was but the beginning of solitude that would accompany him for the rest of his life.

And in this way, Ariel Gimmel, at twenty years of age, reached the place he had been looking for all his life.

He stopped the car's engine. A deafening thunder exploded and echoed through the jungle as in cascades of sound, lightning scratched the air with its electric paws, the spectacle lulled Ariel, and the rain's drumming on the car's roof relaxed him, and he fell asleep like a baby in his mother's arms.

And with the acute pain in his heart of having lost his friend, Werner Mann paid a man to drive him to Campo Grande, the capital city of Mato Grosso do Sul state in Brazil. There, he got into a hotel room, took a long shower, changed his clothes, placed the old ones in a garbage bag, took the bag outside, and placed it in a garbage bin in the hallway. And then, with a broken heart, Werner dialed María Rosa Martinez's number. It was his first call to her since six days before, when he was in the company of Ariel, on September 4, 1983, as they left the city of Asunción.

María Rosa did not answer his calls. Puzzled, Werner insisted on redialing her number. At the other end of the line, only a dead tone responded. Now panicking, Werner insisted, and the long, persistent, yet unanswered ringtone sunk into his heart and left a sour taste in his mouth.

During most of the day, almost every hour, Werner insisted on communicating with her, but there was no answer. *Something must have happened*, Werner concluded. Seated on the bed in his hotel apartment, he scratched his head. And then, in the solitude of his hotel room, slowly in his mind, Werner delved into what had happened to him since he arrived with his dream to Asunción del Paraguay and shared his vision with María Rosa. Unquestionably, he regretted the lightness with which he managed the relationship. And so, Werner felt every moment that he had lost without her. He began remembering all those happy moments, but the ones that came stronger into his memory were those he did not spend with her, or if once, they were together, those moments where he only focused on his problems, never asking her about her problems, her dreams, her projects of life. And he felt so selfish, so wretched.

Because the same happened with his relationship with Ariel. A young man, a pure soul, whom Werner did not listen to as he should have done.

Finally, Werner understood his selfishness had guided his every action, all the time. Why do we not take others seriously? Why do we not love others, as everybody deserves love? And in his act of contrition, Werner cried. The sobs coming from the depth of his life, for he then understood he had lived an empty life. And the diamonds, the money, the richness, all that he dreamed about was but burned paper, which was the pedestal he had sat his life on, forgetting the value of the simple love, the sincere friendship, the humble help, and nature, above all.

And it was then that a beam passed through the fog in Werner's memory and illuminated Ariel's words that he pronounced just minutes before their encounter with the bandits when they were still inside their car.

Ariel opened the glove compartment, took a small copybook and a pen, opened it, wrote a number, and gave Werner the piece of paper.

"What is it?" *Werner asked, reading the number.*

"This number is where we can reach María Rosa just in case she doesn't answer her telephone."

"I have her number."

"Just in case she doesn't answer, Werner! Say, in case of an emergency."

"Shouldn't be any, Ariel. Why?"

"We never know, Werner."

"Okay. Let's go now." *Werner put the paper in his shirt pocket.*

In his shirt pocket! His sight went to a corner where his backpack lay. Which shirt was that? The green one, military design with two pockets in the front. He went, no, he jumped toward his knapsack, turned it over, and emptied it, but only one shirt was there, and it was not green, but a striped one instead. He snapped his fingers. The garbage bag! He left outside in a garbage bin hallway just before taking a shower. And he opened the door and rushed to the garbage bin with his heart tight like a fisted hand, and there it was, the bag still sitting there, the lady housekeeper unhurriedly pushing her cart toward it, just a couple of doors down the hallway.

Alleviated, he grasped the bag, opened it, and emptied it there in the same hallway, recovered the green jacket, checked the pockets, and there it was—the paper between his fingers, like a flower blooming in the worst winter of his life.

IT TOOK Werner three attempts until, finally, he got an answer.

A woman answered at the other end.

"Hola?" the voice said.

"Hello, I would like to talk to María Rosa. Is she there by chance?"

"Who is it?"

"My name is Werner Mann. I'm a friend of hers."

"Mr. Werner! Blessed is the Lord! Where are you? María Rosa has been so worried about you and the younger man. Are you okay?"

"I'm okay. Where is María Rosa?"

"Unfortunately, María Rosa is not here, Mr. Werner. Let me tell you that many things have happened in these last days. Are you safe there?"

"I'm safe. Where is María Rosa?"

"María Rosa may be travelling by bus to Curitiba by now, Mr. Werner."

"Curitiba?"

"She has an aunt there."

"Yes, but why? What happened to her?"

"It's all because of Senator Orozco. She went to ask his help to find you, and the man of Evil took advantage of her."

"Did he rape her?"

"The Senator went to her house, brought some gifts for her—" the woman's voice broke out of emotion.

"Did he rape her?"

"She left everything," the woman sobbed. "She is scared. She carried nothing with herself, just a little money and lots of hope."

The woman paused. Werner was startled.

"There is something more, Mr. Werner."

"What?"

"An anonymous person denounced her of terrorist activities, and the police raided her house. So now, they are looking for her and for you, too. And the young one as well. Ariel, María Rosa told me his name is."

"What? What are you saying?"

"Association with a terrorist. Your photo is all over, Mr. Werner. And María Rosa's too."

"It does not make sense. I was just yesterday in a military compound."

"Where?"

"In Pedro Juan Caballero."

"Are you still there?"

"No. That was yesterday. I'm in Brazil now."

"You are safe then. The order of capture just came today. So they won't touch you there. And Ariel?"

"I don't know where he is. He may have suffered an accident."

"Oh my God! What a disgrace."

"And how about you? Are you safe?"

"I am, Mr. Werner. I'm a nun."

"What?"

"A nun, Mr. Werner. Sister Sandra."

"Sister Sandra!" Werner almost suffocated because of the surprise. "If María Rosa contacts you again, please tell her I will meet her in Curitiba. Tell her to look for me in the Radisson Hotel."

"I will do, Mr. Werner. I have to go now."

"One more thing, please, Sister Sandra."

"Yes?"

"Can you do me another big favour? Can you please contact Ariel's family? They live in Chile in Valparaiso. The family name is Gimmel. G-I-M-M-E-L. Tell them he is missing somewhere."

"Is he hurt?"

"I don't know, Sister Sandra. I hope he is well,"

"I will, Mr. Werner. I will contact Ariel's family through the Chilean Consulate for sure."

"Thank you, Sister Sandra. Keep yourself safe."

"Go with God, Mr. Werner."

She hung up.

As soon as he hung up, Werner called the hotel reception, booked a flight to Curitiba, and requested a reservation at the Radisson hotel. Then, exhausted, he took a shower and slept.

He dreamed of a rabbi visiting him. Werner woke up, agitated from this dream. But then, during the morning, an epiphany struck him, and he understood the meaning of the dream. The rabbi was an emissary of the Lord of Israel who visited him to tell the truth of Ariel's fortune. Werner then knew in his heart that Ariel was alive and well and that he was now living somewhere and in good company, in the rainforest.

It was indeed a miracle. Werner felt alleviated, changed into a new person, now a believer of miracles and the unknown forces of destiny, which he belittled until then, and he promised to focus the rest of his life more on the spiritual rather than on the material.

And on Ariel, Werner thought, and the chances of Sister Sandra communicating with Ariel's family of his disappearance and possible death was indeed a delicate mission, above all in a country like Chile, where informing relatives on the loss of a dear one in strange circumstances had become since the military seized power, but a diabolic routine.

THE NEXT day, Werner took a plane to Curitiba, eager as he was of a happy reencounter with María Rosa to start a new life together and live happily ever after.

And so, self-evicted from the country that helped him fulfill his dream, another episode in Werner Mann's life closed—a chapter that had its beginnings in a laboratory in the heart of Berlin, more than forty years ago at the onset of War World II.

WHEN ARIEL woke up, the rain had stopped. He got out of the vehicle and walked toward the point he had chosen to carry on his objective. And such a point as the geological event that caused them to panic the first time they, Werner and Ariel, confronted it. Yet, at this point, the sinkhole's borders had expanded and destroyed the road. Standing at the edge, Ariel could see the crater's walls were vertical and smooth as carved in the rock by a huge razor blade. One could see only some yards down, and after that, it was all but a dark immeasurable void.

Ariel checked the pocket in his shirt, took the diamond, and held it to the light. The stone sparkled like a miniature sun. Then he cut one leaf from the bushes growing by the side of the road, placed it on the ground, and put the diamond on it. And then he undressed, tossed his clothes inside the station wagon, his camera, his wristwatch, even his gold necklace with the Star of David, and looking at Werner's belongings, the bandits' words came to his mind.

"*Você não vai precissar desta porcaria, dotor.*" And he felt sick, but continued what he was doing.

Finally, he put the station wagon into neutral, placed himself behind the vehicle, and pushed it toward the sinkhole. The station wagon moved, its tires crushing the red dust, and having reached the border of the abyss, Ariel gave it a final push, and the vehicle fell noiselessly into the void.

And then, Ariel collected the diamond from the leaf, put it in his right hand, made a fist, and began walking on the same road he had come on to six days before, Werner and he, on their quest for the diamonds.

And without thinking what and why he was doing it, he began to run. He ran fast and agile, his bare feet leaving a faint track on the road's red dirt. He ran fast, holding his head up high, and he felt light as if he were floating in the warm breeze of the morning. He ran fast and was not surprised to see the Native dwellers standing all together on the road as if they were expecting him.

And he reached them, almost gasping, and the Native dwellers made a circle around him, and the old Native man with the leather belt came out from the group and began the strange ceremony of smelling him as he did the first time over there in the depth of the jungle. And the old Native man again performed those strange bows as if he were laughing and holding his stomach, but with no sound. And the group slapped themselves and embraced each other, but this time, they included Ariel in their celebration.

And the rainforest embraced them all.

Manufactured by Amazon.ca
Bolton, ON

21047399R00210